MW00334478

Also by K. Aten:

Children of the Stars

K. Aten

Silver Dragon Books
by Regal Crest

Copyright © 2020 by K. Aten

All rights reserved. No part of this publication may be reproduced, transmitted in any form or by any means, electronic or mechanical, including photocopy, recording, or any information storage and retrieval system, without permission in writing from the publisher. The characters, incidents and dialogue herein are fictional and any resemblance to actual events or persons, living or dead, is purely coincidental.

ISBN 978-1-61929-432-5

First Edition 2020

9 8 7 6 5 4 3 2 1

Cover design by AcornGraphics

Published by:

Regal Crest Enterprises

Find us on the World Wide Web at
http://www.regalcrest.biz

Published in the United States of America

Acknowledgments

This book was an absolute beast to write and review and I owe a select few folks effusive praise for their help in putting it together. My beta reader, Ted, who sticks with me no matter how many pages I churn out, despite how off the rails my original idea wanders, and regardless of how bloody long the novel takes to write. Ted, I honor you. Two other essential people that slogged through this epic tale and helped clear out the grammar cobwebs are my editors, Micheala and Mary. You two are simply the best! And last on the list are the dynamic duo, Cathy (publisher), and Patty (liaison). As the last line of defense at Regal Crest Enterprises, you two are the real superheroes.

Dedication

This book is for all the people who do the right thing, even when it's most difficult. It's for people fighting to make the world better, and for those who never give up.

"Morality should never take a back seat to fear or convenience."

Also...I believe.

Prologue

IN EVERY WORLD across the known universe, there are multitudes of stories told to entertain the masses. Each place, every pinprick of life scattered throughout the stars, has its own history and language of memory. Some stories are true, while others are so fabricated they border on comical. But they are all cherished equally because love and humor are common languages in any self-aware society. There are tales that extol the virtues of romance and drama while others put words to the actions and adventures of heroes long forgotten. But once in a lifetime, worlds and stories come together and there is no definable genre to the telling. There is no point at which you could pull that tale apart to its individual components. The story simply is as it has always been. And the heroes merely wait for the loving gaze of the reader. This is one of those tales.

THERE IS A galaxy that exists, spiral in shape and teeming with a sea of suns and satellites, masses of rock, great and small, some of them miracles of organic and crystalline potential. In one arm of a lonely spiral, there lies a star. Let's call it Sol. And around that star orbits a handful of planets, each with their own peculiar makeup and orbit. While a total of five orbiting planets and moons hold the capability to sustain essence and esprit, only one swirling ball of green and blue holds the power of organic life.

Carbon-based and requiring oxygen to thrive, reproductive creatures have been growing on the surface of Terra for billions of years. But it has only been in the last two hundred thousand years that humanoids evolved. Ignorant and angry, creative and curious, the peoples of Terra spewed toxins into their own environment, the damage peaking around the same point in time they began to fling radio signals and radiation alike into the far depths of space.

They are primitive, jokes to some and studied by others. Incapable of sustained space travel, the Terrans are left marooned on their planet to wallow amidst the filth of their own creation. But beauty can still be found. With each decade of advancement, the humanoids work on restoring the natural state of their world. And to protect the delicately burgeoning people of Terra from advanced species that would do them harm, one race stepped up to safeguard the planet. The Tau Ceti are the oldest known beings, more advanced than all others and therefore the most powerful. If they said a star or one of its satelites was off limits, the other worlds listened. And in the Terran year of 1952, the Tau Ceti declared the planet known locally as "Earth" to be such.

Those extraterrestrials already on the surface that were living in peace, unknown by the local humans (as the Earthlings called themselves) were allowed to stay. But every single one had to pledge on penalty of death that they would not share advanced technology with the humans of Terra. They had to abide by the Sol-Ceti Pact to remain hidden to the people of the planet and not interfere in the development of technology, society, or biology. Even the humans themselves were not exempt from the ruling by the Tau Ceti.

The Sol-Ceti Pact was essential and more important than the people of Terra would ever know. It kept them stable, and it kept them ignorant of just how small and inconsequential they were in the known universe. But most importantly, it kept them safe. And like many important decisions, treatises, and discoveries around billions of worlds, there was a very good reason for the Sol-Ceti Pact's existence.

Chapter One

LET'S SET THE scene. The location is hot, a desert in the middle of nowhere, or maybe it's nowhere in the middle of a desert. The Mohave spans across four of the United States—California, Nevada, Arizona, and Utah. An inhospitable region, dry and cold at night, hot and deadly during the day, it was a place on Earth you went to for one of two reasons. You either wanted to die, or you needed to hide. And for a government facility with more secrets than employees, the reason was most certainly the second. The drab complex near the Groom Lake basin in Nevada was a high security base and if the desert itself didn't keep out the casual or not so casual observer, the tall, electrified fence was sure to do the trick.

More advanced than ever after the discovery of the ship in Area 51, the scientists on the base were having a banner year. The vessel itself had been gutted and chopped into parts, like a great beast killed in primitive times, each part going to a different family to sustain them through the hardships of life. Only instead of yielding meat, the ship provided so much more. The Aero department got the ship hull, the Engine department was gifted with the propulsion system, and the Tech group received navigation and electronics. But there was one more department listed only as the Organics group. You see, the spacecraft wasn't empty when it crashed. No, besides technology, wonder, and a great deal of fear, it also brought an alien down to the planet's surface. It was the extraterrestrial, a previously sentient organic body, that was given to the black suits.

The crash itself concerned the Tau Ceti immensely. They knew what few others did, that the alien was a fugitive that had come to Earth for two reasons. First and foremost, he wanted to escape pursuers from his home planet. They were intent on sentencing him to life on a prison island for his horrific crimes. Second, the

fleeing alien knew about the primitive aspect of
Earth's natives and their technology. He figured that
if he couldn't oust the Sovereign Queen of his own
world, he would find a new one where his channels of
power would make him a god among the people. Kendo Binn
Havington was meant to rule, one way or another. A fact
passed down from one generation to the next.

It was shortly after the crash and discovery by the
humans that the progenitor race of Tau Ceti formed the
non-interference pact. They saw potential for disaster
when the ship was split up for research and they wanted
to mitigate the damage, as well as warn others who
thought Terra would be an easy conquest. The Tau Ceti
liked the scrappy planet much the way it was and considered the Earth and its people a pet project of
sorts.

The humans of said "scrappy planet" had other ideas
about how innocent they should remain. And it was a
guarantee that the Tau Ceti never informed them of any
non-advancement pact. The various departments investigating each part of the ship typically worked quite
well together. However, the organics lab with its
black-suited agents and scientists was a bit out there
for most of the scientists and division members to
really feel comfortable. The other department's personnel thought they were "spooky" and refused to even
enter that wing of the facility. As for the reason for
black suits over any other color, well they served a
purpose too. Black didn't show alien blood nearly as
much as traditional medical scrubs. So everyone in the
Spook division wore black no matter the type of clothing preferred, from the team of scientists to the
director of that wing. And that is where we find one of
the very first antagonists in this tale.

DR. BRIAN DAGGETT nodded at the guard and pushed
through the high security doors of the research facility. Director
Keene had raked him over the coals for showing a lack of results
in their current analysis. But Doctor Daggett had ideas, he had
plans. And with the threat of unemployment hanging over his
head, and Christmas right around the corner, he was understand-

ably stressed. As if he didn't have enough to worry about right now, he just found out the day before that his wife was pregnant with his second kid. The first one wasn't even speaking yet at three years old, certainly no prize. Never mind the fact that his eldest child was a girl.

Worst of all, Truman had announced that he wasn't seeking reelection. So what if he was prickly and had low approval ratings. Anyone that had the balls to drop a five-ton bomb on their enemy was "jake" with Brian. As for his oldest kid, the best he could hope for there was to marry her off to some enterprising young man with more ambition than common sense. "From my lips to God's ears." He muttered to himself as he unlocked his office.

Brian collapsed into his chair and ran a hand through thinning hair. If he couldn't get results going the official and legal route, then maybe it was time to try another way. His right index finger jabbed and spun around the rotary dial of the phone, numbers he knew by heart. Ringing sounded through the line, then a click as it was picked up.

"Yeah."

The good doctor didn't bother with pleasantries. "Stegman, it's Doctor Black." Clearly a codename, as it wasn't his real one. "We are a go for Operation Spook."

The plan was simple really. Alien DNA was discovered to have ten extra sets of chromosomes beyond the twenty-three pairs a standard human possessed. Brian Daggett was a brilliant man, despite displaying a distinctive lack of moral fortitude for most of his forty years on the planet. He was the one who discovered a way of splicing human and alien DNA together, with some of the "borrowed" technology his man had taken from the Tech wing. And with the best geneticists in the world under Brian's purview, he had one hundred fertilized hybrid eggs waiting for their fully-human incubators. Now all he needed were the "volunteers."

"I'M SORRY, DOCTOR Daggett, but after two years and nearly half a million dollars in resources, you've yielded no quantifiable results from your Chromodec project. You've wasted both time and money chasing a mythical 'super-man.' This isn't a comic strip, Doctor." He paused, his face serious, as Brian had ever seen it in the three months that he had known the new Director.

Brian swallowed nervously. "No, sir. It's not." He'd person-ally witnessed Director Aimes make a man piss his pants, but Brian wouldn't give him the satisfaction of showing fear. No sir he wouldn't.

The new director of the facility shuffled a few papers in front of him on the desk. He was quite disturbed by what he had found when he began reviewing the project files of each research wing. Most could be taken care of easily enough, but the last one was a bit more problematic. He picked up the conversation where he left off. "And as a result of this human genome folly, I'm afraid there are very tangible consequences to that waste. This depart-ment is scheduled to shut down within two weeks and all person-nel will be transferred to fill existing vacancies at other bases around the country. I was able to get placement for your team, with the usual non-disclosure regs in effect. You, however…" He sighed for both dramatic effect and to convey displeasure, exactly as he'd been taught before being assigned this particular mission. "I'm afraid we're going to have to let you go. You have one hour to pack your personal belongings then a guard will come by to escort you to the gate. This is to be a termination with prejudice due to your poor decisions and reprehensible behavior." He was well aware of how Daggett would take the news. The Watchers were counting on a specific response from the man.

Daggett tried to plead his case. "But, sir, perhaps we just need to run more tests on the children — "

Director Aimes raised his voice in anger. "There have been enough tests run, Doctor! I cannot believe you have the temerity to sit in front of me and plead your case given the nature of what you and your team have done. You abducted women from all over the country and implanted alien-human hybrid eggs into them, then returned the women to their families in disgrace!" He pounded on his desk, as if anger had gotten the better of him.

"You even had a team of hypnotists on the payroll to implant false memories of some sort of alien abduction, knowing that not one person would believe them. Not only did their friends and family think those poor girls were liars, but every one of them became an unwed mother. You ruined their chances of ever find-ing good marriage potential, forever shamed as harlots. And on top of everything else, you wasted thousands of dollars on planted personnel with the sole responsibility of monitoring those women and the children they birthed. No, Mister Daggett, we are lucky that there were no dire consequences from your actions. As it is, I personally hope you burn in hell for what you've put those young women through."

Brian's face paled and he began to sweat. How had it all gone so wrong for him? Well here is a little secret. It went wrong when he tried to use alien DNA and technology to alter the biology of humans, to *advance* it. He personally broke the pact that was formed right after Kendo Binn Havington crashed to the surface. What Doctor Daggett didn't know was that Director Aimes himself was not who he seemed. Per the Sol-Ceti pact, there were Watchers placed in every major government of the world. How else could they guarantee that the terms of the agreement were not being broken? Director Aimes had come into the game late, as humans liked to say, but he was going to get the job done, even if that job was the worst kind of cleanup. He leveled a cold look at the man sitting on the wrong side of his desk. "That will be all, Doctor."

There was nothing left to say, nothing left that Brian Daggett could do to plead his case or salvage his career. Getting fired *with prejudice* by the government was bad enough. But all the research he'd been doing for the past decade was covert and nothing he could list on a resume. Without a doubt he knew that Aimes would have him blacklisted in the science community. No, he was ruined. On top of that, his wife was pregnant with their third child. She insisted on trying again the year before, knowing how disappointed Brian had been not having a son. At the time it made sense to suggest using his connections at work to guarantee a son with the Organics lab's "newfangled fertilization" technique. She bought his idea, hook, line, and sinker. And it was fortunate he had one modified egg left. Now the sex of the child mattered not, nor did the potential power of it, because it would grow up fatherless.

Exactly forty-five minutes after exiting the director's office, a gunshot echoed through the corridors of the Organic wing of the facility. Armed guards found the body of Dr. Brian Daggett slumped over on his desk, pieces of skull and nearly-macerated brain matter painted the wall behind him. It was one less loose end to wrap up. Strangely enough, the cleanup team was already on standby to take care of his office.

DECADES IN THE future, and light-years away, there was trouble of another kind. Terra wasn't the only planet full of people grasping greedily at the tendrils of power. Even rulers felt fear when fanatics stirred the people from the safety of reason. But there were other powers in the universe that even escaped fugitives or evil generals could not fathom. Sometimes only the hands of babes can grasp something so intangible and pure. For true power comes from the heart and cleaves to the mind. It does not come from the mind and cleave to the heart.

THE LIGHT WAS weak where it shone through the portal, and the stars glimmered brightly in the darkness beyond. Denii and Selphan Del Rey gazed upon the sleeping infants with equal parts worry and affection. Both babes had the medium hued skin of their races, but where one was of fair hair and eyes, the other had eyes and hair of darkness. Less than a month old and their tiny hands grasped together with desperate intent. A sigh escaped Denii's lips. Her mate gently brushed her nearly black hair behind an ear and moved closer. "What troubles you, sirra?"

Denii looked to her binary queen and gave a smile that did not reach her eyes. "I mourn for them. Neither will grow up knowing their worlds as we did."

Anger pulled Selphan's lips into a frown. "Their worlds are nearly dead, and of their own doing! Perhaps they are not worth knowing."

The shorter queen placed a calming hand over Selphan's. "Without a past, we have no anchor for the future. You know this, 'Phan. Despite the pain the war between our two planets has caused, I regret having to leave. My heart breaks that we could not save them."

Selphan wrapped an arm around her queen and pulled her close. "There was nothing we could do, he refused to go. Even though the planets of Reyna and Tora were sworn enemies, there is at least some hope we can take from the fact that we had finally forged an alliance with Calden and Inir Baen-Tor. It is a shame that factions of our respective planetary governments sought to keep the conflict going until the bitter end."

"We should have saved them."

The taller woman gently stroked the white blonde hair of Zendara Inyri Baen-Tor. "We saved their daughter."

"And ours." Denii smiled and ran gentle fingers through the

dark hair of the other babe, Amari Losira Del Rey. She was the royal heir of the planet Reyna and counterpart to the baby at her side, heir to the planet Tora. After a few minutes of silence, Denii moved her hand to stroke the soft skin where the babies' fists clung to one another. "They've already bonded. I did not expect it so soon."

It was Selphan's turn to sigh then. "It was written in the filtered rose light of Q'orre that the babes of our two houses would be destined for each other. They are Q'sirrahna. Had we not saved the child of Tora, our own daughter would have been bereft, empty of heart and soul her entire life. She would have languished. They are stronger together, and nothing short of death can keep them from finding one another."

"Perhaps together they could have saved our worlds."

Selphan shook her head. "No. Nothing could have saved our worlds. The light of our sun Q'orre has shone down upon a war that is older than our two houses. The war is too old and too profitable to end without a clear victor. No peace or alliance could have been forged without a mutiny of the ruling elites, as we clearly bore witness to. They made their money on the deaths of the common people. I mourn for them all. I weep each night for the people of our house and home."

The smaller woman nodded sadly, eyes wet by unshed tears. "You know I weep as well. That is why we must do our best to keep the last children of Q'orre safe. I like that we've started a video log for them. It's only right that they know the histories of our worlds."

Alarms suddenly rang throughout the ship, startling the women and infants alike. Even as the queens' hearts raced with anxiety, the babies filled their lungs and squalled with fear and discomfort at the loud repeating noise. "We need to secure them then check ship status and coms!" As a precaution, they moved the babes to emergency pods and sealed them away into silence before making haste to the pilot station. The infants calmed while the women became more distraught.

Sitting in the primary pilot seat, Denii punched in new coordinates and the forward screen blurred in space, the tell-tale sign of a faster than light jump. She turned to her mate. "I have only bought us time. While our ship is faster, they have the newest tracking technology and will follow our ion trail wherever we go. Perhaps we have not saved anyone on this journey."

Selphan unclasped from her own seat and stood. "No! I

refuse to believe that. I'm going to check the database to see if there is a safe haven somewhere in this galaxy. I know there are primitive planets, maybe we can find one to hide the four of us."

After a tight-lipped stare, Denii nodded. "I'll stay here and monitor the alerts. Let me know what you find."

The taller woman leaned down and kissed Denii tenderly on the lips. "I will."

THREE DAYS PASSED by with two more near misses of their pursuers. Each time the other ship caught up it was closer than the last, and the queens of Reyna knew they were running out of time. Each day they spent a good many hours holding the infants in their arms, telling them stories of the houses of Reyna and Tora. They fed and comforted the babies of dark and light, and took turns cradling and cuddling with each. But the little ones never stopped trying to reach for each other. As predicted, their soul bond was fully formed, if not quite sealed, at an unheard of age.

On the fourth day, mid-ship time, Selphan finally found a promising biome. She hit the intraship com and called for her mate. "Denii, I've found something!"

The other queen's voice sounded over the com speaker in return. "Be right there."

It took less than two minutes to traverse the corridors between the pilot station and the research room. In it, Selphan had a planet on the view screen. A lush water world, with brown and green masses covered by swirling white clouds. The taller woman spoke as soon as her mate arrived. "The atmosphere looks promising. Their sun is a yellow dwarf, quite a bit different than our own Q'orre. According to their classifications, Q'orre would be considered an ultracool dwarf. That means their light will be significantly brighter than ours, and with a yellow-white focus, rather than the rose tint we are used to. The temperatures are near enough to our home worlds to guarantee that alone should hold no adverse effects for our races, as is gravity."

"What is this?" Denii pointed at a short list of elements and percentages.

"That is their atmospheric makeup. Nitrogen of seventy-eight-point-zero-eight percent, oxygen of twenty-point-nine-five percent, Argon of point-nine-three percent, and a variety of other elements make up the remaining point-zero-zero-zero-one percent. Traces of neon, helium, and krypton are negligible and will not affect our biology."

Denii frowned. "Argon? What is that, I don't recognize it? While only a small amount, it is not an element we have been exposed to. We do not know the effects such an element will have on our alien systems. It could mean slow poisoning — "

"Or nothing at all. This argon is an unfamiliar element to our computer system. I only got the name and molecular structure off the planetary information network. But that doesn't make it bad for us and we don't have time to run experiments, we need a place *now*. We need a planet and society we can hide and assimilate into, where we won't be found by the soldiers of Tal Boraan."

Fury washed over the normally affable Denii Del Rey. "He is a disease upon the society of both planets! Nothing but a mercenary and thief of our world, promoting destruction and misery in the name of a pointless war. We held the treaty in our hands when his ships attacked Tora! And for the betrayal of our own general, the king and queen of our sworn enemy entrusted us with their only child. I am at a loss as to how I should process this. Why didn't they come?"

In an instant, the taller woman was out of the console chair and by Denii's side. She took both hands into her own and held them clasped to her heart. "I don't know, sirra. Perhaps they felt a responsibility to their people. We may never know their motivations, we only know they wanted to keep their child safe. And I worry too. You know I would not even consider such an unknown now if we were not out of time."

"Do we have any contacts there? Is the planet in a protected system?"

Selphan nodded. "Yes on both counts. I have already sent coded transmissions into the solar system and received a response from two pairs of Reynan-allied races that are embedded on the surface. They are working as Watchers but should still be able to help us. The planet is called Earth by its inhabitants. Or more formally known as Terra. The star is Sol. They have beings of power there but they are monitored closely by Watchers. Because the Terrans are not capable of interstellar travel yet, they are under surveillance and protection from the Tau Ceti. As a whole, the Tau try to prevent people from landing on the planet, but if explorers do make their way to the surface they are on their own. As you already know, the Tau Ceti are infamous for their dedication to non-interference. At least when it suits them."

Denii's eyes widened. "Tau Ceti? Are the inhabitants of similar physiology then?" She was curious as to why the humanoid grays would take such an interest in a primitive planet. While they were a curious race, they usually kept to their own.

"No. In physical appearance the people of Terra are a very near match to the races of Q'orre. As you know, even though we consider the races of Reyna and Tora to be different from each other, we truly vary only in coloring. We share a near common ancestor. After reading about the people of this system, I wonder if we share a much more distant common ancestor with the Terrans as well."

"Interesting." Denii tapped her lip while she flicked the screen through details of the new world. The planet's information network was impressive but disturbing with its content. "Despite their primitive technology, they are as much a warring world as our own planets were! Are you sure it is safe?"

Selphan smiled. "The allies I made contact with assure me that they've lived successfully on the surface for a number of years. There are two sets, both mated pairs in the most prominent country. Either can help us acclimate to the planet and society."

"Q'orren?"

"No. Another humanoid species that can subtly alter their appearance to seem Terran."

Denii turned toward Selphan. "Are we close?"

The taller woman punched a few more buttons and it brought up the special overlay to show position of their ship. "We are quite close. We entered the heliopause of their solar system about twenty tics ago."

"I still have concerns—" Denii was unable to finish her statement as the alarm claxon sounded again. She turned to her mate. "Secure the babies!" Then she raced back to the pilot station. When Selphan joined her in the second chair, Denii gave her mate the bad news. "They are within two jumps, the closest they've come so far. I'm bursting us to the far side of the Terran moon to hide our signal, but I fear that we are out of time."

Selphan looked to her mate with tears in her eyes. "The men of Tal Boraan will never stop pursuing us, we need to let them go." It was the look on Denii's face that said clearly she knew who the "them" were that her mate referred to. Parents the universe over were conditioned to provide for their children, to love them. But it was only the best sort of parent that would sacrifice everything for their offspring. Selphan continued. "Amari and

Zendara are what is most important now."

A tear fell slowly down Denii's cheek as her mate's words hit her fully. "My baby, my child — "

"Will live."

With hearts and spirits broken, they made their way to the pod room, and the babies. They each opened a chamber and unclasped a child from the bed. "My baby, my darling, sirra..." Denii whispered the words into the tender place below the dark-haired baby's ear. Amari smiled and kicked her feet at the reassuring feel and sound of her mother's voice. At the same time, Selphan whispered words of love and reassurance against the cheek of Zendara Baen-Tor, daughter of their sister planet and heir to their enemy-turned-ally. Both children would be sent into a strange world without knowing the love of their true parents. After a few minutes, they switched so the two queens could say goodbye to the other child. When both infants were secured in the emergency pods once again, Denii turned to her mate and sobbed onto Selphan's shoulder, both knowing that they could not grieve for long as the trackers were still out there. The babies themselves cried at being separated.

Denii and Selphan returned to the pilot station and prepared for the future as best they could. As much as they wanted to keep the babies together, there was too much risk of discovery. So messages were beamed to both pairs of contacts on the surface of the strange watery planet, and coordinates were transmitted to each pod's navigation system. They delayed the launch because it hurt to send the innocent babes into that unknown, such as it was. The two queens made one last recording for the babies they were sending off to the planet below. But the delay was short-lived as the claxon sounded again. With final whispered words of love, Selphan pressed the launch button. As the matching life pods disappeared from their view screens, they each breathed a sigh of relief that there was no ion trail for their pursuers to follow. The children of Q'orre would be safe.

The tears fell again as the noise clamored around them, echoing down the halls of the nearly empty ship. Denii's words were quiet, barely heard through the alarm. "We are the last of our families."

Selphan responded. "No, they are."

With the risk of discovery so dire, they both knew there was only one way to guarantee the secrecy of what they'd done. The child heirs of the Reyna and Tora royal sovereigns would be a beacon for any wishing to use them in the power struggle between the two warring planets. The Queens Del Rey would never let them be found for such a purpose. As a secondary alert sounded discordantly against the first, the two women clasped hands. Their grip was strengthened by fear and sorrow. There were two matching buttons on opposite ends of the console, guarded by protective covers. With precise movements, they each flipped the cover out of the way and hovered over the buttons. Dark eyes met one last time and words slipped from Denii's lips. "Ahna, me sirra."

They were answered by Selphan. "Me sirra, ahna." Then hands moved in unison and their main screen lit up with a brilliant flash. The ship was gone. Ahna meant forever.

Chapter Two

WE COULD TALK about the time seventeen years ago when two tiny escape pods slipped unnoticed to the surface of the Terran planet. One heading to a remote location in the northeastern part of the United States, the other touching down on the opposite side of the country in the Northwest. You could learn all about the Watchers who took in those small children of the stars, raising them as if they were their own biological offspring. But this tale doesn't belong to the Watchers. This is a story about two princesses, growing up in a world not their own.

IT WAS THE hottest part of the day as the eagle soared high above the canyon surrounding Lake Twenty-two in Mt. Pilchuck State Park. Summer in Washington was Amari's favorite time of year because her parents gave her free rein to hike the trails near their home in Verlot. It was the place she felt freest of spirit. Being homeschooled, some would have thought she'd been lonely growing up, but that was never the case for the dark-haired youth. Her parents moved to Verlot, Washington when she was three so it was pretty much the only home she remembered.

But sometimes those who are different from all others get a sense of that truth early on in life. And Amari had that sense. She never really felt like she fit in. She had a hard time acclimating to the public school when she started kindergarten, and her anxiety in jostling crowds of rambunctious children only grew worse as she got older. Each time a kid pushed her, or grew physical in the harmless way children often did, her muscles tensed uncomfortably and her stomach clenched. Accidents would happen as a result of her anxiety and Amari began to loath going to school. There were also the problems associated with her nearly untestable intellect. By sixth grade she was beyond anything the public school could teach and her mother decided it was best to instruct her at home.

The thing young Amari never told her parents was, while the

jostling and physical contact with other people made her uncomfortable, that wasn't what caused the majority of her anxiety. The
mixed sense of loss and fear actually stemmed from the fact that
she felt like something was missing from her life. In the way of
young minds with too much imagination, she often wondered if
she had been born a twin. But her adoptive parents never mentioned it and she never wanted to ask. Besides, Amari figured
that her adoption records were probably sealed anyway. Whatever the truth was about her past, the emptiness was always
there.

Verlot, Washington and Mt. Pilchuck State Park were places
where people only visited when they wanted to escape from the
pressures and patterns of life. And Amari was no different. She
was taking advantage of a weekend free from responsibility since
she knew they'd all be gone soon enough. In less than four
months, she would be going off on her own for the first time in
her young life. The University of California – Berkeley had the
best biochemistry program in the United States and she was
headed there to complete her doctorate in the fall. She had been
lucky enough to take remote classes for her undergraduate work
but she couldn't stay home forever. The thought was slightly
overwhelming and her parents were worried for her, as always.
She would be significantly younger than the rest of the students
and probably socially ostracized, but that kind of loneliness never
bothered her. Mostly she would just miss her parents and the
mountains of home.

An eagle called out from the blue expanse overhead and
Amari's dark ponytail swung back and forth as she craned her
neck up to watch. The breeze blew little wisps of her hair around
her face but she didn't care. For as long as she could remember,
Amari envied the great birds in the sky. She longed for the freedom they had as they soared through the air high above the
world. She'd seen that same eagle and his mate often enough to
know that they nested nearby. On a whim, the teenager started
up the steep trail that wound toward the top of the ravine. Loose
gravel made the trek slow going but Amari knew it would be
worth the view when she got to the top. She had her cell phone on
her, not because she'd actually get reception, but because it had a
really good camera.

Despite the strenuous climb, the teen wasn't the least bit
tired when she reached the apex of the trail. She stood on the
edge of the path to take a few pictures of the scenic lake below.

No matter how many times she hiked the area, the beauty never failed to amaze her. The eagle called out again and she spun around hoping to get a good picture from the higher elevation. Suddenly more loose gravel gave way beneath her boots, pitching her down the rocky slope.

NOW FREEZE THE scene and what would you see? A phone hanging in midair, destined to become an unidentifiable explosion of plastic, metal, and circuitry against the rocks far below. A girl tipped back over a ledge with one foot up and one foot sliding down a cliff, panic on her face and arms fixed in a desperate windmill motion. An eagle stopped in the sky above, as if it paused to rest in its ever-circling observation of the world below. For anyone but Amari Del Rey, the situation would surely be dire. However, you already know if that were the case this tale would end here. But look, in this instance you are more informed than the young woman who is about to tumble down a ravine. In this very moment, which of you is more powerful?

THE PHONE FLEW from her hand as if in slow motion and was quickly forgotten as panic fully set in. The girl threw her hands up to ward off the impact of the ground she rapidly approached. "No!" Her voice echoed around the canyon as fear of death kicked in. But something strange happened. The impact did not snap her neck or wrists. It didn't bounce her down the cliff like a limp ragdoll. When she hit the side of the cliff, it was as if all forward momentum simply died. She collapsed to the rocks painlessly and began to slide. Then before she could get purchase with her scrabbling hands, she slid over another ledge. That time she didn't land. With eyes screwed shut tight, she stopped. The wind whistled through the trees but the sound was overshadowed by the pounding of her heart.

Seconds ticked by and Amari didn't sense any more movement so she slowly opened her eyes. The world held a strange glow. She wasn't safe on the ground, with only a few scratches to show for her mishap. She wasn't stranded on a ledge, waiting for the slightest movement to send her to her death. Amari floated in mid-air, hunched over as if she were predicting another strange non-impact fall. As soon as she realized she was floating away from the cliff face, she dropped again and the entire cycle repeated itself. When the dark-haired girl finally came to a full stop with all body parts on the ground, she was sitting in a foot of icy snow. The lake was still below her and the sun continued to shine down from high above. The eagle even called again to let Amari know that the world was just as it had been before she did the impossible.

"Well, shit." Unable to process what had just happened, Amari searched around for her phone until she remembered that it was the first casualty of her strange tumble down the mountain.

Before panic could reassert itself in the forefront of her mind, she let curiosity get the better of her. She stood up, with the back of her jeans slightly damp, and tried to remember the feeling from when she was suspended in the air. A tightness washed through her entire body, much like one of her anxiety attacks, and she began to rise. If anyone had been watching that trail in midday, or if anyone had seen the lone hiker who tumbled down the mountain and lived, their surprise would have been eclipsed by the new sight above Lake Twenty-two. Floating in the air over a strip of leftover spring snow was a young woman. Her once dark hair and eyes both glowed a flaming white color. It was as if an iridescent white fog slowly escaped from those two places, like heat from a body in winter. And the person that was Amari Del Rey was forever changed. Amari was energized and full of questions. Her excitement fueled her mad scramble down the hiking trail.

As soon as she made it back to the trailhead, Amari jumped in her old pickup truck and drove with reckless speed to the research station where her parents worked. In all honesty, it was her dad that worked there as a climate scientist. Her mother was a mystery writer and often went to the station to write just to be with her dad. It was sweet in a way that made teenage girls gag. Her dad's Subaru sat parked in the dirt lot and dust settled over it when she slid to a stop. Without thinking, she was out of the truck and slamming the door open in the small one-room station. It bounced off the wall with a lot more force than she intended. "Mom, Dad! Something just happened, you won't believe it!"

"Amari?" Her mother immediately took in the dirty teen with her ripped and scuffed clothes. She was by her daughter's side in an instant, physically checking the younger girl for injury. "Are you okay? What happened?" Her dad stood as well but didn't approach. Rather, he held a peculiar look on his face as his wife spoke.

The young woman brushed her mother's hands away with exasperation. "Mom, I'm fine!" At her mother's concerned look, Amari's features softened. "I promise. But seriously though, something really weird just happened to me."

Finally her father walked over. He pulled out a chair at a small dining table that sat near the kitchenette and waved her toward it. "Well then, have a seat and fill us in."

Not really thinking, she threw herself into the chair in a huff at his perpetual calmness, only to have it shatter beneath her. "What the?" Amari stared at the wood pieces surrounding her on the floor, then moved her gaze back up to her parents. She caught the look they shared with each other and her eyes narrowed. Amari knew she was adopted, but never once in her life had James and Michelle Bennett made her feel that she was anything other than their biological daughter, until the shared look Amari witnessed between them. She never questioned the fact that they chose to have her keep the last name of her birth. Amari never cared to think about their excessive overprotectiveness when it came to strangers in Amari's life. She even knew about the secret journals they kept in a locked safe in the basement, but she never asked about them. However, the look they exchanged with each other said the time had finally come for demanding answers. "What's going on?"

Her mother started. "Amari—" She was quickly interrupted by her dad.

"Not here." He turned away from them wearing the cold look of a stranger and began packing up his laptop and paperwork. Amari's mother did the same as the teenager pulled herself up off the floor.

"Guys? Where are we going?"

Her dad slung the leather satchel over his shoulder and grabbed the Subaru keys from the hook by the door. "Home." He held his hand out. "Give me your keys, it's probably safest for one of us to drive your truck back."

Amari took a step back. "You're freaking me out! And what do you mean, safest? I told you, I feel fine."

"Please, Amari." Light brown eyes were pleading, and the young woman could not resist the tone of her mother's voice.

"Fine." She reached for the door handle and pulled to a stop as two voices called out in a rush.

"Be careful!"

At first she rolled her eyes in response, then thought of the chair incident from a few minutes before and carefully opened the door. Despite the overall feeling of weirdness ratcheting up to an astronomical level, the voice inside Amari's head cautioned her to maintain a sense of calm and rational reason.

The trip home took about twenty minutes. That was twenty minutes of silence in the cab of her old pickup truck where she sat in the passenger seat. She went to grab her phone out of her pocket to check her Instagram account and remembered that she lost it in the fall. She decided to get the bad news out of the way as they pulled up the long drive to their house. "I dropped my phone when I fell. It's probably shattered and scattered down the cliff above Lake Twenty-two."

Her dad's voice was steady with no emotional inflection. "That's fine, we'll help you get another."

Amari worked some evenings and weekends at Becker's, a local grocery where she primarily stocked shelves. It was a job she could do without interacting with people so much. She was proud of the fact that she had saved her own money for the expensive smart phone, but she was also irritated that her parents would have to help her get another. "Thanks." She didn't want to come across as ungrateful but she didn't have to like their help either.

Michelle pulled in last and parked James's Subaru next to her own Jeep Cherokee, opposite the side that Amari's truck rested. The wide turnaround near the house provided plenty of parking for even more vehicles if people came over, but few did. James and Michelle Bennett only held a handful of friends in their close-knit circle, and they didn't host people very often. Amari had accepted years before that both her parents were intellectuals and not particularly outgoing. She understood because she was much the same way.

Once they were inside, James took a seat at the kitchen table and Amari followed. Michelle detoured to the stove to put the teakettle on to brew a few mugs of her and James's favorite drink. Amari was never allowed to have any, given the excuse that it was expensive and imported. The tension in the kitchen finally broke when the teen spoke up. "All right, now that you've thoroughly freaked me out, what's going on?"

Her dad leveled a dark-eyed gaze at her. "Why don't you tell us what happened at Lake Twenty-two?"

Amari's eyes widened because she had nearly forgotten her

amazing story in the wake of her parents' strange behavior. "Holy homeostasis, that's right! So, you know how I went up to do some hiking and take pictures of the eagles that nest nearby?"

James nodded as Michelle joined them with two steaming mugs. "Sure."

"Okay, so I decided to head up the old trail to get some pics from a higher vantage point. It was fine at first but when I got to the top the gravel gave way and I slipped and fell over the edge. But I didn't hit like I thought I would. I mean I did, but I kind of bounced and slid, then just kind of floated above the ground, before falling farther down."

"Oh?"

Amari looked at her mother, curiously. That single word response in no way fit the overprotective mother she had grown up with. "Really? I just told you that I fell off a cliff and floated in the air and you, the queen of overprotectiveness, just said 'oh?' Did pod people steal my parents, or what?" She played it off like a joke, but the intense stare from the two adults across from her at the table left a ball of solid anxiety in the pit of her stomach.

Her mother smiled but the ease Amari normally felt was missing. "Well, we can clearly see that you're not hurt."

The younger woman scoffed and worry made its way into her conscious mind. "Seriously?"

"Amari..." Her dad's deep voice trailed off and he didn't finish whatever he was going to say. He turned to Michelle with his brows drawn down and lips pulled into a frown. "We knew this was a possibility."

Her mother whispered back. "I know."

Suddenly Amari pulled her hands back to her own side of the table. "Gah, you really are pod people! All the Internet videos are right! Where are my real pa—"

The panicked ramblings were pulled up short when her mom laughed. "Honey, there are no such things as pod people."

"Phew, I was starting to get worried." She gave a hollow laugh, still feeling out of sorts by her parents' behavior.

Her relief was short-lived. "Pod people only exist in human movies. However, we *are* aliens." Her father paused for a few seconds before continuing. "All of us, including you."

The teen snorted, convinced her parents were playing the most elaborate prank on her. "Right, sure we are. You gonna unzip your face or something to prove a point now? What, am I one of those Chromodecs that are always in the news?" She said the name of the government-created people of power, with scorn.

"Definitely not Chromodecs." Rather than try to explain the details, her dad pulled his cell phone from his back pocket and set it on the table face up. "Before I start this, I want you to promise that you will not move from your seat. It is for all our safety that you let me answer any questions you have once the video is complete. Okay?"

Amari moved her gaze from the phone up to her father's light brown eyes. "Dad?" Her voice wavered with uncertainty.

He shook his head. "This is not a joke, baby girl. This is real and serious. Promise us, please."

The seventeen year old swallowed the lump in her throat. "I promise." With her consent, James Bennett pressed three buttons at once on the phone and the screen lit with a pure white glow. Amari watched as the glow began to flicker and a hologram appeared about a foot above the surface of the table. It looked like something out of a movie but Verlot, Washington wasn't Hollywood and Amari's fears grew. Two women appeared, each having dark hair and eyes like hers. The image was excellent quality and she was startled to see that she shared physical features with both. The shape of her own mouth and nose looked like the shorter woman's, while the sharp angle of her jaw and her broad shoulders were similar to the taller one. She looked at her parents. "I'm related to them, right? Are they sisters?"

Her mother gave her a sad smile and nodded toward the hologram. "Just watch."

"The time has come for you to learn of your heritage, Amari Losira Del Rey." The shorter woman was the one who spoke but for some reason the image didn't line up with the words coming through the small phone speaker below. It looked like it was poorly edited, or a bad dub job from a B-grade Japanese film.

"Why don't the words line up with the video?"

Her father paused the video somehow while her mother rested a smooth hand on top of Amari's. "They are not speaking English, this is a translation from your native language."

The teenager's eyebrows rose. "My native language? Since English is the language I've spoken since my earliest childhood, I believe *that* is my true native language, correct?"

Her mother didn't blush, the woman never blushed. "My apologies, I meant to say the language of your people."

"Oh."

The video continued. "My name is Denii Losa Del Rey, and I

am your primary mother." She placed a hand on the taller woman's shoulder. "This is Selphan Sirre Del Rey and she is your secondary mother."

The taller woman finally spoke and Amari was soothed by her inflection and tone of her voice. "Hello, Amari."

Denii continued. "Together we are co-queens of our planet, Reyna. There is another inhabited planet called Tora, and we both orbit our sun, Q'orre."

Amari looked up at her adoptive parents with wide eyes. "Does that make me—"

The video continued before she could finish her question. "You are our heir, the Princess of Reyna. And unfortunately, if you are watching this video record it means that both worlds are probably lost, if not to life then at the very least to an unsalvageable war. Though we finally achieved peace through a pact, there was a massive attack perpetrated by a rogue general of Reyna. In the chaos that followed, we were unable to save the King and Queen of Tora. They refused to leave their people behind but instead begged us to take their infant baby to safety. So there are two of you to keep us company on our escape, our journey to a new world and home." The woman smiled serenely in the video, then she continued.

Amari sat in silence for nearly a half hour while both women took turns describing where she had come from, a brief history, and the details behind their escape from the rogue general named Tal Boraan. The video seemed to end but just as Amari thought it was finished another started. There were sirens blaring in the background and both women looked incredibly afraid. Just knowing they were her biological mothers caused Amari's heart to race and her anxiety rose as she took in what looked like the last moments that led to her placement on Earth. It was Selphan who spoke first in the second video. "We don't have much time left. We were hoping to escape with you and your Q'sirrahna to someplace safe, but I'm afraid that safety is not meant for the four of us. The general's men have caught up to us at last and we are sending you and the child of Tora down to the planet in hopes that at least you will survive. We will never forget you, little sirra…"

Denii spoke again when emotion overcame the taller woman. "We love you, dear-heart, please remember that our sacrifices were all for you, and we would do the same again and again if it meant you were safe and happy. Be strong, me sirra, and Q'orre keep you safe. You will find your Q'sirrahna again when you need her most."

Silence reigned for nearly five minutes while Amari processed everything. Strange glittery tears ran down her face. They shimmered in a way they never had before. James and Michelle Bennett didn't acknowledge them or otherwise interrupt the peace of the moment. They understood that it would take time for Amari to come to terms with the grief she never knew she carried. Finally the teen looked up at the only parents she'd ever known. "They mentioned another baby, the heir of Tora? They said she is my...keh sirr-ah-nuh. What does that mean? And where is she?"

James reached over to turn off the glowing screen of the phone, the empty white light was cold after watching the end of the emotional video. "The rough translation to English is something like... spiritual eternal love." He turned to Michelle. "Help me out here, you're the linguistics specialist." Amari's jaw dropped. Clearly she didn't know anything about her parents. Amari felt more than a little betrayed in that moment of realization.

"I believe the closest this planet has to the meaning lies within the mythology of soul mates. Only with the Q'orren races, there is an actual bond that is both biological and psychological. And it is not a myth."

Amari sighed and rubbed her forehead right above the bridge of her nose. While she'd never had a headache or any other sickness that she could remember, she felt something coming on that was as uncomfortable as it was unfamiliar. "Wait, slow up. So basically I'm an alien who was adopted by what...different aliens?" She looked back and forth between them and they nodded. "Not only that, but I'm a princess of my world and I was sent to Earth with another baby, another princess, who happens to be my soul mate. Is that everything?"

"Well..." Her mother hedged.

It was her father that actually answered. "As you've pointed out, you aren't human. And your recent incident at Lake Twenty-two has shown you that your biology is quite different from a human's as well. From the studies we ran on you when you were younger—"

"You what?" Amari yelled and both adults winced.

Michelle held up her hands. "They were non-invasive, non-detrimental to your wellbeing. But in order to keep you safe we had to know how the unfamiliar elements of this biome would affect you. In the missive sent by your mothers, they were very concerned about adverse effects. However, we discovered something quite different. We've been waiting for the day that it would manifest in such a way that you would finally notice your differences."

Amari sucked in a breath. "Differences?"

"We..." He pointed back and forth between himself and Michelle. "...are both carbon-based life forms, similar to humans. However, our cells have a viscoelastic property and we can subtly alter our molecular structure to change our appearance. It has helped us to blend in during our two and a half decades on this planet. However, you are not carbon-based. At least not fully. Your cells, your entire atomic structure, seem to be some hybrid of crystal and carbon. The bottom line is that you absorb all forms of energy, then store and convert it."

"What the hell, I'm a freaking battery?"

Her mother frowned. "Watch your language."

Amari gave the older woman a look of disbelief. "Seriously? All this—" She made a circle in the air to encompass all of them. "All this and you're worried about my language, Miss *Linguistics Expert?*" She sucked in a breath to keep going but the deep voice of her father stopped her in her tracks. His familiar term of endearment brought tears to her eyes.

"Baby girl, appearance is everything. You watch the news, you've read the histories...you're taking college classes now. You know what the world is like here. They can never know about us, about you. Do you understand?" She nodded, meekly. "When I say all forms of energy, I mean it. Kinetic, electrical, thermal, light, nuclear, and many more. We don't know your limit, we only know that if the energy is great enough you gain a lot of potential power. We don't even know the conversion ratio between the energy you absorb and the power you can produce. Until now we had no idea how that power might manifest, other than your obvious health benefits. You've never been sick, or even suffered from cuts or insect bites. We weren't exactly sure why. Flying seems to be another one. Will you bear with me for one minute?"

Amari was dazed by what he was telling her but she agreed nonetheless. "Sure."

James stood and left the house through the French doors, then went down the steps off the back deck and returned a minute later with a fist size rock. He set it on the wood dining room table. *Thud* "You said you slipped from the cliff and when you landed you just sort of dropped to a heap on the ground, before you slid farther down the cliff?" She nodded. "Okay, I want to try something right now. I'm going to hit you as hard as I can, okay?"

"James..." Michelle's voice was a low warning.

He ignored her. "You know it won't hurt, you fell off a cliff for M'genda's sake! Do you trust me, baby girl?"

She thought about all that she'd been told and personally witnessed as her highly intelligent mind put all the pieces together. Two things that Amari Del Rey did not lack for was curiosity and bravery. "I trust you."

He motioned for her to stand and there was no warning. One minute she was staring at him with expectation in her eyes and the next moment a fist came out of nowhere only to stop abruptly against her face. There was no sound to it. Amari felt a rush, similar again to the feeling she'd always associated with her anxiety, and she stared at him in awe. "How did you just stop your punch like that? It was like a Kung Fu movie or something!"

"I didn't. I punched you as hard as I could. I'm going to do it again now." He repeated the first action with the same result. Only the second time she was left feeling completely energized.

"Whoa! I feel strange."

James pointed at the rock. "I want you to pick that up and squeeze as hard as you can."

Amari shrugged and picked up the rock and was surprised to find that it weighed nothing at all in her hand. The hard granite crumbled in her fist as she put pressure on it, and she found that the glow had returned to her vision, just like when she was floating. "No way!"

Her parents shared a look again and the words that slipped from her mother's mouth were anything but comforting. "Dangerous. She is much too dangerous. Which means her Q'sirrahna will be the same way."

Sadness stole over Amari at the fear in their eyes. She didn't want to be different, she didn't want to be dangerous. In exchange for the truths they had shared with her, in return for the fear they shared amongst themselves, she gave something back. "I've never told you this, but a part of me has been missing my entire life."

Michelle's lips parted with surprise at her words. "What?"

"I'm telling you now that I feel her, or rather, I feel her absence. There has been a part of me missing for as long as I can remember but I never said anything. I thought maybe I had been born as a twin or something, and separated at birth. Now I know why." She looked up at them, pleading. "I need to find her."

"Amari..." Her mother's hand was soft against the one that had just crushed stone. Fragile.

The teen shook her head as her eyes welled up with tears. "You don't understand. I can't go through the rest of my life with this hole inside me. Not now that I know. I can't!"

Always the voice of reason, her father soothed her by placing his hand on her other one. Strong and sure with his touch. "You heard your mothers, baby girl. You will find her when you need her most. Or maybe even when she needs you. If you feel the emptiness, then surely she must too. I have no doubt that time will pull you together, that is the nature of your bond."

He waited patiently for her to answer, and finally she relented to his promise. "Okay. But what do I do now?"

Michelle spoke and there was hard edge to her voice. "You leave for university soon but we will train you as best we can whenever you come home. Other than that, you live with your secret and ours. We continue blending in with the humans around us. And no matter what, never show anyone what you can do. If their treatment of those Chromodecs is any indication, I don't think the revelation of our non-human status would fare well for us."

"Appearance is everything." Her father's deep voice drove her mother's words home.

Amari whispered quietly back as she looked down at their joined hands. "Appearance is everything."

LET'S TAKE A moment to talk about the Chromodecs. We nearly forgot about that failed experiment back in 1952, didn't we? It was the work of our original antagonist, Doctor Daggett, which proved the necessity of the Sol-Ceti pact. At the time of his rather abrupt and unfortunate demise, we knew for a fact that the Chromodec experiment failed to yield results on the babies born from host mothers. For all intents and purposes, the program shut down the very month that Brian Daggett died. But the Watchers, secure in their high-level government positions, never stopped watching. No, they were ready when the first child was born from a Chromodec parent in 1971.

A tiny boy came into the world wailing as infants
do. But what was unusual about that particular birth,
about that child born of a failed Chromodec hybrid, was
the strength and nature of his first cry. His little
lungs sucked in that first breath of life and exhaled
with volume to protest being born into such a cold and
inhospitable world. But the volume of it was the very
thing that alerted the Watchers, and all people of
Earth really. That baby's cry ruptured eardrums in the
birthing room, shattered windows throughout the hospital, and killed the very mother that bore him. She was
already in the midst of postpartum hemorrhage. The process that would normally compress the bleeding vessels
of the uterus, called uterine atony, had failed to
occur. Her poor body could not handle that and the
shocking sonic assault. She passed away with a rough
mixture of agony and surprise stamped on her pale and
sweaty face.

It was an awful and bleak birth and the Watchers,
under the guise of United States government officials,
swooped in and took the infant into custody. Other
nations all around the world figuratively leaned in to
see what new race of being this child could be. Many
suspected the government of genetic tampering, a science that was just becoming popular in the seventies.
But without the baby as evidence, there was no real
proof of what happened in that hospital.

To counter speculation, the Watchers released a
very official investigative report that listed an
almost impossible coincidence of natural concurrent
occurrences that led to the event known only as "The
Shattering of St. Johns." Interviews, press, and write-
ups in nationally syndicated publications stated defin-
itively that the baby wasn't responsible for the chaos
that occurred that day. It was the first, but certainly
not the last, massive brainwashing of the people. And
it worked quite well, until the next child of power was
born. And the next.

In the year of 1952, not all the one hundred
implanted hybrid eggs survived to adulthood. However,
the experiment still enjoyed a ninety-nine percent success rate. But some of those genetically altered chil-

dren sired more than one offspring themselves. What
Doctor Daggett, and indeed the Watchers themselves,
didn't realize was that it wasn't the initial hybrids
that carried the power of extra ten chromosomes. It was
their children. It has been said that at any given
time, one percent of the population is of a criminal
mind. That statistic held just as true for Chromodecs.
And once the existence of the Chromodecs was no longer
a secret, the Watchers were not allowed to interfere.
Some Chromodecs chose to live life anonymously. Some
went into science to better understand who they were
and the capabilities of their unique and individual
powers. Others were recruited by the government as a
next level law enforcer.

The Chromodec Office of Restraint and Protection
existed for just such a purpose. The government loved
their acronyms so the C.O.R.P. was born not long after
the first reports of Chromodec criminal activity sur-
faced. Consequently, the government also had their own
special detainment facility. Guantanamo, closed for
nearly a decade at the time, was the perfect place for
such a detention center. Why an entire facility dedicated to containment? Not all Chromodecs were good.
There remained that small percentage that had dreams of
darker intent. Because all of them were born in the
United States, most of the people with power chose to
stay there. But a few scattered around the globe, ever
vigilant not to fall into the hands of foreign governments.

Seventeen years after two princesses fell to Earth,
there were nearly five thousand Chromodecs on the
planet and that heightened awareness of advanced good
and evil was the state of the world. Like ordinary
humans, there were powerful people who sought to do
harm and there were equally powerful people who existed
to stop them. With so much focus on people who were of
different ability, it made it even more essential for
those other races living in secrecy on the planet to
blend in. It could mean life or death if they were discovered since many didn't have superhuman powers like
the Chromodecs. They were weak and fallible, and every
bit as mortal as a human.

Chapter Three

THINGS SEEM PRETTY ideal for our young Reynan princess, don't they? One could imagine that the other child would fare equally well on the opposite coast of the most powerful country on the planet. Taken in and raised by the same race of Watchers, the wee babe from Tora would be cared for and loved just as the queens wished. But some stories aren't all about idyllic trips down paths of self-discovery, with an end destination being happiness. Some stories are about loss and the choices we make after suffering for much too long. And this tale brought to Earth from the stars reads much like a flipped coin. When one lives in the sun, the other will be relegated to the shadows. We move now to another place, roughly the same time of year as Amari's introduction to her origin story. There is a house that is far different from the one the young princess of Reyna grew up in, and that is where we find her Q'sir-rahna.

THE RUMFORD, MAINE police cruiser sat parked on the side of the road at the end of a long driveway. Perched ominously at the opposite end of the gravel track was the Oxford County Group Home for Teens. "You can't keep doing this, Zendara."

The young woman in the back of the car sneered. The rebellious expression fit perfectly with her beat-up black leather jacket and short-cropped spikey blonde hair. She was a punk and Officer Roberts knew it, but she wasn't a bad kid. "I hate that name. I told you to call me Zen the last time you picked me up."

Brian Roberts rolled his eyes. "I swear, kid, you give me a wicked huge headache every time I see you in the back of my car. But let me set something straight for you. Number one, I'm not obligated to do what you tell me. Number two, I've written your full damn name so many times on my paperwork that you're never gonna be anything but Zendara to me. Got it?"

The young woman in the back gave a long sigh but didn't

answer. Roberts spoke like the lifelong Mainer that he was and it grated on the young woman's nerves. Zen's parents never had the local accent so it wasn't something she adopted growing up. She took shit for it when she became a teenager but by that point in life she just didn't care anymore. And the more time that passed, the more she hated the way everyone around her spoke.

Officer Roberts continued with his lecture, not bothered in the least that she didn't want to hear what he had to say. "The problem I see is that this is the third time you've broken curfew this month, and for what? Some dickhead in a band? You're smarter than that, kid."

"What do you know about it, huh?" Her anger was instantaneous and hot. She was indignant that the cop could act like he knew her when the truth was, no one did. At least not since her parents died when she was twelve.

He looked at her in the rearview mirror. "I know that you caused quite a stir when your parents took you to the clinic in Bangor for an I.Q. test back when you were ten years old. You ain't dumb, that's for sure. I also found out that you aced all your placement exams in school yet you consistently refused to turn in homework or participate in class. And despite all your shenanigans, you managed to graduate near the top of your class a few months ago." She looked away from his eyes and he felt himself soften toward the sad young woman. He was nothing but a small town cop near retirement, but that didn't mean he couldn't have a heart. "Zen..." She looked back at him as a semi went by the cruiser, causing the car to sway back and forth.

"What?" Her voice was quiet, resigned.

"It's like you're not even trying anymore. I know Doug and Tammy wouldn't want to see you like this."

She slammed her fist into her denim-clad thigh, but there was no feeling to it other than a twisting in her stomach and a tightening of her muscles. It was always dead when she wished more than anything for the pain. "Well, it doesn't matter, does it? It's not like they're here to say anything. Besides, I've only got three more months then I'll age out of the system and I won't be your problem anymore, Officer Roberts."

He scrubbed a rough hand across the top of his bald head. Finally he turned in the seat so he could see her better through the cage that separated the front from the back of the cruiser. "And do what? You gonna move in with Remy and his crew of misfits? Or maybe work at that little grocery store for the rest of your life? You've got a basic education and a job that will barely keep you fed, Zen. I know people that can help you, there's a half-way house for kids that age out—"

"Save it, I don't need your charity. I'll figure something out. Are we done here?"

He continued to stare at her for a minute longer, but she looked away from his pitying eyes and focused on the lights of the large building in the distance. Finally he sighed and reached down to start the car again. "Yeah, we're done." Sitting in front of the group home, he watched as Zendara Baen-Tor was led inside by a security guard and a member of the staff.

REMY PASSED THE joint to Zen and resumed strumming the guitar that lay across his lap. "You see the news today? About the 'Dec that attacked a government building in Wisconsin?"

Zendara shook her head. "Nope, when have I had chance to watch the news? I came here straight from work." She took a hit off the joint, despite the fact that it never had any effect on her. But she wanted to fit in with the band so she did it anyway. It was all about appearances. "Did anyone die?"

"Not for lack of her trying. She was crushing everything with some sort of telekinesis. The CORP took her down before she could do too much damage."

The seventeen-year-old sighed. "It's bad enough we have to worry about regular criminals, but every time these Chromodec menaces pop up it just stirs people into a frenzy. Even now they're talking about passing legislation that would make it man-datory for people of power to register with the CORP."

A negligent hand stopped strumming and waved through the air. "You know I don't follow any of that. Not like we're going to see any of the 'Decs here in Rumford. Jesus, why do you even care? It's not like it affects us."

Zen shrugged and carefully took the joint that Remy held out again. There was just the barest nub left. "I don't know. It just bugs me that some people are even saying the Chromodecs should have tattoos or implants or something for tracking. That's some bullshit, you know? Even I read enough history in school to know that idea's fucked up!"

Remy played a languid progression of chords and shook his head at her ranting. "You need to chill out. I mean, fuck, you'd think my shit had no effect or something. Weed is supposed to make you mellow, dude. Besides, shouldn't you be focusing on one problem at a time? Like, what are you gonna do about Gould? You know if they catch you again they're gonna send you to the delinquent place up near Bangor. You'll be fucked then, babe."

"I don't know." She watched as the smoke swirled from between her lips. It was heavy and blue where it mingled with the rest in the basement of the house that Remy and his friends rented. The band lived and practiced there. And when they weren't all doing a variety of loser and dead-end jobs, they even had gigs in Rumford and the surrounding towns. Dive bars mostly, but it satisfied the musicians' need to perform. And on the occasion that the gig didn't pay in cash, it usually paid in beer. Sometimes Zendara sang with them during practices, but at seventeen she wasn't old enough to get into the bars where they played. And Remy's sketchy friend had yet to come through with a decent fake I.D. for her. Zendara picked at the frayed hole in her jeans then sighed in boredom. She stood from the ratty garage sale chair.

"Where you goin'?" Remy always kept track of her. Whether it was for possessive reasons, or something more, she didn't know. It wasn't like they were exclusive. He slept with chicks after their gigs, and Zendara regularly slept with Cin, the bassist for the band. The group was all pretty loose and casual like that. There was just something about Cin's dark hair and eyes that drew Zen to the woman more than anyone else. But something was also missing with her as well. As good as Cin could make her feel with those talented fingers, there remained a hole inside Zen that she didn't know how to fill. Drugs, alcohol, sex—nothing worked. And nothing worked well enough on her to dull the pain of losing her parents, or take away the ache of longing that had no name. "I gotta get back soon. After all, I don't want to get sent up to Bangor, right?"

Remy narrowed his eyes and watched as she looked everywhere but him. He knew she wasn't going back right away. He also knew that Cin had the night off from bartending and she was currently in her room, binge watching Netflix on her laptop. "All right. Catch you later."

With a nod, she ran a hand through her long blonde spikes then clomped up the wooden basement stairs, heading for Cin's room with purpose. Even thirty minutes of pleasure was better than nothing. Better than a lifetime of pain. Zendara was never going to fit in and live up to the expectations of the people around her. She missed her parents every single day and nothing was going to change that.

A little while later, Zen walked through the door of the group home to check in, right before curfew. Since Roberts had brought her back that last time, she had been careful to follow the rules. She didn't expect to see two of the home's security officers and the home's administrator waiting for her. "Where have you been?" Damaris Gould was a severe woman with no tolerance for anything but order. She was the sort of woman who wore her business suit like armor and kept her hair pulled back into a bun, even at ten o'clock at night.

Zendara was both confused and worried but she didn't let it show on her face. "What do you mean, where have I been? I had a shift at the grocery today and I was hanging out with some friends after. I haven't broken curfew, Miss Gould. I learned my lesson after the last time." Administrator Gould believed that infractions were best served by idle hands so every time Zen broke curfew, her punishment detail got more and more extreme. The last time Officer Roberts brought her back, Zendara spent two weeks cleaning bathrooms, gutters, and any other foul surface the old bitch could think of.

Ms. Gould scowled. "I'm afraid this has nothing to do with curfew, Miss Baen-Tor. Items have been reported missing by people in the women's dorm and a complaint was filed. That complaint named you as the thief. Now this is a very serious accusation but we gave you the benefit of the doubt and the board decided to do a search of all the rooms in the home. Unfortunately, the stolen goods were found in your possession."

"What? That is total bullshit! I haven't stolen anything from these cows, I haven't even been here all day. It's not like my door is locked, anyone could have put that shit in my room!"

She didn't notice Damaris Gould tense with her outburst, nor did she see the younger officer rest his hand on his Taser. But she did see Brooke Wendt smirking through the window of the door that led into the women's dorms. "If you please, Miss Baen-Tor, the crude language is highly unnecessary from a young woman such as yourself. And be that as it may, the fact remains that the stolen items were found amongst your own possessions. We have decided not to press charges because it would do the home more harm than good to make the local newspapers for such activity. But I see no other course of action than to have you transferred to a more secure facility until you turn eighteen in a few months.

You will have one day to submit your resignation to your employer and pack your things. A car will take you to the Bangor Home for Troubled Youth first thing Friday morning."

Zendara's mouth dropped open in shock. The betrayal of it all was like a punch to the gut. "You can't do that!"

Ms. Gould gave her a tight-lipped smile. "I can. The paperwork has already been submitted. We have given you more than enough chances to conform to our more—" She eyed the rough looking young woman from head to toe. "Our more delicate expectations, but you continue to push the boundaries of our patience. Good night, Miss Baen-Tor."

Angry, Zen took a step toward the administrator but stopped immediately as both security guards tensed. If there was one thing that Zendara Baen-Tor had learned in her nearly eighteen years of life, you didn't mess with the police. And while the group home's rent-a-cops weren't real cops, she wasn't going to go up against someone with a Taser. Just the previous year some kid had made the paper for getting tased by the cops, then later dying from the resulting seizure. No, while Zen was a rebel with most things, she wasn't stupid. She always kept her nose clean and she never started physical fights. If she had, she may have found out about her special powers sooner; however, the young blonde chose instead to spin on her heal and march through the door leading to the dorms.

Once in her room she began packing her meager belongings in the large duffle that she came to the group home with. She picked up the picture she kept on her nightstand and sat on the edge of her single bed. Doug and Tammy Smith stood in the background, while a twelve-year-old girl with nearly white blonde hair and bright blue eyes stood front and center. Her parents told her when she had turned ten that she was adopted. They said she came into their life right after they found out they couldn't have children of their own. They called her a little miracle sent down from the heavens above. The Smiths loved her more than anything, she knew it with certainty.

Zen ran a finger over the image of the little girl. She seemed so light and innocent in the photo. Gone were the dark clothes and punk hairstyle that she currently favored. Those were affectations born of having one's life turned upside down. The picture had been taken a few months before her parents were killed in a car accident in the middle of the school day. She was pulled from her class by the school counselor and Officer Roberts.

Her parents had no will, and no family members were found that could take in the young girl. She was allowed to pick up her clothes and a few personal belongings, but the rest of the household items were sold by the bank to pay off the lien on the house. Strangely enough, when she was going through their belongings, she found a key with a note in her dad's wallet. All that was written on the note was the name of a national bank and a security box number in Rumford. The social worker took her to the local branch of the bank but they had specific instructions not to open the box unless Zendara was eighteen. For all she knew, the box was loaded with gold and cash. At least that was a fantasy she used to tell herself when she fell asleep in each new foster house.

At first, Zendara was bounced between a few different private foster families. But she never adapted well to the loss of her parents and none of the foster families she was placed with wanted to cope with a child who didn't know how to deal with her grief. She suffered anxiety and bouts of clumsiness that left things broken in each new house. She was also much too intelligent and often got in trouble in school out of sheer boredom. Zendara was transferred to the group home shortly before her fourteenth birthday, almost exactly four years ago. And now she was moving again. The question remained, was she going to control her destination, or was she going to be moved against her will?

She could bolt, but Rumford was a pretty small town. The cops would know where to look for her, and she wouldn't be able to go back to her shitty job bagging groceries. She had some money saved up but not enough to live on until she turned eighteen. The other option was to spend her last few months in the system at some state run facility for troubled youths. Zen heard her share of horror stories about what went on there and she didn't like that choice either.

"I heard what happened."

Zen jerked her head around to look at the girl standing in the doorway. Her heart slowed again when she saw that it was her friend. "Hey, Cam." She circled a finger in the air. "Did you know about this?"

The redhead looked back at her sadly. "No. I would have said something if I did. You know it was Brooke. I hate that bitch!"

Zendara carefully wrapped the picture in her hand in a soft t-shirt and placed in the top of the duffle bag before she zipped it up. "Yeah, me too. Now I need to figure out what I'm gonna do."

Cam cocked her head slightly, confusion drawing the center of her brows upward. "What do you mean? I heard they're sending you up to the state home. You don't exactly have any choice in the matter."

Zen shrugged and looked away from her only friend at the group home. "I could run. I'll be eighteen in two months, they won't care after that."

"But if they catch you it will be even worse!"

The blonde slapped her bed covers in frustration but the bed didn't move at all. "Worse than what? We both know what State is like, we've both heard about the crap that goes on there. Running away might be my safest option and that's saying something."

The other girl walked all the way into the room and sat on the bed next to Zen. "Hey, it's only two months. You can stay safe that long. Just keep your head down and blend in. Try not to be such a troublemaker, yeah?"

Zendara sighed. "Yeah, you're probably right." She quirked a smile at Cam. "What are you going to do without me here, huh?"

Cam rolled her eyes. "Probably be bored. Nobody else tells me the crazy stories that you do." She paused then threw her arms around Zen. "I'm going to miss you. Seriously, of all the people I've met here you're the finest kind."

The blonde with the haunted pale eyes returned her embrace. "I'm going to miss you too. And hey, I'll put in a good word for you at the grocery store if you're interested. They're going to need someone to fill my position once I'm gone." She knew how much Cam had been dying to get her own job, but they were hard to find when you were under eighteen and living in a small town.

There were tears in Cam's eyes when she pulled away. "Sure they won't think I'm too gawmy?"

Zen grinned at her perpetually clumsy friend. "Naw. If you drop the cans when you're stocking just turn the dents to face the back of the shelf."

Cam giggled. "Thanks."

The redhead left after that and Zen settled down to sleep. The next day was going to be busy, but she'd manage. It wasn't as if she were leaving forever. Two months was practically nothing in the grand scheme of things. She just needed to keep her nose clean and play the part. She'd do whatever she needed until she was free, be whomever she needed to be.

NOW YOU KNOW that while one of our young women was fully aware of her birthright and power, the other was left in the dark and wallowing in a place that was less than ideal. The saying that "when life hands you lemons you should make lemonade" doesn't always apply. What if you have no sugar or water? Your end product will remain unpalatable. One thing both women *did* know, there was a hole that begged to be filled inside each of them. A yearning possessed both Amari and Zendara, and that emptiness would not be assuaged until they could at last meet on the face of this tumultuous world.

Chapter Four

AMARI'S EXCITEMENT GREW with each new item she packed into her suitcase. Her electronics, snacks, and hoodie were already stowed away in the backpack. In less than two months, she would be graduating with her doctorate but that wasn't what put the smile on her face. It had been an entire semester since she'd gone home to see her parents and her next visit had finally arrived. It wasn't simply that she missed them, because that was a given. Even after everything she'd learned about herself and about Michelle and James Bennett, they were still her mom and dad. No alien biology or princess birthright could change that. But beyond seeing her parents, she was also excited to be away from civilization for a few weeks. As promised, whenever she was home she had a free pass to use her powers. She and her parents spent hours a day testing and honing her skills.

"Hey, almost packed?"

Amari was so in her head that she didn't even hear her roommate coming down the creaky hall. "I am. Thank you for giving me a ride to the airport." Amari observed Jordan's blonde hair and blue eyes for a second. They had only been occasional lovers for the past few months. Jordan seemed fine with the casual arrangement but Amari still worried that the other woman would put too much emphasis on their sexual relationship. Amari knew she didn't want to make a life with her roommate because somewhere out there was her soul mate. She could feel her every day like a physical ache. However, the young alien princess hadn't met her Q'sirrahna yet, and there was a world of experience that Amari longed to gain. Despite her homeschooling and the fact that she lived in a place that was so remote, the young Reynan woman had taken to her sudden immersion into the university culture with gusto.

Jordan shrugged and smiled. "You know it's no problem at all."

Being a certified genius, Amari's classes were never any challenge, which was why she was graduating so young with a doctorate in biochemistry. Even Jordan, who would graduate with her in a few months, was six years older. So on the weekends, while the rest of her classmates were stuck with homework and large projects, Amari was traveling around the city, trying new food, and taking in all the people and things that she'd previously only ever seen on TV, YouTube, or Instagram. Many were surprised to find out that she was both homeschooled and a genius because she acted so completely normal, if more mature, than others her age. Amari was fine with that, fine with the assessment of strangers. She had to fit in and it was all about appearances.

And that was how she found herself occasionally sharing a bed with her roommate. A few months back Jordan convinced Amari to go to a party with her. The older woman was bi and promised Amari that it was a very inclusive crowd and also assured her that no one would mess with her for being too young. Amari agreed to be the driver of Jordan's car since she wouldn't be drinking. The end of the night found Amari consoling Jordan because her roommate's ex-boyfriend was at the party, with his new girlfriend. That was when Jordan confessed that she missed sex more than the boyfriend and Amari confessed that she'd never had sex. Shortly afterward they worked out the details of a mutually beneficial arrangement and worked their way into bed. Amari found it a lot of fun and Jordan was a great teacher.

Amari slipped into the straps of her backpack and hefted the suitcase, though admittedly it weighed practically nothing to her. "So what are your plans for the break?" She followed Jordan out of the room and waited for her roommate to respond.

Jordan gave her a giddy smile and held the front door to the apartment they rented, while Amari walked through with her bags. "Actually, I have a date tomorrow night."

Amari whipped her head around in surprise. "You what? Is it the woman from the coffee shop?"

Her roommate nodded shyly. "Yeah. Chloe."

Suitcase momentarily forgotten, Amari pulled her into a careful hug. "That is so awesome, you've been talking about her for weeks now. Are you excited?"

A big sigh met her question as they continued walking down the stairs to the main entrance of the building. "I am, but I'm also nervous. You know I haven't gone on a date since Jake."

The sound of the locks disengaging on Jordan's car was the cue for Amari to open the trunk. She rolled her eyes. "That guy was such a tool. The way he acted at the party," Amari shook her head. "I have no idea what you saw in him in the first place."

The Oakland International Airport was only fifteen minutes away from their apartment and Jordan didn't say anything for a few minutes. Then she finally conceded a point. "You're right, he was a tool. I'll have to fill you in on my date when you get back." She glanced down at her GPS, then shot Amari a curious glance in the passenger seat. "Have you gotten any offers for after graduation?"

The younger woman smiled. "Surprisingly, despite my age I've gotten a handful of offers from around the country. My paper on the single metal catalyst with both organic fuel cell and solar cell functionalities was well received. I've already accepted the position of Senior R & D scientist at a company in Indianapolis after I graduate and I start working there in three months."

"Twenty dollars says they call you Doogie Howser on the first day."

The young genius frowned. "I don't have to tell them my age, you know. It's illegal for a company to ask."

Jordan rolled her eyes, a terrible habit she picked up from her roommate. "Kid, while your brain is scary intelligent, you *look* like you're still in high school!

"I interviewed with them last month and the board of directors didn't say a word."

Laughter met Amari's response. "I've read your papers and seen all the stuff you've accomplished over the past few years. No one is going to turn down that head!" She paused and sighed. "I'm not going to lie, I'm only giving you grief because I've gotten exactly two offers. One for Cleveland, and the other for a company in New Mexico."

"What's wrong with either of those places?"

Jordan gave her a look before switching lanes on the freeway. "Really? New Mexico may as well be the seventh level of hell, it's so hot. And Cleveland is known for two things, losing sports teams and pollution." She shrugged. "I'm ninety percent certain I'll go with Cleveland though, just because it's closer to my family."

Amari laughed. "Minnesota girls have to stick to the cooler climate, huh?"

"Something like that. So anyway, about my date..." Her words trailed off. She had brought them back to the previous topic but didn't know how to continue.

The younger woman gave her roommate a big smile. "You should text me, or send cute selfies of the two of you. I've been in the coffee shop a few times and I think I know who it is, but I'm not certain she's the one I'm thinking of."

"Chloe has short red hair, in a pixie cut, and the cutest green eyes I've ever seen!" Jordan gushed and Amari knew her friend was smitten.

She laughed. "Yup, that's the one I was thinking of. And she *is* cute!" They chatted for a few minutes longer until Jordan pulled up in the drop-off lane at the airport. Amari unbuckled her seatbelt and gave the other woman an awkward hug across the center console. "Okay, you got my itinerary for my return trip, right?"

Jordan pulled her phone out of her pocket and brought up the calendar. "Yup, two weeks from Sunday, ten thirty at night. You're lucky I love you, I have an exam first thing that Monday!"

Amari laughed. "I am. And in case I forget to tell you, you're the best!" Ten minutes later, Jordan's car was gone and Amari sat slumped in a chair with dozens of other passengers waiting to head north. Her final destination was Everett, Washington, where her parents would pick her up. Then they'd have an hour and a half drive to their house in Verlot. She pulled out her eReader and waiting for the boarding call.

AFTER SPENDING THE day testing new avenues of energy absorption, Amari's clothes were once again left in a state of shredded disrepair. She'd been home for a week and both her and her parents felt like they'd made great strides in understanding more about her capabilities and strength. Unfortunately the last test led to a granite boulder the size of a house coming free from the cliff face and rolling right over top of her. They discovered a few important things after that incident, the most important being that energy absorption didn't just give her strength and allow her to fly. She could also move significantly faster than a normal human. That was how she stopped the boulder. When in hyper-mode, as her dad called it, perception, reaction, tracking, and balance all increased to match her speed.

The other thing they learned was that her clothes and shoes could not stand up to the abuse caused by rogue boulders and hyper-speed. Once back at the house, she removed her shoes with an irritated look on her face and tossed them in the trash. Her mother had disappeared into the basement as soon as they walked in the door and re-appeared around the corner into the dining room a few minutes later.

"What is that?"

Michelle held a vaguely humanoid shape of black material in her hands and had more material draped over her left arm. It was so dark that it looked like a shadow, as if it absorbed every bit of light that touched it. "These were our ship suits, the ones we came to this planet in. They absorb light and other radiation, the super black color is a side effect."

Amari moved closer, thoroughly intrigued. "That is very cool, I watched a video about stuff like this a few years ago. It was made with carbon nanotubes that are ten thousand times thinner than a human hair."

"Yes, well I can assure you that these are not made the same way. These have special polymers that allow the suit to change with us as we alter our shape. Being capable of faster than light travel, our race is significantly more advanced than that of the humans on Earth."

James took one of the suits from his mate's hand and held it out to Amari. "While it is nearly indestructible because of its elastic polymer properties, it also has the benefit of being self-healing with the added ability to neutralize caustic chemicals."

She took it from his hands. It was lightweight and surprisingly soft. "So how does that help me? These suits were clearly made for you." While she was near enough to her father's height, she did not have his exact build or dimensions.

Michelle Bennett grasped the neck of the suit she still held, and with a movement that Amari couldn't quite catch, the suit suddenly split apart down the middle. She couldn't tell if it was front or back because the fabric was so black. "Those same elastic properties will allow the suit to mold itself to the wearer. The suits that your father and I have are identical to each other."

The younger woman moved closer. "Show me how you did that."

After her mother repeated the move a few more times, Amari was able to easily open the one she held. She looked at her parents excitedly. "Can I put it on?"

Her dad's soothing voice held a hint of humor. "That's why it's in your hand, baby girl." He nodded toward her room. "Go on. I'm tired of buying new shoes every time you come home."

A dark eyebrow went up when Amari glanced back at him. "And how will it help my feet?"

Her mom answered. "The soles are reinforced and the material will react as you move, giving you cushion and extra push as you walk or run."

"Of course it will." Amari rolled her eyes as she walked toward the bathroom. She wasn't mocking her mom or the suit that she'd just been given. But she'd complained many times to her parents about them not sharing more alien technology and information with her. They insisted it was for the best if she were truly going to blend in. But here they were giving her this seemingly magical suit. She had the sudden thought that it probably wasn't so much that she'd worn them down with her begging but rather they were both frightened by the boulder incident. At the size of a house, and being made of granite, it was easily twelve hundred tons.

Yet she shrugged it off as if it were nothing. Much to Amari's surprise it didn't even hurt, but the amount of kinetic energy she absorbed was unfathomable. She felt so full of power that her vision immediately took on that glowing quality it had when she was expending energy. Since the boulder had continued rolling down the hill, she decided to race along the ground to catch it. Not only did she reach the speeding rock easily, but with a single punch she was able to split it in half. Of course it took more than one punch to reduce the massive stone to harmless rubble and when she was done she was even more "juiced up" from the rebounding kinetic energy. That was her own term for the feeling.

Unsure how to work off the uncomfortable amount of power, her dad told her to run around the house as fast as she could and he clocked her speed on a radar gun that he had in storage. At least she thought it was a radar gun. Running worked to expend her energy but it wasn't a long-term solution. Her shoes were destroyed and the ground around the house was significantly worn down, so they knew they'd have to think of another way, and soon.

When she came out of the bathroom wearing the suit, her dad's eyebrows went up. "It's been years since I saw one on a humanoid. You look like a shadow."

Her mom laughed. "I think you've been using your earth sight too long, James."

"Can I try it out?" The words came out in a rush of impatience and excitement. Her dad nodded and they followed Amari out of the house. The sun was setting as she took to the sky, hair and eyes glowing bright white. James and Michelle watched as she soared high above, much like the eagle she had admired a few years before. They were afraid that the life that had been entrusted to them by the Reynan royals twenty years prior was heading down a path of peril. But in the starlit sky, Amari had never felt so free.

NOW WE SEE that the first of our protagonists has started down her path, heading vaguely and slowly in the direction of her soul mate on the other side of the country. But what was the other woman to do? When we last saw Zendara Baen-Tor she was being forced into a possibly dangerous state-run group home. She had a negligible amount of money, no family, and her friends were being left behind. And three years is a long time to feel that ache of emptiness.

ZENDARA SAT IN the back room at Pete's computer, checking her email. She hadn't heard from Cin in about a week and her texts went unanswered. Zen was currently on her thirty-minute break before closing out her shift at the bar, so she had plenty of time. She never went back to Rumford when she was released from the foster care system. Instead she opted to stay in Bangor and found a job working a sleazy strip club, six of seven nights a week. Waiting tables for horny old men barely paid the bills but she still managed to tuck away money here and there throughout the week. She wanted to get out of Maine and head west. She wasn't sure why, but something pulled her in that direction. Before losing contact, Cin had been texting Zendara about her sister's cleaning business and how fast it was growing. And the former bassist was sure she could get Zen a job working nights cleaning office buildings in downtown Detroit. Anything had to be better than working at a titty bar in Bangor. The good thing was that being part of the wait staff, she didn't have to go topless. The bad news was that she also didn't get the tips that the dancers did either. It was a fine line between self-respect and starvation.

After logging in, she read Cin's email and her face broke into a wide grin. Her friend hadn't dropped off the face of the earth after all, she had only dropped her phone and shattered the screen. She read the email twice and each time the middle line caused her stomach to flutter with nervous anticipation. It was the one that insisted that Zendara should move to Detroit. It continued by saying that Cin's sister had a job for her when she got there. She even offered an empty room in the house she was renting with two other women. They'd split the bills four ways and it was guaranteed that Zen could afford it while she was working for Cin's sister.

It all worked out so well in thought. And she didn't have to worry about any drama with Cin. While they never continued their sexual relationship after Zen was sent away, the two women remained friends over the years. Sometimes she thought her old friend from Rumford was her only friend left, which made it especially hard when Cin moved back to Michigan to help her sister out. There was nothing left to hold Zendara in Maine any longer and that persistent ache of longing that radiated within her heart continued to pull her west.

"What are you doing in here?" Donnie, the assistant manager, stood in the doorway to the back room with his normal constipated look on his face.

"I'm on my break, what's it to ya?"

His irritated features turned to sour anger. "Listen you little cunt, don't get an attitude with me! And what are you doing on Pete's computer anyway?"

Zendara scowled. "He gave me permission. I've still got seventeen minutes left of my break, will you quit riding my ass already?"

Donnie had never been a trim man, but he didn't even have the reassuring bulk of active fat either. He wasn't some athlete who was put out to pasture after high school, playing rec league softball one night a week. No, he was well and thoroughly sedentary. She doubted he'd ever done any lifting other than a beer can. He sneered and jerked a thumb back toward the door he came through. "Well I'm in charge tonight and I say get the fuck out of here already. Take your break somewhere else!"

The younger woman muttered a few choice words and logged out of her email before shutting the computer down. "Fine. Whatever you say, *boss*!" She made to stomp past him, muttering even more. "Enjoy your spank session, you rancid piece of sh—"

He roughly grabbed her arm before she could pass him and escape out the door. "You know, you'd be pretty if you used that mouth for more than just bitching all the time."

Zendara grew livid and jerked her arm free. "Eat a dick, asshole!"

"You can't talk to me like that, you ungrateful little whore!"

"Oh, fuck off, Donnie!"

Before she could exit the door, he pushed it shut and blocked her escape route. "Not so fast there, chicky!" The unappetizing specimen of human genetics eyed her up and down and gave his crotch a slow rub just below the spot where his belly hung over his belt. "You know, if you polish 'Little Donnie' real good for me before you go back to work, I'll forget you said that and I won't tell Pete you've been skimming the register."

"I've never stolen anything in my life!"

His smirk was pure evil. "No?"

She knew he wasn't going to move, and she had heard a few of the girls talk about how they'd been blackmailed into giving Donnie blowjobs. Thinking about the email and her savings for a split second, Zendara made a choice. As he started to reach for her one more time she surprised him by stepping in close. Then before he could say another word, she kneed him hard in the crotch. "Polish this, Asshole!" As he crumpled to the floor in agony, Zendara calmly untied her apron and threw it over his writhing body. "I quit!"

Chapter Five

A LITTLE FUN fact, 23 is one of the most commonly cited prime numbers, which is a number that can only be divided by itself and one. 23 is also the quantity of chromosome pairs the average human is born with. There are dozens of coincidences that all center on this double-digit wunderkind of the number world. It is the smallest prime that contains consecutive numbers. There is even a self-declared religion, called Discordianism, which believes 23 is the Holy Number. They say it is a tribute to the Goddess Eris, the one who surveys a world of chaos. But for two babies who have grown up separated by fate and circumstance, 23 is a magical number of possibility. Their lives have been circling each other, spinning ever closer as the pull of their bond brings them together. For much too long, they have been waiting to meet, waiting to fill the void that exists when Q'sirrahna are kept apart.

"DID YOU SEE we had another shooting last night, at a mall down in Texas? It's all over the news today. The thought that someone could do that just makes me sick!"

Dr. Amari Del Rey looked up from where she was making notations. "I saw and I agree. I also saw we had another gang related shooting here in Chicago last weekend, not that it was much different than nearly every single day of the week. They said an off duty CORP agent jumped in front of some kids and saved their lives. Supposed to be a ceremony this weekend. I swear, the violence makes me want to just unplug from life for a while. There is no making sense of the human race's need to perpetuate such brutality on one another." She shook her head.

"It's not all just normal humans stirring up trouble! Look at the Chromodec that tried to take over the Willis Tower last month. He blew the windows out and had twenty hostages when the CORP finally caught up with him. I mean, it's terrifying to think that a person with an automatic gun can fire it off into something like a crowded mall. But these 'Decs are really danger-ous without weapons at all!"

Amari rolled her eyes. "Didn't he call himself Zeusifer or something?"

Her associate, Dr. Stephanie Young, snorted at the stupid name. Then she continued clicking through the data results of their live cell engineering project. "Yeah. He could draw lighten-ing from the sky or something. Nearly took out a city block down in the loop." She sighed and shook her head. "Sometimes we humans really suck, you know?"

Stephanie laughed and Amari chuckled half-heartedly with her. After all, she couldn't truly agree because she wasn't human. "Yeah, funny how that is."

Stephanie looked up with a grin and switched gears conver-sationally. "Speaking of funny, my niece told me a new joke when I went to my sister's last weekend. Two chemists go into a bar. The first one says, 'I'll have an H-two-oh.' The second one says, 'I'll have an H-two-oh too.' The bartender serves them up and both chemists drink. The second one dies."

Amari barked out an abrupt laugh, not expecting her associ-ate's joke to be any good. While Stephanie thought herself hilari-ous, she wasn't known for much more than sarcasm and bad puns. The other doctors and internists usually just humored her. "That was good, actually. You can tell your niece well done the next time you see her."

The Reynan princess had been working at the University of Chicago for about six months. She was in Dr. Andrea Evan's lab as a post-doctoral research associate. The associates in Evan's lab were tasked with working on ongoing molecular tool develop-ment projects. They did a variety of other projects as well that required mastery of a broad spectrum of skills from protein engi-neering to live cell imaging. It was very similar to what she had been doing in Indiana.

After a little more than two years at her position in Indianap-olis, Amari felt the need to move again. While the aching absence of her Q'sirrahna no longer pulled her east, something told her that it was time to move north. She took the job at the University of Chicago because the laboratory with the job opening was focused on the manipulation of signaling pathways that were responsible for cancer metastasis. One of the main current direc-tions, as stated by Doctor Evans, was in the development of new tools for manipulation and detection of protein activity in living cells. Bottom line, cancer was a huge problem for humans and Amari wanted to do her part to solve that problem. Even though she couldn't use her powers to help the human race without risking exposure, there was no restrictions about using her brain.

"You have any plans for the weekend?"

Amari shook her head. "Nothing major, why?"

"I'm going with a group of friends to try a new club down in the loop tomorrow night. Want to come along?"

Amari contemplated her own plans for the weekend. The last time she went home to visit her parents, they gave her a thumb drive that contained the histories of both Reyna and Tora. It had taken them years to download the information from the computer in her pod and translate it into a format that could be played on Earth systems. It wasn't like the movies where the protagonist could just plug into an alien ship and make it work. She compared the two activities in her head. She thought of staying in her apartment and listening to the history of her home world and then considered the idea of going to some club in downtown Chicago with a group of people she didn't know. She shook her head slowly while Stephanie looked on. "You know what, thank you for the invitation but I'm still unpacking boxes from my move. Plus I'm reading this really good history series right now. I'm just going to stay home and chill."

Stephanie shrugged. "Suit yourself. But text me if you change your mind. We live close to each other, and I'm going to take the red line downtown after work Friday night to meet the rest at the restaurant. So if you change your mind you'd be keeping me company on the train. We'll go to the club after dinner."

Amari shrugged. "Thank you, but maybe some other time."

The older woman paused for a second and Amari looked up, sensing her eyes. She waited for Stephani to speak her mind. It never took long. "You know...you're pretty young to just stay home every weekend. How old are you anyway?"

"Twenty-three." Amari made a face and waited for the comment from her colleague. Just as Jordan predicted, it took her old colleagues in Indiana all of a day to start calling her *Doogie* as soon as they discovered her age. She found it annoying because she'd never even seen the show about the young genius medical doctor. But Amari refused to hide something so trivial when she had much bigger secrets to keep.

"Jesus Christ, you're just a kid!" When Stephani saw the look on Amari's face she toned down her reaction a bit. "Sorry, I just meant that. I have more than ten years on you and you're the one staying home reading the history of the world every weekend. Don't tell me you have a couple of cats at home too."

The younger woman shook her head and smiled. "No pets. But it's no big deal really. I've always been the solitary type, you know? If I get out, it's usually just wandering around and doing my own thing. I like people-watching, I'm just not a big fan of people." That was the most personal thing she'd admitted to anyone working at her current lab. But she trusted Stephanie. She felt comfortable with the woman who had immediately taken her under her wing when she started.

Stephanie took a few steps closer to Amari. The hand she settled on the younger woman's shoulder was warm and comforting, and it reminded Amari that she hadn't had any physical contact with anyone since she moved to Chicago. "Hey, it's cool. But if you do want to get out and make some friends, my crowd is pretty diverse. Young, old, gay, straight, intellectuals, gamers, geeks, I know a little bit of everyone." She cocked her head when Amari didn't answer. "It's funny, we've worked together for six months now and I barely know anything about you. And here I've been telling you all about my family, my cat of nine years, my ex-boyfriends, and my collection of troll dolls."

Amari laughed and patted Stephanie on the arm. "It's all right. If it makes you feel any better, you're my only friend in Chicago."

"Then I've been a terrible friend!" A buzzer sounded nearby and both women glanced toward the source before looking back at each other. Stephanie was undeterred. "Come on now, it's your turn. You can give me the deets while we check slides."

"Fine." Amari shook her head at the other doctor's persistence then saved her document and followed Stephanie over to the incubator. "Where should I start?"

Both were busy gowning up in sterile clothing and Stephanie waved her hand haphazardly at Amari. "I don't know, just the basics."

They began removing and analyzing slides and Amari gave her colleague the deets, as requested. "Hmm, I'm adopted and grew up in Verlot, Washington. Homeschooled with remote undergrad until seventeen, then I went off and got my doctorate from the University of Southern California – Berkeley. I took a position in Indianapolis when I was twenty, a month after graduation—"

"Twenty! Jesus." Stephanie shook her head and snorted behind her mask and Amari finished her sentence.

"And I moved here six months ago. Pretty boring life really, not much to tell."

"Any boyfriends or girlfriends?"

The young Reynan woman felt a familiar pang of loss sweep through her as she thought of her Q'sirrahna. "No, neither."

Stephani's wide eyes were comically visible over her mask. "Nothing? Um, are you a virgin or ace?"

While Amari knew well what the first one was, she'd never heard the second term. "What's ace?"

Stephanie rolled her eyes. "Boy, you really don't get out much, do you? Ace is just slang for someone who is asexual. A person who has no sexual feelings or desires—"

Amari held up a gloved hand. "Stop, stop, I already know what asexual means. I just wasn't familiar with that term. And no, I'm neither a virgin nor am I asexual. I just haven't had a girl-friend or boyfriend."

Once her hands were free, Stephanie turned fully to face Amari and pointed at her. "Wait, I'm confused. You haven't been in a relationship, you're not ace, but you're also not a virgin?"

The older doctor watched as Amari's face flushed pink where it was showing above the surgical mask. Amari sighed and rolled her eyes. "Surely I don't have to explain friends with benefits to you, Doctor Young."

Stephanie didn't answer but she gave her a look of disbelief.

"Why do you find that so hard to believe?"

"Man or woman?"

Amari hummed and smiled unseen behind her mask, remem-bering all the curves of Jordan's body. "Woman."

"Is—" Stephanie started hesitantly, then continued after a gap in her words. "Is it your parents? Are they against you being gay?"

Amari shook her head, touched that Stephanie cared. "No, it's not that. Mom and Dad are really cool. As a matter of fact, they're more open to diversity than anyone else I've ever met." Amari laughed to herself. Dr. Stephanie Young truly had no clue just how diverse her family was. "No, I know it's not usual for someone my age. But it really has nothing to do with my parents, or anything that's happened to me in my past. While it's true that I am pretty solitary, that's not the reason I've avoided relation-ships." Her thoughts turned inward to the message from her birth mother. *You will find your Q'sirrahna again when you need her most.*

"Well, what is the reason then? Now I'm curious and I'm going to bug you until you tell me."

Amari pulled out another slide and placed it delicately into the machine. "You know what they say about curiosity."

Stephanie snorted and rolled her eyes. "I have a cat so I know all about curiosity. Spill, or I swear on all that's holy that I'll take the little mice from Kendall's lab and load up your locker if you don't."

The younger woman shrugged. "I happen to like mice, but fine, I'll tell you. The truth is that I'm waiting for someone."

"You're kidding me! Who?"

From one second to the next, it seemed as though Amari changed topics. "Tell me something, Doctor Young. You're a woman of science, do you believe in soul mates?"

Stephanie's gaze focused on the far wall of the lab as she thought about the question. "You know, I've always wanted to believe. I mean, I grew up watching Xena and reading science fiction and romance. Wouldn't it be nice if there was someone out there just meant for us? Someone with whom you connected with on such a deep level that you could never be split apart? Realistically though, I'm not so sure something like that is possible, but—"

Her words cut off as her eyes grew distant with thought. Amari prompted her. "But?"

"But who am I really to determine what is possible and impossible? For instance, look at the Chromodecs. People one hundred years ago would have thought they were magicians, or gods. Science has a way of explaining the unexplained but we don't know all the science and some mysteries have yet to be solved." She paused. "I try to keep my own relationship goals a little more down to earth. I'm a thirty-five year old single lady looking for a boyfriend, or possibly a girlfriend, in a dating pool that is only interested in women two-thirds my age. I'd be happy to find a man who knows how to do laundry and doesn't send a dick pic as a way of asking me out. The idea of a soul mate seems a bit out of reach."

Amari put a latex gloved hand over her mask to muffle the laughter. "Tell me that didn't really happen."

Stephanie rolled her eyes. "I'd like to but I can't. I still have the evidence on my phone."

"What? You didn't delete it?"

"Psshh, are you kidding me? I was amazed at it. But I didn't respond because I'm sure the guy is a total man-whore and I wasn't going to touch that with a ten foot pole."

Stephanie and Amari finished the last of the slides nearly at the same time and closed the machine. Then Amari took off her mask and gloves and turned to her friend. "I don't believe you! Let's see it."

The other woman looked at her, shocked. "Are you serious?" Amari nodded and made a "hand it over" motion with her fingers. Stephanie removed her own gloves and mask before sliding her cell phone out of the pocket of her lab coat. She scrolled through her photos then handed it over to Amari. "There you go."

Amari took the phone and her eyebrows went up as she gazed at the picture. She turned the phone horizontal, then vertical again. "Well. That is certainly impressive!" She handed the phone back to the other doctor who pocketed the device and started laughing.

"And how do you even know if you've never been in a relationship and have only been 'friends with benefits' with a woman?"

The younger woman shrugged. "If it's on the Internet, I've seen it."

Stephanie's eyes crinkled at the corners with her mirth. "Doctor Del Rey, you are a kinky woman!"

"Not kinky, just curious."

The older woman came right back with Amari's own words. "You know what they say about curiosity. But anyway, back to your question about soul mates. Why did you ask? Do you believe there is one out there for you?"

Amari's voice was filled with certainty and for a second, Dr. Stephanie Young was jealous. "I know that my soul mate is out there, I can feel her every day. It's like there is a piece of me that is missing." Amari unconsciously rubbed the center of her chest where the ache was usually strongest. She knew she was admitting too much, but it was also a lonely life that she led. The only people she had to talk with about her unique situation were her parents. And they always cautioned her to be calm, be patient, and to wait for her Q'sirrahna to come to her.

"Do you know who it is? Is this some random idea or is there someone you've met that leads you to believe you are soul mates?" Stephanie's words were far from teasing, as Amari initially feared when she admitted her beliefs.

Amari shrugged and moved to a cabinet to grab another tray of samples to load into the incubator. "Yes and no. I don't know who she is but I know of her and while it may seem crazy, I can feel a pull to her. It's nothing precise, just a vague general direction."

"That does sound crazy, but cool too! Well, for your sake I hope you find her."

Amari sighed. "Me too." Suddenly, her loneliness became unbearable and she looked up at her colleague and friend. "You know what, you're right. I do need to get out more. If the offer still stands, I'd love to hang out with you and your friends tomorrow."

Stephanie gave Amari a wide smile at the younger woman's sudden change of heart. "That's the spirit, kid!"

AMARI'S DECISION TO accompany her friend and co-worker Friday night would prove to be significant in more ways than one. You see, per her parents instruction, Amari Del Rey had always tried to fit in. The world was a dangerous place, made even more so by the existence of the government Chromodec experiment's progeny. It was hard enough for people to cope with the average horrors and atrocities perpetrated on them, let alone crimes caused by people with superhuman ability. Citizens were scared, the government was scared, and frightened people passed immoral laws based on a panicked response.

The young Reynan read the news, she followed the bills being introduced in the House and Senate, and she read every report on the Chromodecs that she could get her hands on. That included the redacted ones published by the government as well as the top secret files she got from her parents. She well understood the power potential of the hybrid humans with their extra ten chromosomal pairs. On one hand, the biochemist side of her was fascinated. On the other hand, she was even more worried that public opinion would eventually sway everyone against all people of power, even the heroes that served with the CORP. And there was no telling what they, or the government, would think if they knew

actual aliens were in their midst. Specifically one
holding the power that she did. Amari Losira Del Rey
was no Chromodec, she was something far superior and
frightening with her potential.

SINCE IT WAS still spring and the wind coming off the lake
was chilly at night, Amari wore a pair of skinny jeans with industrial looking zippers sewn into the legs, and a thin and tight black
turtleneck sweater. She left her hair down to help keep the wind
off her neck. While she didn't feel the cold quite like a human
would and it certainly wasn't capable of killing her, Amari still
didn't find it comfortable. She had less than ten minutes before
she was supposed to meet Stephanie. The other doctor also lived
along Washington Park so was fairly close. Amari put on a pair of
sturdy black boots with zippers in the sides. Then she grabbed a
black jacket from her coat hook before pocketing her wallet and
keys and walking out the door.

Stephanie was hopping on one foot, putting her shoes on
when she answered the door. "Hey, you made it! Give me just a
second and we can go." The Garfield subway station was only
two blocks away, luckily for Stephanie. Amari could never understand why women would want to wear such uncomfortable
shoes. They weren't warm or practical, and tall heels had been
proven to have a number of adverse effects on the human body.
Joint disease of the feet, shortened Achilles tendons, osteoarthri-
tis of the knees, hip pain, and chronic back soreness were all signs
that a product should never have been invented. Amari blamed
her newly discovered penchant to judge human cultural idiocies
on her recent exposure to her home world histories. The planets
of Reyna and Tora were significantly more advanced in every
way. Of course, they apparently had their own share of violence
and war, so clearly no race was perfect.

There were about ten women total in the group, counting
Amari and Stephani. But they were the only two that lived so far
south, by Hyde Park. That's why everyone just made arrangements to meet at Girl & the Goat, an eclectic restaurant that had
gained in popularity over the past few years. Jill, a physicist at
Loyola, had called ahead and made a reservation for twelve so
they were covered. Stephanie was right, her group of friends was
pretty diverse. They also had a habit of playing musical chairs
around the table throughout the casual tapas-style meal, so

Amari got to meet and chat with nearly all of them. Afterward they ended up at a speakeasy down on Dearborn, where they had drinks and took turns singing bad karaoke. Amari couldn't remember the last time she'd had so much fun.

It was after two a.m. when Amari and Stephanie found themselves perched gingerly on dirty plastic seats, riding south on the red line back to their station. For reasons only the CTA would know, the train didn't stop at Garfield like it was supposed to and Stephanie swore as the train cruised by their station. "Goddamn it! Of course it would skip on the night I have to pee so bad I can taste it."

Amari looked at her, alarmed. "What do you mean, skip? Does this happen often? How do we get back?"

The train started to slow so she followed Stephanie's lead as the older woman stepped toward the door. "It means, young grasshopper, we get off here to take the next northbound train back to our stop. It's a pain in the ass because it could be fifteen or twenty minutes before the next one comes along at this time of night."

Bing Bong "Doors are closing."

They stood on the platform for a second as the train pulled away, then Amari cut a glance to her friend. Stephanie wore a pained expression that wasn't entirely due to the uncomfortable heels. "Is your bladder going to last until you get home?"

Stephanie grimaced. "I don't want to talk about my bladder right now." She led the way down the stairs, then over to the other side and back up. There was one man in a ratty hooded-jacket waiting on the northbound platform. They were in luck because the digital sign hanging above said the next train was due in five minutes. Unfortunately that was the only thing that was lucky. As they stood there waiting, the man stalked toward them. His face looked pale in the light of the platform, his hair a tangled mess where it stuck out past the hood. Before Amari even realized what was going on, the man had pulled a knife and held it toward them in a threatening manner. "Give me your money and neither of you bitches gets hurt. Got it?" He glanced around nervously to make sure no one else was near then focused back on the two women.

Amari wasn't sure if her friend was brave or stupid because instead of doing as the man asked, she pulled out her cell phone and snapped a picture of him. "No way, asshole! I'm dialing the cops now." Maybe it had worked before, or maybe Stephanie was usually a good judge of people and their motivations but either way, she was wrong about that particular man. Rather than take off as Stephanie was hoping, his face contorted in rage and he shoved Stephanie backward, sending her phone flying out of her hand even as she stumbled past the yellow safety line. He seemed to realize what he'd done when Steph's panicked face disappeared over the edge of the platform. He took off back down the steps to exit the station.

"Amari!" Stephanie called from below, her voice high and frightened. In the distance, a light appeared signaling the approach of the next train. There was no question as to what Amari had to do but she knew it would have repercussions.

With a controlled jump down to the platform, she saw where Stephanie sat on the timbers just to the side of the actual tracks. Her shoes were gone, scattered somewhere in the darkness. Amari stumbled over one of the timbers when she landed, causing her step past the closest rail, subsequently touching against the third rail. Stephanie screamed, then stopped and looked confused when nothing happened to her friend. Amari just shook her head at the massive jolt of energy and came back in rush. Far from doing nothing, the current from the rail had juiced her beyond belief. "Hold on."

A horn sounded much too close so she quickly scooped Stephanie up in her arms, then leaped straight up to the platform above. She set the older woman back on her feet and the high-pitched sound of brakes startled Stephanie from the shocked stare that she gave the younger scientist. "How did—"

Amari grabbed her by the arm and practically pulled her onto the train as the doors opened. "Come on, we have to go!"

"But—my shoes! My phone! And you..." Her words trailed off.

Knowing her own feet were immune to both the temperature and any damage they'd receive while walking barefoot in the city, Amari calmly removed her boots and handed them to Stephanie. "These might be a little big but they'll get you home."

Instead of taking the boots she leveled a gaze at the younger woman. "I don't understand." The fearful set of her mouth and eyes had been replaced by that familiar look of curiosity.

Amari sighed. "I can explain, just not here." The train started to slow and she shook the boots she held out. "Put these on, we're nearly to our station."

Stephanie grabbed the offering and quickly stuffed her feet

in, then zipped them up. She groaned and stood as the train pulled to a stop. As they made their way through the doors, Stephanie in Amari's boots and Amari in her socks, the older woman said the first inane thing that came to mind. "This is the best my feet have felt all night."

Then the events of the previous fifteen minutes caught up with them and both women started laughing. They didn't get control of themselves again until they turned onto the block of Stephanie's apartment. It was Amari who broke the silence. "I'm sorry I didn't save your phone."

Stephanie stopped walking. "That is what you have to say to me? You're sorry that you didn't save my phone? Are you aware that just a little bit ago you jumped off a train platform, touched the goddamn *third rail*, which should have killed you by the way, and you lifted me into your arms and jumped back up onto the platform acting as if gravity didn't affect you in the least?" She paused and ran a hand through her carefully styled hair. "Are you kidding me right now?"

Amari looked down, noticing for the first time how there was a small hole in one black sock, perfectly displaying the big toenail of her left foot. "I'm sorry."

The older woman wagged a finger at her. "Screw sorry, kid. You're not getting these boots back until you tell me what's going on. So, walk and talk, babe."

Amari didn't say anything until they were about twenty yards from the entrance to Stephanie's apartment building. Finally she spoke. "Do you believe in aliens?"

Stephanie was busy digging her keys out of the purse that was slung across her chest beneath her coat. She pulled up short at Amari's words and looked at her in dawning amazement. Their conversation about soul mates earlier came back to the forefront in her mind. She pointed a finger at the younger woman and Amari slowly nodded. "Holy shit, you're a Chromodec!" Stephani shouted the words and Amari quickly hushed her.

"Keep your voice down. And I'm not one of those government hybrids. I'm asking you if you believe in Aliens, with a capital 'A,' Steph. X-Files, little gray men, and anything else the movie industry has thought up and only gotten half right."

Stephanie didn't shout the words, but they felt right given the situation at hand. "There are more things in heaven and earth, Horatio, than are dreamt of in your philosophy."

For Amari, she felt a mixture of relief and anxiety. Her

silence had been broken, at last.

SO OUR FIRST protagonist has "outed" herself in the
tale, but will her life get better or get worse? And
who can say whether or not her new human friend will be
trustworthy? But at least she has followed her heart
and continued in the direction of her Q'sirrahna. When
last we observed our other protagonist, she too was
following her heart. Headed to Detroit, you had to wonder how the young Toran baby, grown into an orphan
punk, fared in such a dark and dangerous city. After
all, revitalization only took a town so far. Unfortunately for both young women, the motor city was still
nearly three hundred miles from the windy one. The ache
persisted.

"YOUR SHOT!" ZENDARA called out to Cin where the other
woman stood at the bar ten feet away. They had the night off and
were spending the evening shooting pool at a place called
"Gears" in Royal Oak. They had been working for Cin's sister,
Gloria, for the past few years and by request were usually on the
same shift. Urban Cleaning Solutions had become quite a name in
the Detroit area for their quality of service in cleaning the office
buildings downtown. While the job wasn't challenging in the
least, it was easy and it allowed Zendara to work nights, which
she preferred. But that familiar ache was starting again, and
something told her she needed to keep traveling west. She knew
that Gloria's company had just expanded to West Michigan, ser-
vicing the greater Grand Rapids area. And Zendara was hoping to
transfer.

Cin returned with two beers and two shots, neither of which
would affect Zen in the slightest. It was just one of many strange
facts about herself that she never could explain, nor would she
ever tell anyone else. She just assumed it was a metabolism thing.
It's not like she had health insurance to go get checked out.

"All right already, Jesus! If I'm going to lose I at least want to
have a good buzz doing it."

They both laughed as they downed their shots then chased
them with swigs of beer. Zendara stepped back from the table
while Cin lined up her pool cue. "You'd think that after all these

years messing around in dive bars you'd be better at pool."

"Hey!" Cin protested, right as she managed to sink a ball. "I do well enough at the game. You're just a freak of nature who is unusually good at playing with sticks."

Zendara snorted. "Maybe I should have been a drummer, huh?"

Cin laughed so loud people turned to stare. "You also have no rhythm, so no. You can safely cross that one off your list."

"Fuck you." Despite her words, both women knew that Zen wasn't mad. When Cin finally missed, the punk stepped up to the table. "So, I've been thinking…" Her voice trailed off as she shot, but she didn't pick up her sentence again on the other side.

"About?"

Zendara stopped playing and leaned on her stick, the butt of it pressing against the floor near her right combat boot. "I'm ready to move on again. I want to go west."

A dark eyebrow lifted as Cin took a calm swig of her beer. "West? That seems kind of vague."

Zen sighed and walked over to grab her own beer. She propped the stick against the wall by their table. "Grand Rapids. I want to move and I was wondering if you think Gloria would let me transfer to the new UCS location over there."

Much to Zendara's surprise, Cin let out another loud laugh. "Let you? She'd probably cream her pants if you asked to transfer. She was just complaining the other day about how hard it was to expand and train a new team on the other side of the state. She'd probably kiss you and give you a raise if you agreed to relocate over there. She wants people in Grand Rapids who are familiar with her company and the quality expectations she has. She's been over there so much lately that my nieces are starting to miss their mama."

Zendara chuckled at her friend's choice of words. "I'll pass on the kissing, thanks. I think one sister is more than enough experience on that front. But seriously, you're not mad? You're my best friend and I hate to just leave you."

Cin set her beer down and reached a hand across the table to grip the younger woman's shoulder. "Hey, it's fine. I promise. I mean, I left you a few years back so I understand that life takes us where it wants sometimes." She paused for a second as she let her hand drop, then she lowered her voice and leaned a little closer. "Is this about…you know, the ache that you were telling me about? Is it pulling you again?"

Zendara had told Cin about the aching emptiness when they still lived in Rumford. When asked why Zen never wanted to date anyone, Zen was forced to explain the feeling she had, the one that pulled her and made her think that someone was out there on the other end. Rather than make fun of her like most probably would have, Cin just nodded and told her it was all cool. There was a reason they had stayed friends for so long. They just knew how to get each other and let the other person chill when they didn't get them. Coming back to the present, Zen nodded. "Yeah. It's a lot stronger now, which makes it better and worse. I wish—" She broke off her words and sighed in frustration, running a hand through her long blonde spikes. "I wish it were more accurate. I wish I could just find whomever is on the other end and know."

"Know what?"

Zen shrugged. "I'm not sure. But I'm convinced it's a person and I need to find her."

Cin grinned and clapped the younger woman on the shoulder. "Well then, why don't you come with me to Sunday dinner tomorrow and you can ask Gloria for that transfer."

A return smile spread across Zendara's lips and she stood to grab her stick again. She lined up her next shot, not looking at her friend. "And you really think Gloria will say yes?"

"I do. And for what it's worth..." Cin trailed off until she got Zendara's attention again. They locked eyes in the dark bar. "I hope you find her. Your mystery girl."

Zendara smiled sadly, even as she paused her shot to rub the achy spot in the center of her chest. "Me too."

IT HAS MOST definitely been confirmed that the two women, grown from babes born in the light of another star, were actively searching for each other. It almost gives a person hope, doesn't it? While Grand Rapids still wasn't Chicago, it was significantly closer than Detroit. And with Zendara's continued trek toward her Q'sirrahna, we've also learned that the closer they get to each other, the greater the pull they feel. It was only a matter of time before one of them was forced to move again.

Chapter Six

THERE IS AN island country in the Caribbean known best for its missile crisis and succession of Communist dictators. The United States has always had a contentious history with Cuba, but despite that they continue to maintain the 46.8 square mile scrap of land surrounding Guantanamo Bay. And on that little scrap of land is a place with no international rules, no typical government oversite, and too much ambition. The Guantanamo Bay Naval Base was converted into the place Americans used to house their most dangerous criminals. It was a place to put terrorists where they could be forgotten. Legal and ethical policies of the facility were always in question, and for good reason. Publicly and officially, the camp was closed nearly twenty years ago. Covertly, it houses the criminal Chromodecs who are brought in by the various CORP teams around the country.

Camp Delta and Camp Echo were the most well-known detention centers. But there was one other located about a mile outside the main camp perimeter. Camp "No" is a black site that is officially known as Section Eight. The unacknowledged area was previously used to interrogate the worst of the worst of decades past. It is also the perfect place for Marek Maza, aka Oracle, to start building his future.

"PRISONER ZERO ZERO six seven nine, please state your full name for the record."

The prisoner in question had his wrists and ankles shackled together via a length of chain and wore a gleaming metal collar with blinking indicator lights around his neck. He was tall and lanky, unshaven, and had recently lost a tooth in the events that took place at the top of the Willis Tower in Chicago. "The name is Zeusifer. Who're you?" One of the two guards at the door snorted before controlling himself again.

The interrogator continued. "I'm going to ask you again, what is your full name?" He had a metal briefcase open in front of him. The case wasn't empty but rather was merely a protective outer shell for one of the many Hieronymus machines that the Agency utilized.

The device itself was simple. Two large dials placed near the center of the machine face top, labeled Rate One and Rate Two. A sample well was set down in the machine, toward the hinge side of the faceplate and centered snugly between the two Rate dials. It already contained a snip of the prisoner's hair. A power toggle switch with its red indicator light, a green light to indicate whether the sample well was clear, and a small knob for intensity, rounded out the basic Scalar Adjustment Machine. It was usually just referred to as the "ScAM" by CORP agents, which is ironically what history and science had always determined the Hieronymus machines to be, until Chromodecs with their powers of scalar energy manipulation showed up.

The man self-titled as "Zeusifer" scowled. "I already told you my name, if you don't like it then you can go fuck yourself. You and all your little gooney-men in black. I don't owe you shit!" He struggled with his shackles for a few seconds before finally cursing and looking up at the interrogator again. "As soon as I get out of these cuffs I'm gonna call the power of Zeus down on you! The power of Zeus with the temper of the Devil, that's what I am! And y'all are in for a world of hurt when I get loose!"

The man in the black suit sitting across the table from prisoner zero zero six seven nine smiled at the other man's words. "It's quite unlikely you'll be going anywhere, Leroy Oliver Landon. You see, around your neck is an eloptic collar, meant to prevent you from manipulating scalar energy." He paused and cocked his head at the surprised look on the man's face. "Are you so ignorant about your origins, Leroy? You are a Chromodec, the result of alien and human DNA testing by our very own government. And since we don't want you to cause any more destruction, the collar is a necessary precaution. Wouldn't you agree?"

"I don't agree with nuthin'!" Leroy Landon spit on the floor next to him causing a look of disgust to twist the features of the interrogator.

Two things that Colonel Marek Maza hated with a passion were disrespect and filth. "Oh, I think that will be enough out of you, Mister Landon." Maza, with the confident calm of a seasoned interrogator, flipped the power switch and the ScAM came to life. He set the rate knobs, then moved to the intensity. The dial was adjusted fairly low at two because he didn't want to damage the prisoner.

Sweat immediately beaded on Leroy's forehead and his face paled. "What are you doing to me? I don't feel so hot..."

"Prisoner zero zero six seven nine, please state your full name for the record."

Anger drew down Leroy's brows and his lips twisted into a grimace. "Fuck you, Fed!"

Colonel Maza increased the intensity to three and watched the prisoner's hands clench into fists. Leroy started to pant and his eyes widened as he tugged frantically at his restraints. "This is not a game, Mister Landon. If you do not cooperate you will be culled." Maza paused for a few seconds to let the other man experience the full effects of scalar warp that the machine was inducing. "Prisoner zero zero six seven nine, please state your name."

At forty-five seconds of level three intensity warp, Leroy Oliver Landon started blubbering. "Oh gawd, oh gawd, please stop! Please make it stop, I'll do anything. Anything you want!" The man in the orange jumpsuit strained against the chains as his eyes rolled wildly in his head before he vomited down the front of his clothing.

"Prisoner zero zero six seven nine, please state your full name for the record."

Seeming to find a moment of clarity, the prisoner complied. At fifty-seven seconds of three intensity scalar warp, he broke. "M—my n—name's Leroy Oli—Oliver L—Landon. Pl—please make it stop!" Foam dribbled out the left side of his mouth. Sixty seconds into the first standard interrogation tactic, and the criminal Chromodec, Zeusifer, sat drenched in sweat with tears running down his face. It seemed that even the bad guys had someone to fear.

With a quick twist, the man known to the CORP groups worldwide as Oracle, turned the intensity back to level two. Leroy shuddered but didn't fully relax. "There's a good man inside you, Mister Landon. Now if you would carefully place put your hands within the outline on the table we can begin." Leroy opened his mouth to speak but his interrogator cut him off. "No talking, just do as I command."

Tentatively, rough and scraped hands slid onto the table in the places that had been outlined for just such a purpose. The chain that connected the wrist and ankle shackles sounded like a low growl as it slid along the edge of the black resin surface. With the press of a button beneath the interrogator's side of the table, electromagnets engaged beneath the prisoner's cuffs to trap him in place. Leroy panicked at first then settled at the look on the man in black's face. "What are you gonna to do to me?"

Oracle slowly removed the thin black glove from his right hand and reached out to touch the back of Leroy's knuckles. At first contact Leroy stiffened and his eyes rolled back in his head. "It's not what I'm going *to* do to you, Mister Landon. It's what I'm going to do *for* you." After a minute and a half of telemetric reading, Oracle pulled back with a smile on his face. "Oh, I certainly have plans for you. I hear L.A. is a nice place to live but we should get you trained first..." As his words trailed off, laughter started. The guards in the room joined their colonel, knowing he had found another suitable candidate.

OVER THE PAST few decades a number of people have wondered what happened to the criminal Chromodecs that were apprehended by the CORP. Some even speculated that perhaps the criminals were brainwashed to become CORP agents themselves. By funny happenstance, that is exactly what the facility at Guantanamo Bay was doing. Much history had been divulged about the Chromodec project, at least as much as the government thought the public could handle. Of course many people wondered why no other aliens had crashed in the decades since. Conspiracy theorists often speculated that the United States government was collaborating with an alien race with the end goal being world domination. But no, it wasn't the government that had that goal, it was one man.

As for the information that wasn't divulged to the public, that was a little more complicated. You see, there was a very good reason why no aliens came to claim the nearly destroyed spaceship in 1952. The alien on board, a Psierian, was an escaped fugitive that the government of Psiere was trying to keep secret. When their bounty hunters discovered that the alien was dead, they made their report back to the military ship *Endara* and called it a day. The alien man didn't even die in the crash. He died slowly afterward because he was trapped in the wreckage and a predecessor of the eloptic collar prevented him from using his powers. The American government, being the resourceful sort that they were, reverse engineered the collar decades later to create more.

But the collar and its origins are neither here nor there in the importance of this tale. What is important is that the eloptic collar was a very useful tool during Chromodec apprehension and conditioning. By negating their powers, it was easy enough to use the ScAM to weaken a Chromodec's will. After that, basic indoctrination techniques were used to adjust the criminal's mental behavior and moral disposition. It was a well-researched process with one hundred percent initial success for all Chromodecs. Occasionally one would go rogue and break conditioning, thus requiring them to be brought in for "re-adjustment," but overall it worked quite well. The conditioned Chromodecs were then placed in various roles throughout the CORP agency. More than seventy-five percent ended up on CORP enforcement teams.

Unfortunately for the CORP agency and the country as a whole, not all were conditioned to improve their moral disposition. Since he was the man of power at Guantanamo, Oracle had been testing the incoming prisoners for their potential use in his plot of ascendancy. And people followed him willingly because Col. Marek Maza was a visionary and a very charismatic man. At six-foot-two, with blond hair and blue eyes, Maza was like a superhero among soldiers and superiors alike. They saw him as a failsafe, a stalwart protector against all that was evil in the world. He was the Chromodec that pioneered the conditioning program, and he had a perfect record. Unlike other would-be villains, Oracle didn't shun the spotlight. On the contrary, he wanted to win over as many people as possible.

But Colonel Maza wasn't just in it for the fame and the power of success and popularity. No, for him it was much more personal. His own mother was born back in 1955, her father dead and family in disgrace. But despite Sally Daggett's inauspicious beginning, she

still managed to marry well and have children of her
own. Unfortunately for Marek, she died in childbirth
with his younger brother. As you may now realize, Marek
was the grandson of an infamous man and he had intent
to erase the legacy of disgrace from his past. If all
went as planned, the world would thank him for taking
over.

TWO YEARS LIVING in Grand Rapids only did one thing for
Zendara, it made the ache grow stronger than ever before. Zen
spent her evenings cleaning office buildings, getting as many
hours as she was allowed so she could save up some cash. Years
before, when she knew she would spend her life chasing the hollow emptiness in her chest, she got used to living lightly. The
young woman still carried the large black duffel bag from home
to home, and she merely rented rooms instead of actual apart-
ments to save money. She practiced the art of serial transience.

That wasn't to say that she didn't love her current town.
Grand Rapids wasn't the dirty and sprawling example of urban
decay like Detroit. Over the past decade it had become a role
model for urban advancement. The arts were alive and well in the
vital and modern downtown area, and people flocked to the
region from all over for some of the best medical care in the country. The only thing Zendara didn't like was the influx of people
with power.

Against all common sense and reasoning, a Chromodec had
come into the city with the sole purpose of organizing the largest
group of thugs in a nest of local gangs. After months of robberies
and murders, local law enforcement finally enlisted the aid of the
CORP. Agents in black suits rolled into town with their armored
black SUVs, causing chaos among the local populace. Her previous run-ins with law enforcement and other official government
organizations left Zen with a bad taste in her mouth where the
CORP was concerned.

She often wondered what happened to the Chromodecs that
they captured. Wasn't the CORP itself comprised of those same
hybrid humans? It seemed a little sketchy to her. But Zendara had
learned over and over again that the saying, "If you can't beat
'em, join 'em," was all too true more often than not. Perhaps the
super-powered criminals were merely brainwashed, then forced
to serve as Agents. Wouldn't that be funny?

What she also discovered while living in her newest city was how often she found herself staring southwest. Zendara went to the beach on Lake Michigan every few weeks, winter or summer, and the pull always drew her gaze across the water. There was only one place it could be, a large city that was sure to hold the person she longed for.

"I'd like to give my two week notice, Gloria."

The older Hispanic woman looked back at her in surprise. "What? Is something wrong?"

"No, nothing is wrong. It's just time for me to move on. I have loved working for you, but UCS is doing really well in West Michigan now and I'm feeling the itch to move on to Chicago."

"Well, okay. You've been with me five years now and your help has been invaluable with the expansion. If there is anything you need..." She left the statement open-ended.

Zendara shook her head. "No, you've been great. I'm going to start scouring the job sites to find something similar to what I have with you. I just hate leaving you in a lurch."

Gloria smiled. "I've got contacts in the Chicago region, people I've met in the industry. Let me see what I can dig up for you, okay? It may take longer than two weeks, but that will give you time to train Jose as your replacement. He has been a good assistant manager over there but I want to make sure he's really got the whole thing down before I turn you lose."

A slow nod met the company owner's words. "Okay, I can do that. And thanks."

"THAT WAS PRETTY cool that Gloria was able to get you into the Campus Services department of the University of Chicago." Cin stood with her at the Amtrak station in downtown Grand Rapids, waiting for the train that was due in ten minutes.

Zendara smiled. "Yeah, she's great. I'm actually going to miss working for her. I'm going to miss you! But you know you didn't have to drive all the way across the state to see me off."

Cin punched her shoulder. "Are you kidding me? No way would I let my best friend move out of state without saying good-bye!" The brunette stuck her hands in her pockets. "So, you're all squared away with a place to stay when you get there, right?"

"Yeah, I found an appartment to rent in Bronzeville, about a mile north of the university. I got online at the library and looked up public transportation information and found the platform I'd have to exit for the school. The rent is surprisingly affordable and doable with my salary. Of course, it is only a room and my neighbors will probably suck."

The other woman looked a little concerned. "What if you're in a sketchy neighborhood? There is a lot of crime down there you know."

Zen raised an eyebrow and smirked. "Really, dude? I lived in Detroit for three years. We eat those Chicago gangsters for breakfast!"

"But you're from Rumford, Maine, you numpty! I'm sure those Chicago gangsters eat you east coast newbs for lunch and dinner!"

They both laughed and Zendara checked the time on her phone. She still had a few minutes before the train was due. "You never told me how you ended up in Maine when your entire family lived in Detroit."

Cin shrugged. "I thought I was going to be a big rock star, I was following the dream."

"In Rumford?"

The older woman laughed. "Yeah, well, life. You know?"

Zendara laughed too. "Probably a girl."

"You're probably right." Cin admitted. The telltale sound of a train horn signaled the end of their conversation. After exchanging a long hug, Cin stepped back and picked up Zendara's duffel bag to hand it to her. She staggered under the weight. "Jesus, that thing weighs a ton!"

Thinking her friend was playing around, Zendara grabbed it from her with ease. "Whatever, dude. You're such a drama queen. Tough Detroiter my ass!"

Cin raised a dark eyebrow at the other woman. She hadn't been joking but let it slide. There were a number of weird things about Zendara that she just played off. Instead she snorted and made a shooing motion. "Yeah, yeah. Now get on the train before they leave you behind."

"Yes, ma'am!" With that, Zendara gave her best friend one last hug and spun on her heel to join the boarding line.

AND JUST LIKE that, the downward spiral that held our two soul mates draws them ever closer. With both in the same city, working at the same institution even, it is only a matter of time before they meet. But life on

Earth is ever so unpredictable and there are a multitude of potential problems that could arise. Amari and
Zendara are two completely different individuals. Both
princesses, yes, but life has also taken them down very
dichotomous paths. What happens when a jaded Zendara
meets with the affluent Amari? What will Zen say when
she finds out that she isn't as human as she thought?
And how will their carbon/crystal cell bodies react
when two beings of such immense power resonate closely
together for the first time?

FRIDAY EVENING FOUND Amari ready to blow off some
steam. She was going out with the girls again, having dinner and
hitting the same karaoke place that they had on many occasions
before. The only things that ever changed were the restaurants
they tried. With her colleague's urging, Amari had become a regular in Stephanie's group of friends. For the first time in her life,
the Reynan princess finally felt she had a place to call home and
friends who were more than just casual acquaintances. She went
back to Washington to visit her parents twice a year, and they visited her once a year, but it wasn't the same as having people she
cared about and counted on where she lived.

Best of all, she had developed a deep friendship with Stephanie. Rather than get weird after the incident on the train platform,
their bond grew and the other doctor agreed to keep Amari's
secret. As a doctor and scientist, Stephanie Young well understood what would happen to Amari should her origin get out.
Best case scenario, the regular government types would get
involved. Worst case, the CORP would come knocking, being the
de facto agency for all things superhuman. Then Amari would
disappear and probably never be seen again.

James and Michelle were understandably upset that Stephanie discovered her secret but there was nothing that could be
done about it. Amari even asked if there was some fancy thing
that could erase memory like in the movies. They assured her
there was not, at least not in their possession.

Over the course of the two years they had been friends following the incident, the women conspired together to study
Amari's blood and biochemistry beyond what the younger
woman's own parents had done. They had the right training for
it, as well as a lab at their disposal. They just needed to keep it a

secret from their colleagues and the head of the lab. The findings were remarkable but not anything they could share or utilize. Besides her evolving friendships and expanding knowledge about her race, every month during the new moon and darkest nights, Amari would don her ship suit and fly above the trees of Washington Park. She had to focus to dampen the white glow of her hair and eyes so no one saw her, but the freedom made the effort worth it.

At quarter after six, Amari stood on the northbound side of the Garfield platform next to Stephanie, who was raving about her new boots. The northbound train approached from the south at the same time the southbound train pulled up to the platform. As the passengers began disembarking, a flash of warmth spread throughout Amari's chest. She rubbed the spot, disoriented at the unfamiliar feeling.

Her eyes searched the crowd desperately, knowing that something important was occurring. She missed the sound of her own train arriving because in that moment her eyes locked on those of another woman. A blonde, sporting biker boots and long messy spikes, was rubbing her own chest and searching the platform as well. Pale blue eyes met her own dark ones and Amari shivered. She was certain she saw the other woman mouth the words "it's you," then Amari was abruptly pulled onto the train and the doors closed.

"Amari, snap out of it, I called you twice! We almost missed our train and I'm starving!" As soon as the doors closed Amari rounded on her. Stephani instantly took a step back at the strange look on her friend's face. "What?"

Amari's expression was indescribable and her voice laced with emotion that she'd never before felt. "That was her!" She unconsciously rubbed her chest as she gazed back in the direction of the platform they had just left.

"Her who?"

Amari turned her attention back to her friend and her hands started to shake. "My Q'sirrahna!"

Dr. Stephanie Young was shocked, her growling stomach and evening plans momentarily forgotten in the wake of her friend's revelation. "Oh shit. What are you going to do?"

The younger woman thought about her dilemma for a minute. There was no way she'd be able to find the woman if she went back to the platform. She was clearly on her way somewhere. But she hoped that her soul mate either lived or worked nearby. She met Stephanie's expectant gaze. "I'm sure she's long gone by now so there's no point in cancelling our plans. Maybe I'll stalk the platform this weekend and see if she turns up. I mean, she has to feel the connection the same as me."

Stephanie made a face. "Well that sounds incredibly — "

Amari smiled. "Dull? But it's not. It's probably the most exciting thing that's ever happened to me. And I'll bring a book to keep me occupied while I wait."

ZENDARA STOOD CLUTCHING the pole near the train door. It was her fifth day of riding the L to her evening shift at the university and she still wasn't comfortable with the crowds of other passengers around her. Sure, she'd ridden the public buses in Grand Rapids and Detroit but it wasn't the same as a train. She felt more on guard than ever before. As each new person bumped and jostled against her, it gave Zen a rush of feeling in the pit of her stomach. It was like anxiety, but not.

At least the ride from where she lived to her work was a short one. And Zendara liked her coworkers and her manager in the university's campus services staff. She was told that she would do a variety of jobs, depending on her previous training. Her parent department, Campus, Building, and Residential Services, was responsible for a lot more than just cleaning. They also handled snow removal, pest control, landscape services, engineering and utilities, building maintenance, mail, and more. But she didn't mind cleaning. It gave her a lot of time to think and listen to science podcasts on her phone. Despite her lack of effort in high school and her failure to attain any sort of secondary education, Zendara remained a genius. Most of her life, secret from everyone that knew her, was spent reading books from the library and listening to science-based podcasts.

She got on the red line at the Indiana platform and took it four stops south to Garfield. It wasn't a busy ride and for that she was grateful. Zen couldn't imagine having to fight the crowds heading into the loop everyday if she were working in the downtown area. Though typically, her shifts were later than any office worker's commute.

She fell in love with Chicago as soon as she emerged from the doors of Union Station on her first day in the city. It was new and fresh, and it felt a little surreal at first. Rather than immediately make her way south to where her new apartment was located on the day of her arrival, Zendara spied a water taxi across the river and purchased a ticket for the city tour. People gave her strange looks as she hauled her oversize duffel bag around but she didn't care. It was grand, nothing like anyplace else she'd visited or lived. And adding to the magical feeling that her first day inspired, the familiar pull in her chest mellowed and changed. While it didn't ache as it usually did, it felt stronger somehow. Softer. Zendara Baen-Tor didn't know what that meant but she was certain she was in the right place.

Now she was starting her fifth night of work, seventh night in Chicago overall, and had yet to get any kind of direction when it came to the familiar emptiness. The train jostled and brakes squealed as it approached her stop. Before the doors had even opened Zendara knew something was wrong. She'd never been sick a day in her life but something felt different, off. Heat infused her chest as she exited the train with a dozen other passengers. She rubbed the place over her heart and searched around for something or someone that could be causing the reaction. Two women stood waiting for the northbound train that was just arriving. The dark-haired one of the two searched the crowd on the platform, hand held to her own chest. That's when Zendara knew. Their eyes met and words whispered unbidden from between Zen's lips. "It's you." Then the woman's friend pulled her through the doors of the train and she was gone.

"No!" Her hand reached out and people around her were startled by the loud cry. Then, as if they saw such dramatics every day, they continued walking around her. She wasn't sure what to do. She tried rationalizing with herself, her muttering keeping the area around her clear of train passengers. With less than a week at her new job, she certainly couldn't miss any time. Besides that, the woman and friend looked dressed up. It was Friday night and they were probably heading downtown for the evening. "She must live nearby!" There was only one way to find the woman again. Zendara would ask her super if she could get off a few hours early, maybe fake a sickness or something. That should get her back to the platform in time to wait for people returning from the clubs. She'd wait all night if she had to.

A shoulder knocked into her and Zendara felt the familiar rush, snapping her out of her daze. She pulled her cell phone out of her pocket to check the time. "Oh shit, I'm gonna be late!"

ZENDARA DID MANAGE to get out of work a little early but it was still nearly one thirty in the morning by the time she was changed back into her street clothes. There was a new moon in the sky as she cut through Washington Park, and the greens-pace seemed darker than usual. She'd been told the area around the university was pretty safe but that didn't stop Zendara from pulling her unzipped jacket a little closer. At five-foot-nine she wasn't small by any means but there was always someone bigger. Her thoughts were distracted by the memory of the woman on the platform and she didn't see when a shadow split from the rest of the trees. The shadow resolved itself into the shape of a man, a lit-tle taller and broader than she was. She pulled up short when she noticed that his right hand stayed in his pocket. The man looked strung out, his voice rough in the dark night.

"You got any cash you can spare?"

Zen got used to not carrying cash on her when she lived in Detroit. Pretty much everyone accepted bank cards so she only had that, her ID, work badge, and her CTA pass. "I'm sorry, I don't."

She made to move past the man but he stepped with her to block her way. "I'm not asking again. Give me your wallet and cell phone, now."

"Or what?" She was pretty sure she could outrun him. He didn't look like he was in great shape. At least she was sure until he pulled the gun out of his pocket.

His hand shook as he pulled back the slide to cock it. "Please, I don't want to hurt you. I just need your money and stuff, then I'll leave you alone." Zendara put her hands up and stepped back out of reflex. She'd never had anyone pull a gun on her before, not even in Detroit.

"Hey!"

A shout from farther down the path drew both their atten-tion. Zen watched as the man spun around and raised the gun toward the newcomers and she didn't even think before reacting. She took a few steps and tackled the guy to the ground. The sound of the gun rang loudly through the night and she felt an adrenalin rush go through her body like nothing she'd ever known. All those times she tried drugs and alcohol, chasing that feeling of power and euphoria that others talked about, all those times she failed to find it. But in that moment it was everything. Zen punched him in the jaw and knocked him out before the gun could go off again.

The sound of running steps came toward her and she looked up to see a guy and a girl a few feet away. The guy spoke first. "Are you okay?"

The girl, maybe his girlfriend based on how close they were standing, spoke up as well. "Was that a gun? Are you hurt?"

Zendara shook her head. "No, he must have missed me. The dude's pretty messed up, I think he's strung out or something. When I saw him raise his gun toward you I knew I had to do something."

"You saved our lives!" The woman looked down to the man on the ground, then back up to Zen.

"We need to call the cops." The guy pulled his phone from his front pocket and Zendara stood there in shock. Her body practically buzzed with energy and she almost laughed that it took nearly getting shot in order to finally feel an adrenaline rush. It felt as if she could run a hundred miles or bench press a car. It was amazing. Her thoughts were brought back to the moment when the guy spoke again. "They said the cops'll be here in five minutes."

The man on the ground moaned faintly and Zendara thought to move closer and shove the gun out of reach before he came to. She shook her head as the gravity of the situation took hold. "If you hadn't distracted him..." Her voice trailed off.

"Hey, you're going to be fine. Everyone's good now and the cops are on their way." The woman held out her hand to Zendara. "I'm Sara, and this is Scott. We're both science majors at U of C."

Zen shook her hand, then Scott's when he offered it. "I'm Zen. Nice to meet you." The silence after their introduction didn't last long. They heard the sirens before the lights appeared, and within no time a patrol car arrived. Two officers got out and approached the scene, flashlights in one hand and guns in the other. Zen watched as they both took in the three people standing near the body on the ground.

"Who called in the report of the armed attacker?"

Scott spoke up. "It was me, Officer. We were cutting through the park, heading back to the residence halls, when we saw this guy—" he pointed to the unconscious man "—confronting a woman. She had her hands up and was stepping back from him so I was pretty sure he wasn't a friend. But I didn't know he had a gun when I yelled."

The other cop spoke up. "What happened then?"

"He turned toward us with his gun raised. He must have

been aiming it at her first." He pointed at Zendara. "When he was distracted she took a couple steps and tackled him to the ground. The gun went off, luckily missing everyone, and she punched him in the face."

"I knocked the gun away when it sounded like he was going to wake up." Zendara pointed about five feet away, near a big oak tree.

They spent some time at the scene collecting evidence and asking a lot of questions. Ever conscious of time slipping away, Zendara grew more and more agitated. She was asked to come down to the station the next day and file an official statement. It was two thirty in the morning by the time the cop car drove away and the student couple continued in their original direction toward the residence halls. Zen practically vibrated as she took off at a sprint through the park, heading for the train platform. She stopped only seconds later. Seconds and hundreds of yards.

"What the *fuck*?" She looked around and knew that what she'd just done was impossible. The world had blurred when she started running and that was why she pulled up short next to a north wall of the fitness center, off the corner of South Martin Luther King Drive and East Garfield Boulevard. But the surprise came only when she realized how far she had traveled in such a short span of time. Then she remembered the rush of feeling as the gun went off. Zendara pulled her jacket open a little further and began searching her shirt for anything that could tell her what happened. Her hands stilled as her right ring finger slipped into a hole in the fabric. The hole was near the center of her body, just under her left breast. The skin was smooth behind the rent.

There was no way she could go to the subway platform with so much uncertainty swirling in her head. And the anger at her missed chance seethed inside her. With a cry of frustration, Zendara lashed out at the brick wall. Even as she punched she knew it was a stupid move guaranteed to earn her a broken hand. But she didn't care. Much to her surprise, not only did the impact of skin on brick not hurt, but her hand left a hole in the blocks. Even as the familiar rush coursed through her, a curse and question escaped her lips. "God *damn* it! What's happening to me?" Partly in shock, partly out of fear, Zendara leaned against the side of the building and slid down until she was crouched in a shadow. The hole from her fist was dark and obvious on the expanse of brick above her head. All thoughts of finding the woman from the train were lost in the realization that she was not like everyone else. No matter how many questions she asked herself, Chromodec was the only logical answer.

EVEN IF YOU don't feel the same way, you can understand what it's like for people without power to fear and hate those that have it. An important thing to understand is that, just like humans, Chromodecs are not born good or evil. And even a good Chromodec can hurt a person accidentally, or many people. Back in the eighties, there was an unfortunate young man who had been born on the wrong side of the tracks. New Jersey was full of youthful toughness in any decade and it was no different for Jacob Johnson. Every day after school, bullies would taunt him, would beat and humiliate him. Then they'd leave the sobbing boy in the street. He'd eventually pull himself together, gather his books, and head home to an alcoholic mother and a house without food. You see, Jacob's dad was a first generation Chromodec that took off before he was born. It was the genetic legacy passed on by his absentee father that was the key to this particular tale.

It was an average school day and Jacob had to serve detention after last class for a prank that he didn't even pull. It was later than normal as he walked by the construction site and no workers were around. That was when the bullies struck again. But that time something changed inside Jacob. One kid, Barry, kicked him hard in the head when he was on the ground. Jacob saw a bright flash and sharp pain began to throb behind his ears. A rumbling and creaking sound from the construction site drew the other kids' attention. Then a crane with a load of steel I-beams tipped precariously toward the little group. Before they could even think to move, the load swung around and dropped on top of all of them. Including young Jacob.

He probably didn't mean to hurt anyone. The boy was simply reacting to the pain, fear, and built-up frustration. But even so, they were all dead. No…Chromodecs were neither good nor evil but they had the power to do both with abandon.

Chapter Seven

THINGS APPEAR BLEAK for the women hailing from the Q'orre star system. Let's pause on Zendara right in the moment of her colossal self-discovery. A shadow could be seen sitting in the grass against the fitness center building. With head down, she sat with her right cheek rested on her knees as the chill gradually seeped through her jacket and seat of her pants. She stared vaguely off toward Martin Luther King Drive. While not uncomfortable in the cool night air, the feeling couldn't exactly be described as comfortable either. She wasn't lost or hurt, but the young self-proclaimed nomad was so very alone in this strange new city. And the emptiness that had plagued Zendara her entire life, remained. She didn't know why the dark-haired woman was important, she only knew that they passed each other like two trains in the night. Figuratively and quite literally. And now Zendara has found out that she's what? A Chromodec? It was certainly the only logical answer. She rubbed her chest as a vague heat settled in.

Now we move to observe Amari. Distracted, yet emboldened from the quick glance at her soul mate, she wasn't nearly as engaged in the night of revelry as everyone else. A few noticed, but she just said that she was tired and most didn't question further. Only Dr. Stephanie Young knew the truth. Later that evening, Stephanie humored Amari for a few minutes at the Garfield station. The younger woman wanted to linger in hope that the blonde would have returned. But alas, the stop was empty at two thirty in the morning. After walking Stephanie back to her apartment, Amari wasn't sure what to do. She didn't want to go home. While she had built a good life for herself in Chicago, there was still a hole inside her that had yet to be filled. A strange feeling of hopelessness and fear washed through her. She had never felt so alone in her entire life. Despite the wave of emotion, Amari walked aimlessly toward Washington Park and rubbed her chest as a vague heat settled in.

Denii Losa Del Rey knew what she was talking about twenty-five years before on that small fleeing ship.

"Be strong, me sirra, and Q'orre keep you safe. You will find your Q'sirrahna again when you need her most."

If there was only one certainty in the world, it was the fact that a Q'sirrahna pair would always find each other if they were both alive and in control of their own fate. And sometimes even fate intervened with situations that were less than ideal. What Amari and Zendara didn't know was that in just such a short chance meeting on the Garfield platform, their bond was woven even tighter than before. Both their bodies and souls were as one, and nothing could keep them apart. That bond would prove invaluable in the future of these two brave and powerful women.

NORMALLY, IT WOULD be a quick couple of blocks walk after Amari left Stephanie at her apartment building on Prairie Avenue. But something about the night and the near meeting with her Q'sirrahna earlier had her out of sorts. The ache of longing returned after she left Steph on her doorstep. Rather than head to bed after a long and tumultuous day, Amari opted to walk toward the park. She didn't have her suit, but she wasn't planning on any tests of her power either. The woman from Reyna just wanted to clear her head. Her chest had gotten warm and tight since arriving back in her neighborhood and she didn't know what it meant. She only knew to follow that familiar pull.

Zendara had her own issues to deal with. She hadn't been sitting in the grass very long when she felt her own chest warm and constrict. The feeling was accompanied by a rush similar to what she felt after getting shot. With her head resting on her knees, she could easily see the normally busy street through the sparse trees at the corner of the park. And what she saw caused a hitch in her breath. A lone figure crossed the street to her side then continued into the park itself, and the shape of the person grew more defined as they drew closer. Zen's head came off her knees when she saw the woman pause, then alter her path. She was walking directly toward Zendara.

Amari didn't know where she was going, she just followed the pull in her chest like it was a string between two points. She knew that there could only be one person on the other end. Once she crossed into the grassy expanse beneath the trees, she paused and adjusted her direction slightly. The feeling was taking her toward a shadowed area next to the fitness center. She eventually slowed to a stop and Amari's words came out mumbled and quiet, unsure in her confusion. "There's nothing there. This can't be right."

A voice that seemed too loud in the darkness, broke the semi-silence of a big city at night. "I suppose your correctness depends on what you're looking for."

A shape emerged from the shadows and Amari startled. A resonating warmth spread through her limbs as she took in the woman in front of her. The darkness hid the features that she'd already glimpsed on the train platform. But she didn't need a clear view to know who was standing twenty feet from her. "You're here."

The ache soothed and Zendara answered her. "Yes, but who am I to you?"

"You're my Q'sirrahna, my soul mate."

Lines appeared between Zen's brows, unseen by the woman that had yet to come any closer. "Are you a Chromodec too?"

The confusion was contagious. "Chromodec? Why would you think that? I'm definitely not a Chromodec, and neither are you."

Stubborn, Zendara shook her head. "How do *you* know? I have power, a power I never even dreamed of. And I've only just discovered it tonight."

"What?" Amari's surprise was so great, her voice came out at nearly a yell. "Didn't your parents tell you anything?"

Harsh words full of long-held anger ground out into the night and Amari felt a sharp pang of sorrow in her chest. "My parents are dead."

She couldn't keep her distance any longer. But rather than run toward the other woman like her heart demanded, Amari took slow and measured steps. They would not miss each other again. "Please, can we talk? I think there is much I need to tell you."

"Stop! Stay back, I don't know who you are but some shit has gone down tonight and I don't think I can deal with any more weirdness." Zendara took a step toward the main road, hoping to head back to the train platform. "We can talk tomorrow."

Amari's heart leaped into her throat. "No, you can't leave

yet!" She took a few more rushed steps forward and only succeeded in making Zendara panic. But rather than take off for the
L in her uncertainty, Zen bolted toward the center of Washington
Park. Determined not to lose her, Amari activated her power and
followed. She ran after Zendara but the other woman proved just
as fast when on the ground where there were trees and other
obstacles to avoid. With that thought in mind, Amari took to the
air. She knew she had to catch her Q'sirrahna as soon as possible
to avoid having anyone see them.

Zendara made the mistake of heading for the lagoon and had
to take a circuitous route along the path around the dark water.
After a quick glance behind her, she didn't see her pursuer and
slowed to a stop. She never thought to look up. Amari slowly
lowered from above mere seconds later, startling the newly
empowered woman from Tora. Realizing that she was out-
matched by someone who could fly, and not sensing aggression
from the person who pulled her heart like no other, Zendara
didn't bother to run again. The two women observed each other.
Zendara stood in a small grassy area just off the path where it cut
across Bynum Island. She was unaware that both her eyes and
hair were glowing black like ethereal flame, the opposite of
Amari's bright white hair and eyes. But while Zen's feet were
planted firmly on the earth below, Amari floated in the air. "Who
are you?" Zendara's voice held both fear and awe.

Amari floated closer until she was right in front of the
blonde. "It's not who I am that matters. It is who we are
together." She paused. "We are Q'sirrahna. My name is Amari
Losira Del Rey. I'm an adopted orphan and princess of Reyna.
And you are Zendara Inyri Baen-Tor, the princess of Tora and my
soul mate. I have been waiting for you my whole life." She slowly
floated the few feet back to the ground and her dark hair and eyes
returned as the power faded. Both women felt something resonate
within them at the nearness of the other.

"Ho-how do you know who I am?" Zendara's own power
winked out as well when she relaxed slightly. She had not had the
easiest time growing up and she'd seen her share of darkness
from people. But despite the completely strange turn of events
the night had taken, something inside her screamed to trust
Amari. And if intuition weren't enough, the pull of longing that
spread heat from her chest outward certainly was.

Amari took a step forward and Zendara took a step back.
Amari tried again. "Please, I can explain everything, but not here.

I live only a few blocks away from the park. Will you come with me?"

"You promise you're not just fucking with me?"

"I swear I'm not."

After a few seconds pause, Zendara nodded. Amari held out her hand. At the blonde's wary look she tried to explain. "I'm sorry. I can't explain it but I have a nearly irresistible urge to touch you. May I?" At Zendara's curious look, Amari rushed to explain. "It's just that I've only known your name for the past eight years, but I've felt your absence my entire life. I just—it doesn't seem real. You know?"

Zen's voice was a whisper. "I know."

WHILE IT MAY have come across as a strange request to most people, it made sense under the circumstances. After all, both women felt the pull toward the other. Both of them had felt the ache of longing for something, someone, who was missing in their life. But there were many things they still didn't know. Even with all Amari's research on herself and the information she'd gathered from her parents, her life on Earth had changed their biology beyond that of her mothers' comprehension. Two crystal-carbon beings of power had never come into physical contact with each other on Earth before, let alone shared a soul bond. Q'sirrahna were rare on their respective planets but not unheard of. However, none of those Q'sirrahna had ever been changed by an alien atmosphere, had never been tasked with a fate so grand. That resonating warmth they both felt had been building their entire life. And much like two magnets in the dark, they will be brought together abruptly as soon as both hearts and minds opened to the other.

What they didn't know was that such a long time spent apart had caused their biologic processes to run slightly out of synch from one another. The touch of each other's skin would cause something later called, "resonance flash." The moment when the frequencies of their individual crystal-carbon cell resonances were abruptly pulled into synch. Such a rapid change of resonance would have the effect of resetting Amari and

Zendara's power level. Curiously enough, a resonance flash would instantly expend their power. Then as they synched up, it would be absorbed into the other person. It was to be both telling with its intensity, and damning to their secret existence. They were not the only people of power wandering the city that night.

ZENDARA COULDN'T RESIST the pull of the dark haired beauty and she found herself reaching out. In an abrupt and frightening turn of events, their fingers jumped together, interlocking like pieces of a puzzle, tight and fast as two strong magnets. A great boom echoed around them as a beam of light enveloped both women and shot straight into the sky. At once, Amari Del Rey and Zendara Baen-Tor expended the accumulated energy stored within their cells and absorbed the other person's. It was the greatest rush either had ever felt and the women were left dazed. Amari and her parents determined years before that the conversion rate between the energy she absorbed and the amount that was actually amplified and stored by her body was frighteningly high. So that single instance of resonance synch left them incredibly "juiced."

Amari licked her lips, still buzzing from the event, but Zendara was the one who spoke what they were both thinking. "What was that?"

"Power." The word breathed from between Amari's teeth as she took stock of her own body. Then a smile washed over her face. She didn't know that part of the emptiness she felt her entire life was due to being out of synch with her Q'sirrahna. The aching feeling disappeared with a flash of light in the night sky. "I feel whole!" She opened her eyes and looked into the shining blue of Zendara's. "Do you feel it too?"

Zen nodded. "Yes. I feel powerful, and complete. And this has never happened to you before? The beam of light and boom?" Despite her earlier misgivings about the stranger in front of her, she was loath to let go of Amari's hand. The other woman was completely unknown to her yet at the same time she was everything.

"No, never. As a matter of fact I—" Amari's eyes suddenly grew wide as she realized the attention that their little display would draw. "Shit! We have to go right now! They'll come looking for the cause of the flash." She tried to pull Zendara's hand with her but the other woman resisted. Amari turned back to her with fear coloring her words. "Please, Q'sirrahna, we must go or we'll be found out. Trust me."

The blonde nodded and together they ran. The white glowing eyes for the princess of Reyna was purposely dampened as they fled back to Amari's apartment at speed and on foot. The dark glowing hair and eyes belonging to the princess of Tora were unseen in the darkness.

It took only a few minutes for the two women to end up back at Amari's apartment. Zendara entered behind her, eyes wandering around the nice place curiously. It was a far cry from anything the less-affluent woman was used to. They spent a few minutes standing on the balcony that looked out toward Washington Park, searching for anything that would indicate their power display had caught the attention of the authorities. There didn't seem to be any lights or sirens converging on the area so Amari led the way back inside.

"I think we're safe." She nervously waved toward the couch. "Please, have a seat. Would you like something to drink?"

Zendara looked up from where she was fingering a framed picture of what she assumed was Amari's parents. "No. Thank you."

They both took a seat, Zen on the couch and Amari on the recliner. Then without warning, Amari stood and moved over to the couch, following a strong urge to be near her soul mate. Zendara didn't say anything and it took a long sixty seconds for Amari to work up the nerve to look up and meet the other woman's eyes. She sighed and ran a hand through her hair before resting it back on the couch, mere inches from Zendara's. "I'm sorry, this is awkward." Her eyes moved carefully back down to stare at their tanned fingers where they rested next to each other, carefully not touching. "It's just that you're finally here and I don't really know how to process everything. And I have this overwhelming need to—anyway, it doesn't matter. I can only imagine how you feel." She raised her head and met Zendara's light blue eyes, caught in the moment and unable to pull away from her intense gaze.

Zen was just as overwhelmed, but a part of her felt completely at ease, relaxed and content for the first time in her life. She too had been staring at their hands, then moved up to watch Amari's dark lips. She unconsciously leaned in. The attraction between the women went beyond that of their soul bond. It was physical and emotional. She leaned closer and heard Amari's breath hitch. "I don't think you need to imagine anything. I believe you know exactly how I feel right now. Don't you?" Amari swallowed thickly and gave a slow nod. "The question is, what are we going to do about it? Do—do you have someone in your life? Are you single, married, or dating? Because I'm going to be honest, I don't think I can be around you if you are." Zen shuddered at how close their bond had wound them together. She wanted to crawl inside Amari's skin, she wanted to drink from her until they were turned inside out, until they had merged into one person. It was the strangest yearning she'd ever experienced.

"What do you think? Do you honestly believe I could know about you my entire adult life and choose to be in a relationship with someone else?"

Zendara let out a sigh of relief. "I guess not."

"Thi—this need we have—" Amari drew in a shuddering breath. "I, um, I think this may be a side effect of being Q'sir-rahna. Maybe it's because we are so close together now, or maybe it was due to the flash from earlier. I don't know what any of that is, but I know the basics of our anatomy. We have a cell structure that is both carbon and crystalline based, which is how we are able to absorb and store power." At Zendara's slightly confused look, she tried again. "Keep in mind, this is not my area of study but I've been reading about it for nearly a decade. So, in physics, resonance is the phenomenon in which something vibrating, a system or external force, causes another system to oscillate with greater amplitude at specific frequencies. And if the responding amplitude for a given frequency is at the maximum for that material, then it is called the 'resonance frequency.'"

Amari watched the other woman for some kind of reaction, anything that would indicate she understood the science of the description given. Zendara's parents had apparently died before telling her anything about herself, and she didn't exactly dress or act like a professional but looks could be deceiving. While the doctor of biochemistry wanted to help her Q'sirrahna understand, she didn't want it to seem like she was lecturing either. "Are you following me so far?"

Little lines appeared between the blonde's brows, and her gaze turned inward and unfocused. Finally she sighed and addressed Amari's question. "I think so. Mechanical resonance is similar. Buildings, bridges, and stuff all have a natural frequency of vibration. For instance, if an earthquake happens, or even high winds, a bridge is built to accommodate a certain amount of sway. But if the frequency of oscillations of the earthquake or high winds matches that of the bridge, it will cause the swaying motion to amplify and be violent. Bridges and buildings have famously collapsed because of it and modifications need to be made for buildings in certain areas of the world."

Surprised that the punk-looking woman was able to apply Amari's broad explanation to a mechanical example, she blurted out the first thing that came to mind. "Are you an engineer?"

Zen snorted and rolled her eyes. "Hardly. I never went to college after high school. I clean office buildings at night." At the other woman's incredulous look, she admitted one of her personal habits. "I like to listen to science podcasts while I'm cleaning. And when I don't understand something that's said I'll jot it down in my little notebook and look it up at the library later." She shrugged deprecatingly. "I don't know, I've just always had a knack for understanding stuff. My parents had me tested before they died. They made a lot of plans for me when they discovered the results."

Amari sensed that they had traveled far from the impersonal world of physics and science, and into the deeply personal place of pain that Zendara held. "And after?"

The blonde shrugged and stared at their hands again. "After they died I didn't care anymore."

"I'm so sorry that you never got the childhood you deserved. I wish I had known you growing up, or better yet, I wish you had known me. Even though I have been aware for a long time that I'm adopted, I couldn't imagine not having my parents in my life. What you must have gone through..." She couldn't finish. Amari wanted to grab hold of Zendara's hand and never let go. She even went as far as raising hers from the couch but caution froze it in place. They had no idea what would happen if they should touch again. She had a theory, but nothing that was proven or concrete. And a scientist trusted proof over irrational action.

But despite the fact that Zendara had intellectual potential that was equal to Amari's level of genius, if not training, she was no scientist. And what she may have lacked in composure and patience, she more than made up for with bravery. Before Amari could pull away, Zen turned her hand over palm up and pressed them together. Breath froze in their lungs as they waited for something to happen, but all was quiet in Amari's condo. As if it had been planned out and choreographed ahead of time, they both sucked in a breath and turned to each other. Micro sparks of crystalline energy caused their tears to shimmer in a way that Zen had never seen before and their smiles were matching beacons of hope and remembrance. Zendara didn't let go, but she turned slightly and drew her leg up to get more comfortable. Her face was a study of curiosity and wonder. "Tell me about us."

DR. AMARI DEL Rey was beyond any measurement of genius that existed on Earth, and she was scientifically trained. It was understandable that Amari would have formulated theories over the years by analyzing her own blood and using oscilloscopes to measure the power absorption rate between her body and various types of energy. Just knowing that her cells were both carbon and crystalline in nature were major clues to solving the mystery of her abilities. She didn't tell Zendara those theories at the beginning because they had much more important and basic details to discover first. But after years of study, Amari was convinced that her cells could alter their own frequency to the resonance frequency of any energy type. That allowed for the instantaneous transfer and amplification of power.

But the detail she hadn't put together yet was how their individual bodies reacted with each other. It was one thing to resonate at the frequency of a foreign body, it was completely different if a foreign body resonated at her own natural frequency. That flash from earlier in the park was their bodies synching to the same natural frequency, shifting each of them to something new. But it was also the final step necessary to permanently bind them together. They now shared the exact same frequency as their natural state, one that was completely foreign to anything else in the known universe, thus amplifying each other. Any power potential they had separately would be immeasurably greater when they were together. Neither the world, nor our two protagonists were ready for the consequences of that moment in the park. At least not yet.

UNSEEN BY THE two women on Amari's balcony, a portal opened in a darkened section of trees on Bynum Island, in Washington Park. The local CORP computer algorithms flagged an uptick of social media posts about a strange beam of light shining into the night sky at the same time their computers also registered a massive energy anomaly. The anomaly and accompanying sonic boom disappeared nearly as quickly as they occurred but agents were able to pinpoint its origin point within ten yards. The strength of the energy burst was something they'd never seen before, which was why the eight member Chicago team stepped through the portal on high alert. Seven Chromodecs and one human comprised the unit, all wearing standard black uniforms with built-in light body armor. Because they didn't want their identities made public, every agent wore something that looked like a modified black motorcycle helmet with built-in coms, HUD, and tinted face shield.

They were a well-rounded and highly capable CORP team. As soon as they had boots on the ground, the team leader leaped into the sky to gain observation height. Code-named Rocket, she was only five and a half feet tall but her personality and commanding presence made her seem like a giant. Coms activated, she called out instructions to the rest. "Voda, Chinook, Blaze, spread out and look for anything unusual or signs of a struggle."

"Yes, ma'am!" Blaze engaged his headlamp and began walking roughly east from their position. Voda didn't bother with the headlamp, she simply went right up to the water and started walking west across the surface. Chinook went north, using wind to clear the path of debris and leaves.

"Minder, use your telepathy and see if you can pick up anyone lingering in the area. Take Lingua with you."

A single male voice replied over the com link. "What about us?"

"Rocket, I've got a patch of scorched earth over here!"

Rocket flew toward Blaze, their team pyrokinetic, and gazed down at the burn pattern near the center of the island. "That's the spot! I want Vision's hands on that scorch to see if he can get a psychometric reading. Shyft, you guard him until we're ready to 'port out of here. The rest of you, spread out through the park and see if you can find anything else."

"How are we supposed to find anything in the dark, this park is huge!"

Special Agent Romy Danes scowled as the familiar whine of

Chinook's voice came over her speaker. Sometimes leading her team was like herding toddlers. The wind-manipulating Chromodec had only been with their unit seven months and his attitude was never something she would choose to add to a solid team. But unfortunately, they had no say in who was assigned to the CORP enforcement units. The Special Agent in Charge, her, merely had to make the best of it. She didn't bother to answer Devin, aka "Chinook." Instead, she hovered above the lagoon and watched the headlamps of her various agents as they searched. "Vision, anything yet?"

Julian Hill was a smaller man, one of the shortest agents on the team. With dark skin and darker eyes that frequently crinkled at the edges when displaying his infamous biting wit, he was crouched down with their teleporter in the area Blaze had found. Shyft was keeping guard, as directed. Vision's gloves were off while he focused entirely on his non-physical senses. Finally he straightened and snatched his gloves off the burnt grass. "It was two people for sure just based on the boot prints. But I can't get a read on anything more personal than that. It's like a blank in my vision when I focus on the owners of those boots. Instead I'm getting the psychic imprint the disturbance of their passing left behind. Very impersonal. They came in from the northwest. I saw blue water, and a building with a hole." He shook his head as if that alone could clear up the fuzzy vision he had of the ones they were searching for.

Rocket zoomed her HUD map of the park and found what she was looking for. "Heads up! The Washington Park pool and fitness center are northwest of here near the intersection of Martin Luther King and Garfield." She was happy to see the headlamps below change direction to converge that exact location. Vision and Shyft disappeared below her and popped up on her HUD between the fitness center and the pool. At the speed of her namesake, it took Special Agent Danes seconds to cover the distance, unlike the rest of the team on the ground.

When she landed, she saw Vision once again crouched with his hands on the ground, most likely trying to get a new read. Shyft remained back so as not to disturb him. After a few seconds, Agent Hill stood and pointed farther out, closer to the edge of the park and the intersection. Blaze arrived first at a light jog, and Rocket made a circling motion in the air with her gloved hand. "Blaze with me, Shyft and Vision paired, the four of us will split up and search around the fitness center. The rest of the team is to pair up and do the same with the pool facility."

Agent Dara Smith joked over the com in reply. "You definitely know the way to a girl's heart, sir!"

Blaze snorted where he stood next to Rocket. He didn't cue his com but she heard him just the same. "Kiss ass."

She turned to look his way with her face shield up. "Stow it. You know she's just joking around."

He didn't raise his face shield in return. "Yeah, well she ain't funny." Rocket didn't bother to say any more. Voda and Blaze came to their team about the same time but the two Chromodec agents never got along. It probably had something to do with opposing scalar manipulation powers, one being water and the other being fire. Predictably, they got along like cats and dogs.

Rocket and Blaze covered ground faster than the other pair and before long they found themselves staring at a fist-sized hole in the fitness center's external wall. "Damn. Chromodec for sure, boss."

Rocket didn't answer, instead cued her coms. "Shyft and Vision, double-time to the north side wall."

Mere seconds later Agent Traverse teleported himself and Agent Hill to Rocket's location. They stepped through the portal and the smaller man grinned. "We cheated."

The rest of the team arrived about five minutes after that and stared at the hole. Vision had both gloves off. His right hand grasped the hole while the palm of the left hand pressed flat against the brick surface below it. "I sense a lot of anger and confusion. Loneliness, like someone is lost while not being lost."

Minder spoke up in the silence that followed. While her words were all too familiar, they weren't ones that the team wanted to hear. "Shit, looks like we have a rogue. Possibly newly discovered."

Rocket shook her head slowly, unconvinced. "I don't know. Something in my gut tells me this is different. Can you get anything else, Vision? Age, physical description, anything?"

Agent Hill closed his eyes and focused again, moving his hands along the rough surface of brick like he was reading braille. "I get nothing at all about the person. Again, it's like they leave an afterimage of their passing but nothing of the individual remains."

"Not even gender?"

Vision shrugged. "Telemetry is not an exact science, as you well know. But I'll be honest, I've never had anyone show up as a null, let alone two people. I think your gut is right on this."

Special Agent Romy Danes stood with one hand on her hip and moved the other hand up to rub her forehead with worry, forgetting about the helmet. She huffed as her fingers met the raised face shield. Unfortunately, leading the CORP team came with an extreme level of responsibility to the general public and rubbing her forehead with worry was a habitual mannerism for her. "All right, looks like we aren't going to get any more here. I want samples taken from the brick wall and the scorch on the island. Lingua and Vision can start collecting the samples while Shyft 'ports everyone back to HQ." She looked toward Agent King, aka Lingua. The woman was an invaluable resource to the team because she held advanced degrees in linguistics, forensics, and computer science. "After Shyft returns and takes the two of you to collect the scorch sample, I want a full analysis done as soon as possible. This much power means our rogue is priority one right now. Dismissed!"

When it was just Agents Julian Hill and Sara King left on the ground, Romy Danes addressed them specifically. "I want these findings coded for my DNA only. No one else gets access. Understand?"

All their face shields were in the clear and untinted state so it was easy enough to see when Vision narrowed his eyes with concern. "Do you have a reason you don't want the rest of the team seeing the results?"

Rocket shook her head. "Nothing concrete, but I've had a gut feeling for a while now. However, after ten years and a stint in Black Badge together, I trust the two of you implicitly. I just hope I'm wrong about the rest, especially with a powerful new potential threat on the horizon." Both nodded in agreement. With that, Agent Danes leaped into the sky and rocketed away, searching the Chicago skyline for answers.

Chapter Eight

YEARNING, LIKE TWO celestial bodies caught in the gravity well of each other, sometimes people can find themselves drawn inexplicably together. For Amari Del Rey and Zendara Baen-Tor, their chemistry was not so unexplainable. It was more biological than even a human's laws of attraction. You see, the women of the Q'orre system were linked at a very young age, a destiny predicted by prophesies of both Reyna and Tora. As Q'sirrahna, they were connected on not just a cellular level but a spiritual one as well. Amari and Zendara's natural frequencies were perfectly in synch with each other and would always be so as long as they stayed in regular contact. As a result, not only did they feel comfortable in each other's presence like no other person in their life, but they craved the other person's touch.

An individual could say the two women didn't know each other well enough to be romantically inclined toward one another. However, it was the very nature of their bond to be drawn emotionally, as well as physically. That attraction was a feeling that was reinforced by the natural empathy they shared. It was a truth that Amari and Zen discovered slowly, with each hour that ticked by on the night of the great resonance flash. But despite their Q'sirrahna bond, the women were very different. Time would tell whether that difference was more nature or nurture when it came to their past and their biology. By nature, the people of Reyna were considered the more hesitant race. Reynans were typically thought of as long-sighted intellectuals, compared to the people of Tora with their penchant toward action and quick thinking. Two very opposite traits to have. Couple that with their very disparate upbringings on Earth, and you have the makings of an intriguing and potentially volatile match.

TWELVE HOURS AFTER the incident on Bynum Island saw a remarkable amount of information exchanged between Amari and Zendara. It was early Saturday afternoon by the time the two women ran out of words in their initial volley of introduction, each feeling infinitely more connected to the other through the simple act of sharing their past histories. Minus the occasional break for food or drink, or other more mundane bodily functions, they never left each other's side. Nothing untoward happened as their hands remained clasped tight, no agents in black knocked on Amari's door to investigate the incident in the park, and their cell phones were blissfully silent. But their introduction and acquaintanceship had come to an end and they were caught in a moment of silent awkwardness.

Amari stared down at their joined hands. "What happens now?"

"What would you like to happen?" Zen looked up to meet Amari's dark eyes.

"I don't know." Sudden nervousness went through Amari and she fell into her old habit of wanting to stay busy when she was uncomfortable. "I should probably get some stuff done around here, and call Stephanie. Then maybe I'll head into the lab—"

The kiss took both of them by surprise, despite the fact that Zendara initiated it. Slow and languid, it started as a mere caress of lips that grew with each pair of breaths in and out. Eventually Amari couldn't take the temptation any longer and opened her mouth to Zen's questing tongue. Smooth like silk, her Q'sirrahna tasted like the sweetest of fruit. It was a quiet moan that brought the intimate kiss back down from the summit of passion and rewarded the two women a measure of control. Mouths pulled back but rather than separate, their foreheads pressed together by some mutual and unconscious decision while they caught their breath.

"Fuck." Zendara's face was flushed and she panted with unexpectedly intense desire. "What was that?"

Amari gently released the breath she'd been holding and willed her heart to slow. "I suspect that was just another facet of our Q'sirrahna bond."

Zen pulled back and broke contact with Amari and a light shudder ran through both. "Is it always like that for you?"

A slow shake of Amari's dark head was answer enough, but her awe-tinged words drove it home. "It's never been like that with anyone but you."

Dusky lips curved into a smile. "Same." She took a deep breath before releasing it and looked away to gather her wits before speaking. "About the kiss, sorry if I kind of jumped in there like that. I didn't even ask permission, I just—I mean, I get that we're meant for each other but I still should have waited. But sitting here with the way we're being pulled together...I had to know."

Amari rushed to reassure her, placing a hand on the other woman's arm. "No! It's fine. It's not like I wasn't thinking about doing the same thing. But I was afraid."

"Afraid? Why?"

"It's disconcerting to be this drawn to someone I've only just met. Realistically, we're complete strangers."

Zendara grabbed her hand after Amari nervously ran her fingers through her shoulder-length dark hair. "But we're not strangers! I may have only just met you but I've known you all my life." Seeing the uncertainty in Amari's eyes, Zen backed off. "Listen, perhaps we should take some time to come to terms with everything. I should probably get back to my apartment. I need a shower and we both need sleep." She turned to grab her coat from the back of the couch and Amari cried out at the sudden impending loss.

"No!" Zen turned back and raised a finely arched pale eyebrow in a curious expression, prompting Amari to explain her outburst. "I don't want to lose you."

A tender smile met her words. "You'll never lose me. Let's exchange cell numbers and addresses. I mean, we both work at the university but it's not like we're there at the same time." She shrugged. "I'm not trying to pretend like I'm unaffected by all this, because I am. I think that's why I just need to take a minute and let it all soak in. You know? Plus I need to stop by the police station today and make a statement about the attempted robbery last night."

Amari nodded. "Yeah, I get it. It's a bit overwhelming, especially for someone who was completely in the dark like you were. Would you like to come over for dinner Sunday—er, I guess since it's now Saturday afternoon, would you like to come over tomorrow?"

"I would love that."

"Is there anything you don't eat?"

Zen grinned at her. "Worms."

They made their way to the door of the condo where Zen turned to look back at her soul mate. Just the impending short separation caused a little spike of anxiety to flare in her chest. But she had to do some thinking and to do that she needed space. She wasn't like Amari, she hadn't been aware of her background and powers for nearly ten years. It was a lot to take in. Soul mate. No, Q'sirrahna. She looked into Amari's liquid dark eyes and watched as the other woman licked her lips and moved closer. Zen held up a hand to forestall her.

A hurt look flickered across Amari's face. "What's wrong?"

"Nothing's wrong. Actually, things are more right than they've ever been before. But I'm going to be honest with you, I don't know what will happen if you kiss me like that again."

Amari sighed and looked down. "You're right. I won't want to stop." After composing herself, Amari looked back up with a smile and held out her arms. "How about a hug instead?"

"I think I can handle that." Zendara leaned into the embrace, her arms tight around Amari's back. Then as she sensed the hug was about to end, her lips whispered softly against the side of Amari's ear. "I'm so glad I finally met you, Q'sirrahna."

Amari shuddered and when they pulled away from each other, her eyes were bright with sparkling unshed tears. "Ahna means forever."

Zen smiled. "I think I already knew that." Then she was gone, out the door like a dream, before she could lose her resolve.

MEANWHILE, BACK AT CORP headquarters, a figure dressed in an armored black bodysuit paced back and forth in the main control room. Despite her lack of height, Special Agent in Charge Romy Danes cut an impressive figure in her uniform. While she would never be known as cruel, she could be a stern taskmaster at times. Because of that, the rest of the team had abandoned the room hours before. After working most of the night, they were all due some downtime anyway. But Rocket was the epitome of a responsible team captain and she took her duty far too seriously. Many tried to maintain a life outside the five-story CORP building located in Lincoln Park. But SAIC Danes held no such illusion. Her life was the CORP, her family was her team. Chicago was her city and no one threatened her city without meeting justice head on. And strange energy readings in the middle of the night usually only meant one thing, a rogue Chromodec.

"SIMoN, any other anomalies detected?"

"No anomalies have been detected since the original incident, Special Agent Danes. Shall I run a deep scan analysis of all other forms of energy emission?"

SIMoN, or Synthetic Intelligence Monitoring Network, was the heart and soul of the CORP, tracking and controlling information from all over the world. The HUD in their helmets was tied to SIMoN, so too were all other defense protocols for the facility. They had full access to government networks as well and the local city and state official systems. They could monitor police and military communications, flight paths for anything in the surrounding airspace, power grid usage for the entire state, communications, transportation, and so much more. It would probably frighten most people to know how much power was at a CORP agent's fingertips at any given time.

"Have we seen any strange communications, or spikes in the power grid for the metro Chicago area?"

"All current CORP-monitored systems are operating within normal parameters."

"Damn it!" Rocket slammed the bottom of her fist into a nearby wall. Even though it was made from a metal alloy, her impact left a slight indentation in the surface. It was one of the hazards of being a levikinetic with a strength boost. As described by her name, Rocket could indeed fly via her levitation but the scalar energy also surrounded her in an unconscious, nearly-impenetrable, bubble when she utilized the power. Special Agent Danes could blast through just about anything and was hard-pressed to be injured while midflight. The strength also came in handy when on the ground as well. With her specialized combat training plus her powers, she could duke it out with the best of them. Of course she also had to be careful around people and equipment too, so very careful.

"You see, this is why we can't have nice things."

Rocket spun around, then relaxed immediately when she saw it was one of her longtime friends. Agent Sondra Shields, aka Minder, graduated at the CORP academy two years after Romy. They served together for years on the Dallas unit before Romy was offered a promotion and new post in Chicago. They were even lovers for a short time, but just as with all of Agent Danes's romantic interactions, duty pulled her away. Minder's transfer to Special Agent Danes's Chicago unit was only approved once it was verified that more than five years had elapsed since their physical relationship had ended. But while they were no longer lovers, Rocket considered the other agent a friend and a valuable addition to the team.

"I won't tell if you don't. Though I should probably dock my own pay for the damage." Rocket grinned at her.

Minder shook her head. "No matter the rank, you still have that same core of blazing duty within you. Doesn't it get tiring?"

Romy gently threw herself into a nearby control chair and spun around to watch her friend. She knew that Sondra was talking about more than just the wall. "It's exhausting but I do what needs to be done in order to keep the city safe."

Sondra took a seat in the next chair. "You are troubled. Is it the rogue Chromodecs?"

Rolling eyes met her words. "Come on, Sonny, you don't have to be a mind reader to know that. I know you. Say what you've come to say."

The subordinate agent frowned at the old nickname and the memories it stirred. She couldn't afford to be distracted when so much was at stake. "You need to get some rest, and you need to get out of the building for a while." She held up a hand to forestall any protests that Rocket could give. "I'm telling you as both your resident telepath, and as your friend. You're mentally weary and that will make you a liability in the field. We need you in top shape out there, Danes."

Romy eyed her friend, analyzing her words and possible motivations. Perhaps the other woman was right. She had an apartment, she should probably use it sometime. She could also stand a pint or two and some company if she were lucky enough to find it. "Fine, you're right. I could use a night off." The problem with being a CORP agent was that they were always on call if they were in the city. However, the odds of anything happening were pretty low. She glanced at the main screen one last time before rising from her chair. She purposely didn't look at Agent Shields. "SIMoN, continue full scans every thirty minutes. I'll be available via communicator should you get a hit on our energy anomaly, or if any other emergencies arise. Otherwise the team on premises can handle any minor emergencies that crop up. Agent Shields is senior on duty, please log that in the records."

"Log has been noted in the duty records, Special Agent Danes. Analysis instructions also noted. Evening records will be stored in your secure file for review later, if you so desire."

"Confirmed, SIMoN. Shunt records of all monitoring into my private DNA-locked disk. I'll go over the data tomorrow."

Minder sighed. "Is that really necessary? You don't trust us for one night?"

Rocket went to the wall and opened a cabinet that contained dozens of high-tech communicators. They were so small they fit inside the ear and were molded to look as natural as possible. She removed a pair and popped them into her ears, then activated a switch on her smart watch. She would be able to hear just fine with the ear buds in, but she would still be able to respond within seconds should an emergency arise. Even when she was off duty, she never left it far behind. Romy shut the cabinet and walked back toward Sondra. She slapped the other woman's arm on the way by and called over her shoulder. "I trust you just fine, it's the city I don't trust. Night, Minder!"

"Have a pleasant evening, Rocky." Minder waited for ten full minutes in silence after Rocket left the control room. Once she had determined that no one was near, she walked over to the computer console and typed in a series of alpha-numeric digits. The screen flashed red and SIMoN's voice sounded through the room.

"Security override, protocol delta, initiated. Awaiting manual input." She typed in a few more commands and the screen flashed again. "Access granted."

After typing in the network ident and computer key, the red camera light blinked on. Nearly at the same time, the screen also brightened to show the smiling face of Colonel Maza. "Ah, well done, my dear. Report!"

Minder frowned and addressed the man on the screen. "We have a situation..."

EVIL COMES IN many forms and flavors. For some, their evil clings to them like an odor, obvious to anyone who comes near. But for others, their evil is buried beneath a charismatic smile and kind eyes. Their evil is old and emboldened, built over years of indoctrination and reinforced with each new betrayal. The Chicago CORP team certainly did have a problem but unbeknownst to its leader that problem could mostly be found within. How many walls could they lose before the entire castle crumbled to the ground? Their team and many more were soon to find out.

SPECIAL AGENT DANES'S first stop was her condo in Washington Park, near the university. She rode her motorcycle home, the helmet she used as Rocket doubling as a bike helmet for the trip. Her suit was rolled up and locked in panniers on either side of the machine. She wanted to be fully prepared in case something came up. Since it was early afternoon, she caught a few hours' sleep before heading out for a beer at a little bar nearby. Bender's had cheap draught beer and an open attitude, catering to just about anyone. She knew if she wanted to belly up to the bar for some drinks no one would bother her and conversely, if she wanted to look for a little company for the night, there was a good possibility for success with that as well.

A little after seven p.m. she was exactly where she wanted to be, sitting on a padded stool at the end of the bar and nursing a cold brew. Romy Danes traced the sweat from the glass with the tip of her finger, catching the droplets before they could hit the napkin below. She enjoyed watching the people come and go, seeing the connections men and women made in the darkened atmosphere. But Romy wasn't only in the bar for a little R & R, she had an agenda. Her willingness to go home for a few nights was less about her own comfort and more about the fact that she lived near the very park they had been exploring the night before. Bender's was on East Garfield Blvd, just southwest of the Garfield train platform. She planned to use her time asking around about the strange light from the night before. Even though the energy anomaly occurred in the wee hours of the morning, Bender's was one of the hundred plus Chicago bars that had a license to serve liquor until four a.m.

Romy was still on her first beer when a woman came in and sat two stools away from her. She was what Romy considered "intellectual cute," and appeared to be close to the same age and height. The drink she ordered looked complicated and sinfully delightful, and the agent used it as her opening. "That looks more like dessert than anything else."

Startled, Stephanie looked up with the cherry held firmly between her teeth as she popped the stem off and set it on the napkin beneath her martini glass. The other woman was attractive, her short dark hair cut into a sleek crop with side-swept bangs. While Dr. Stephanie Young had only ever been with men, she was in fact bisexual. She'd just never found a woman that was interested in her at the same time she was interested in them. On one hand, Steph had a voice in her head cheering that someone so hot was initiating conversation. On the other, she was lamenting the fact that Amari would arrive any moment for promised girl talk therefore making it impossible to socialize with anyone else. However, a simple introduction and small talk in the meantime couldn't hurt anything.

"It's a chocolate covered cherry martini. With both chocolate and regular whipped cream floating in the top. And yes, it's so good it's almost a crime." Stephanie sipped her drink and took notice of the way the other woman followed the line of her throat down to the cleavage peeking out at the top of her shirt. It was a gesture of interest that pleased the very single Doctor Young. "I haven't seen you in here before, are you new to the area?"

Romy shook her head and took the initiative to move over a seat. "No, been living in Washington Park about five years. Though I'll admit that I'm a bit of a workaholic and I'm always at the office." She held out her hand as if it were an absentminded afterthought. "Sorry, my name is Romy."

Stephanie accepted the handshake with a smile. "Steph. I live in the area too. So does my friend, Amari. Who—" She glanced at her cell phone screen to check the time. "Should be here any time."

"Well I don't want to intrude…"

"No, it's fine. You're definitely *not* intruding." She stared at her barely touched drink then looked back at Romy. "Would you like to try a sip? I'm afraid it won't go with your beer but it's definitely worth a try." She gently nudged the glass toward her new acquaintance.

Dark brown eyes and a quirky smile met her action. "What the hell, why not?" Romy gently lifted the martini glass and took a sip, getting a little whipped cream on her upper lip, which she immediately licked off. "Oh, that *is* good! Perhaps I'll order my own a little later, when I'm ready for dessert." She winked at Stephanie, who had the good grace to blush.

Before either of them could speak again, the bartender walked over and nodded toward Romy's nearly empty pint. "Want another?"

"Sure." When he brought it back, she used the opportunity to bring up the occurrence in Washington Park. "Hey, uh, someone in the bathroom was talking about a strange light in the park last night. Did you see it?"

He shook his head while Stephanie watched intently. "Naw, I was still working my shift. I don't even get out of here 'til five a.m. because of our late closing time."

The bartender walked away and Romy turned her attention back to her new friend and shrugged. "I was just curious. I mean, I know I'm not home very often but I don't want my place wrecked by some crazed Chromodecs, you know?"

Steph nodded. "Oh, believe me, I get it. I didn't see it myself but my friend told me about it. We were out last night but got back to Garfield platform around two. My friend walked me home after that, but I would have been inside long before the flash I heard about."

"Your friend walked you home? What is he, some big burly dude or something?" Romy was hoping she hadn't misread the woman's interest.

"No, my friend Amari. She always walks me home. She's the one that told me about the strange light in the park."

A fine dark brow lifted at Stephanie's words. "She walks you home, then walks herself home alone? How is that any safer?"

Stephanie laughed loudly. "Oh, no one is going to touch Amari, she—" She stopped abruptly, realizing that she was about to say things that shouldn't be said. But damn, Romy was so easy to talk to. The doctor shook her head slowly. "What I meant to say is that Amari has had a lot of self-defense or something. So, you know, she's, uh, pretty safe."

The woman in question heard the last part of her friend's sentence and was curious why she was the topic of conversation between Stephanie and the attractive woman next to her. Amari couldn't help being a little paranoid after their light show in the park the previous night. She had no doubts that the Chicago CORP team would be investigating the incident in the coming days. Maybe even the cops. Even if they hadn't seen any movement in the park last night from her condo balcony, that didn't mean no one was there. "And just what is it I'm pretty safe from, Steph?"

Stephanie spun toward her good friend in surprise. "You're here!"

"As opposed to? I mean, we did arrange to meet at seven thirty, or did you forget?"

"No, no! I didn't forget. Shit, where are my manners?" She gestured toward Romy. "This is Romy, she was just keeping me company until you got here and we could commence with some girl talk. Romy, this is my very best friend in the world, Amari."

Romy laughed good-naturedly and held out her hand. "Amari the baddass, apparently. It's nice to meet you. I don't know a lot of people in the area but I'm glad I came out tonight." She paused for a second. "So, Stephanie tells me that you saw the strange light in the park? Was it crazy? Should I be worried when I'm out of town for work?" That had always been the cover story for many CORP members to explain their frequent social absences. It was easiest to claim they had jobs that required them to travel a lot for work.

Leery, Amari answered the woman's question. "You're probably fine. My balcony faces the park—"

She was cut off by Stephanie's mumbled word. "Lucky!"

"Anyway, I got home and stepped outside and that's when I saw this crazy, uh, beam of light or something. It just shot into the sky, then disappeared. I don't know what it was and it was so fast I didn't even have a chance to pull out my cell phone. Being a scientist, I'm naturally curious but I wasn't about to head over to the park in the middle of the night and check it out. Call me a coward if you want."

The agent laughed at Amari's words. "So, not a baddass then?"

Amari shrugged. "Even I know my limits."

Awkward silence fell for about thirty seconds before Romy decided it was time to move on. She stood from her stool and grabbed the fresh beer and left the empty glass sitting there. She raised it to her two new friends. "Well, I'll let you two continue with your evening. It was nice meeting you both. Perhaps I'll see you around here again. You know, since we all live in the neighborhood."

Amari gave Romy a wary nod. "Yes, good to meet you too." But before she could pull Stephani away, the good Doctor Young was already handing Romy a business card from her purse.

"My cell number is on there, just call or text if you ever want to hang out. It was nice meeting you too, Romy."

Romy took the card, her fingers grazing against Stephanie's as she pulled her hand back. "The pleasure was all mine. Have a nice evening, ladies." She watched the two women walk toward a booth in the darkened back corner of the bar. Animated whispers, punctuated by jerky hand motions told the agent that Amari was not happy with her friend for some reason. But that wasn't the only reason that Romy had her eye on the two long after they left her presence. Based on Amari's body language alone, she was certain the younger woman had been lying about seeing the light in the park. Something about her tale rang untrue, and Special Agent Romy Danes was going to find out why.

Chapter Nine

IT WAS HOT in L.A., even in the springtime. While California was known for its sunny weather, it wasn't so idyllic in America's second largest city. Smog was an unfortunate side effect to the combination of high population and pollution mixed with the heat of a massive concrete jungle. Even so, a California CORP gig was pretty sweet if you could get it. Having just graduated from the rigorous two-year training course, Agent Olly Landon was feeling nothing but excitement as he walked into the L.A. headquarters. He had to show his badge and submit to a retinal scan and hand scan before security would let him through the armored steel door. Five men and four women greeted him on the other side. All wore the distinctive black uniforms of a CORP agent. One man with blonde hair and blue eyes strode forward and held out his hand.

"I'm Special Agent in Charge Collin Bremmer, code named Shockwave. Congrats on your program success and welcome to CORP-LA." After he finished shaking Olly's hand, he waved toward the eight other people in the antechamber. "This is your new team."

Agent Landon gave everyone a wave and a smile. "Hey."

Shockwave pointed out each member as he went around the room. "That's Doc, his power is healing so you'll want to be real nice to him." A few chuckled at his statement. "Then we have Gauss and Sinter, our brother and sister magnetism twins; Glacier who can freeze just about anything; Wildfire, our resident pyro; Python with her telekinetic squeeze; our flying man Jet; and lastly we have Portis, our teleporter."

Bolt smiled nervously and waved back at them. "Very nice to meet you. I'm Bolt and I can shoot lightening. I'm really excited to join you all in LA. Your team is supposed to have one of the best track records in the CORP."

Shockwave clapped him on the shoulder. "One of the best? Try *the* best!" More laughter followed his braggadocios words. "Okay then, now that we've all put names to faces, I want to run some simulations in the warehouse so we can all get a feel for our new member and his power." He smiled at Bolt, showing movie star quality teeth. "Sound good?"

"Yes, sir, sounds great!"

The SAIC shook his head and laughed. "None of that here, we're a lot more laid back than those suits down at the Guantanamo training center. You can just call me Shockwave, that's formal enough for me." He turned to the rest. "Let's go people, daylight is wasting!"

One by one they filed through another secure steel door. Before they could step past, Shockwave paused and looked back at Bolt. "Say, do you know Doctor Daggett?"

A strange look came over Agent Olly Landen's face. It was as if someone had taken a cloth and wiped away his previous expression, leaving a stoic façade behind. "Yes, we met in Nevada a few years ago."

Special Agent Collin Bremmer's Hollywood smile turned feral and he nodded once. "Welcome to the team, Agent Landon. You'll do just fine in LA. We have quite a few friends of the doctor here."

DOCTOR DAGGETT, OR Dr. Brian Daggett, if you prefer. Now that is a name that keeps popping up, isn't it? You see, much like any other secret society over the years, the agents that were part of Oracle's grand plan needed a way to recognize each other. You couldn't have mass communication between individual cells. It was too easy for the sleeper agents to be compromised that way. No, things needed to be kept on the micro level for the plan to succeed. While Col. Marek Maza had quite a few telepaths swayed to his mission, not all were able to be conditioned to his needs. It wasn't a matter of power. Oracle either had to overpower and brainwash the Chromodec in question, or the CORP agent had to be morally corruptible and capable of betraying a team that they would be serving with for years. That took a special sort of personality, which was why not all agents trained and placed in teams all over the country were sleepers.

But there was still the problem of the sleeper agents recognizing each other without the aid of a list or compromising symbol. That was how Oracle came up with the code phrase that fell from Shockwave's lips.

"Do you know Doctor Daggett?" It was simple and innocuous while still paying homage to the man who created their race more than half a century before. Of course someone could legitimately know a Doctor Daggett and *not* be an agent of Oracle. That was why there was a counter phrase. "We met in Nevada a few years ago." It too was simple, easy to remember, and once again referenced the place where the Chromodecs all began. The secret facility in the middle of the Mohave.

And let's not forgot about the newest member of CORP-LA so soon. After all, you may remember him with a slightly different name. Before he spent two years in the rigorous CORP agent training program, Agent Olly Landen was none other than the rogue Chromodec, Zeusifer. Once broken by the Hieronymus machine, Leroy Oliver Landon had passed Oracle's test with flying colors. Reconditioned and rebranded as Bolt, he was sent to the other side of the country from where he was initially apprehended. Lucky for Oracle, or perhaps it was all part of his master plan, the CORP teams rarely ever met other agents outside their home team. So the shadier aspects of the program had yet to be discovered. It also helped that all agents had to go through a two week refresher course at the Guantanamo facility every other year. It was then that Oracle fished for more accomplices and guaranteed the loyalty of his existing ones.

Things were progressing as planned, and with more than forty percent of the nation's active CORP agents being sleepers, action was surely imminent.

"WHO WAS THAT?"

Stephanie glanced at Amari as they made their way to a darkened corner of the bar. "Her name is Romy, she seems nice enough. And cute!"

Amari grimaced. "And why was she fishing for information? You can't say anything about what I told you, Steph!" She sliced her hand through the air as if to cut off future discussions on Stephanie's part.

Once they were seated, they paused when a waitress came around to take Amari's order. When she was gone, Amari spoke in a whisper that was just loud enough to be heard over the juke-box music. "I don't have to be a rocket scientist to—"

"You're not a rocket scientist." After interrupting what was sure to be a diatribe about safety and secrecy, Stephanie popped the second cherry from her glass into her mouth.

The younger woman froze mid rant, nonplussed at the inter-ruption. "What?"

Stephanie rolled her eyes. "I said, you're not a rocket scien-tist. And you're pretty adorable when you're fired up, but go on." She waved for Amari to continue and tossed the stem on the fresh napkin.

"Fucking hell, this is not funny!" People glanced at them when she yelled, including the mystery woman at the bar. Romy, whatever her last name was. Amari felt more than a little pleasure as Dr. Stephanie Young looked back with wide eyes, but she apol-ogized anyway. "Sorry for swearing at you. But this is serious. After that flash of energy we put out last night, the CORP has to be looking for us."

Steph gave her a curious look. "Why would the CORP be looking for you? You're not Chromodecs."

"I know that and you know that but how would anyone else know? As far as the world is concerned, the only people on Earth with powers are Chromodecs. Even Zendara thought she was a Chromodec. Can you believe she had no idea that she even had powers until last night?"

"What?" Before Amari could answer, Steph held her hands up in a stop motion. "Wait, start from the beginning. Tell me what happened when you left my place last night."

Amari spent thirty minutes and almost two drinks giving her friend the abbreviated version of meeting Zendara and the infor-mation they exchanged. "She just left a few hours ago and we have plans to have dinner together tomorrow night."

"Whoa, whoa, whoa, time out!" Steph made a tee with her hands. "You mean to tell me that the woman you're destined to be with, your soul mate and person you can't keep your hands off of, just went home by herself tonight? Girl, what were you think-ing?"

Amari drained her beer. "I was thinking that I dumped a lot of information on her since last night and she probably needs to process a little."

"The only thing she needs to process is dat ass—"

Amari's hand prevented Steph from finishing her statement.

"Stop. Do not let whatever you were going to say past those lips!" She sighed. "Listen, you're my best friend. And I know the secret I've asked you to keep over the past few years is huge. And I probably haven't done a good job of explaining to you how dangerous it is for me or anyone who knows about me. My adopted dad filled me in a little bit about what goes on with the CORP division. I've also done my own research. Did you know that every single rogue Chromodec that is apprehended just disappears? They are taken to Guantanamo and never heard from again. Not only that but we continue to see new graduates from the esteemed CORP academy that go on to be placed on CORP teams all over the country. We're never given the agent's names, just their code names. And we can't see their faces."

Steph looked at her curiously. "So what's your point? You're starting to sound like one of those conspiracy theorists."

"The difference between me and them is that I *know* the truth. And my point is that I don't like how the government can just make people disappear. And what happens to those people with power that they consider rogues or threats? Where is the due process? I read the official documents on Chromodec origins and it was not pretty."

"What do you mean you read them? I thought that info was top secret? Even the news agencies who got copies of the info couldn't get much out of them because they were so heavily redacted!"

Amari shrugged. "My dad. He's been here for decades, and while he's legally my guardian in Terran terms, his official job is to be a Watcher for the Tau Ceti. You remember, I told you about them a long time ago? They're the ones that keep us from being overrun by other alien races and prevent premature technological and biological advancement." She shook her head as she realized she was getting off track. "Anyways, the Tau Ceti tried to sweep the entire Area 51 Chromodec experiment under the rug. It would have worked too, at least until the first child of a Chromodec was born. We've all seen old news reports, I mean that's the world we live in now. But Dad says that the government has extremely high security on the entire CORP program. They have more power than any other government agency, even the CIA."

Steph sobered and finally nodded. "So we have to be even more careful than we were before."

Amari placed her fingers on the back of her friend's hand. "If they find out about me, they'll investigate everyone who knows me. They'll investigate my parents, and they'll find out about so much more. We can't take any chances right now."

"Would you still save me if I fell off that platform today?"

"I would save anyone if my intervention meant the difference between life and death."

The other doctor tilted her head to the side to stare at her all-too-human alien friend. "Why? If you're so afraid of discovery for you and your parents, why would you still take that risk?"

Amari blew out a breath as she studied the empty beer bottle in front of her. Finally she looked up and met Stephanie's blue eyes. "Because it's the right thing to do. Morality should never take a back seat to fear or convenience. Because this isn't a damn movie or comic book, and I'm not some unfeeling monster. If I have the power to save someone's life, I'm going to utilize it."

Stephanie gave Amari's hand a light squeeze. "You're definitely not a monster. And I don't think I can ever tell you enough how grateful I am for what you did. You saved my life and I'll never forget that. I'll be careful, I promise."

"Thank you."

A glint suddenly came into the older scientist's eyes and she abruptly circled the topic back around to Amari's soul mate. "So, you should definitely text her and invite her back over tonight."

Amari protested. "But we already have plans for tomorrow!"

"Do you want to see her?"

Amari sighed wistfully and nodded.

"Does she want to see you?"

"I don't know."

Steph raised an eyebrow. "Really?"

The younger woman smiled. "Okay, you're probably right. I'm just afraid..."

When she failed to finish her sentence, Stephanie prompted her. "Afraid of what?"

"It's just so frightening, the depth that we connect. It's extremely intense. From the moment we touched in the park, I knew she was a part of me."

"Hun, isn't that a good thing though? Isn't that the connection you've been searching for your entire life?"

Amari nodded. "It is, but we know so little about our connection. Neither of us expected that huge energy release and flash of light from simply clasping our hands together. What happens when we actually sleep together?"

Stephanie snorted. "Talk about explosive sex!" Amari looked

at her as if she'd just grown a third head, then abruptly broke out into laughter. That set them both off and eased the building tension. As they calmed down again, Amari let out a long sigh, thinking about the attraction she felt for her Q'sirrahna. Stephanie leaned over and tapped Amari's phone. "Text her."

"But what about you? We're supposed to have girl's night. I'd be a terrible friend if I just left you hanging on a Saturday night!"

Steph cut her gaze over toward the bar to the lone figure still seated at the end. Romy looked up and met her eyes with a smirk. "Oh, I think I'll be just fine." She waved her hand toward Amari's phone. "Go get the girl!" Then she leaned a little closer. "That's what I'm gonna do." When it dawned on Amari what she was talking about, Steph winked. "Don't worry, I'll be careful."

Amari rolled her eyes. "Fine! But we are so going to talk about you and her and how it goes on your end." As Steph's BFF, Amari knew that the older woman was bisexual. She was also quite aware that Steph had never actually been with another woman. Part of her hoped that things worked out for her friend just so Steph wouldn't be so alone. With Steph's nod, Amari picked up her phone and sent a quick text to Zendara. She didn't even get a chance to set it down again before it vibrated in her hand. When she read her Q'sirrahna's response, a wash of giddy pleasure went through her. "Flag down the waitress, I need to go."

Stephanie started laughing. "Don't worry about it, it was only two beers. You can owe me."

Suddenly Amari looked worried. "But what about you? I can't leave you to just walk home alone."

"Who says I'll be alone?"

Amari groaned. "You're going to take her home the night you meet? Which one of us is supposed to be the millennial here?"

Steph defended her actions. "Hey, I'm single and I don't have some special soul mate to keep my hopes up. A girl's got to do what a girl's got to do! I'm thirty-five years old and live with my cat, and the last four men and women I dated were duds. Relationship prospects are drying up before my eyes."

"Oh please, you're goddamn cute and you know it! But fine, just be careful and I'll try not to worry so much. Now you better go snag that sexy lady before someone else does. She keeps looking over here." Something about the woman at the bar still left Amari feeling uneasy but she attributed it to her overall paranoia of being found by the CORP. Romy looked small and harmless enough so she thought Steph was probably fine. She stood and put on her jacket. "All right, I'm out. Wish me luck!"

Stephanie waved her hand to flag down the server. "You've already got your girl, wish me luck!"

"Fine, luck then." They exchanged a quick hug then Amari weaved briskly in and out of patrons toward the exit near the front.

Once Stephanie paid their tab, she made her way back up to the bar. Boldly, she took the stool next to Romy. With a flirty smile and a fresh drink in hand, she turned to her new friend. "So, do you have any plans for the evening?"

Trying her best to separate duty from attraction, Romy flirted back. "I do now."

I KNOW WHAT you're thinking. But no matter how it seems, Special Agent Romy Danes is not a bad guy. She is simply a woman who is trying to do the right thing, keeping the city and its citizens safe from harm. She really did want to dive into Steph and Amari's story from the night before, convinced that some bit of information was being withheld. And Stephanie's approach after her friend left the bar was an unexpected boon.

But beyond the duty weighing on her from being the leader of the CORP-CHI team, she still had human emotions and human needs. And it had been a long time since she'd connected with someone outside the job. She found Stephanie extremely attractive and she was clearly intelligent if the PhD in biochemistry listed on her business card meant anything. So intelligence and nerd cuteness, two things that drew Romy like a moth to a flame. And technically she was on her downtime. Might as well make the most of it. She had no idea exactly what she was getting into, or the level of intrigue one simple love interest could bring. But in the days to come, she would certainly find out.

AMARI LOSIRA DEL Rey was an upstanding and responsible citizen. She was a doctor of biochemistry and a princess of

Reyna, one of the fabled lost daughters of Q'orre. And she was definitely *not* one to take reckless risks in exchange for personal reward. Oh but she wanted to. Her pressing need to reunite with her soul mate tempted her to use powers that were best kept hidden after the incident in the park. Realistically she knew it would take Zendara fifteen minutes to get from her apartment to Amari's place. Even so, nerves had her wanting to rush.

Amari was home only five minutes when the knock came. She opened the door and Zendara stood there looking disheveled and a little wild. She wore baggy sweats, a hoodie, and a smile. Feeling self-conscious at Amari's scrutiny, Zen waved at her clothes. "I was getting ready to take a shower when you texted me. I grabbed what I planned on wearing for an evening in."

Amari returned her smile with one that had a bit of playful heat, then reached out to pull the other woman inside by her hood strings. "Well, it's a good thing we're staying in then." Once the door was shut, she moved in to kiss her Q'sirrahna only to be held back by strong hands.

"Wait. We're not going to—you know, go boom again, right? I know you said we have to maintain a low prof—" Amari's lips were soft and the silence was abrupt as they molded to her own.

The kiss eased to an end and they pulled back. "Does that answer your question?"

Suddenly feeling like the cautious one, Zen frowned at the risk Amari had taken. "I don't know."

The Reynan princess grinned. "Are you complaining?" Zen shook her head. Getting the answer she expected, Amari led her Q'sirrahna farther into the condo. "I wasn't taking a risk you know."

Zendara startled and pulled her hand away. "What the fuck! Can you read my mind now?"

"No, but I can read your face well enough. Not to mention, I was thinking about it too. I have a theory and can explain my reasoning if it makes you feel better."

"Please, I don't like to be in the dark. So many things are confusing enough right now and I don't want be lost anymore."

Amari snagged her hand again and pulled her along. "I will never lose you." Zen sat on the couch where directed but Amari didn't follow her. "I'm going to grab a bottle of water. You want some?" Zen nodded. "Be right back."

The condo was open with high ceilings and Zendara followed the other woman with her needy gaze. "I thought you had plans tonight? When did you find time to come up with a theory about our big boom?"

The doctor of biochemistry laughed at her Q'sirrahna's phrase. "I did have plans. It was my best friend who convinced me to text you tonight instead of waiting to meet tomorrow."

"Does this best friend know about you? About us being, uh, special?"

Amari returned with the water and sat on the couch next to Zen. "Yes, but I only told her under extreme circumstances." When she saw Zen's pale eyebrow rise with inquiry, she elaborated. "I saved her life. Someone tried to mug us on the way back from the loop one night."

Zen snorted. "And you played the hero?"

"Mmm, no. Steph did. She took a picture of the guy and told him to beat it or she was going to call the cops."

Both eyebrows went up. "Brave *chica*!"

Amari shook her head. "No, stupid. He shoved her off the platform before taking off. Our train was coming so I had no choice but to jump down for her. When I landed I touched the third rail and she saw it. Then I lifted her into my arms and jumped back up to the platform."

"Holy shit, the third rail? Were you..." She struggled to think of the right word, understanding the effect after Amari's explanation of their powers the night before, and her own experience with being shot.

"Juiced? Yeah, totally. So anyway, she had a ton of questions for me and wasn't going to let me go without an explanation. She's very intelligent, and curious."

Zen grinned at her. "Sounds like someone else I've recently met. How long has she known? And she's kept your secret?"

"About two years, and yeah. We've actually run some tests on my blood and cells on the sly. Not all my information came from my parents. Some of it came from our work at the lab."

"Okay, fair enough. Now tell me about your theory."

Amari sat up straighter and moved her water bottle from her lap to the end table. "So if you remember our cells are a mix of carbon and crystal, and you know that according to my real parents we bonded as babies. Perhaps even before that if you believe the recorded prophesy about us. But anyway, we initially bonded as babies but then we were separated shortly after. Now if we were vibrating at the same natural frequency when we were separated, it would stand to reason that decades on Earth would affect each of us in a slightly different way. And that ache we felt, the emptiness, was merely discordance as we both slowly moved away from the initial frequency. I think that when we touched in the park it was a reset of sorts, like magnetic poles snapping together. We met in the middle and melded back to the same frequency once again."

Zendara started laughing. "Scientists! All that to say no more boom?"

"You're being purposely difficult right now."

"I'm not, I swear. But I get it. We shouldn't have another of your 'resonance flashes' unless our natural frequencies diverge again. How else could that happen, besides another long absence? Because I can tell you right now, that's never going to happen if I can help it."

Amari smiled and squeezed the hand that had found its way into her grasp. "No, I'm certainly not going to let you out of my orbit again either. And I don't know how exactly the dissonance could happen besides time and distance. Steph and I have done a lot of research but most of it was on establishing the scope of my abilities. External force, energy, is absorbed into our cells and it powers a multitude of capabilities. But could something affect those cells and pull them to a different vibrating frequency? I don't know."

Curious, and always questioning the reality around her, Zen couldn't hold back her questions. "So how does our power work? I know you said that our cells are carbon and crystal, but how do we absorb energy? How does the energy transfer work?"

"All right, this one isn't theory. It's something Steph and I have measured with equipment 'borrowed' from another lab. But we discovered that when we measure the frequency of an energy source and monitor my own frequency when I touch it, my body instantaneously matches the object's resonance frequency and I absorb the power. As for how I hold that power, the only thing I could come up with was that our carbon crystal cells act like a battery. They convert, magnify, and store whatever energy we absorbed."

Zen cocked her head. "Convert how?"

Amari shrugged. "I don't really know that. Sorry. I haven't discovered an answer that makes sense using any of today's current science understanding or technology."

Zendara sighed and took a slow sip of her water before wedging it between her knees and screwing the cap back on with her left hand. "So..."

Clasped hands squeezed tighter. "So."

Shy smiles met across the tiny bit of air between them. Zen spoke first. "Basically, I don't have to worry about any more explosions when I kiss you."

"Well, I guess that depends on what else you're doing at the time."

"Oh really?"

Amari turned so she could lean in close, so close their lips brushed together. Zen shivered as Amari whispered into the blonde's exhale. "There's only one way to find out."

The will of their bond was not going to be denied again. This time when their lips met it was with the unspoken promise that it would not end anytime soon. Neither one dominated the exchange. At least neither did completely. Control of the kiss went back and forth between them, until they came up for air gasping and thoroughly aroused. Zendara cupped Amari's cheek gently, never breaking eye contact with her soul mate. "Can we..." She trailed off as her eyes glanced around, unsure exactly which door in the condo was the one leading to Amari's bedroom.

The two women, fair-haired and dark, wanted exactly the same thing. Amari stood from the couch, pulling Zendara up after her. "Come on." Amari led her soon to be lover to the farthest door, and subsequently the larger of the two bedrooms in the condo.

Zendara spared a second to move her gaze around the room, taking in the sparse decor and neatly made queen size bed. She didn't have long to observe though with Amari's impatience pushing at her back. She turned to her Q'sirrahna. "Are you sure you want to do this now? I mean, we haven't known each other very long —" The second kiss came as Amari walked her slowly backward toward the bed. It only ended when the bend of Zen's knees hit the mattress and Amari gave her a little shove. Zen fell back and began laughing.

"What's so funny?"

The prone woman shook her head. "You're much more forward than I thought you'd be."

Amari grinned at her. "And you're wearing too many clothes. What's the matter, sirra, are you shy?"

Zen paused at Amari's words. "Sirra...love?"

"Yes. Don't you feel it too?"

The look on Zendara's face softened and her lips turned up into a gentle smile. "I do. I don't even know how to explain the feeling, but it's not something I've experienced before. I, um..." Her words trailed off again as she watched Amari begin to undress.

"Too many clothes."

Amari was down to her bra and underwear and Zen had only managed to remove her hoodie. She wasn't even wearing a bra and Amari groaned as she climbed onto the bed and sat across Zendara's hips. She gazed longingly at Zen's small breasts with their stiff pink nipples. She often marveled at how similar her own body was to the humans of Earth, despite the fact that she came from so far away. But given the expanse of pleasurable flesh in front of her, Amari decided that was a mystery for another day. She reached her hands out and stopped when she saw the rapid breaths of the woman below her. She wasn't sure if it was anticipation that had Zen's respiration and heart rate elevated, or apprehension. Instead of touching Zendara like she wanted, Amari leaned forward and rested her hands on either side of the panting woman's head. "Are you okay?"

Zen smiled and threaded her hands through Amari's shoulder length dark hair. "Sorry. I am. I'm just nervous."

Amari pulled back but Zen tightened her hands. This caused Amari to readjust her position and move closer until she was nestled between Zendara's legs. Her upper body rested along Zen's torso. The contact of skin on skin was electrifying but she tried her best to ignore it. "I thought you said that you've had other lovers."

Strong hands moved from Amari's hair and caressed down her shoulders. Zendara's breathing increased again at the feel of her soul mate's silk covered breasts rubbing against her very sensitive nipples. "I—uh, I did. I have, but—" Her words ended in a hiss as Amari moved against her.

"But what?"

Blue eyes came open and Zendara pulled her closer. "You're evil!"

Amari started slowly pressing their lower bodies together, ignoring Zen's statement. Her own breathing increased with her excitement and she wanted nothing more than to kiss every single inch of her Q'sirrahna. But for some reason she couldn't resist taunting the attractive woman just a little. "You didn't answer."

Before Amari could resume her undulating movements,

Zendara moved a leg farther to the side and quickly flipped them over so that she was on top. She grabbed Amari's hands and held them above her head in an attempt to still the teasing woman's caresses. "I can't think or answer when you do that."

Suddenly turned on by Zendara's position, Amari panted. She was intimately aware of the other woman's new position between her legs. "Can — can you answer now?"

Zendara met her gaze steadily, unrepentant for her actions or the words to come. "Those other lovers weren't you. There is no one like you for me in the universe. Show me the stars, Q'sirrahna."

Amari's reply was tender, perhaps the most important one she'd ever spoken. "We'll show each other."

No more words were needed after that. As they moved together, both women realized the truth of Zendara's earlier answer. No matter how many people they had been with previously, none could have hoped to match the emotional and physical connection they now shared as soul mates. It wasn't just the bond that made the experience so uniquely fulfilling. It was a sensual dance that was older than most races possessing both emotion and biological urge. But as they touched each other, kissing and rubbing their bodies together, something else started to happen. The natural frequency that they both shared began to move, the resonance changing harmony with each hitched breath and kiss-quenched sigh.

Fingers of each found and merged into the other. Movement pulled passion higher and still the harmonies modulated to match the moving bodies of the two women of Q'orre. It was as if their souls were serenading each other, singing in unison. It was beautiful, both a beginning and ending, yet the song continued to rise higher the closer they came to release. They developed a cadence to their pleasure, but like any great masterpiece, the song was bound to come to an end. It was Zendara who reached that point first and she called out to her lover as her heart hammered in her chest. "Sirra..."

Amari slowed but did not stop. "What's wrong?"

"N — nothing. But I'm nearly there. Are you close?"

Rather that answer, Amari sped her fingers as she played her Q'sirrahna. She listened with something other than her ears as their resonance change pitch. A keening erupted from Zen's mouth as the orgasm tore through her. The sheer force of her pleasure reverberated through their soul bond and pulled Amari along into her own pleasure feedback loop. Shudders rippled through them as wave upon wave of bliss wove into and through their cells and played harmoniously across their skin. The reaction itself lasted for nearly five minutes before they both collapsed to the bed in exhaustion. Sweaty and content, Zendara turned her head to meet Amari's nearly black-eyed gaze. "You are in my heart now, my soul."

Amari smiled and traced Zen's pale brow with her finger. Then she shifted to cuddle into her soul mate's side. "Sirra, I've always been there."

Too tired to even worry about a blanket, the lost princesses of Q'orre fell asleep in a tangle together. Their bond was infinite and unbreakable.

NOW SOME MAY think it impossible for two people to fall into love so quickly, barely knowing each other as Amari and Zendara did. There are others who truly believe in things like kismet and serendipity, and love at first sight. But for the two babies sent to Earth decades before, it was none of those things. They didn't just fall in love, as it may have appeared to the casual observer. No, they've always been in love. They are soul mates and some bonds simply exist from the beginning. Not just of their lives but from the start of time itself. They were not two beings who had fallen in love. That is much too human a concept. They were one eternal love, which was composed of two beings. Q'sirrahna.

Chapter Ten

SEVEN A.M. WAS exceptionally early to be waking up after an evening of pleasure with a beautiful woman, but Romy was a creature of habit. She lay in bed feeling the pull and slight discomfort of muscles that been neglected for too long, and thought about the woman next to her. Dr. Stephanie Young was an astounding bed partner, and no slouch when it came to witty conversation either. But even after a night of wonderful distraction, Rocket was unable to shut off her mind to the problems at hand. She considered the two rogue Chromodecs and what the great beam of light would mean to her city. Her thoughts also touched on the woman next to her, and Stephanie's friend. The agent's instincts told her that there was more to the women's story, but confusingly enough, those instincts also told her they were trustworthy.

The last problem was something that had been tickling at the back of her brain for nearly a year. It was the feeling that things were not right with her team. She started encoding many of the computer checks to her private login six months ago though she had no concrete reason why. It was just a gut feeling.

A sound to her right drew Romy's attention and she turned her head in time to see Steph stretch and let out a little squeak of waking. It was remarkably cute. When the doctor of biochemistry opened her eyes, she was faced with Romy's dark brown ones gazing at her from the next pillow. Steph gave her a shy smile. "Hi." Her voice was sleep-rough and sexy.

Romy returned it, feeling only slightly awkward. "Good morning."

Steph turned onto her back to stare at the ceiling of her bedroom. "I wasn't sure you'd be here."

"Really?"

Stephanie's shrug was stifled by the fact that she was lying down. "Well, I don't normally do this sort of thing, maybe a handful of times. And honestly, that was only with men." She paused, then took a chance with the full truth. "Actually, I've only been with men before you and they usually bolt first thing. Good enough for a night apparently but not for a follow up date."

Instead of reacting negatively to the idea that Steph was bi, Romy smiled and moved closer. "Well, I'm definitely not a man. I'm also even more convinced of the idiocy of the opposite sex if they run from your bed in the morning. How foolish of them."

Steph blushed and gave her a delighted smile in return. "You are a smooth one with only a few hours' sleep."

The agent replied in a more serious voice than expected. "Smoothness is only skin deep, honest goes to the bone."

Equal parts flattered and embarrassed, Stephanie changed the subject. "You look like you need to leave. Back to work for you?"

Romy turned to her side to face the woman who had thoroughly caught her attention the day before. "Not necessarily. Rising early is a habit that I've had for decades though."

"Military?"

There was a pause but Romy saw no reason not to answer honestly. "Uh huh."

Steph rolled onto her side as well. "You never said what you do yesterday, just that you travel a lot for work."

"I'm a security specialist, working for a firm which has satellite locations all over the country. That's why I travel so much and frequently get called away." She glanced away for a split second. "It also makes for bad relationship material."

A pale blonde brow went up at Romy's words and she chose to ignore the last part, for now. "What company?"

"I'm afraid I can't divulge that information. We have contracts with the government that preclude anyone with high level security clearance to their facilities from divulging the name of my employer. It could make me a target. I'm sorry."

Rather than be put off, Steph grinned. "So you've got high clearance. Romy Danes, security specialist extraordinaire. All the mystery makes you pretty damn sexy.

Romy swiftly rolled over to pin Steph to the bed. "And you don't need any mystery at all to be sexy, Doctor Young."

"Charmer!" They stared into each other's eyes with stupid grins for a second. "So you're up, but you don't have to leave?" The feel of Romy's body pressing into hers left Steph breathless as she remembered the previous night.

"Well I think that depends entirely on you. I can go if you want me to. Or we can both go and maybe get some breakfast?" Romy took in the blonde hair that spread across the pillow, framing Steph's head like a halo.

Blue eyes looked up with a slight bit of insecurity. "What if I want you to stay for breakfast?"

Romy laughed quietly with delight. "Well, then I'd say I know how you got your doctorate because that's a very smart idea. Now all we have to do is..." Her words trailed off as she leaned closer.

Steph's voice came out as nearly a whisper when Romy's lips all but caressed her own. "Is?"

The kiss was soft and slow. With both women running on little sleep from the night before and feeling relaxed, the urgent passion from the previous evening had tempered significantly. Instead it was surreal and sweet, a perfect way to wake up the body and mind. Romy's eyes twinkled as she answered the question. "All we have to do is work up an appetite."

Fingers tangled in the short dark hair above and pulled Romy down until their lips could meet again and again. Steph spoke around a grin when they pulled back for air. "Keep that up and we certainly will."

SUNLIGHT SLANTED THROUGH the blinds and hit a pale green wall above the large bed. The owner of the bed was the first to stir. Amari had always been a type A personality. Despite the level of her genius and seeming ease of her education, the doctor of biochemistry had been driven and hardworking from a young age. She was passionate about her career and often put in long hours studying the intricacies and mysteries of the world. But just because she was used to waking at an early hour didn't mean she had any desire whatsoever to stir from her bed in that precise moment.

Amari turned to her side so she could better study her Q'sir-rahna. Nothing could have prepared her for the connection she felt during the most intimate moments of her night with Zendara. Amari's statement of completeness had not been a lie. But it was so much more than simply experiencing the absence of ache for the first time in her life. It was emotional, spiritual, and physical connection of the highest level. She could *feel* Zen deep inside her mind and heart. The woman in question stirred as if she could sense she was the subject of regard. A small part of Amari saddened when her soul mate didn't go through a slow and peaceful awakening like she herself had. One moment Zendara was asleep and the next her eyes were wide and alert, with a tenseness to her body that didn't fit with the lassitude such an amazing night brought on. Amari could see she wasn't fully aware yet, just that she was prepared for...what, the young scientist wasn't sure. The tension melted immediately as the blue eyes fixed properly on the brown ones Zen had fallen into so thoroughly the evening before.

"Hi." Zendara's voice was rough from little sleep and the events of the previous evening. Amari wasn't surprised really, Zen had been especially loud the night before. Any soreness and deepening of timbre wouldn't last long given their healing capabilities but the sound of it triggered something primal in the Reynan princess. Amari flushed as she remembered the noises that came from her lover's mouth, over and over again. Her parted lips and red face gave away her thoughts more than any words and Zen chuckled, bringing Amari out of her daze.

Amari cleared her throat. "Good morning."

"What are you thinking about?"

She glanced away and reddened further. "Nothing."

A snort was Zen's response at first. "You know, it's weird but I can almost *feel* your lie inside my head. It has a thick, too-sweet flavor in the back of my throat. But even if I couldn't feel it through this connection we have, I'd still know."

Amari brought her gaze back to Zen. Her look was a mix of curiosity and hunger. "How?"

Zen's eyes crinkled at the corners as she held back a smirk. "You have a terrible poker face, for one."

"And?"

Zen licked her lips. "We've already established that we feel the same pull toward each other, the same attraction." She reached out to cup Amari's cheek tenderly. "Do you think it will always be like this?"

Amari closed her eyes and exhaled slowly. "Like what?" Her voice had a breathless quality to it, a side effect to the overly sensitized feeling of Zen's skin touching hers.

The other hand came up from between their bodies and Zendara cupped both sides of her lover's face before surging forward and capturing Amari's lips in an intensely deep kiss. Minutes went by as their tongues caressed one another. Zen nipped lightly at Amari's bottom lip, scraping teeth over soft flesh. Amari's response was a whimper and a desperate clutch at Zen's bare skin, just below her ribs. Unfortunately, alien or no, they were forced to pull away to suck in deep and rapid breathes of air. But even as she retreated from the bounty of passion before her, Zen carefully caressed Amari's bottom lip with her thumbs, reveling in the softness. She whispered into the morning light. "I waited so long, without even knowing what or whom I was waiting for. And you—" She shook her head slightly. "You have been more than I ever imagined. I've never known anyone like you."

Amari laughed lightly, trying to control the riot of her emotions such a simple touch against her lip provoked. "I should hope not since I'm an actual alien."

"No," Zen frowned. "I mean where I grew up. Rumford, Maine is small, just a stain on the map really. And without my parents it was a really lonely place for someone who felt things differently, who craved—" She broke off her words and swallowed thickly. "After my parents died I wanted my outside to hurt like my inside. I never wanted to do anything truly wild, too afraid I'd be caught. I had friends who cut themselves but I was under too much scrutiny while in foster care. Instead I'd slam my hand into my own thigh and feel nothing but sick twisting in my stomach. Eventually it got easier to ignore the pain in my heart. I never stopped missing them though it did get better with time."

Amari looked at her curiously, trying to understand. "How did it get better? Was it the friend you told me about, Cin? Or just time itself?"

"It was you."

Amari's smile was gentle, not at all mocking. "Now that's just impossible. You didn't even know I existed."

Zen glanced down to where there hands were clasped together. Their tan skin formed a nice contrast against the cream-colored sheets on the bed. "This is going to sound weird—" She rolled her eyes and laughed. "Who am I kidding, *all* this sounds weird and yet it's true!" She huffed and continued. "Anyway, it's funny but I used to think I was actually a twin or something, like I had that crazy twin empathy that you always read about. I brought it up once to my parents but they got really weird so I never said another word about it. But—" She brought their hands up and pressed the back of Amari's knuckles to her own heart. "I always felt you. Even when I was lonely, I was never alone."

A reddened bottom lip pinched between Amari's teeth as she struggled to control her emotions. The words were quiet when they finally came. "It doesn't sound crazy at all. I thought the same thing only I never asked my parents. I didn't understand it until the day I fell off a mountain and they were forced to tell me everything. As soon as I learned of you, everything clicked and all those feelings throughout my life suddenly made sense." She sighed. "I'm sure the reason your parents freaked out was because they knew of my existence." Amari tilted her head, causing it to slide along the pillowcase. "You know, I'm really surprised they didn't have some sort of plan in place in case something happened to them. It makes no sense that Watchers would be so unprepared. They left nothing for you, no clues?"

Blonde hair mussed even further as Zen shook her own head. "No. I was told to pack a duffle bag and everything else had to be put up for auction. There were no—" She stopped, as a forgotten memory came back to her. "The key!"

"Key?"

"Yes! After my, um, my parents died I was given their personal effects, which was surprisingly little. But my dad had a business card from the local bank in his wallet, as well as a safe deposit box key. When the caseworker took me to the bank, they said I had to be eighteen to access it so I put the key away and just forgot about it."

Amari was so excited she pulled away from Zendara and sat upright in bed. "Do you still have it? I'd bet anything it contains information about who you are and your pod's data crystal!" Zen sat up as well and Amari's gaze flicked down her body as the sheet pooled at her waist.

"Data crystal?"

"Yeah, that's what my mothers' recorded the history of our planets on, as well as personal messages for both of us. It took my Watcher parents years to create a system that could download the data from the crystal and put it into an Earth-compatible format."

Zen swallowed and looked back at her soul mate with awe. "Do you really think that's what it is?"

A shrug. "Only one way to find out. We could take a road trip."

"I can't take time off work, I just started my job! Not to mention it's a little too far for a car ride and I'm not exactly flush with cash right now since I literally just moved here from another state."

"I could—"

Zen cut her off with the wave of a hand. "No! I'm not going to let you pay my way. I've survived this long without someone taking care of me. I can manage just fine, it will just take a little more planning on my part to get back to Rumford and that security box."

A hurt look washed across Amari's face. "I thought we were supposed to take care of each other."

"This is different, sirra."

"How is this different?"

Zen sighed. "I don't know, but even if it isn't I still don't have enough time to go. Its Sunday now, which means you have to go to work in the morning and I have to report to my shift tomorrow night. It's just not possible."

Amari sat in silence for a few seconds while Zen was certain the other woman had finally begun to understand. She was surprised when Amari reached over to her nightstand and grabbed the phone off the charger. She tapped the screen for a few seconds then looked up at Zen with a grin. "What if it weren't impossible? What if I told you we could get there in a little over an hour at no cost at all?"

Zen reached over to feel her forehead. "I'd ask what you're smoking."

Amari batted her hand away. "Stop that. We can fly ourselves there. It's nearly the new moon so it will be plenty dark to hide us if we leave a few hours after midnight. We'd get there in time for sunrise and some breakfast while we wait for the bank to open first Monday morning. What do you say?"

"You still have to work." Zen pointed out.

"I have loads of sick and vacation time. I'll call in."

Zendara ran her hand through messy blonde hair. "How will we get back? I still have to report to work tomorrow night."

Amari tapped a few more times on her phone screen. "Sundown is at eight-oh-seven p.m. As soon as the sky starts darkening we can take off, you'll be back in plenty of time to make your shift. Are you in?"

Zen shook her head, not to deny the other woman's suggestion but rather with bewilderment. "Amari..." She sighed. "Sirra, I would have never guessed you were so adventurous. It just seems like an awful big risk to take for a box that I completely forgot about for years. And after what happened Friday night in the park, it seems especially risky. It's no big deal, really."

"But it *is* a big deal! You lost so much, let me help you regain some of your history."

"The risk—"

Amari slapped the bed in frustration. "I've been careful my whole life! You need your past. *We* need it to move forward. I'm pretty sure there will be another recording from my mothers', different from my own message. I...I would like to see it. *Please*, Zen."

Zen grumbled but finally acquiesced. "You're crazy, chica. But we can leave tomorrow at sundown. So what do we do now — " She was bowled over by a very excited lover. As Amari peppered her face and neck with kisses, Zen's laugh ended in a whimper. "Never mind."

Around noon, Zen finally fought free of the gravity-like pull to be near Amari and took herself home for a shower and change of clothes. She also had to get the key and business card where she'd hidden them in the frame of her family photo. While she was gone, Amari took care of her own personal needs and listened to Steph gush for nearly forty minutes about her evening with the mysterious woman from Bender's. Amari was worried of course, but she couldn't deny Steph's happiness and hated the thought of being anything but positive about her friend's evening. After all, despite how amazing her best friend was, the woman had a terrible track record with romantic partners.

"Wait, you two are flying to Maine tonight? Like, *flying* flying?"

"Yes."

"And you're not going to be back 'til — Curie! Put that back, you asshole! Sorry, you're not coming back until tomorrow night? What about work?"

Amari rolled her eyes at Steph's outburst toward her curious cat, unseen over the phone. She was used to Steph yelling at the recalcitrant feline. "I'm going to call in, duh."

"But you never call in!"

Laughter met her words. "Extenuating circumstances. And before you bring it up, no, I'm not just doing this to get out of the scheduled lab inventory tomorrow. Sorry to stick you with Jones on that, by the way."

Stephanie sighed dramatically. "Fine, whatever you need to do. But just so you know, Jones wears so much cologne I'm surprised he doesn't trip the PPM sensor in the clean room."

"It does make one's eyes water."

The older woman's voice turned serious. "You two need to be safe, okay? After that little lecture you gave me last night, I'll worry about you the entire time you're gone!"

"We'll be fine, I'll promise."

"But what if you hit a plane or something?"

Amari laughed. "We'll stay below eight-thousand feet, which

is the lower threshold that most airlines operate at. It burns more fuel to fly in the lower, denser air so they stay above that point. Besides, our senses and reaction times are all heightened when at speed so I promise not to wipe out any domestic flights."

Steph snorted. "Thanks for the TED Talk, Captain Del Rey. Does she even know how to fly?"

Amari rolled her eyes. "I'll give her a crash course tonight."

"Not literally I hope."

"Funny lady. Now if you're done gushing and worrying, I have to go. She should be back soon and I'm going to start giving her flight pointers in my living room."

"Oh, God, good luck with that. I know you've got those fancy high ceilings but you should probably still move your lamps when you're practicing those excelsior powers of yours."

"Thanks for the tip, Stan Lee." Amari shot back, wryly.

The women dissolved into laughter before saying their good-byes and hanging up. Not long after that Zen arrived back at her doorstep with a duffle bag of clothes and Chinese takeout. And as much as they wanted to touch and connect, per the demands of their bond, both women refrained. It was time for Zendara to learn what it truly meant to be from another planet.

Amari and Zen made sure to catch some sleep before getting up at three a.m. for the flight to Maine. After they took turns in the bathroom, Zen rifled through her duffle bag for clothes. "Do you think plain black jeans and my leather coat would be all right for the trip? Will I get cold? I mean, it's not like I've ever flown at altitude under my own power. Jesus, what am I saying? I've never flown at all until just a little wh—"

Amari's finger cut off the nervous woman's rambling. She gave Zen a sly smile. "I think I have something even better we can put on." The super black ship suits would be perfect for their little witching hour jaunt.

IN THE EARLY hours of morning they took to the sky, heading northeast. The flight was shaky for Zendara but with Amari's help they kept on course. Only once did she have to catch Zen when she saw a low flying plane and abruptly lost focus. After that Amari stayed near just to keep her steady. Their plan worked exactly as intended. Both women changed into clothes they had stuffed into backpacks they wore beneath the pliable ship suits. They grabbed a long breakfast at a diner near the bank and Zen was glad that she didn't recognize anyone inside. Though to be fair, it had been years since she'd last been in Rumford. The bank was empty of other customers at nine a.m. when they arrived. The tellers themselves looked half awake.

"Can I help you?" A clean-cut young man stood behind the counter wearing a checkered dress shirt and a light blue tie. His smile was as polished as the name tag that sat near the teller window. Neither laughed at his name but Zen did snort.

The punk woman got scrutinizing looks from Joe Banks and one of the women who stood near the drive-through window. But she was used to the narrowed eyes and cool dismissal from career professionals. Perhaps it was her wind-blown blonde hair that was cut in a near mowhawk, or the leather boots and jacket. She clearly didn't look like their regular clientele. "Yeah, I'm here to pick up the contents of a safe deposit box." She slid the card with the number across the counter toward him.

He picked up the old and battered business card. It was yellowed with age but still had the pertinent information on it. He flipped it over to read the back before looking up at Zen. "I'll have to call my manager for this. I've never handled safe deposit box withdrawals before."

Joe left and returned a few minutes later with a woman in her mid-forties. She had shoulder-length brown hair and a pleasant enough smile. As soon as she neared the younger women, she held out her hand toward Amari, assuming the more put-together of the two was the one with business at the bank. "My name is Roberta Lloyd and I'm the manager here at the Rumford branch of First American Trust. Joe tells me you'd like to access a safe deposit box?" She was obviously taken aback but recovered quickly enough when Zen scowled and shook the hand instead.

"Yes, I have a box my parents opened when I was younger and I'd like to retrieve the contents now."

Roberta looked at Zen with new interest. "Oh? And who are your parents, Miss…"

"Zendara Baen-Tor. My parents *were* Doug and Tammy Smith. They died thirteen years ago."

A minute flicker of expression crossed the bank manager's face but it was quickly schooled to polite condolence. "My apologies. Let's see if we can get that box for you. Of course, you'll need the key to open it. You did bring the key, correct?"

Tired of the conversation and feeling a little off about the woman's questions and demeanor, Zen's response was less than patient. "I wouldn't be here if I didn't. May I have the box now?"

Amari squeezed her free hand, feeling how unsettled her Q'sirrahna was through their bond. She tried to pull Roberta's attention to her instead. "Please, we'd really like to see the box and have some privacy. This is very hard for Zendara. I'm sure you understand." Amari met the woman's gaze unflinchingly and sensed something different about the other woman. She had her suspicions but it wasn't worth acknowledging, let alone bringing up in a public place. You simply didn't ask someone if they were a Watcher and expect no retribution.

Roberta's piercing gaze swung to Amari and she gave a curt nod. "Of course. If you could both follow me."

She led them to a private room, then left to retrieve the deposit box in question. Within minutes they were alone with the locked gray box sitting innocuously in front of Zen. They weren't quite sure what to expect considering it took two strong looking bank employees to carry it in and it made a loud *thud* when placed on the table. Zendara held the key in her shaking hand but stopped just shy of inserting it. Amari gently covered the trembling fingers with her own to soothe her shaking. "Take your time, sirra. There is no rush."

Zendara swung her pale gaze to her soul mate. "I've been waiting half my life for this. No, my *whole* life if you consider my true past. I want to see, I'm just scared."

"Hey," Amari called softly and the single word brought Zen's gaze back into sharp focus. "I'm here with you. We're together now and there's no more reason to fear."

A brilliant smile broke over Zen's face as she realized the truth of Amari's words. Most of her fears in life stemmed from being alone, abandoned. And with her Q'sirrahna by her side, she'd never have the same fears again. Suddenly ready to face the unknown, Zen shoved the key into the lock and turned.

Two pairs of greedy eyes took in the contents of the fairly small box. It was standard bank size of five inches wide by five inches tall and twenty-four inches deep. Zendara's jaw dropped as she suddenly and inexplicably recalled her childhood fantasy. It wasn't the thick white envelope sitting inside the top of the box that shocked them. It wasn't even the strange narrow eight inch blue crystal that left both young women with their jaws open in mute surprise. It was the six standard size gold bars stacked neatly inside. Zen's voice was a whisper. "Holy fuck." She was unable to break free from her shock. "Is that—" She swallowed the word that she was afraid to say.

Amari reached out and pushed into one of the bars with her fingernail. "It's real."

Zen turned haunted eyes back to her love. "I don't understand."

"Open it, sirra." She nodded toward the envelope with Zen's full name written on the outside.

The envelope contained a five page letter that both women read quickly, certainly faster than human speed. It detailed Zendara's past, as well as her parent's duty as both Watcher and guardian for her. The end of the letter also mentioned that they had set the box up to make sure she was taken care of through life, and that they planned to sit her down when she was thirteen and explain everything. It was dated just three days before the accident that killed them. A lone tear tracked down Zen's face. "They never got the chance to tell me. They didn't abandon me. They cared, they just didn't get a chance to set everything up before they were killed."

"Did you really think they didn't care?"

Zen shrugged. "Sometimes, when things seemed darkest. I wondered if they ever loved me at all."

Amari recalled the letter she had just read and looked back to the open box. "They loved you, sirra."

The laugh she received for her dry words was a little broken. "Yeah, I guess they did. I don't even know what to do with this, or how much it's all worth."

Amari pulled out her phone and did a little research. "Standard gold bar size, which it appears you have, is four-hundred ounces. With six bars at current gold prices...holy shit!" She turned wide eyes to Zen. "You have more than three million dollars in gold right there."

"No." Wide blue eyes glanced at the gold, then at Amari, then back at the gold.

"Yes."

"This can't be real."

"It's real, sirra. You're rich."

Zen sighed. "I don't even know what to do right now, how to process this." Tears pricked Zen's eyes.

Amari reached out and caressed her cheek, garnering the shocked woman's full attention. "I have a suggestion."

"What's that?"

"Quit your job."

Zen's face scrunched up with dismay. "What? No, I can't do that! What will I do, how will I—" Panicked words were stilled with a single index finger.

"My love, what do you love doing most in the world?"

A quizzical expression came over Zen's face. "We discussed this. I love to read, to learn every chance I can get."

"Then why didn't you go to school, get a degree?"

"Because I didn't have anyone but myself to rely on. No one was going to support me but me so I got a job and...oh."

"Yeah?"

Beautiful breathless laughter came from between Zen's lips. She turned wide eyes toward her soul mate. "I'm free. I can go to school, learn as much as I want. I don't have to worry about missing a rent payment or buying new shoes."

Amari smiled back. "You don't."

In a move that was too quick for human eyes, Zen spun around and grabbed the sides of Amari's head and pulled her in for a desperate kiss. When they broke for air again Zen whispered against Amari's too-soft lips. "I'm free."

"I love you too."

Once both women had gotten control of themselves, they pulled back to investigate the last item. "What is that?"

Zen pulled out the crystal and felt a low vibration resonate into the palm of her hand, up her arm and through her entire body. She dropped it onto the table again, half expecting it to shatter. "Whoa!"

Amari picked it up and while a dark eyebrow went up, she made no other motion to indicate she felt the same reaction that Zen did. "That's what I thought. It's one of the crystals from your pod." She glanced back in the box. After placing the crystal on the table she bypassed the two necklaces inside and reached over to remove a business card. It was for a storage company that listed a local address and phone number. The card had a unit number written on the back. Also in the box was a key ring with two Stanley lock keys and a third brass one securely attached. "And I suspect this is where your pod is stored."

"What should we do?"

Amari looked at her and smiled. "You should call in."

"Sick?"

Laughter met Zen's skeptical response. "Call in *quit*. You don't need that job. Go to school, find what you really want to do. I plan on calling in as well but I'm going to take the entire week off. I've got so much vacation time saved up and we don't have any major projects going this week. Just inventory." Zen scowled again and Amari could already read the look and emotion that pulsed through their bond like waves. "Sirra, I'm not telling you what you *have* to do. I'm telling you what I would do. It's your call to make. Literally."

A snort. "And if I quit? What then?"

"Well, we could take a few days here to investigate the pod, then make arrangements to ship it someplace more secure."

Zen nodded. "Your parents?"

"Mmm hmm. Then we should fly to Washington if you're up for it."

Zen started to nod again until she realized exactly what Amari was saying. "To meet your parents? I—" She swallowed thickly. "I don't think I'm ready for that." She looked away, hating the fact that she was probably disappointing her lover.

Amari shrugged and surprised the other woman. "Then we won't go to see them. It's not that big a deal, really. We have all the time in the world, sirra. Let's just wrap up affairs here first then you can decide. Okay?"

Zendara's smile was wide and happy and she heaved a sigh of relief. "That sounds great. Thank you."

The two women split up the contents of the lock box into their bags to spread out the weight. There was a little concern because while Amari had a special heavy-duty pack that could carry a lot of weight, Zen's was just a standard JanSport and not really equipped to hold her half of the one hundred fifty pounds of gold bars. Beneath the gold there was a certificate ensuring both, their authenticity and the legality of ownership. They were in Zendara's name. The crystal and keys went into large zippered pockets of Zen's coat but she paused at the two necklaces. The chains, if you could call them that, were made of shimmering strands that were near enough to metal without quite being anything she was familiar with. Each strand featured a pale lavender crystal pendant. It didn't look as though there were clasps to get the necklace open but when Zen held the strand pinched between the finger and thumb of each hand the filaments separated. She pushed them back together and they immediately formed a seamless connection. Two mouths made a little 'o' shape of amazement. Amari was the one that said what they were thinking aloud. "Now that's cool!"

Zen looked to her in surprise. "So you didn't get anything

like this from your parents?"

Amari shook her head. "No. That must be something from your family, the King and Queen of Tora."

Not wanting to be in the bank any longer, Zen grabbed the necklaces and dropped them into one of her inside pockets. "I can figure out what to do with these later."

After they closed out the safe deposit box and left the bank, Amari called an Uber with her phone app. From there they went to the nearest sporting goods store where they purchased reinforced lockable cases for the gold, three bars per case. Their next stop was the rental unit on the outside of town. It was a small place, older, but the surrounding lawns were kept up. The brass key unlocked the gate and when they found their way to the unit number written on the back of the card, one of the Stanley keys unlocked the heavy padlock. The inside was like something out of a science fiction movie for Zendara, but Amari was completely unfazed. After all, the pod was the exact same one as her own, which she had seen many times before.

"Whoa, this is baddass!" Amari smiled as the other woman ran curious hands over the silvered skin of the eight-foot long craft. Zen glanced back at her lover and saw the smirk. "What, you don't think so?"

"No, I agree. But I've seen my own pod many times since my parents told me the truth. They have it stored in a shed behind the house in Washington. There is room for yours when the time comes to transfer it."

"How would we even go about something like that? Do we hire a company and tell them it's just a movie prop, or what?"

Amari shrugged. "It's no big deal. I'd call Mom and Dad and they'd take care of it. The Watchers have people all over the world and they would make sure something like this is kept quiet. You wouldn't have to do anything but allow me to make the call."

Zen thought for a few minutes, chewing her lip. Finally she nodded. "Okay, I think I'd feel better knowing it's secured with yours rather than sitting in some storage locker in backwoods Maine a thousand miles from where I live."

Seeing that her Q'sirrahna looked more than a little overwhelmed at the thought of so many unfamiliar things, Amari smiled and stepped closer to place a kiss on Zen's cheek. "I'll take care of it. Now —" She moved toward the ship and placed her hand against a slightly off colored section of the hull just below the portal. There was an abrupt hiss through the storage unit and a large section of the top lifted to show a bed of sorts inside.

Amari stepped back to let Zendara peer inside. "Is that..." Zen's words trailed off as she reached out to touch the soft surface.

"That is where you first came from the stars down to Earth, sirra. It's one of the last things my mothers' touched before they...they..." She drew in a deep breath and let it out in a long sigh.

"Do, um, do you know exactly what happened to them?"

"No. When my adopted dad showed me the recording of last few minutes before we were sent down to the planet, there were lights flashing and sirens blaring and they both looked incredibly worried. The fact that we've never heard from them since is probably most telling of all. I don't think they would let me go, let us go, if they had any other choice." She swallowed hard and finally met Zen's eyes. "I don't know for sure if they were killed, just that a rogue general was after us and they had been on the run from a ship sent to follow and retrieve the Reynan royal family. My adopted parents said the Watchers detected an explosion on the far side of the moon shortly after our pods hit the atmosphere so they assumed that Queen Denii and Queen Selphan were aboard when it happened."

Zen immediately stepped close and wrapped Amari in her strong embrace. "I'm so sorry for their deaths. I know it's not the same when neither of us have met our real parents but it's still hard knowing the women who brought us to this planet, or my parents who stayed behind on their own to try and quell unrest, paid the ultimate sacrifice so that we could live." She pulled back to look into Amari's dark eyes. "I'm glad I have you. I don't think I could have gone through my whole life feeling as alone as I was. Until that night in the park, it was like half of me was missing."

"I know exactly what you mean. But I would never have given up on finding you."

Zen flushed lightly, barely coloring her tan skin. She opted to change the subject. "Is there a way to use the crystal that was in the lock box here in the ship, in order to see what's on it?"

Amari shook her head. "I'm afraid not. While there are crystal ports on the ship, they are only for navigation crystals, which have a different kind of data."

"What's the difference exactly?"

"Okay, imagine the crystal is a flash drive." Zendara nodded.

"Now you can put a lot of different files on a flash drive and plug it into your computer, or even a car. But certain systems can only play certain kinds of data. The pod is programmed to read navigational data, but that's not what is recorded on the crystal in the lock box. My parents tried to read the crystal that was enclosed in the pod with me, on the pod systems, and it didn't work. They had to reverse engineer some of the tech in my pod to create a computer that would be able to read the crystal and transfer it into a format that could be played on standard Earth computers."

"Jesus! How long did that take?"

Amari snorted. "The pod recording was easy enough. That was the first thing my dad showed me when I first learned I was not who I thought at seventeen years old. But that was just a matter of recording what was played from the pod onto his phone. However it took them years to figure out how to get the data from the crystal and format that into a disk that I could use in my computer. They finally finished it a few years ago and sent me the last of the histories of Reyna shortly after I arrived in Chicago. I suspect that yours will have the same type of histories for Tora."

"And they'll be able to get that for me if we send the pod and crystal to them?"

"Yes. Until then, let's see if we can bring up the pod recording of the last few minutes." She leaned into the pod and tapped a few buttons next to a faceted screen that was at the tapered front of the inside of the pod. The screen flickered and cleared before flashing red. Unfamiliar writing appeared on one the largest of the facets for about ten seconds then it disappeared and the strange screen turned black again. "Damn. There is an error." Amari and Zen backed out of the pod at the same time but Amari grabbed the other woman's hand when she saw how sad Zen looked. "Hey, don't worry. I'm sure my parents can fix it and get the missing data. Let's just make the calls and get all this stuff into their hands, okay?"

Zen sighed and scrubbed a hand through her pale hair. "Yeah, that sounds good. I'm ready to get the hell out of this town anyway."

They stepped outside into the morning sunshine and Amari pulled out her phone and smiled. "Why don't you call the university while I speak with my parents about making arrangements for transport of your pod?"

Confusion washed over Zen's face. "But if we have the keys, how will your parents get someone here to transport it? I don't want to leave the unit unlocked!"

Amari shrugged. "A little lock won't make a bit of difference. They'll even make arrangements with the management company to cancel the storage unit."

They stared at each other for a few seconds before Zen sighed and pulled out her own phone. After looking up a number and dialing, she cleared her throat nervously and spoke. "Yeah, can you put me through to the maintenance supervisor...?"

Satisfied that Zen was busy with her own call, Amari hit the saved number for her parents. She felt bad that she hadn't had a chance to speak with them since she'd connected with her soul mate. And now she was calling to drop, not just that information on them, but to also request they make arrangements to get Zen's pod back to a house all the way across the country. Once that call was finished, Amari made a call to her own boss to take the rest of the week off work. At the end of her second call, she stuffed the phone in her pocket and turned to watch Zen stare thoughtfully back at the small ship. "Now that we've wrapped up all the details, what do you say we catch an Uber to the nearest large city and grab a nice dinner before finding an airport that will take us home the old fashioned way?"

Zendara grinned and delighted Amari when she affected a heavy northeastern accent. "I'd say if you're from away and want good seafood, then Maine's the place to be. Question is, you want steamers, chowdah, quahog, or bug?"

Amari sputtered before bursting out laughing. "Oh my God, I don't think I've ever heard someone sound so, so...so much like a Mainer!"

"It's Mainah and I'll have you know that people from these parts are the finest kind."

"I think *you're* the finest kind."

Zen rolled her eyes. "Yeah, now you know why I tried real hard to never pick up the accent. My parents didn't have it and after they died I stubbornly refused to speak any way but theirs." Her eyes grew unfocused for a second before she shook off past memories and smiled back at Amari. "All right, call us an Uber and we'll head for Augusta. It's the nearest city with an airport that will get us to Chicago and it's just down the road apiece. I also know a place there that has wicked good food and shouldn't be right out straight this time a year."

Amari shook her head and laughed again at Zen's local vernacular. "You're too much."

Zendara smiled. "And you're exactly enough. Thank you for sharing this adventure with me, for finding me."

Their eyes caught and held as deep and abiding emotion flowed between them beneath the surface of their bond.

"Always," was Amari's reply.

Chapter Eleven

EVEN WITH A world so uncertain, sometimes good sur-
prises still happen. For Zendara, her declaration of
being free wasn't just based off some childish notion
of what it meant to be rich. Abandoned to an imperfect
system at a young age and lacking any kind of understanding about what it means to be loved and supported
by a family as you grow into adulthood, she had been
trapped in the web of her own circumstance. When you
grow up poor, you stop hoping for something better. You
stop wishing for more. And the reality of working and
scraping by meant that Zen had to give up a lot of
childhood dreams. Education, love, and security fell by
the wayside with each year that passed and she filled
up with uncertainty and loneliness. And you can certainly say that money can't buy happiness and be correct for the most part. But when happiness can be found
in education, in a decent pair of shoes, and food on
the table? Oh yes, it can be definitely be bought then.

Financial worry was a soul-sucking monster that had
been vanquished with the appearance of six gold bars.
Best of all, Zen could safely accept it since it was in
her name. The money was both a balm and a penance for
all the years she was deprived of love and safety after
the death of her parents. More importantly, it helped
sooth the rawness she felt upon the discovery that
truth was just another staple of life that she'd been
missing as she grew up in Rumford, Maine. With the boon
left inside that lock box, Zendara Baen-Tor had the
resources and time to discover exactly who she was and
what she was capable of.

THE REST OF the week saw a lot of bonding time between
the two women. They didn't get back to Chicago until late Monday evening so Zen just stayed the night with Amari again. They
watched hours of video about the history of Reyna and Amari
began teaching Zen the Reynan language as well. She promised
that when the history of Tora was retrieved, they'd learn everything there was to know, together.

On Tuesday they went to Zen's bank to see about exchanging

one of the bars for cash she could deposit and renting a safe deposit box for the other five. Given the amount in question, the bank was more than happy to upgrade Zen's account, assign a personal account manager, and put her in touch with a financial advisor. That took nearly half the day but when it was all said and done, Zen felt more secure than she ever had in her life. No more low paying strip club jobs, no more nights cleaning offices, and no more missing meals to save money. She really was free. They celebrated with a trip to Navy Pier and spent the rest of the afternoon and evening exploring, eating, and having fun.

Zen went back to her apartment Tuesday night, much to Amari's displeasure. But even with everything they'd discovered together, Zendara didn't want to impose. The separation didn't work out as planned for either of them. Instead, Zendara showed up on Amari's doorstep the next morning with tired eyes and an anxious look about her. Amari simply pulled her inside and led her directly to the bedroom where they curled up together and fell into a deep sleep. The yearning between the two soul mates was too great with their bond being so fresh. When they woke again, Amari suggested the other woman pack a few changes of clothes and stay the rest of the week. Zen readily agreed.

Amari finally called Steph on Wednesday evening to see how her best friend was fairing with her absence. Steph's first words had her feeling immediately guilty. "I hope you're happy, I've been pulling doubles all week so far. Besides you, Doctor Khogali is out sick this week with chicken pox. And we were told in no uncertain terms that inventory must be complete by this coming weekend. Who even gets chicken pox nowadays?"

"Oh no, I'm really sorry. But you know I wouldn't have called in if it weren't so important."

Stephanie started laughing. "Oh, don't I know it. You had to get your freak on with your newly discovered soul mate! Have you even left the bedroom since you got back from Maine? Wait, you *are* back from Maine, right?"

Amari laughed at her best friend. "Yes, we got back Monday evening. And before you have a coronary, we flew back the normal way in a plane."

"I thought she was all against you paying for plane tickets or something."

"About that..." The call went on while Amari explained all the strange things they found in Zen's hometown. The older scientist was speechless when she learned of what all was in the lock box but it didn't last long. "So is she gonna be your sugar mama now?"

"You know me better than that!"

Steph smiled on her end of the line. "I know, hun. I just like messing with you. I'm so happy you found your soul mate. It's just so crazy and unbelievable how it went down, you know?"

"Yeah. I really want you to meet her. Maybe we can get together this Friday night or something." Amari sighed. "And what about you? Sounds like you enjoyed your time with a certain Romy Danes last weekend. You two have plans to see each other again?"

Steph giggled, which was so incredibly unlike her, and Amari immediately knew her best friend was smitten. "We've texted on and off all this week so far but she got called out of town on business. However she's supposed to be back in time for us to go on a proper date on Friday night. Can you believe it? Me on a real date? It's been—" She paused to count back in her head. "Eight goddamn months since my last one, and that was a wreck!"

"You'll be fine. And since it looks like you'll be busy Friday night, maybe we can get together Saturday so you can meet Zen."

Steph's laugh was less than innocent. "If we're out of bed by then."

"My virgin ears, Steph!"

"Oh please! Maybe I should say if *you're* out of bed by then, hmm?"

Amari blushed and made a noise low in her throat as Zen walked into the living room wearing nothing but a towel. The heat and pull of their bond increased exponentially as the two women from the Q'orre system locked eyes. "I have to go, Steph, we'll catch up later."

Steph snorted. "Make sure you let her up for air once in a while, though death by sex would certainly be a way to go." The line went dead with no response from Amari. Steph just rolled her eyes, happy that her best friend was so happy.

COLONEL MAZA WAS a patient man. After all, he had been in charge of the Guantanamo facility for nearly a decade, every single year devoted to the advancement of his plans. Rogue Chromodecs were dangerous, at least that was what he had been convincing the upper brass for years. The truth was that all Chromodecs were dangerous and he wanted every single one of them under his control. You don't need to be an accountant to realize that numbers are very important to his plan. As any mathematician can tell you, numbers are power. You may be curious what kind of power Oracle is looking to grasp. Let me break it down for you with a little lesson.

In 1952 Doctor Daggett had one hundred viable embryos, ninety-nine of which went to full term. By 1975, all ninety-nine of those original test children had gone on to produce three hundred and two children with powers. The government did a study decades later, calculating the propagation rates of Chromodecs and the numbers were astounding. The Chromodecs were highly fertile and every single one, male or female, was responsible for an average of four children each over their lifetime. Now factoring in birth outliers and death rates, the current Chromodec population was right around five thousand across the country. However, the majority were never known by the people around them. Only about a third served with the CORP program, and of those fifteen hundred, only five hundred were actual trained CORP agents.

But five hundred fully trained agents with super human powers? That was the strength that the Oracle sought to control. With them, he could command the rest. And with five thousand, there was little he couldn't do.

By the time Amari and Zendara had discovered the full depth and nature of their bond, forty-two percent of the active CORP agents had been conditioned to Colonel Maza's cause. You may think his need to harness the power of nearly five thousand super-humans was just one massive ego trip. But in all actuality it was about the end game. Marek Maza wanted to change the past, and to do that he needed to control the future. When Oracle's plan was consummated from start to finish, Dr. Brian Daggett would be remembered as a legend, and Col. Marek Maza would be hailed as the savior of the greatest nation on Earth. It was time for the culling to begin.

LIKE ANY GREAT tactician, the Oracle had a firm grasp of all players on the field, minus a few outliers. He sat in a secure room observing monitors displaying the CORP control room for every major city across the nation. When Minder contacted him the previous week, he patiently listened to her concerns and assured her that a few rogues wouldn't interfere with their plans. Nor would one suspicious lead agent. Instead he cautioned that action was imminent and asked her to warn the other sleeper agents to watch for the sign to begin. The official order was to subdue if possible, kill if necessary. After all, you couldn't recondition a dead Chromodec. He had given none of his sleeper cells the intel on what the sign would be, but they would know exactly when to start. Everyone would know.

ROMY DANES DID indeed follow through with her promise to be back in time for a date on Friday night. Leery of her teammates still, she went off grid again for her and Stephanie's liaison. Agent Shields seemed happy that she was getting out of the CORP building as well. "It's about time you started taking some time for yourself. And don't worry about us, we'll hold down the fort."

Rocket looked at her longtime friend and teammate. Despite their history together, worry still tugged at her subconscious mind and left her feeling off-kilter. Minder had seemed especially distracted lately but with Romy's plans for the evening, there wasn't exactly time to sit her down and see what was bothering her. "If you're sure..."

Agent Julian Hill, otherwise known as Vision, gave her a little push. "Seriously, boss! Get out of here, we've got this. We'll call you if SIMoN picks up any more spikes of power. Go get a drink, take a bath...hell, read a book."

She rounded on him but couldn't keep the smile off her face. "Fine, I'll make myself scarce. But I'm only doing it because I agree with Minder that a few days off last weekend had me feeling a lot better, a lot less stressed. I'll check in tomorrow. SIMoN, Agent Shields is senior on duty. Please log that in the records."

The computer's reply was prompt. "Yes, Special Agent Danes." With that taken care of, Romy grabbed a set of communicators from the cabinet on the wall and left the control center. She didn't bother turning them on just yet.

Romy met Steph at her apartment and neither woman had any qualms about taking the elevated train from where they lived in Washington Park. They switched to the brown line and got off at Segwick and from there it was a reasonable walk to the Second City comedy club. They had a casual dinner at 1959 Kitchen &

Bar, which was located upstairs, then afterward caught a comedy show that had been getting rave reviews. It was after one a.m. by the time they arrived back at the train platform near Steph's apartment. It only made sense for her to invite Romy upstairs once they were standing in front of Steph's building.

The next morning was nearly a repeat of their first one together, though Steph had gone to sleep feeling significantly surer of herself. When Romy woke a little after sunrise, she lay in bed staring at the woman whom she had grown to like immensely in such a short amount of time. She had a private phone that was off SIMoN's network and used that for all her personal calls and liaisons. It wasn't professional to use her work phone for such things. She and Steph had been texting all week, even sharing phone calls on two separate occasions. It was safe to say they were well on their way to getting to know each other.

It was rare for the agent to feel such an immediate connection to someone but there was something about Dr. Stephanie Young that drew her in. As soon as Steph's sleepy blue eyes opened, Romy smiled. "Hi."

Steph cleared her throat. "Hi." She raised a hand to brush the dark strands of hair out of Romy's eyes. "I had a great time last night."

Romy's look turned tender. "I'm not going to bullshit you, last night was one of the best evenings I can remember."

"I feel the same way." Stephanie glanced to where their hands had come up to clasp together. They were on their side facing one another. "I know you said that your job makes it really hard to have and maintain a relationship but—" She paused then looked up to meet startled brown eyes. "But I really like you and I'd be interested in regularly dating you."

Concern, relief, and affection washed through Romy. Part of the CORP agent's mind was in complete denial that she could ever make such a thing work with a sweet woman like Steph, always having to hide who she was and disappearing at all different times. The other part of her, the human part, wanted a chance at love just like everyone else. And she saw potential with Stephanie Young, something she hadn't seen in a very long time. Romy made the decision to follow her heart. "I think—" Unfortunately for both of them she was interrupted by the communicator in her ear. She had turned the beacon off the night before but never turned off the receiver. It wasn't seen or heard by her bedmate but Romy paled at the tone that repeated. It was a nationwide

CORP alert of the highest priority. "Shit!" She shot a panicked look at Stephanie. "I'm sorry, but I have to go, something has come up."

The biochemist sat up as Romy did, both paused for a brief second as the sheet pooled around the waist of their nude bodies. Steph snapped out of it first. "What do you mean something has come up?" Stephanie gave her a look of disbelief.

Romy shook her head. "I'm really sorry, Steph, but I have to go." She hurled out of the bed before Steph could ask any more questions. Less than two minutes later, the attractive agent was out the door and running for her bike.

"What the fuck just happened?" Disappointed and hurt, Stephanie dressed in a sweatshirt and pajama pants and left the bedroom to make some coffee. There was no point in going back to bed now, she'd never get to sleep. She wandered into the kitchen searching for some bitter brew and decided to fix breakfast as well, having worked up an appetite the night before. Even though she was hurt by Romy's abrupt departure, her body hummed from her second night of intimacy with the attractive woman. It was exhilarating and mind-blowing, and an entire thesaurus worth of other pleasurable words. She thought about calling Amari to gush once again but decided against it. There was no point in ruining Amari and Zendara's time together to talk about her own with a woman she'd probably never see again. So much for trying to date someone, clearly her words had sent Romy running scared. Stephanie really thought the other woman was different too.

Fifteen minutes later she sat down at her coffee table to eat and turned on the TV. The first bite barely made it into her mouth when screen beeped with a news alert. "Breaking news, the CORP headquarters in New York City has been attacked. The entire facility was reduced to rubble from an unknown explosive device around seven a.m. No survivors are expected. Government agencies are on the scene to determine the cause." She muted the sound but the ticker continued to scroll across the screen while she sat in shock, omelet forgotten on her plate. Steph was riveted, watching the scene of devastation. "Holy shit!" She jumped up to run to the bedroom to grab her cell phone but was interrupted by urgent pounding on her front door. "What the—"

"Steph, please let me in. Hurry!" Romy's voice was muffled but laced with worry.

For a second she was tempted to not answer, but the tone of

the other woman's voice and the news she had just seen convinced her otherwise. Cautiously, she left the chain lock attached but opened the door far enough to see Romy. Her previous night's romantic partner was scanning behind her but quickly spun around at the sound of the door. "I didn't expect to see you back here."

Romy had a panicked look about her, something that didn't fit on the calm and seemingly unflappable woman that Steph met the night before. "Please, I need to come in. I'm in grave danger."

Steph frowned but quickly shut the door and unlatched the chain before opening it up again. Romy wasted no time pushing her way in before shutting and locking the door behind her. She wore a slim fitting black backpack, had a black helmet in one hand, and a pistol in the other and Dr. Stephanie Young slowly backed away. "Who are you?"

Out of sight and slightly calmer, Romy blew out a breath and tried to decide her best course of action. The punishment was severe for any CORP agent to reveal their true identity to a civilian, but all the rules had flown out the window over the course of thirty-minutes. With the Chicago headquarters compromised and her trustworthy team members either dead or captive, she needed help in contacting another CORP group for backup. Making a decision, she stood straighter and looked Stephanie right in the eye. "My name is Romy Danes and I'm the Special Agent in Charge of the Chicago CORP headquarters. My code name is Rocket. My facility has been compromised and the members of my team are either dead or subversives. Doctor Young—Stephanie, I need your help."

Recalling Amari's words from the week before, Steph spoke quickly, her words laced with fear. "Am I in danger?"

Romy moved forward to reassure her, but the gun and helmet in her hands had Steph stepping back just as fast. "I'm sorry." She set the helmet on the table next to the door and tucked the gun into the inner pants holster that clipped into the back of her jeans. She had locked it in the seat compartment on her bike before going into the bar the previous night. Once her hands were free, she stepped forward again and Steph didn't move. "You shouldn't be in any danger, I promise. I shut the tracking beacon off before I even left my apartment last night, and they don't know about you. But they do know about my apartment and any other places I normally frequent. And SIMoN's facial recognition software guarantees they'd pick me up within thirty minutes, no matter where I go." She shook her head ruefully. "And to think I used to rely on the abundance of cameras all over the city to apprehend criminals..." Her voice trailed off and a quiet sigh took its place.

"Simon?"

"Sorry, it's the computer backbone for everything CORP does. Synthetic intelligence monitoring network. SIMoN for short. The program came out of OAS Laboratories." Rather than respond, Steph sank into a nearby chair and thought about the strange turn her morning had taken. Mistaking her contemplative reaction for one of being overwhelmed, Romy strode over to the chair and dropped to a knee in front of her. "I'm sorry, this must seem strange and crazy and beyond anything you could comprehend happening to you. I didn't mean to bring all this to your doorstep, I just didn't know where else to go that would be safe."

Much to the agent's surprise, her words only served to garner laughter from the doctor of biochemistry. "Agent Danes, I think you have no idea what I could comprehend when it comes to strange and crazy things." Her eyes were suddenly drawn to the television and she grabbed the remote to turn the volume back up.

"This just in, CORP facilities all around the country are reporting attacks. Some have released statements saying that their situation is under control, while other cities find their citizens hiding in fear as super-human battles rage on the ground and in the air. A state of emergency has been declared for the following locations: Houston, Austin, Indianapolis, Charlotte, New Orleans, Boise, Seattle, Wilmington..." They continued to listen as the newscaster read off all twenty cities where the Chromodecs battled each other. After that announcement, they switched to the cities that had given the all clear, meaning CORP facility had things under control. "Los Angeles, Chicago, Philadelphia, Phoenix, San Diego, Dallas, Jacksonville, Boston, Denver..." Steph muted the sound but both women continued watching the ticker display the list of cities that were no longer supposed to be in danger.

Romy stared at the screen with dread. "Jesus, it's like the fucking apocalypse out there. And clearly my facility wasn't an isolated incident. Something much bigger is going on here."

Steph turned to Romy. "I don't get it. Chicago is listed as being all clear, so why are you hiding?"

Romy bowed her head, feeling the closest she's ever been to

defeat. "Because it's not." Making a decision, she stood and moved back a foot to the couch, then took a seat. "I left because an emergency alert came across my com. You couldn't see or hear it, but that's why I left when I did. Again, I'm sorry for that. Anyway, when I got to my bike I tried calling in but SIMoN wasn't responding. I tried accessing my security files through my HUD but my access was locked out. Finally I called the one person I trust above all others on my team. Vision—er, Agent Hill. He said that he was previously with Agent Smith, that's Voda, when they were fired on and she was hit. By the time I called him they had already gotten her but he was still trying to exit the facility. Sleeper agents had taken over and were searching for him level by level. He said Agent King, another trusted friend, was able to get out but he lost contact with her com shortly after."

"And did this Agent Hill make it?"

"No." Romy gave a pained look, unsure of the fate of her long-time friend. "I heard the report of shots fired over the com, then nothing. He's either dead or captured now. As far as I know, it's just me and Lingua on the outside."

Steph gave her a piercing look. "What are you going to do now?"

Rocket shook her head. Her entire team was lost, her facility and data access was now gone, and she had no idea who she could trust. With at least one city reporting all clear that she knew for certain was compromised, it made sense that there would be more that had been taken over by rogue agents. Sadly, the secret nature of their organization meant that the public would probably never know. The question was, how would she be able to tell the good guys from the bad? There was real fear in her eyes when she met Steph's questioning gaze. "I don't know."

Dr. Stephanie Young smiled back at the displaced agent because she knew something the other woman didn't. "I'm sorry about your team um, Agent Danes, but I think I can help."

"Please, call me Romy, or Rocket even."

"Fine, Romy then. As I was saying, I know some people who can help you if they are so inclined, and if they are promised immunity from CORP investigation."

Rocket sighed, sure that Steph didn't fully comprehend her situation. "I don't mean to belittle your offer, but who could possibly help when our nation is being overrun by enemy Chromodecs? It is an impossible amount of power to face and I know this city like the back of my hand. There is no one on that level here."

Steph merely smiled and repeated a line she had muttered years before. "There are more things in heaven and earth, Horatio, than are dreamt of in your philosophy." Then she left to get her cell phone from the bedroom. It was time to make that call, only girl talk wasn't exactly on the agenda. Their deep discussion right before Romy's unfortunate exit would have to wait until the emergency was over.

A NATION IN chaos, and those who were once protectors were now suspected to be on the wrong side of society. Average citizens didn't know what to think about the Chromodec attacks happening all over the United States. World leaders held their breath, waiting to see how it would all play out. Many whispered to their advisors that they knew something bad would eventually occur in a country that would let so many superpowered humans run amok. Of course their whispers were always in secret because you never wanted to offend the nation that held the most power.

However, if there was one thing that Doctor Young was not, it was an average citizen. After years of being privy to Amari's secret, she was definitely more stoic about the Chromodec uprising than most of her peers would have been. And now, regardless all her previous reassurances, she was about to break Amari's trust. But after their conversation the night before, she thought her friend might understand under the circumstances. After all, it wasn't everyday a person got to save the world. All the doctor could hope for was that Amari actually meant what she said, that if she had the opportunity to save a life she would take it despite the danger.

AMARI BLINKED BLEARILY as synthesized chords and rhythm drums blared from her phone on the nightstand. She originally programmed "She Blinded Me with Science" by Thomas Dolby as Steph's ringtone as a joke but left it on her phone because it annoyed her friend so much. She was still half asleep when she answered. "This better be good! You're the one who told me to get the girl and I'm still getting the gir—"

"We have a problem. I'm not going to say your name but I have someone who needs your help." Steph was being as careful as she could with Amari's identity, in case the younger woman didn't want to risk herself or her family.

Amari sat up abruptly, wide-awake in an instant. "Where are you, what's going on?"

Zen slowly followed with confusion as she listened to one side of the conversation. "What happened?" Her Q'sirrahna put a finger to her lips, asking for silence and waited for Steph to answer.

"Go turn on the news."

Amari put the phone on speaker and got out of the bed to pull on a nearby shirt that was discarded the night before. Zen followed her lead. "Which station?"

A sigh came over the line. "I don't think it will matter. This is a nationwide problem." Her words had both women making their way toward the living room and Amari grabbed the remote to turn on the TV. "Holy fuck!" Zendara perfectly summed up what Amari was feeling as they observed the chaos being reported by the news.

After taking a second to get over her initial shock, Amari spoke into the phone again. "Steph, I don't understand. Are these rogue Chromodecs? Where did they all come from?"

Steph's voice was as serious as the younger woman had ever heard it. "Not rogue Chromodecs, rogue agents."

"Shit."

Amari cut her gaze toward Zen, watching the other woman as she watched the television. "So what does this have to do with us? Are you safe? Where are you? I don't know what's going on right now but you can stay with us until it's over."

While Steph appreciated the offer, that wasn't why she called. She started explaining the reason to her best friend, careful not to give away Amari's identity to the woman sitting a few feet away. Romy just watched her curiously, wondering who the mystery person was on the other line. "I'm home so don't worry about that. As for what it has to do with you, well that's for you to decide. I went out last weekend to meet Amari for a girl's night. She left early to spend time with her girlfriend and I met a woman at the bar who came home with me."

"I knew it! That woman was trouble, wasn't she? If you're not safe so help me —"

Steph cut her off. "Easy there, tiger. I'm safe, I promise. But the woman —" She looked at Romy and the agent nodded, knowing Steph was going to blow her cover. " — she's the Special Agent in Charge of the Chicago CORP headquarters. She says rogue agents have taken over the facility and either killed or captured all but one of her loyal team members. She needs help."

Zendara's eyes widened and she looked up to meet Amari's gaze. Amari was just as dumbfounded but there was a good bit of anger mixed in. Unlike Zen, she had read the history of the government CORP program and knew there was an underbelly of darkness. "And why should I help those that would gleefully hunt us down to lock us away somewhere?" Amari was torn. She had just found the one person she needed more than life and was desperately afraid to lose her again. In her mind, coming out of hiding to fight in a battle that ultimately wasn't hers was not a safe option.

Stephanie cast a worried glance at her new lover. "No, she's not trouble, she's *in* trouble. And people are going to die, have *already* died. It wasn't too long ago that you told me you weren't some unfeeling monster. That if you had the power to save someone's life you were going to utilize it. Well you both have this power!"

Unsure what to do, Amari muted the phone and looked to her Q'sirrahna. Her spiky blonde hair was in disarray from another night of passion and Amari felt herself fall a little more in love with the woman who shared her destiny. Zendara swallowed thickly. "I don't know anything about fighting, and even less about my powers, but I'm willing to fight if it means we can quell the chaos on that screen." She pointed to the television. "I lost my parents to the carelessness of one normal man. How many other kids out there are going to lose their parents to whatever evil is going on? I want to help."

Amari watched a few seconds of the news coverage on the TV before reaching for Zen's hand. "I want to help too."

With one last glance at her soul mate, she unmuted the phone and sealed their fate with Stephanie. "Neither one of us knows anything about fighting nor does Zen have any amount of experience with her powers, but we're both in. Go ahead and give *Agent* Danes the short version of our history and we'll be at your place in forty-five minutes. I expect your famous omelets, so get cracking!" Amari snorted at the pun.

Stephanie gave Romy a triumphant look and spoke clearly back to her friend. "Ha-ha, cute joke. And thank you…Amari. We'll see you soon." The agent gave her a startled look as Steph hung up the phone. "Would you like some breakfast? Looks like

I'm cooking for everyone. Oh, and I have a story to tell you."

THE TIME HAS finally come, hasn't it? The country is in jeopardy, nay, the world, and heroes are needed. And no matter what you may think, there is plenty of risk for our two women of Q'orre. While powerful beyond anything the people of Earth have previously seen, they are not invincible. And unfortunately for them, years of testing have given Amari plenty of insight as to her strengths but it has shown her none of her weaknesses. She and Zendara would be essentially flying blind and hoping for the best.

Chapter Twelve

ORACLE SAT IN front of a row of monitors, deep inside the Guantanamo bunker. He felt fairly secure on the island but a person could never be too sure. There were a number of reasons why the generals or even the president wouldn't send troops to apprehend him. The first and most important was because they still had no clue what was going on and assumed Colonel Maza was on their side. The second was that even if they figured out something had gone sideways in the Chromodec program and the CORP had been infiltrated by an enemy of the state, Oracle was protected in Guantanamo. What would they do, launch an attack on his location? Not hardly! Cuba would take that as a sign of aggression and surely retaliate. No, if and when the government figured out that he was responsible for the Chromodec uprising, they would have to be a lot more discrete in their counter measures. And if Maza had control of the CORP agencies, none of those measures would lead to success.

"Sir! There is a call coming in from General Johnson on the external line."

Oracle grinned. "Take a message." He watched as another CORP facility engaged the coded beacon that he had provided, letting him know the takeover was successful in that location. He was so close to victory he could taste it and wanted nothing more than to tell General Johnson to go fuck himself.

The lieutenant swallowed hard. "But sir, he says its urge—"

Piercing blue eyes turned toward the nervous man in the doorway. "What part of—wait," He held up his hand and paused to consider his options. "Tell him I'm in the middle of something. Explain that I'm doing my best to handle the situation and that I'll call him back in sixty minutes to report." The soldier awaiting Maza's orders nervously gave a salute and spun around to carry out his directive. He was one of the newer ones assigned to the facility. And admittedly, one of the few non-Chroms that Maza had at Guantanamo.

Colonel Maza had been slowly replacing personnel with Chromodecs over the past few years and his senior officers never even noticed. While plenty of people were clueless as to the goings-on at the Guantanamo Chromodec reconditioning and detainment center, occasionally Marek Maza stumbled across ones who weren't. But he always had a plan. A lot of things could make good men turn a blind eye to less than good activities. Money, blackmail, and simple threats of violence all made for excellent motivators. Another beacon flashed on the map of the United States and Marek smiled. He was happy that nineteen cities had come under his control, but he was irritated that thirty-nine were still in question. Oracle turned to a loyalist that was manning communications for the initial Chromodec offensive. "Give me LA on the coms."

ORACLE WAS CERTAINLY a man with a plan. He seemed to be ready for all contingencies and had a respectable network of communication and strategies to aid in the push for control over the most powerful people on the planet. However, there was one problem he couldn't prepare for, one thing he was unable to predict. See, despite his extensive knowledge about the Chromodecs and the program that originally spawned them, he didn't know anything about the Tau Ceti, their Watchers, or alien refugees. Granted, the Watchers wouldn't interfere, nor would the Tau Ceti. But there were two very powerful refugees who were about to throw a wrench in Oracle's plans. That is, if they can learn to work as a team and control their powers.

THOUGH THEY PROMISED forty-five minutes, it took a little over an hour for Amari and Zendara to show up at Stephanie's condo. After the initial knock, Steph pulled the door open and the two would-be saviors were met by an intense agent standing defensively with her pistol cocked and ready. Zendara just snorted and rolled her eyes before following Amari inside. Her previous experience with the law gave her a healthy dose of disrespect for the people enforcing it. And her recent experience with a gun had shown her there was nothing to be afraid of concerning the agent's weapon.

Romy saw the reaction and bristled at the woman dressed in combat boots, black jeans, and a black hoodie. "Do you have a problem?"

Zen scowled. "I don't like cops."

Amari filed Zendara's attitude away for future reference. While she was a little put off by it, she mentally reminded herself that not only did they have very different backgrounds, but she really didn't know her Q'sirrahna very well. You could only learn so much in a week. Amari called out to the tense agent as she walked by Romy to give her best friend a hug. "Put your gun away, Agent Danes, you can't hurt either one of us with it."

Stephanie wrapped her friend in an embrace and whispered in her ear. "Thank you."

"No. Thank you for reminding me of my words and responsibility."

The two colleagues and best friends stared at each other for a second then Steph shook her head and turned toward the kitchen. "Well you're late, so I put your omelets in the oven to keep warm. Come eat and we can talk."

"Oh good, I'm starving!"

Zen's unfamiliar voice stopped Steph in her tracks. She'd forgotten that she hadn't actually met Amari's soul mate. Reversing course, she abruptly turned to the younger woman and held out her hand. "I'm sorry, where are my manners? I'm Stephanie Young."

Zendara took her hand and appreciated the other woman's firm grip. "Zendara. Thanks for breakfast. We actually forgot to eat dinner last night so we're both pretty hungry right now."

Amari's best friend moved her gaze up and down the blonde woman and smirked. "I'm sure you ate plenty."

Amari swatted her arm, albeit lightly. "Oh my God, Steph! You did not just say that."

The room quieted in an awkward pause before Steph turned to lead the way to the kitchen and called over her shoulder. "Oh please! Despite the situation at hand, it took you more than an hour to make it a few blocks to my condo, and even then you both show up wearing wrinkled clothes? I'm not an idiot." She pulled the warm plates out of the oven and set them on the table.

"One, we're wearing the ship suits underneath. Zendara's only worn it one other time before so I had to show her how to put it on again. And we did some last minute power instruction."

Steph grabbed silverware and paper towels as the hungry couple took a seat. Rather than look at their hostess when she set the eating utensils down, the two women appeared to be caught in each other's gaze. "Mmm hmm." She snapped her fingers in front of Amari's face and pointed at the plate. "God, you two! Eat your damn breakfast so we can come up with a plan to stop these assholes already."

Both newcomers began eating but Amari kept glancing at the Chromodec out of the corner of her eye. The woman, Romy Danes, looked uncomfortable—wary even. Though she supposed that was to be expected given the circumstances. While her perusal was discrete, Zendara's was less so. "I've never met a 'Dec before. What's your power?"

"Zen!" Slightly embarrassed, Amari punched her in the arm, which only succeeded in giving her soul mate a slight rush.

Zendara swallowed her bite of food and grinned. "Thanks, that was nice."

"You're incorrigible!"

"What, is it rude? How would I know? I've never met one before!"

"Excuse me!" Both younger women abruptly stopped talking and looked up at Romy. Satisfied she had their attention, she answered Zendara's question. "For future reference, 'Dec' is considered a derogatory term and not politically correct. And while it's not rude to ask a Chromodec what their power is, it is rude to talk about me as if I'm not in the room."

Looking chagrined, Zen apologized. "Sorry." Then she stuffed the last bit of food into her mouth and swallowed before speaking again. "So what is your power then? I'm assuming you have a cool code name like all the other D—Chromodecs I've seen on TV."

Steph startled the assembled women when she cracked up laughing. When she met Amari's eyes she shook her head. "Wow. She's not what I expected at all. You two are like polar opposites!"

Before her friend could answer, Stephanie scooped up the empty plates and loaded them in the dishwasher and took a seat at the table. Awkward silence returned, but Rocket knew they didn't have time for feeling each other out. "I'm capable of levitation powered flight with a nearly impenetrable TK field while I'm flying. I also have kinetically boosted strength." She needed to know more about her potential allies so redirected the questions back at the two younger women across the table. "So you're both aliens? Is that your natural form, um, do you normally look like that?" She waved vaguely toward their very human-seeming bodies.

Zen smirked. "Well, I went through a goth phase back in high school, but for the most part sure."

Steph giggled and Amari sighed, getting a better feel for the person she was bonded with each passing minute. While a week of near constant contact seemed like a lot, there was much they hadn't learned about each other yet. She had seen Zen's impatience at the bank in Maine but wrote it off as nervousness given the situation. Amari was starting to think that her Q'sirrahna was a little wilder and rougher that she originally thought. "Zen, please. Agent Danes doesn't know any more about us than we know about her." She addressed the agent next. "To answer your question, as you can see we can easily pass for human, or Chromodec. But while human and Chromodec cell structure is all carbon based, ours is a crystal-carbon hybrid."

Romy tilted her head. "What does that mean? I'm assuming you have power of some kind, or Steph wouldn't have called you — wait! You were the cause of the explosion and bright beam of light in the park last weekend, weren't you?"

Amari nodded. "Yes. That was a result of a, well, something I'm calling a resonance flash. As for our power, that depends on what you throw at us."

"Meaning?"

Zen was content to let Amari do all the talking, mostly because she didn't actually know much about their powers. At least, not on the same level her soul mate did. Not only that, but she couldn't help feeling a little insecure about her place with Amari based on Steph's reactions. Her Q'sirrahna was a brilliant and esteemed scientist, she had friends and family who loved her, and she had been using her powers for the past eight years. As she watched the light from Steph's livingroom window bathe Amari's dark hair with a warm glow, she also couldn't ignore what Steph had said about them being opposites. It wasn't until they were around other people that Zendara noticed the differences in their personality, but it became glaring in the presence of Stephanie and Agent Danes. Zendara was impatient, impulsive, and had never had any higher education. Amari was a child genius, introspective, and well-spoken. Why would she want Zen above all others?

A hand crept into Zen's grasp below the table and her fears calmed instantly. Warm affection came through her bond with Amari. With that simple touch, her question was answered. Amari didn't just want her, she needed her. And the love they felt for each other, one that had been seared into their cells before birth, was stronger than any fear or failing. Together they were stronger. Zendara only came out of her reverie when Amari's voice slowed to a stop. "...basically, we are only as strong as what we face."

"Wait—" When Zen had their attention she continued. "Didn't you say that we don't just match resonance and absorb all energy, but we also augment it? We amplify whatever we absorb before storing it in our cells?" Amari and Stephanie both nodded. "Then we are stronger than what we could face."

As impressed as Romy was with the description of their powers, she had her share of concerns as well. "What is the amplification? What kind of energy can you absorb—nuclear, heat, cold? What powers do you get from this stored energy and what are your weaknesses? I need to know what sort of resources I can count on from you both before I can formulate a plan."

"The amplification proved difficult to calculate, especially since different types of energy transfer, such as electrical, kinetic, etcetera, are hard to compare. It's not exactly apples to apples. As of yet, we have not discovered my personal limits for absorption."

Rocket jerked her head toward Zendara. "What about her?"

Zen shrugged. "I have no clue. All I know is that I got shot and all it did was give me a massive rush that let me run really fast. Oh, and apparently I can fly but I'm pretty antwacky still. Amari has assured me that we have all the same powers though."

Steph raised an eyebrow at her best friend and mouthed, "Antwacky?" Amari merely shrugged, not having a clue at the odd words that Zen sprinkled into her vocabulary. Maybe it was a punk thing.

The CORP agent's brows wrinkled with her confusion. "How is it possible you don't know your own powers?"

Zendara gave a short laugh. "I only just discovered that I had powers the night of the resonance flash. So a week now."

Finally Rocket moved her gaze between the two women who had volunteered to help her win back the city. "How long have you two been together?"

Zen's answer was laced with levity at the agent's confusion. "Since the night of the resonance flash."

Amari chimed in then. "Even though I'd felt her absence my whole life, I'd never met my Q'sirrahna until last Friday night. We grew up on opposite coasts of the country and while I've known about her since I was seventeen, she had no clue who she was or that I actually existed."

Romy sat back in her chair. "Wow, talk about some luck that you two found each other here of all places."

"No, Agent Danes, it was fate. Born within minutes of each other on different planets, prophesy was written that we would be Q'sirrahna, bonded. We are soul mates and were always meant to be together." With those words Amari brought her and Zendara's tightly clasped hands above the table. "There is nothing that can break our bond. And I know you are wary, but no matter who we are or where we are from, everything we have is at your disposal."

"Fine, I'll stop with the third degree. My instinct is screaming for me to trust you, so I will. What are your powers exactly, besides energy absorption?"

"Superhuman strength, meaning I once reduced a house-size granite boulder to rubble in just a few minutes and all it did was make me stronger. Truthfully though, it ran me over first so I had a lot of absorbed kinetic energy. Anyway, I've been clocked around seven hundred miles per hour while running in my suit, and about eight hundred miles per hour while flying. We don't get sick, and if there is an injury it heals fast. That's most likely due to the constant absorption of sound and radiant energy that fuels us."

Zen perked up. "Injured, how?"

Amari leveled a serious look at her. "We're not impenetrable, sirra. We can be cut and stabbed if the motion is slow enough, if there is no energy to absorb. We still need to breathe and eat. While we gain much from absorbed energy, we still need sustenance like a carbon-based organism. We need to be careful."

Romy brought up the one thing she was afraid of. "What about scalar energy? Does it affect you in any way? That is the source of Chromodec powers, and consequently our greatest weakness."

Steph had been watching and listening closely to the conversation but didn't have much to add before. "Weakness how? I've read about scalar energy and how Chromodecs actually manipulate it, which gives them their individual powers. It's not on the electromagnetic spectrum, right?"

"Yes, I remember reading my father's reports on it as well. Scalar energy, sometimes referred to as eloptic, is responsible for assembling physical matter from the ether. Protons, neutrons, and electrons are assembled and disassembled using scalar manipulation."

Romy turned her intense focus to Amari. "Who is your father and why does he have reports on us?"

Amari shrugged. "I'm afraid that is information you don't have clearance for, Agent Danes."

Rocket waited for a second, then came to the conclusion that it wasn't worth alienating her new allies for the sake of satisfying her curiosity. She continued without pushing for answers. "Yes, well concerning weaknesses associated with scalar energy, it can be affected two ways. The first is obviously by a Chromodec, the second is by using a device. The ScAM is a machine that is used in Chromodec interrogation and conditioning. It doesn't manipulate external scalar energy exactly like a Chromodec can, but rather it can manipulate the internal energy of whomever the machine is genetically coded to. All it takes is a snip of the person's hair to work."

"What does it do?" Steph found the discussion extremely interesting, especially the parts that intersected with her own biology research that she had done with Amari.

The SAIC of the Chicago CORP facility swallowed hard. "How about I tell you what it's used for. Years ago when I first completed the CORP training I went through a battery of tests. Both physical and mental, they were easily as rigorous as anything I completed when I served with Black Badge. Anyway, on top of the standard CORP testing, they also use a variety of interrogation techniques on you, including the ScAM. The scalar adjustment machine is really nothing more than an updated version of the Hieronymus Machine."

Zendara sat forward. "That was the machine created by Thomas Galen Hieronymus." At the blank looks around her she elaborated. "He was the electrical engineer who lived from 1895 to 1988. The machine was patented in 1949 to use in the 'detection of emanations from materials and measurement of the volumes thereof.' Everyone thought he was a quack."

Amari shook her head and smiled. "I'm not even going to ask how you know that bit of esoteric fact. More audio books I presume?" Zen grinned and shrugged.

"I'm actually pretty impressed with your knowledge. Not just some punk kid after all, hmm?" Zen scowled but Romy held up her hand to forestall any retort. "I'm not trying to jerk your chain. How about I elaborate on the machine. Hieronymus was considered a quack but what everyone didn't know was that his machine was fully functional. It simply had nothing to measure yet since beings who could manipulate scalar energy didn't exist. Even then, it was a happy accident that led to the discovery of the machine's effects on Chromodecs."

"And those effects?" Amari was curious because she hadn't read anything on the subject in her father's archive.

"I can tell you from personal experience that it's not something anyone ever wants to go through. There are two dials that are connected to variable capacitors. Those are used to adjust the radionics rates. Radionics are based off the idea that living matter emits detectable electromagnetic radiation, and can be interpreted diagnostically. The dials are used to tune the machine to a specific person. Think of it like a pair of binoculars. While the snip of hair in the SCaM may show the individual, the rates allow the biological image to focus." She blew out a breath at the wide eyes facing her. "It sounds crazy, I know. Anyway, there is one other dial and that is for intensity. That is what determines the level of effect the machine has on a subject." She shuddered. "As far as I know, only six people have made it to level five, and only one to level six."

Seeing that the agent had paled with the memory, Steph instinctively reached out her hand to lay it on Romy's. "Does it hurt?"

Romy shook her head. "No, not specifically. It's quite hard to explain. The best I can do is tell you that level one starts with a slight nausea and dizziness. Level two makes you feel like you're running a fever and that your powers are pressing on you from the inside, even though they lock a collar around your neck to prevent you from using those powers."

Amari held up her hand. "A collar?"

The agent nodded. "Yes, an eloptic collar. It emits a scalar frequency that negates our powers."

"What about level three?" Romy had all three women riveted with her descriptions of scalar energy and the conditioning techniques for the CORP agents. Every person in Steph's condo was curious by nature.

"Level three makes you feel like your skin is crawling off your body and you start to lose autonomic function."

Steph made a face. "Eww! All function, such as respiratory, bowels, and the like?"

"Usually the subject vomits, cries, and sometimes defecates. On rare occasions respiration or hearts stop, and the subject seizes." She took a sip from the water glass Steph had set on the table earlier. "Level four makes you feel like you're turning inside out."

Amari chimed in. "How do you know so much about the levels, are they well documented?"

"Because I made it to level five before I passed out. I have no idea how Col. Marek Maza went all the way up to six. But I suppose he is the head of the Guantanamo facility for a reason, he knows more about Chromodecs than anyone else alive —"

"Marek! Now why does that name sound familiar?" Amari wracked her brain trying to puzzle it out.

"Could it have to do with the information your parents sent you about the Chromodecs?"

Amari shrugged at Steph's suggestion. "I don't know. It wasn't nearly as detailed on some things as what Agent Danes is telling us right now."

"Amari..." Zendara's voice was quiet, tentative. Her thought was only half formed, more gut instinct than anything. "I think you're onto something. You know I read a lot about a variety of science subjects. I definitely remember that name connected with Chromodecs somehow, but I doubt it has to do with this Colonel Maza. It's a long shot connection but we should look into it." She turned to Romy. "Does he have any famous family? How old is he, first or second generation Chromodec?"

Romy looked thoughtful. "Well, as you know Chromodecs age slightly different than humans, or perhaps we age the same and are longer lived. But while I'm not certain of his birth year, I'd peg him as probably first generation."

"Is there any way to find out who his family is? My friend Brian over in the genetics lab has an account for the National Ancestry Registry. I can text him for the password —"

Zen slapped her hand on the table. "Brian! That's it, that's how I recognize the name. Dr. Brian Marek Daggett. The infamous founding father of the Chromodec program."

"Holy shit." Romy's reaction startled everyone at the table. "Are you implying that somehow Colonel Maza is connected to Doctor Daggett?

Amari took her cell phone from her hoodie pocket and began texting. "Only one way to find out."

Steph gave her a look. "Your parents?"

The younger woman nodded. "If they don't know then no one will." She set the phone on the table after sending the message.

Ever the good hostess, Steph slid her chair back and stood. "While we're waiting, does anyone want anything?"

Zen thought about how tame her life had been until the previous Friday night. "Got any beer?" Not that the alcohol would affect her in the least.

"Do you have anything stronger?" Zendara and Stephanie looked at Romy in surprise. She shrugged. "What? I have a feeling we're going to need it."

"Good point. Shots it is." Then she walked over to the cabinet where she kept her liquor bottles.

Everyone jumped when Amari's phone vibrated on the table. She opened up the document her dad had sent her and tabbed through the various pages. "Damn."

"What, no go?" Steph had rushed back with a bottle of top shelf vodka and four shot glasses when she heard the noise.

Amari looked up at the group. "Actually, just the opposite. Doctor Daggett's youngest daughter is Marek Maza's mother. The morally bereft doctor must have implanted one of his altered embryos into his own wife while he was running the Chromodec program. Maza is his grandson."

"Oh hell, things are starting to make sense. And we're in worse trouble than I originally thought. He's been running the CORP program in both a training and reconditioning capacity for the past ten years." Rocket rubbed her temples and waited for Steph to pour the shots. They had a lot of work ahead of them.

LIKE ANY GOOD investigative team, our group of heroes is starting to put the pieces of the Chromodec uprising puzzle together. While the picture was less than ideal, they at least had some idea of what they were facing. Unfortunately the four women were severely outnumbered with only one CORP agent, two aliens with no combat experience, and one normal human. How would such a small group even think to win out against an unknown number of trained rogue Chromodec agents? And Marek, surely he had even more plans once his faction had taken control of the most powerful facilities in each city. Would he have a contingency in place for those outliers that would think to rebel? We can only wait and find out.

Chapter Thirteen

TROUBLE OFTEN FINDS those who go looking for it. But sometimes it is doled out from the top down. You may wonder where all the other heroes are. The country's CORP facilities could safely be split into thirds where it concerned Oracle's successful implementation of his plans. Approximately nineteen cities were safely under the control of his rogue agents, and twenty were reporting fighting between the legitimate CORP agents and the rogue faction. That left nineteen cities that were successful in fending off the attack from the sleeper agents and were making plans to help nearby facilities. LA was not one of those cities. As a matter of fact, it was one of the first to initiate Oracle's beacon. It was no surprise really since six of their ten member team were all sleeper agents. It was easy enough for the rogues to take out Doc and Wildfire but the twins proved tricky. While both heroes were newer graduates of the CORP training program, they were still masters at magnetism. And they were exceptionally bright. Sinter and Gauss, or Agents Imani and Isaiah Bell, knew they couldn't take back the city on their own. With the country in chaos and unsure who was on the right side, they fled to the two people they trusted above all others. With magnetism-powered flight, it took about four hours to make the trip to Dallas.

"WHAT IF THEY'VE been taken?"

Sinter sighed. "That's why we're at the house."

Both twins had skin color somewhere between that of their two parents, and lean swimmer builds. Though Gauss was a few inches taller, he was still younger, if only by a minute. Being born second, Isaiah was used to his sister's penchant toward taking the lead. She'd done it all their life. "But what if they haven't been taken and there are rogue agents waiting at the house for them?"

"That's why we're not going in. We'll hide in the panic room in the back shed." Imani motioned for him to follow as she slipped over the fence that surrounded the property. They were still quite a ways from the house, nearly out of sight. After entering the shed at the back of the property, they found the trap door and keyed in the security code. The panic room was nothing more than an old fallout shelter that had been converted before the twins were born. The second generation agents were only marginally surprised by the two people already down there. "Mom, Dad! Imani threw herself into her dad's arms, while her mom wrapped Isaiah in a tight embrace. The two people that the younger Bells trusted above all others were none other than their own parents, Agents Jaxon and Shawna Bell. But they were best known as Augur and Hatch on the Dallas team. Augur was gifted with telepathy and telesthesia, which were the abilities to speak mind to mind and to remotely view a distant or unseen target. His wife, Hatch, was the resident teleporter.

Augur's deep voice had them at immediate attention. "Your team?"

Isaiah shook his head. "I'm afraid there were only four of us that weren't part of whatever faction is attacking. They got Doc and Wildfire right away."

"Did they kill them?" Hatch's voice was as light and melodic as their father's was deep.

Imani answered. "No, they locked them up. When they came for us we were able to escape. Once we made sure no one was following, we headed here." She paused with worry weighing on her shoulders. "What's going on?"

"We're not sure. But it looks like someone on the inside is making a grab for power." Augur shrugged. Jax was a big man at six-foot-five, and he was covered in a hard-earned layer of muscle. With dark skin and nearly black eyes, he was like a mountainous shadow and intimidating without even trying. He rubbed the top of his bald head in obvious concern. It was unnerving for his kids to see the big man so worried.

It was Isaiah who voiced both twins' fears. "How can we fight effectively if we don't know who to trust?"

"I can think of one person who is above reproach, and she's not one to be taken easily."

Hatch looked at her husband, understanding exactly who he was talking about. "Rocket."

The twins looked at each other, then spoke at the same time. "Rocket?"

Augur's voice was a reassuring low rumble. "You might not remember her. She's the Special Agent in Charge of Chicago. We served with her in Black Badge, before they started funneling all the Chromodecs into the CORP program. Or rather, before Black Badge effectually became the CORP."

Sinter smiled. "I think I do remember meeting her when we were little. And that's great to hear because an agent named Minder was on the news reporting that while Chicago had some casualties, everything was under control."

Hatch shook her head. "If it wasn't Rocket reporting then I wouldn't believe any of it. We're going to have to do this the hard way." She looked at her husband and got a nod. "First thing though, we all need to get some rest and food in us. Your father and I haven't had any downtime since this all began and we're going to be no good to anyone if we collapse. They won't find us down here so let's take the opportunity to take care of ourselves." She looked at her son and daughter. "How are you both feeling?"

Isaiah responded first. "Truthfully?" Hatch nodded. "I'm wiped. We had to fight our way out then fly a few thousand miles here. I think I've been running on—"

"Adrenaline. We both are." Even in their twenties, the twins still finished each other's sentences.

"All right, that's settled then. Let's set our chronos for seven hours from now. That will give us some much needed sleep and still allow us time to shower, eat, and gear up before heading out after dark." Augur quickly set the time on his watch then looked up at his family. "As you know, every major city is loaded with cameras, per the CORP directive. There is no way I want to walk around during the day in Chicago right now."

They all nodded then each went their own way to find a bunk for the next few hours though it was anyone's guess if they would actually sleep.

"WE AREN'T SAFE here."

Stephanie's head jerked up. "What? You told me that I was safe!"

Rocket shook her head. "You were safe from my team. But now I know this entire affair is nationwide it's only a matter of time before the bad guys start pooling their resources to bring in the rest of us. I need a base of operations and I need Lingua."

Amari cocked her head. "I understand your need for a head-quarters, but why do you need Lingua specifically?"

Rocket sighed and sat back in her chair. "Because my team

doesn't have anyone who can far sense but other teams do. A Chromodec with telesthesia could easily track me down with just a photo. I need Lingua because she's the only one I know who can use an eloptic collar to create a buffer field that will prevent Chromodecs from using their powers in its general location." Zendara raised a pale eyebrow and Romy elaborated. "Human genius. She can speak more than thirty languages and is a hacker and cracker. That woman has forgotten more about computers than I'll ever learn."

"And you have one of these eloptic collars?" Amari was curious about the device.

"In my backpack. It's standard kit for every agent."

"What can we do to help?" Stephanie's mind was racing with everything Romy had laid out for them. Part of her felt a twinge of jealousy at the level of admiration in Romy's voice when she spoke of the other agent, but the logical part knew that any sort of jealousy after two nights of intimacy was irrational.

"I need a place with computer access that's hidden and out of the way. I also need to find a way to the rendezvous point I set up with Lingua years ago. I told her and Julian that if things ever went south to meet there at noon, every day for a week. And if one of us doesn't show after the week is up, consider the agent lost."

Amari frowned. "You think she'll make it then?"

Romy nodded. "Despite the fact that she's human, she's one of the best I've ever worked with. If she wasn't taken back at our headquarters, then she'll be there."

"You shouldn't go out in public! You said it yourself, they're looking for you everywhere and every camera in the city will be scanning for you."

Romy leveled a serious gaze at Steph. "I'm going, she won't trust anyone else."

"Steph's right, it's not safe for you in the city right now. You definitely shouldn't go without backup."

The agent snorted. "Who's going to be my backup, you?"

Amari smiled. "I may not have your strategic mind or combat training, Agent Danes, but I have more power than anyone you've ever met and I've been learning how to use it for the past eight years. So, yes."

Zen didn't like the fact that Amari was going off without her, but she had little to contribute with the situation. She knew nothing about Chicago other than what you could read in the tourist brochures, nor was she familiar with her powers. But she could do something to help. "Agent Danes..."

All heads swung toward Zendara and Romy cleared her throat. "Please, all of you, call me Romy or Rocket. This 'Agent Danes' business gets tedious after a while."

"Fine, Rocket then. I was going to say that I think I know someplace you can use as a base. I'm on the maintenance and janitorial staff for the University of Chicago. Or rather I was until I quit on Monday. Anyway, my second day we were called in to transport some old computers down to the basement of the Ryerson Laboratory. It's the Computer Science building."

Rocket sat forward. "And?"

"The basement's primary access is through an unused stairwell. It's locked and only the maintenance staff badges will get you in. There are tons of computers and other electronic equipment stored in there. It's an old lab they shut down a decade ago when the new building was built. We would just need to get you on campus. They practically have security cameras on every building." Both Amari and Steph nodded, suddenly ruing the security measures that had always before made them feel safe. After a few seconds pause, Zen turned to her Q'sirrahna. "Unfortunately I doubt my badge will still work. I'm sure they deactivated it the very same day I quit."

The agent shrugged. "If it comes down to it, I can have Lingua hack the system and reinstate security clearance for your badge. The real problem will be sneaking onto a campus full of people."

Steph held up a hand. "Hold on, we may all be okay on that front." After grabbing her cell from her pajama pants pocket, she quickly tapped out a text. She got a reply about thirty seconds later and smiled at the group. "As I suspected, with the state of emergency being declared in so many cities across the country, including a few within two hundred miles of Chicago, classes have been suspended for the next week."

Amari met her eyes. "Evans?" She mentioned the name of the doctor whose lab they both worked in.

"Yup." Steph's lips made a popping sound on the p. "He'll be gone as well."

Romy blew out a little sigh of relief. She rubbed the back of her neck, feeling better about the situation than when she first arrived at Steph's. All in all, their help was beyond anything she could have imagined. "Okay, so we have a relatively safe and private place to go and somewhat of a plan in place. All that's left for me is to meet with Lingua. I'm going to need a disguise, and a ride. I don't dare take the train because every platform has a camera."

"We can take my car, that's no problem. Where is the rendezvous point?"

Rocket looked at Amari, extremely uneasy about having to trust people she didn't know. "The Crane Girl."

"Is that a bar?" Stephanie was a native of Chicago and even she'd never heard of the place.

"It's a statue in Millennium Park."

Everyone turned toward Zen, startled by her words. "How did you know that? I've lived here all my life and I don't know every bit of statuary in the city!" Steph looked at Amari "Didn't you say she just moved here?"

Zen shrugged. "I read all about Chicago before I moved here. Then I went all around the city the weekend I arrived, hitting every major attraction that I could before starting work two weeks ago."

When Rocket still looked skeptical and more than a little suspicious, Amari spoke up. "While Zendara may not have the education I've been lucky enough to receive, she shares my genius. Our advanced intellect covers logic, kinesthetic, and spatial ability, and we also have eidetic and photographic memory."

"Wait—" Steph held up her hand. "Isn't that the same thing?"

Rocket shook her head. "Photographic memory was debunked decades ago."

"I read all the studies on it I could find at the library a few years back. It was debunked for humans, true. And before I found out I had powers, I just assumed I was a one-off and never mentioned it to anyone."

"Your parents never realized what you could do?"

Zen's face darkened. "My parents died when I was twelve. And no one cares what you can do in a foster home. They only care about what you can't do."

"I'm sorry." Something in the tone of Rocket's voice made Zen look up at her. "I know what it's like to lose your parents young. It was just me and my mom growing up, never knew my dad. He was the original carrier of my Chromodec genes. She died when I was sixteen and I went to live with my grandparents. Two years later I was recruited into Black Badge, then eventually got shuttled into the CORP. I can only imagine what it must have been like for you so young, with no other family to take you in."

"Thank you. I don't like to think about it much. I'm just glad I found Amari when I did."

Rocket nodded. "Well I'm glad I found both of you when *I* did." She glanced at the chrono on her wrist. "We have an hour before the meetup and I need something different to wear." She glanced at her black CORP suit that she hastily put on before taking off on her bike earlier. "Do any of you have something normal that will fit me, and maybe a hat?"

Amari shook her head as she took in Romy's five and a half feet of height. Both she and Zendara had at least four inches on her. "Nothing either of us have would fit you."

"Not to mention most of my stuff's up in Bronzeville where I rent a room." Three sets of eyes aimed their gaze at Stephanie.

She smirked at Romy. "Yeah, I think I can hook you up." Knowing her friend's look well, Amari snorted.

Rocket stood up and so did Steph. "I'm not going to like what you put me in, am I?"

Steph led them toward the bedroom. "Think of it this way, at least no one will recognize you."

Twenty minutes later Rocket found herself in the passenger seat of Amari's car, wearing a light pink tracksuit and hot pink sneakers. She lifted one of her feet off the floorboard and looked at the shoe in disgust. Amari smirked but wisely remained silent. Rocket looked up again seemingly resigned to her fate of fad fashion and pointed out a sign just ahead. "Grant Park South Garage is going to be the closest to the Buckingham Fountain. I would like to avoid wandering around in public as much as possible."

Amari tried to think of something safer than having Rocket roam around the park. "What if I met with her instead—" She held up a hand to cut off her passenger even as Romy was gearing up to protest. "Isn't there some sort of keyword or something I could give her that she'd recognize?"

"No. We purposely didn't have anything like that. Even a moderately trained mind psi could pull a name out of our head under interrogation. No, it has to be face to face or we run. I need to be there."

"All right." Amari looked at the agent and sighed. "Well, at least with that ridiculous getup and the blonde wig Steph had in her Halloween bin, it's not likely you'll be noticed as anything other than a—"

"Skanky soccer mom?" Rocket interrupted with a snort and Amari shook her head.

"I was going to say low-grade hooker, but yours works too."

Romy grinned. "Doctor Del Rey, I didn't know you could use such language."

Amari shrugged, suddenly serious. "I use whatever language I like, Agent Danes. But my parents brought me up to observe and follow social norms, to not call attention to myself. So I usually play it safe in both words and deeds."

Rocket unbuckled her seatbelt and exited the car. Amari quickly followed. "Yeah, well if things go sideways in the park, feel free to toss those rules out the window to keep yourself safe."

An uncharacteristic laugh from, what Rocket had come to consider a serious young woman in such a short time, burst from Amari's lips. "Don't worry about me. From what I've seen on the news reports, none of your CORP team has a power that can do more than juice me up."

Rocket glanced at her. "Someday when this is all over I'd like to speak with you more about your powers."

Amari paused, then nodded.

As they exited the parking garage and made their way into the park proper, Rocket tensed, her body language screaming wariness. Her eyes never stopped moving from person to person as they made their way discretely toward the statuary near the giant fountain. The agent threw out one last cautionary comment to the confident young woman walking at her side. "Unfortunately for both of us, we don't know if my team is the only one in Chicago now. If they were smart, they would have immediately requested reinforcements as soon as they secured the city."

Amari looked at her curiously. "Why is that?"

Rocket took notice of an average-seeming Asian woman leaning against a tree near their meeting point. The brunette appeared relaxed as she casually scrolled the screen of her phone. Rocket took the time to answer Amari's question before altering course to interact with the stranger. "Because they haven't caught me yet." Then, in a seemingly instantaneous transformation, Amari watched the highly trained agent become someone else completely. "Kim? Oh my God, I haven't seen you in forever!" Romy's voice had morphed into that of a higher pitched lilt. She had become the soccer mom referenced just a few minutes before in the car.

On first seeing Romy, a look of relief crossed Lingua's face, until she caught sight of Amari. There was a split second look of panic until she noticed the discreet all-clear sign given by her commanding agent. "Jennifer! Yes, it's been ages. What have you been up to?"

The three women stood near the statue looking as casual as possible, though Amari was not feeling it in the least. Rocket smiled at her friend. "Oh this and that. I've been really active in the school lately." She gestured toward Amari. "This is Joan, we met though the PTA and usually go for a walk and coffee once a week. You busy right now? You're more than welcome to join us."

Lingua gave a quick glance around the park then obviously checked her phone. "Actually, I'm free 'til five and I could definitely go for something that will perk me up."

"Did you drive here? If not you can ride to The Bean Bag with us."

"I took the bus, so a lift would be appreciated. Thanks."

The ride back was tense for all three women on the car. It was Lingua who broke the silence as soon as they pulled out into traffic. "Did anyone else get out? The last I saw Julian, we were separated and..." When Amari glanced at the woman sitting behind her through the rearview mirror, Lingua's mouth was drawn down and her eyes were tight with pain.

Rocket answered the question that trailed sadly from Lingua's lips. "No, just you and me." She swallowed hard and continued. "I was on the com with him when he was taken. Shots were fired and the line went dead so I don't know his status. He was the one who tipped me off that you had probably made it out." She turned in her seat to look at her long-time friend and teammate.

Lingua met her eyes then flicked her gaze to Amari. "And her?"

"An ally, but let's get someplace secure before I start answering questions."

The woman in the backseat scowled. Humans didn't join the CORP unless they were highly capable and perhaps a bit crazy. And humans didn't survive the CORP unless they were wary to the extreme. Lingua was all of them. After a long pause, she begrudgingly nodded. "Fine."

It wasn't long before they were back at Steph's apartment, safe for the moment. They had no issues on the way downtown or back, which made Rocket uneasy. The only thing she could assume was that if the Chicago team of rogues wasn't out in force looking for her or Lingua, then they were either awaiting backup, or awaiting orders from whomever was at the top.

Introductions were made all the way around when the new agent was added to the little group. But learning of the additional allies only served to make Agent Sara King tenser. They were unknown actors and while they were supposed to be on the side of the good guys, she didn't trust them at her back. Once Amari and Zendara's powers were explained and Rocket mentioned that they were the cause of the massive power flash from the park, Lingua could no longer keep quiet. "You didn't consider that your little stunt could have put the entire city in danger? Had that *flash* of yours went outward instead of straight up, who knows what kind of damage you could have wrought?"

Amari answered first. "I apologize, Agent King. But we had no idea that would happen, none. What would you have had us do?"

Lingua was intense on a good day and she didn't care for the carelessness of the two younger women. Their actions had directly endangered the city she vowed to protect with her life. "You could have come to us! The CORP facility has the capability of dealing with people of power, of helping them. What you did was irresponsible and selfish to the extreme. People could have died from your little experi—"

A fist slammed onto the table, putting a hairline crack in the butcher block top. Everyone took in Zendara's furious countenance with wide eyes. "Turn ourselves in to the CORP? Are you trying to make a joke here? How do you think the CORP came about in the first place? Some fucking government agency decided to dissect another unfortunate alien who found their way to this planet. And that turned out so well, didn't it? I don't think so, Agent King. I won't be a lab rat because of your fucking fear!" She leaned toward the startled human agent. "While I don't know much about my power, or even about Amari Losira Del Rey, I know my heart and I trust that my Q'sirrahna would perceive her capabilities well enough. She would never put others in danger like you seem to suggest."

Stubbornly, Lingua persisted and after a glance toward Amari, Rocket let the little confrontation play out. She trusted the scientist to keep her soul mate from doing anything rash. "You just said it yourself, you know nothing about your own powers, and by your admission you've only known Doctor Del Rey for a week. How are you so certain what she's capable of?" Everyone at the table knew that she referred to more than just Amari's physical abilities.

Zen took a deep breath and calmed her heartrate. "Because, I've felt her my entire life. I know what's in her heart because she has always lived inside my own. I trust her implicitly."

Lingua pushed harder. "With your life?"

Zen nodded.

"She's already saved my life, so I trust her as well." Steph felt the need to defend her friend from Lingua's verbal attack.

"Sara..." Romy called to her teammate in a voice that was softer, rife with the weight of shared experience. When she had the other agent's attention, two words followed. "*Político Libre.*" The tense set to Lingua's shoulders relaxed immediately. Decades before, when both women were still with Black Badge, their team found themselves in a remote location in South America. Their gear was lost when they were ambushed by a group of guerrilla fighters and knowledge of the area was spotty at best. They had nothing to rely on but Rocket's instinct and her firm leadership. Despite the fact that she led them farther from their extraction point, toward the area that intel said was the heart of rebel territory, they all made it out safe. A small jungle airport yielded an old cargo plane, large enough to get the team out and one crucial political leader. As they were flying away they could see explosions in the distance, exactly where they were sent to be extracted. Lingua had trusted Rocket's instincts over anyone else since that very day.

Lack of sleep and worry for Vision had given her an immense headache and she rubbed her temples. "Fine. What's our plan then? Should we try to get to the school, or wait until we know more then make our separate ways to the lab?"

While Lingua was a genius, as well as two other women sitting at the table, no one knew each other very well. Rocket was the planner of the group, the strategist. She seemed deep in thought so Lingua took the time to really look at her new band of allies. As much as she studied computers, Lingua also studied people. Part of her question was a test, to see exactly what nature of minds her and Rocket were working with. Her gaze flitted from unknown to unknown. Romy looked as she always looked — closed, stoic, and calm. The woman, Stephanie, appeared frightened but resolute. And she kept splitting her glances between

Rocket and the brunette that drove them back from the park. While Zendara seemed like nothing more than a hardened punk, Lingua wasn't sure what to make of Amari. She appeared calm and mild-mannered but there was a whiff of power to her gaze that Lingua would have missed completely had she met her under any other circumstances.

Rocket knew exactly what Lingua was trying to do and appreciated the effort of analysis of their allies, but they didn't really have time for all that. However, she didn't get a chance to shut down the call for suggestions before Zen answered. "It seems risky to be seen coming and going from the lab a lot, even if classes are cancelled and the foot traffic is significantly less than normal. Maybe especially since classes are cancelled. "

Rocket furrowed her brow. "That is a very astute and practical observation. I agree with you. Despite the risk, we should probably wait here for the time being."

Lingua glanced toward Zen with something akin to begrudging respect, then looked to her leader. "How long?"

"Despite the abundance of cameras on campus, there are a lot of shadows after nightfall." Zen again, with her insightful advice born of hiding from those that would do a person harm, living below the radar in a life that had been devoid of true happiness until Amari entered her orbit.

"Nightfall it is." Rocket looked around the decently-sized apartment. "Do you have room enough for us all to catch some rest? I have a feeling we're going to need it in the days to come."

Steph smiled. "Sure. I have my room and a spare room, help yourself to whichever you like." She looked down the table to her newest guest. "What do you want more, food or sleep?"

Agent King's shoulders slumped with exhaustion, having spent the entire night before on duty. She had been running on nothing but anger and determination since the takeover of their facility. But she also knew she needed fuel. "Food first, then sleep if you've got someplace for me to crash."

Rocket watched as Amari and Zen went to the couch and sat pressed together. They rested their foreheads together and Amari stroked the finely-shorn blonde hairs on the back of Zen's head. Their position and facial expressions grew a little too intimate and she turned away again. That was when she found her glance fixed firmly on the one person who had surprised her most of their unlikely little group. Human, doctor of biochemistry, and oh so fragile. Stephanie flitted around the kitchen with what seemed like boundless energy, despite the fact that she'd had no more sleep the night before than Romy. And running counterpoint to her natural inclination toward disassociation from her romantic partners, Steph's question from earlier reverberated through Romy's head. Perhaps if they all survived the next few days, she'd re-evaluate her stance concerning relationships and commitment to anyone but CORP. After all, the CORP had failed her, betrayed what mattered most. Perhaps someone closer to her heart would do better at protecting it.

HOURS LATER AND nearly a thousand miles south, a family was gearing up for the conflict to come. After everyone had gotten their fill of rest, food, and showers, the setting sun found the two generations of Chromodecs dressed in their black CORP suits.

"How will we find this Rocket if she's gone underground?" While Gauss was the stronger of the two twins, he was also the worrier. Sinter was the more decisive one, and the strategist. Both watched as Augur moved to a large safe that was bolted into the concrete in the corner. The door swung open and they equipped themselves with the weapons, armor, and tech found inside. While Chromodecs had superhuman powers, many of them were still susceptible to a good old-fashioned bullet, and all of them bled as red as any human. It was Hatch that answered their question with another directed at her husband. "Are you thinking of a sight and send?"

He nodded. "That's exactly what I'm thinking."

"Sight and send?" As usual, the twins spoke at the same time, but everyone in the room was used to it since they'd done it as long as they had been speaking.

"Your dad is going to see if he can get a prescient lock on Rocket, and if it's all clear I'll open a portal to her. It's something we've been working on for a while now."

Twin "Cool" echoed in the bunker.

It took years to perfect the specific sight and send technique that the husband and wife team used. But they had gotten exceptional at it. Once Augur made a mental lock on a specific person, he was able to telepathically impart the location and image of the space to his wife. Normally, a teleporter couldn't send anyone to an area where they didn't have line of sight. It would be fatal to be teleported into another object, be it living or inanimate. While most used remote cameras, satellite feeds, and enhanced HUD images, none of those would work in their situation. There were a lot of reasons that Augur and Hatch were considered two of the best agents in the field.

The family spent vital time eating and cleaning up in the bunker before doing one last check of the news. It was grim. Finally they gathered around in the open space, Gauss and Sinter each had a heavy duffle with supplemental gear and ammo in their hands. Augur looked at the younger agents. "Be ready." Then he turned to his wife and at the same time, they reached out to touch their fingertips to each other's temples. It facilitated his telepathy.

ALL FIVE WOMEN in Steph's apartment gathered just after dark, trying to decide on the best way to get themselves to the lower lab at the school unseen. It was Lingua who spoke first when no one could come up with a viable answer. "All this waiting is making me twitchy. All it takes is one half-assed psi and our position is compromised. I feel like a sitting duck waiting here!"

"I agree." Both Lingua and Zendara looked at each other in surprise at the realization that they finally agreed on something.

Rocket sighed and ran a hand through her hair in frustration over their situation. "Settle down, both of you. We're fine here for the time being. No one should come knocking for us just yet." As if she had the power of clairvoyance, pounding sounded at the door seconds after she finished speaking. Suddenly, everyone was in motion at once. Rocket had her pistol out and was standing next to the door of the apartment. Zen had taken a protective stance in front of Amari until Amari tapped her shoulder and nodded toward Steph. Chagrinned, she moved to stand in front of the lone un-trained human. Lingua stood behind the door with her own pistol out.

Steph whispered into the tense room. "Guys, it could be my neighbor."

Before anyone could respond to her statement, a deep male voice called through the door. "Rocket, open the damn door! We're sitting ducks out here."

"Holy shit, yes!" She quickly unlocked the door and ushered the four people inside that had been waiting.

Leery and on edge, Zen said the first thing that popped into her head. "Who the hell are they?"

Augur's southern accent coupled with his deep voice cut through the silence of the room, tinged with a bit of grim humor. "We're the cavalry, kid."

Chapter Fourteen

ZEN GAVE AN eye roll before stepping closer to her Q'sir-rahna again. Steph looked over to the woman that had turned her life upside down overnight. "Romy?"

Rocket's own eyes were in motion, taking in the unlikely assembly of allies. "It's okay everyone. We'll all on the same side here. Steph, like Lingua, I trust these four more than nearly everyone else in my life." Augur and Hatch grinned when they saw Lingua. It was practically a Black Badge reunion.

"Pardon, Agent Danes, but you don't know us."

Rocket's gaze swung to one of the tall young agents that came in with Augur and Hatch. All four of them were wearing the traditional black uniforms of the CORP with their city badges on each shoulder, though none of them still had their helmets or communicators of any kind. She was also glad to note that all four appeared to be well armed. "You must be Imani, and that would make the LA teammate to your left your brother, Isaiah. You might not remember me because you were about six the last time I saw you. I've known your parents for a very long time and I trust them with my life."

Lingua spoke as well. "Same."

"Damn straight."

Augur's deep voice was a soothing balm to Rocket's frayed nerves. It was one thing to have an ally of great but unknown power. It was another thing altogether to have a team of people at your back you knew and could trust in any situation. She quickly strode forward and wrapped Jaxon in a great hug, then moved over to do the same to Shawna. "It's truly good to see you, my friends. We've got a bit of a mess to clean up."

Augur took in the three people he didn't recognize, non-agents, and turned back to Rocket. "Yes we do. Where do we start, boss?"

Rocket was startled at first then gave a nod to Augur's defer-ment of leadership to her. It made sense since she was their unit leader in Black Badge, and she was currently the Chicago CORP SAIC. "Our first priority is getting somewhere secure where we can share information amongst ourselves and set a plan of action in place." Romy glanced around at the motley group of people. "Zendara, that's the blonde over there—" she pointed at Zen "—gave us intel on a secure room below the University of Chicago. Once there, I expect Lingua to use the eloptic collar in my bag to transform the room into a sightless bunker, so we don't have anyone show up on our doorstep like you just did."

Augur looked around Steph's living room, before fixing his gaze on her. "Everyone?"

Rocket nodded. "I'm afraid so. Even when we leave here you know that we can still be traced to this apartment." She looked at Steph. "You can always go stay with a friend or relative until this blows over."

"How safe will she be at a different location? Let's say a Chromodec pings this place and comes here, would they be able to sense Steph in this place and locate her that way?"

"Damn, the girl is right." Augur ran his hand across his head out of sheer frustration. "That's exactly what they'd do."

Amari walked over to the large muscular man and held out her hand. "This girl has a name too. I'm Doctor Amari Losira Del Rey, princess of Reyna. Pleased to make your acquaintance."

Four sets of eyes blink in surprise, and Lingua exhaled a loud snort of laughter. "Damn, princess has teeth." Amari ignored the cynical woman and continued over to shake hands with the newly-arrived family of agents.

Zen stepped forward next. "My name is Zendara Inyri Baen-Tor, princess of Tora."

"What country is that?" Isaiah tilted his head quizzically.

"Not countries, planets." Stephanie joined the greeting train to welcome the CORP agents into her home. "Neither one is human or Chromodec. My name is Steph and this is my place. I work with Amari." She looked around the room and stopped at Rocket. "And I'm definitely not staying by myself so wherever Amari goes, I go as well."

Rocket sighed. "Fine. Now we just need to get the nine of us to the center of the campus without being seen."

"I can get us there, I just need a visual on the place first. If Lingua can hack the campus cameras I can port us right to the door of the building. Even better if there are cameras inside."

Lingua rolled her eyes. "Hack with what? I barely made it out of headquarters before they locked it down. It's not like I had time to grab a kit."

The agent in charge thought for a few seconds before

addressing Steph. "I'm assuming you have something we can use?"

She nodded. "I do, but it doesn't have a lot of computing power. Amari has a badass computer, she brags about it all the time."

They all turned to look at the woman in question. "I do have a top-of-the line model with some added hardware. However, I'm afraid I can't let any of you use it. There is sensitive information contained on the hard drive, and I can't chance that your hacker here won't access the data files."

"Are you fucking kidding me right now? What makes you think your data is more important than saving the people of this city? Who are you to—?"

Amari took a step forward and cut her hand through the air, suddenly rigid with irritation. "Is it worth your life, Agent King?"

"What?" Lingua stopped mid rant.

"The information contained on my computer is secured, and for a reason. I have no trust that you won't go poking around in the machine, if only to determine its capability."

Rocket held up a hand to forestall further argument between the two women. "What is preventing you from sharing information with us?"

Amari rubbed her right eyebrow, aware that she was being forced to say more than was probably wise. "The Tau Ceti Pact of 1952."

A lyrical voice added to the line of questions as Hatch spoke. "And that is?"

Amari remained silent for nearly a minute until she felt a hand slide into her own. She glanced toward Zendara and smiled that her soul mate knew when she needed comfort and quietly offered her support. "After the incident which led to the creation of the people you call Chromodecs, the Tau Ceti decreed that no one was allowed to further advance the humans beyond their natural capabilities, under threat of death."

Surprise registered on every person's face in the room. Amari had never even told Stephani about *that* particular detail in her abbreviated Tau Ceti explanation. There were some things she was better off not knowing.

Lingua could barely contain her curiosity. "Who are the Tau Ceti?"

The next rapid fire question came from Romy. "How do they

know if the pact has been broken?"

And the last question was rumbled in Augur's deep voice. "Who carries out the punishment?"

Amari whined slightly, muttering under her breath. "I am in so much trouble."

"Q'sirrahna, if you can't answer then don't."

Dark brown eyes met pale blue and the soul mates froze in place. Their connection was so complete, so palpable that everyone else held their breath in expectation. "It's fine. I'm not advancing anything or anyone with this information." Amari turned back to where the six Chromodec agents had grouped together unconsciously. "Tau Ceti are the oldest race in the universe. They observed the events of 1952 and declared Terra off limits to further manipulation. Think of this planet as a nature park of sorts. Anyway, to be sure the pact is followed there are thousands of Watchers all over the world, from the lowest of maintenance workers, all the way up to high level government positions. As for the punishment..." She trailed off and shrugged. "I'm not really sure. My parents never told me that. But they did say that the Tau Ceti have access to any piece of tech that carries their data signature and that they always know when information has been divulged to an Earth native. And the punishment doesn't just go to the person receiving the information, it is also for the person from which the data originated. While I have no problem risking my life for the people of my adopted home, I'm not risking it for one woman's curiosity."

The staring contest between Amari and Lingua lasted for a few seconds before the abrasive agent relented. She turned to Steph. "Fine, I need your computer."

Minutes later Lingua had it set up on the kitchen table and was logged into the university server. Then seconds later she brought up the video feed from their security cameras. "What building was it again?"

"Computer Science Building. It's probably coded as something—"

Lingua's voice cut off what Zen was going to say. "Got it. All right, gather your gear, kids, because Aunti Hatch is going to take us on a trip."

Steph was first to speak up. "What do we need in the way of supplies? Should we bring food, or anything else?"

"Hmm, good point. Why don't you take Gauss and Sinter and fill a few bags with some non-perishables."

Remembering something important for the first time all day, Amari grabbed Steph's sleeve. "Wait! What about Curie?" She looked around, noticing for the first time that Stephanie's cat was nowhere to be seen.

"Curie?" Multiple voices sounded at once.

"My cat. And she's next door at my neighbor's place. I sent her off for a sleepover last night."

Amari was confused. "When did you do that?"

Steph smirked. "I texted Julie to come get him halfway through my date last night. I wasn't sure if Romy was allergic and rather than chance it I sent her next door. Besides, you know she never lets me sleep in." Everyone suddenly looked at the door, Romy putting the pieces together and making sense of Steph's earlier statement that the person knocking could be her neighbor. "Don't worry, I texted her again a few hours ago and asked her if Curie could stay longer. Told her I had an important project to work on and would be gone a few days."

Rocket nodded. "Good thinking, Steph. Now that the question of the curious cat has been solved, let's get this show on the road. I want to leave in T-minus five." She turned to Amari and Zen. "Do either of you need something special from Amari's condo? Do you have special, um, requirements? Dietary or otherwise?"

"Frog legs and steel wool pads."

Of the four CORP members in the remaining group that weren't busy securing food and supplies, only Augur made a face. "Really?"

Amari shook her head at Zen. "She's kidding. We only need each other. And we're wearing my parents' ship suits beneath our clothes."

"Ready!" Steph and the twins returned from the kitchen each carrying a large bag of supplies. "Wait, be right back." The doctor ran back toward her bedroom and into the bathroom, before coming back to the group less than two minutes later wearing a backpack. At Amari's raised eyebrow she huffed. "What? It's toiletries and clothes for myself and to share. Just because I'm being forced to flee from my home doesn't mean I'm going to walk around like one of the unwashed masses."

It was the eldest twin who laughed out loud. "I like her, she's got—"

"Spunk!" The statement was of course finished by her brother.

Rocket glanced at her chrono. "Time's wasting, let's go!"

Seconds later, after studying the computer screen, Hatch had her trademark portal open. Visible through the opening was a dark hallway lit only by the faint glow of security lights. One by one they filed through carrying bags of equipment, food, and anything else they thought they would need, with Rocket and Hatch bringing up the rear. Lingua bent down to peer at the badge reader next to the locked lab door. "Give me a few minutes and I'll have this open."

"Let me try this first."

Lingua moved back in surprise when Zen held out the maintenance badge from her wallet and swiped it across the panel. The light on the panel turned green and the sound of the lock disengaging seemed criminally loud in the quiet hall.

Zen grinned. "Let's hear it for bureaucratic holdups when it comes to processing my termination paperwork."

Lingua grumbled. "Will it keep working though?" She paused then waved a hand through the air. "Never mind, I'll reinstate you once I'm back in the system. The badge will be handy to have."

It didn't take long for the experienced team to take in the lay of the lab. There were two shelves full of computers off to one side of the large room. Other machines and equipment of unknown use took up space at the end. A few worktables and an assortment of rolling chairs were in the center of the room. One door led to a small room with a kitchenette complete with a sink and table, another led to an office, and a third door led to a fully equipped bathroom with an industrial shower. Imani jerked a thumb over her shoulder as she walked out of the room. "What's with the heavy duty shower setup?"

Steph was the one who answered on her way to the kitchenette. "It's in case of a lab accident. A lot of these old labs had many uses over the years. Notice the drains in the floors and industrial venting throughout the main room. It was a chem lab back in the eighties, then a physics lab, and I think most recently a computer lab. But since they built the new science building with its state of the art labs, most of the classes are over there."

Lingua gazed around at the computer equipment, tools, and spools of wire that took up a fair amount of space. "It'll do." She looked back at where the rest were gathered. "Any of you handy with computers? Or networking? If I'm going to get this place converted to a safe base from the rogue agents, I need more hands."

One person slowly raised a hand, much to the surprise of everyone, especially Amari. Lingua squinted in disbelief. Seeing everyone's reaction, Stephanie shrugged. "What, my undergrad was in IT, it's just not something I have to use in my real job."

"But your computer is pink!" The self-proclaimed punk shook her head in disgust.

Amari just smiled, loving the new information that she was learning about her friend. She nudged Zen's shoulder. "You shouldn't judge. After all, you're a genius, but you don't even own a computer."

Agent King rolled her eyes. "Fine, whatever." Then she looked to Rocket. "I need paper and a pencil, the eloptic collar, and time."

"I've got some supplies in my backpack, including the collar. How long? Every single minute counts here."

Dark eyes flitted around the room while Lingua did mental computations in her head, analyzing what materials and tools she'd need. "I could probably rig something up within an hour, but it will take me longer to make something more secure."

Rocket nodded. "Make it happen then. In the meantime we need to find out exactly what our new friends are capable of. I want to suggest some excercis—"

"Wait!" Amari's interruption was unexpected. "You mentioned that someone could track Steph from her own home, could they also track to my place the same way?"

"It's a definitely possibility, depending on the strength of the psychometrist they bring in." Augur's deep voice was anything but reassuring.

Amari sighed. "I need to run to my condo."

The leader of their small band understood immediately. "You're concerned about your tech, your laptop, getting into the rogues' hands?" Amari nodded. "All right, work with Augur to get a sight read. You and Hatch can go but come right back! I want you gone ten minutes tops."

"Yes, ma'am!" Hatch walked over to her husband and waved Amari closer. "He's gonna need to read you to get the location and layout of your place, then he'll link me in so I can open a portal. Savvy?"

"Sure, sounds good."

The large African American man placed his hands near Amari's temples as he prepared to read her. "Think of your place on the map, think of the inside so I can see it."

"Okay."

As his hands made contact with Amari's skin, a frown appeared on the older agent's face. "I've got nothing. Are you shielding?"

Amari looked up into his dark eyes. "No, I'm not sure I'd know how to do that."

"What's the problem, Jax?" Rocket looked from the dark-haired young woman to her longtime friend.

He shook his head. "She's completely unreadable."

Shawna frowned at her husband's words. "That's not possible. You're the highest rated prescient in the CORP!"

Rocket thought on the problem for a few seconds, then turned toward Zen. "Zendara, can you come here?"

Suspicious and wary, Zen walked over. "Why do you need me?"

"Sirra, I think they want to test a theory. Right agent?"

"Exactly! Try reading her, Jax."

He touched Zen the exact same way and swore beneath his breath. "Still nothing. It's like I'm touching air. Even inanimate objects will give me prescient images, glimpses into their past and ownership. But these two don't register at all."

The Agent in Charge made a humming sound. "Vision had the same problem in the park last week. He couldn't read them per se, but he picked up the telemetry of their passing. Didn't you say your cells were both crystal and carbon based?" They both nodded and she turned back to Augur and Hatch. "I suspect it has something to do with their alien biology."

Amari let out a sign of relief. "So my place is safe?"

"Nope." This was called out as Lingua walked by carrying a CPU piled high with spools of wire.

"What she's trying to say is that we did get a partial reading from the place that both Amari and Zen visited, and even tracked them from the island to the pool building. Also, I'm sure Steph has been to your place enough times to leave a well-worn psychic path. So I can't guarantee that your tech is safe."

Hatch walked over to the laptop that Lingua had brought along to the lab. "What's the wifi password in this place?" Steph told her the school wifi for teachers and then gave the agent her password. After Shawna brought up a map of the area, she turned the computer toward Amari. "All right, show me your place."

After a spate of typing and clicking, Amari was able to bring up the street view image of her condo building. "There." We should be able to get in and out quickly under cover of darkness.

"Nuh uh, no way is Hatch porting out in the open without someone watching her six! It was different when I thought they'd pop into Amari's place, but this is too risky. I'm going with."

Rocket shook her head. "No, I need you here. We can send —"

"Hey, where are the wonder twins? I'm going to need more hands to run these spools of cable. And I need plates formed to go up on the walls." Lingua called from where she and Steph were sorting different tools.

Both Isaiah and Imani came back into the room from the kitchenette, eating granola bars that had been ported from Stephanie's apartment. "You called?"

"Jesus Christ, Auggy! Your kids eat as much as you do! But fine, get over here and help. The sooner I get this done the safer we all will be."

Rocket ran a hand through her short hair as plan after plan shifted below her feet like sand in a desert. "Jax, I need you here. We need to come up with a plan going forward, and I want to fill you in on some things. Zen and Amari will keep her safe, and if they're not back in ten, then we go in for them and all hell will bust lose." She turned to look at the two alien women and the tough agent standing near them. "Got it?"

Hatch rolled her eyes. "Who's to say I won't be the one protecting the green girls over here?"

Zen bristled. "Are you making a crack about us not being from this planet?"

The black woman laughed, then in a split second she foot swept the blonde woman causing Zendara to land hard on her ass. "Please, you girls are as green as you can get. Y'all have no experience with any kind of combat or self-defense. Rocket says you're powerful but a bomb does no one good if it blows up the friendlies."

Rocket cut the banter as Zen floated up off the floor, unhurt. "Fine, protect each other but get there and get right back. Now."

As soon as the three women disappeared through the portal, Rocket turned to Augur. "We need a plan, and Hatch brought up a very good point. Amari and Zen could be our ace in the hole here, but they could also be —"

"A liability."

She threw herself into a nearby chair at the table and rested her forehead on the palm of her hand before answering Augur. "Yes, exactly that. So what are we going to do about it?"

The big man sat across from her and set his chrono. "We have ten minutes, some of our best plans have been laid in less. Give me a quick rundown on what you know."

Rocket started with the worst news first. "Colonel Maza is behind it all. He's Doctor Brian Daggett's grandson."

Augur's eyes widened in shock. "The creator of the entire Chromodec line?" Rocket nodded. "Well fuck me running! We are balls-deep in some shit now."

Despite Augur's colorful and somewhat disgusting turn of phrase, Rocket couldn't help agreeing with him.

LIKE GENESIS AND the God of Creation, it always seems to circle around back to Doctor Daggett, doesn't it? While we can't exactly say that things are going well for our team of heroes, certainly not all is lost. They've got Lingua, Steph, Gauss, and Sinter working on creating a psi-proof base of operations. Amari, Zen, and Hatch are off to make sure no alien technology or information falls into enemy hands. And finally we have Rocket and Augur plotting their next move. There were three things the team would need in the days to come, assets that would help them fight back against the rogue agents taking over cities all over the United States. They required intel, weapons, and allies. But on top of that, they needed to discover the scope of Amari and Zen's powers. As the two top-notch agents made a list of their resources and plotted the order of action when the three women returned, someone else was just as busy hundreds of miles to the south.

ORACLE WAS MAKING his own list, recording the names of all the cities that had successfully been overthrown by his people. He did eventually speak with his commanding general, and even President Lee. She seemed suspicious but had another call and didn't talk to him for long. His commanding general was a little more work. Colonel Maza put on his best all-American smile. "Yes sir, I am aware of the political implications of this problem. Sir, I have my best teams out helping the battling cities as we speak. We've already confirmed sixty percent are stable, we just need to mop up the rest. I will keep you updated every hour. Yes, sir." The smile morphed into a triumphant grin as he hung up the secure phone. It had nothing to do with the comfort of his chair or the pleasure he felt as each new city set off their beacon.

He spent nearly an hour on the phone, reassuring the most powerful men and women of the world that he had the best agents in place and soon the Chromodec insurrection would be quelled. They didn't have to know that the insurrection was his, or that the people coming out on top in the days to come would be his as well. Once the cities fell and he had full control of the CORP agencies in each location, nothing would prevent him from taking over the other government agencies after. He could digitally blind them with the power each CORP facility had, and troops would be no use because every building was surrounded by civilians going about their day-to-day lives. No, the government would not risk civilians so foolishly so the top elected officials would be powerless to stop him. As Oracle kicked back in his chair he fingered the lighter in his hand before lighting the Cuban cigar. He yelled out to the agent manning the coms across the room. "Digilous!"

"Sir?"

"Refresh those screens, I want to tally my cities again."

Chapter Fifteen

"MY CONDO IS right there." Amari pointed toward a balcony on the third floor of the building. They were standing on the sidewalk with South Martin Luther King Drive and Washington Park at their backs. Street lamps illuminated the cars parked nose to bumper up and down the road on their side.

Hatch looked around for witnesses then quickly teleported all three of them up to the balcony. She cupped her hands so she could see into the sliding glass door before opening another portal inside. The agent checked the time on her chrono then met Amari's eyes in the dim light shining through the large glass door. "You have five minutes to get what you need or destroy it, then we're out of here. Savvy?"

Zen stayed out of the way next to Hatch while Amari grabbed her laptop bag from the floor near the end table. She stuffed the computer and power cord inside, then went over to a small stand near the wall-mounted flat screen TV. She withdrew a stack of external hard drives and two thumb drives and quickly added those to the laptop bag as well. Amari paused, acutely aware that her time was ticking away. There were too many personal items in the place that could potentially lead the rogue agents to her family. Making a quick decision, she zipped the bag, grabbed a duffle from the closet, and then walked over to stand in front of Zendara. "Hit me as hard as you can."

"What?" Zen looked at her with dismay.

"Y'all are wasting time, let's go!"

Amari shook her head. "I have personal items that are scattered around in here and the Chromodec psychometrists could use any one of them to get to my parents. I need speed to gather everything quickly. It won't hurt me, sirra." Understanding completely, Zen complied with a massive punch to the jaw. They both felt the rush of power as soon as her fist made contact. "Again." Once more, Zendara followed her instruction and Hatch looked on curiously.

Then in a blur of motion, Amari raced through each room, filling the duffle with private items like pictures, gifts, and jewelry. Basically anything her parents touched, she shoved into the bag. Having lived away from home for a number of years, there was surprisingly little to collect. "Done. Let's get out of—"

A shriek pierced the quiet night right before the main door to the condo exploded inward with a shower of splinters as the hinges and locks gave way. "Shit! Times up, ladies!" Before Hatch could teleport the three of them away, a blur raced through the door and landed a blow hard enough to knock her unconscious. "Hatch!" Zen caught the agent before she could hit the ground and didn't see the same blur target the back of her own head. The super-fast Chromodec received a shock when his punch not only failed to knock her out, but every bit of his momentum was drained. He found himself completely still with his fist resting gently against nearly white blonde hair. Zendara turned to look at the man who was less than twelve inches from her, momentarily frozen in shock. Misjudging her juiced power, she backhanded him so hard he crashed through the sliding glass door. The shattered glass flew outward, landing next to his body on the street below. Shrieking sounded again and Zen quickly picked up Hatch from the floor, carefully cradling the unconscious woman in her arms. When she looked toward Amari's front door, she saw her Q'sirrahna facing off against three agents in black.

One agent was the source of the powerful shriek but rather than incapacitate either woman of Q'orre, the energy from sonic attack filled both of them with power. Being the main target of the shrieking woman, the influx of energy and its conversion caused Amari's hair and eyes to glow bright white. Another woman teleported behind Amari to strike her from behind but the blow had no effect. Noticing Zen just standing there, the last agent raised a gun in her direction. The Zendara turned and let the bullets hit harmlessly against her back but the action didn't go unnoticed by Amari. "Get her out of here, I'll catch up in a minute!"

Zen looked torn, not wanting to leave her soul mate behind. "Where?"

Amari spun and grabbed the teleporter, throwing the woman into the kitchen before she could react. The agent slumped unconscious against the stainless steel door of the refrigerator. "Where we first met. Go!"

Zendara had no choice but to trust Amari to keep her word, so she quickly lifted Hatch over her shoulder and ran out the broken slider onto the balcony. In her panic she couldn't really remember all that Amari had taught her about flying so she jumped down instead. The speedster was either unconscious or dead on the street below, so she ignored him and ran as fast as possible to the corner of Washington Park.

Back in the condo, Amari reached a point where all the power she was absorbing from the shrieking Chromodec had to go somewhere. In a move that was more instinct than anything else, she pointed her fist at the woman and a beam of energy hit her straight in the chest. It blew her back through the doorway and into the plaster wall on the opposite side of the hall. A small part of Amari took note that the energy blast looked very much like the beam of light that shot into the sky the night of her and Zendara's resonance flash. With both the teleporter and the sonic-powered rogue agent unconscious, that only left the one with the gun. Amari tried to reason with him. "Why are you attacking us?"

The man in the standard black CORP suit kept the gun pointed at Amari, even though he was certain it would do no good against whatever manner of person stood before him. She had to admit that the black helmet and suit did make the CORP agents look intimidating. But she had nothing to fear from these ones. "We were called in to Chicago to track the rogue Chromodecs that are on the news right now. We traced a rogue named Rocket to an apartment near here, and I got another prescient vision that led the team to this place. If you don't turn over the rogue agent, we will be forced to take you back to headquarters."

Amari looked to the left, then looked to the right, before staring back at him in the murky light of the condo. Sirens in the distance grew louder as they approached and she smiled. "Who is 'we' exactly? It looks like just me and you and *we* both know you're out-classed. Let's cut to the chase here. I know that you're actually one of the rogues. Even better, I know that you're all under the direct command of Colonel Marek Maza. The Oracle."

The man's body tensed as he fully realized the current state of his team. The other rogues were either dead or unconscious and the woman with the glowing white eyes and hair had proven to be invulnerable to everything they'd thrown at her. The man licked his lips nervously. "Who the hell are you?"

Rather than answer, Amari asked a question of her own. Her time was short but she had a few loose ends to wrap up. "Tell me the names of you and your teammates and I'll let you go unharmed."

He was quick enough to answer against the threat of something he'd never seen before. "Sonica, Sprinter, and Jump. I'm Reader."

Amari used her speed to snag the gun out of the man's hand and crush the barrel. Then she darted over to pick up both the laptop and duffle bags that she had dropped earlier in the initial attack. "Good. Now I want you to do me a favor, Reader. You tell Maza that the real CORP agents have powerful allies and that he started his little war at the wrong time. His only option is surrender because there is no place in the world safe from us." From the noise outside, the cops had finally arrived and a groaning sound off near the kitchen let Amari know that the teleporter was waking up. Without another word she rose into the air with the bags and flew like a shot out the broken balcony door. She no sooner touched down in the darkness near the pool house when she found herself engulfed in a crushing hug. "Easy, sirra, I'm all right."

"I was worried, freaked out that they would have some secret weapon that could hurt you."

Amari shook her head and brushed a kiss across Zen's lips. "They didn't. They don't. I gave the shooter a little warning to take back to Oracle. Let's see if he actually listens." She peered through the darkness to see Hatch slumped against the brick wall. "How is she?"

As Zendara and Amari fixed their gaze on their companion, a moan came from the black woman and she slowly stirred. Hatch sat forward, rubbing the back of her close-cropped head and looked around with confusion. "What happened? I remember—" She made a face, trying to recall exactly what happened when she went down. "I remember an explosion."

"Rogue agents found us. Sonica, Sprinter, Jump, and Reader. All of them tracked Agent Danes to Stephanie's apartment then they followed the crumbs from Steph's place to mine. Reader claimed to be hunting rogues so I left him a message for your Oracle."

Knowing that it was past the time for them to be back and more than a little freaked out by the big agent that was married to Hatch, Zen prodded Amari. "We need to get back before that Augur guy comes looking for her."

Hatch groaned again and stood up. She gingerly rubbed her neck and moved her head slowly back and forth and up and down, getting a feel for her range of motion. "She's right. That asshole Sprinter didn't scramble me so much that I can't get us back to the base." Seconds later a portal opened up and they all stepped through. Their destination was the corner of the lab that they had designated for teleportation in and out. The location was the first thing the team set up when they arrived, to prevent accidental injury and dismemberment by teleporting into an area that wasn't clear.

"What the hell took you so long?" Augur's voice was laced with worry, which quickly morphed to anger when he noticed his wife's obvious discomfort and the state of Zen and Amari's clothing. Ripped, singed, and full of bullet holes, they looked like they'd gone through a war zone.

Hatch held up a hand to stop his charging bull routine. "We're fine, but we got jumped just as we were getting ready to port out." She addressed the entire group that had gathered around. "Sprinter was there and knocked me unconscious nearly as soon as the door blew open and I don't remember anything after that until I woke in the park across the street."

Augur rounded on the other two in his wife's little recon party. "I should have never trusted you!"

Amari held up a placating hand. "I understand your anger, Agent Bell. But while we couldn't stop the speedster, I had Zen get her out as soon as possible. I dealt with the rest."

Rocket swore under her breath as Isaiah and Imani went over to reassure themselves that their mother was okay. The defacto leader called out to Lingua. "What's the status on that collar mod? We need to go dark right now!"

The irritable agent didn't bother looking at her as she continued typing into the reconfigured computer. "Ten."

"Ten what, minutes? That's too lo—"

"No, seconds. And done!" With a final keystroke she turned around in a flourish.

Amari looked around, as did Zen. Both seemed nonplussed. Zen's eyebrows wrinkled with confusion. "I don't get it, nothing feels different."

Sinter laughed, her voice carrying a lot of her mother's lyrical quality. "As well you shouldn't, you're not a Chromodec. The collar is made to disrupt eloptic, or scalar energy, if that term is more familiar. By connecting it to the wiring placed around this lab, giving it a power boost, and making some program modifications, Lingua was able to create an eloptic barrier of sorts. So while we can use our powers in the center of the room, and outside the lab, we can no longer use powers to push through the eloptic barrier or sense anything through it."

Amari's expression when she looked at Lingua said that she was impressed. "So none of the rogue Chromodecs can see in, or get in?"

Zen scowled. "No one can see out or get out either. It means we're blind."

Stephanie shook her head. "Actually, we're not. Using my password, Lingua tapped into the university's security network and she's got eyes on every corner of this campus through the cameras. We're as safe as we're possibly going to get right now."

"All right people, let's take five to catch our breaths then I want a meeting at the conference table." Rocket wandered to the kitchenette and Steph went over to stand next to Amari.

"I'm guessing your condo is toast?" Amari made a face and nodded.

Zen snorted, finding humor in the darkest things. "Big time!"

"What about my place?"

Amari shrugged. "I don't really know but I doubt they messed it up. My guess is they knew we were inside and that's why they attacked. Honestly, most of the damage to my place was done by me and Zen. I guess I'm not getting my security deposit back."

A single blonde eyebrow went up as Steph looked at her in disbelief. "*That's* what you're worried about? I may never see my baby again and you're concerned about your damn security deposit!"

"Obviously I'm joking, and I'm sure Curie is fine. I also got my stuff so my parents should be safe. I'd call them but I don't want them to worry about me. Not to mention I'm sure they're busy with their own stuff right now with the way everything has gone down. Their job as Watchers will always take precedence over anything else."

"Who's making a call?" Lingua walked up as they were talking and practically pushed through Zen and Stephanie to hold out her hand palm up. "If either of you have phones I want them right now."

Zen gave her quizzical look. "Even if they're off?"

"Even if, genius. Our tech can track the phone no matter what, unless the power source or the network chip is removed. And they'll have SIMoN tracking all cell transmissions right now, filtering out anything they think may lead them to us."

The punk-looking woman quickly unzipped her hoody

pocket and pulled out her phone. Seeing that it was an older model, Lingua took it and flipped it over. Seconds later the battery was removed and Zen had her phone back in hand. The agent looked at Amari next. "Your friend—" she jerked her head at Steph "—already gave me hers for deactivation."

Amari smiled but didn't move to hand over her phone. "Yes, well I guarantee my friend doesn't have a phone like mine. Have no fear, Agent. It's not on any network that your CORP can track."

"I'll be the judge of that. Hand it over, *Doctor*."

After eyeing the self-proclaimed hacker of Rocket's CORP team up and down, Amari shook her head. "I don't think so. It's safer with me."

A dark look crossed Lingua's face at a civilian's refusal to obey a CORP command. "Listen you b—"

"Is there a problem here?" Rocket interrupted what was sure to be a tirade from her long-time friend and fellow agent.

"She won't give up her phone!"

Amari sighed and addressed Rocket rather than the volatile human agent. "Did the CORP know anything about the Tau Ceti before I told you?" Rocket shook her head. "Which means the CORP doesn't know anything about the thousands of Watchers stationed all over this world, placed in nearly every capacity. Trust me, if the tech I got from my parents can keep all that a secret from your *CORP*, then my phone is safer with me than with your hacker."

Rocket tilted her head and contemplated Amari's words. "Aren't you afraid it will be destroyed when you're fighting?"

Finally consenting to a small demonstration, Amari pulled what appeared to be a modern smartphone from her front jeans pocket. Then before any more questions could be asked, she threw it hard at the concrete below their feet. It bounced harmlessly and slid across the floor, coming to rest near a drain in the concrete. "It's a replica of a popular brand, made from non-Earth materials, and running on proprietary Watcher technology. While it's not indestructible, it can definitely take a beating. I also keep it inside my suit when I'm using my powers, which protects it even more."

"Fascinating..."

If anything, Amari's words had the opposite effect of dissuading Lingua from possessing the phone. She eyed the phone hungrily and looked even more excited to explore the previously unknown bit of tech. Understanding exactly how her friend thought about most things, Rocket was quick to head her off. She looked right at the other agent. "Leave it alone."

"Fine." Lingua growled out the word then stalked off to sit at the previously designated meeting table. "Let's get this show on the road, I'm not getting any younger here."

Everyone took her words as a sign and wandered over to join her. Amari stopped to pick up her phone off the floor then sat between Zen and Steph. Rocket started the meeting. "Augur and I sketched out a quick list of the things we need and a plan of sorts. First of all we need gear. The Agents Bell brought a good amount of weapons and ammo but all any of us have is our base suit. That leaves our heads completely unprotected so we need helmets."

Stephanie tentatively raised a hand. "Didn't you say all your helmets were tied to SIMoN, so wouldn't it be dangerous to run around with those if we're trying to hide ourselves?"

"Excellent point! However, Chicago is also a shipping hub and the CORP maintains a warehouse near the airport, in West Elsdon. Nothing inside is keyed to an agent or activated yet, Lingua can do the rest with the equipment here."

Augur took over speaking and everyone's eyes moved to him. "The next thing we need is an accurate idea of our resources. We need to head north quite a ways to get off the CORP radar and run some tests."

"Resources?" Zen seemed perplexed, thinking that he was still talking about gear.

"I believe he's talking about us, sirra."

Zendara nodded. "Ah, right. Gotcha."

The big man continued. "Exactly. There's an area of open land near Dubawnt Lake in northern Canada that I think would suit our needs. Rocket and I have taken other new recruits out and tested them in a similar manner and I think that would be the safest place for all of us."

Stephanie interjected. "We're not recruits here."

Rocket easily picked up on the scientist's concern. "No, you're not. But you're allies and we're all caught up in this just the same. It's better to be prepared for anything and right now we don't know what Amari and Zendara are capable of. And by her own admission, Zendara doesn't even know what she's capable of. We need to know what to expect if we're to work as a team and take down Oracle."

"Any questions?" Augur again.

It was his wife who asked. "Who's going into the ware-house?"

Rocket turned to the twins. "Which one of you has the great-est lift capacity, if say I had a large metal storage container?"

Gauss raised his hand then jerked a thumb toward his sister. "She's best with the small manipulations, the detail stuff. Girl's got finesse, I'm just the brute strength."

The young black woman laughed at her sibling's words. "Don't forget about brains. I've got the brains too." Rather than having short-cropped hair like her mother, Sinter wore hers in a jaw-length tight twist of braids, dyed bright red. In retaliation for her dig, Isaiah Bell lifted her metal chair two inches off the ground then let it drop. She punched him. "Asshole!"

Rocket shook her head and smiled. She wasn't annoyed at their antics, on the contrary she found that sometimes a mood needed to be lightened even when the situation was as serious as theirs. "Now that we've established who has the biggest stick – "

Zen whispered to Amari. "I think she means dick."

Steph snickered and Rocket continued. " – we can finalize the warehouse team. I want Augur and Hatch to stay here and see if they can put together a list of anyone else who may be loyal to the real CORP. That means old teammates we trust and those that we know are solid and suspect they may have evaded capture by Oracle's people." She turned to Sinter, Steph, and Lingua, and Zen. "I want you to start digging. I need lists of every CORP facil-ity and their exactly location. That's public information and should be easy to pull up. Lingua said the printers still work so I want maps printed of each CORP city and Guantanamo."

The human scientist of the group raised an eyebrow with skepticism. "Isn't Guantanamo a famously 'black site?'"

"Lingua can do it." Rocket pointed at the agent in question. "And don't leave a trail that will lead them to our location!"

"It was one damn time! You people are never going to let me forget that."

Augur looked at her in exasperation. "King, you got our transport blown up."

Lingua shrugged. "And yet you're all still here to yap about it. Don't worry people, I know my job."

"Don't you need me to get you to the warehouse?"

Rocket shook her head at Hatch. "Not this time. That was quite a knock you took and all three of us that are going are capa-ble of flight."

"Three?" Amari glanced from Zendara to Gauss, then back to Rocket.

The lead agent pointed back at her. "You're going, Zen is staying." Her face was almost apologetic when she looked at Zen. "I'm sorry but you said it yourself, you don't know enough about your power yet. I promise we'll work on it when we head north to Canada."

Zen nodded. "It's okay, I understand." She sighed, feeling more useless than ever. But the feeling was quickly dispelled by a rush of — something that she couldn't explain as her Q'sirrahna's fingers intertwined with hers. She turned and gave Amari a grateful smile.

Knowing and understanding Zen's fear of separation, Amari leaned close and whispered in her ear. "I'll be back. I promise. Nothing will keep us apart again." Zen nodded and looked up to find that she and her soul mate were the center of the group's attention. She didn't try to explain their exchange nor did she apologize for her fears.

Rocket glanced at her chrono, noting that it was a little less than two hours until midnight. "Okay, we've got about seven hours of darkness left to get the equipment we need and catch some shuteye. Tomorrow we'll head north. One last thing..." She trailed off and looked at the three non-CORP personnel in the room. "You three are still civilians and I'd like to protect our anonymity as much as possible from the public. I don't want someone seeing you flying around fighting what they think are 'good' CORP agents, and recognize your faces."

Stephani held her hands up and shook her head vehemently. "Oh, I'm not leaving this lab for anything."

She got a smile from Rocket. "Nor would I expect you to. But Amari and Zendara on the other hand —" She switched gaze to the two women of Q'orre.

Amari smiled. "No one will recognize us when our powers are activated."

The deep voice of Augur broke the silence that followed her declaration. "How do you mean?"

Rather than try to answer him, Amari slid her chair back and stood. Then she moved away from the table and began removing her damaged jeans and hoodie until she was standing in nothing but the ultra-black ship suit gifted by her parents. She removed the cell phone from her discarded pants and made it disappear into the fabric near her hip. When she turned back to the table of watchers, she let the gathered power in her cells flow freely. Amari's eyes and hair glowed bright white as she rose and floated a foot off the ground. The top of her head was only inches from the drop tiles in the ceiling.

Gauss whistled. "Damn, son!"

He got an elbow to the arm from his sister. "You're an idiot." Then she turned back to the display of power Amari was putting on. "But shit though."

Rocket turned to Zen. "You glow white too?"

"Uh—"

"No. For whatever reason the power seepage causes a negative image effect on our hair and eyes. So while mine glow bright white, hers are black."

Zen looked stunned. "They do?" Her Q'sirrahna nodded.

Hatch tried to picture the younger woman with glowing black eyes and shuddered. "That's some creepy shit, y'all."

"Oh, but it's a damn effective disguise." Rocket nodded with approval. "Now that we have the physical recognition covered, you two need code names."

Amari floated down and retook her seat as Zendara rolled her eyes at Rocket. "We're not one of your damn agents."

Rocket frowned. "Maybe not but at least one of you has loved ones to protect."

Zen's expression darkened with anger. "That was low, especially coming from you."

After a stare down, Rocket finally sighed and scrubbed the back of her neck. "You're right, I apologize. But here are the facts. I know you aren't agents but right now you're allies and you're in the minority. We need to work together as a team and the best most efficient way to do that is working within a system that is well-established and was proven decades ago. So please, can I get some cooperation?"

The younger woman looked away from the agent's eyes and glanced around the table full of worried individuals. "You're right, I'm sorry too. So do we get to pick our own names? I want something cool."

Hatch laughed aloud. "Girl doesn't even know what her powers are and she's already gunning for a *cool* name."

"This *girl* already saved your ass once so I'd shut it over there."

Augur bristled but Hatch only laughed again and nodded. "Fair enough."

Zendara turned to her soul mate. "Can we just use the names of our planets, paying homage?"

"Didn't y'all say you were from someplace called Reyna and Tora? Those are short enough to work easily in the middle of a fight." Rocket nodded her head, silently agreeing with Augur.

Amari massaged her right temple, trying to think. When she looked up her head was already shaking. "I don't think that would be a good idea. My mothers brought us to Earth for a reason. They gave their lives to protect us from whatever was happening on our home planets. We shouldn't risk exposure if knowledge of who we are and where we're from gets out."

"Space names would be—"

"Pretty cool." In synch as always, what Gauss started his sister finished. Then she added to the idea. "Amari, your eyes glow bright white, what about something like Nova?"

Steph looked at her friend with a big smile. "Ooh, I like it!"

"And for me?"

Both twins shrugged their shoulders and Steph contemplated an entire list of terms in her head. "Hmm…"

Amari caught their attention with one quiet word. "Sirra." When she had Zen's attention, she continued. "Your father's name was Calden T'al Baen-Tor. Calden T'al means Brave Warrior. Your mother, Iniri Allo, was named for 'beautiful darkness.' If you want to pay homage without giving us away, why don't we combine the names? T'ala for dark warrior?"

Zendara fought against too human tears at the thoughtful way Amari had met her needs. It was a small thing compared to most others in life but it meant the world to Zen to be able to connect to those parents she would never know. Even if the connection was as ephemeral as a name in the grand scheme of things. "Thank you."

Augur slapped a big meaty hand on the table, startling everyone except for his wife. She was used to the man's abrupt ways. "Now that we have that bit of business settled, welcome to the club, kid!"

Zen met his eyes and grinned. "The name is T'ala, not kid."

"Hey, why don't all of us get to pick our own names?"

"Yeah!"

The leader of their little group rolled her eyes. "Who gave you and your brother the codenames of Gauss and Sinter anyway? Were they assignments or did you get to choose?"

Imani sighed. "Assignments."

"You know that you are allowed some input. If you didn't like your codenames, why didn't you say anything?"

She gave Rocket a strange look. "When you go into the program, you don't question the guys in charge. Come on, Rocket, you've been in for decades. I thought you'd know that better than most."

She grinned at the younger woman. "On the contrary, Agent Bell, I *always* question the people in charge."

The newly christened *T'ala* snorted. "Rebel G-man, you're not as bad as I thought."

Rocket just laughed. Letting out a breath she didn't know she was holding, the Special Agent in Charge pushed her chair back. "Come on people, time is wasting and it's not going to stay dark forever." Taking a cue from their leader, everyone staggered up from the table and she pointed at two young heroes, Gauss and Nova. "You and you, with me. Everyone else knows their jobs so get to it!"

Before Amari could walk away, Zen grabbed her wrist and pulled her into a short embrace. The kiss was deep and desperate. When Zen pulled back, she whispered into her beloved's ear. "Be safe, sirra."

Rather than answer the request with words, Amari kissed her soundly again and gave a wink. Then she followed the two agents in black toward the main door of the lab, thinking idly on how she almost matched them with her outfit. Except hers was definitely "cooler."

FOR A WOMAN like Zendara Baen-Tor, orphaned and raised on a life of disappointment and skepticism, it was a new feeling to be part of a group, just as the group in question found it difficult to welcome an unknown into their ranks. CORP agents had a special bond. They forged themselves into a family in a world that mostly feared them. And for Amari, she had grown up with all the love and support she could imagine. The privilege that ensured her security was unlike any Zen had known, and also afforded her with a special insight as to her role in the world. And the more she learned about her power and the injustices found on her adopted planet, the more her heart longed to make a change. Every day that went by with her immense abilities shuttered left her with a growing sense of un-fulfillment. But that unease was soon to end. The time had come for the heroes of Earth to be born, and even re-born. By sweat or by prophesy, a ragtag group of men and women were about to find themselves as saviors in as dark a time as any that had come before.

Chapter Sixteen

LINGUA DEACTIVATED THE cameras in the area around their temporary headquarters as Rocket, Gauss, and Nova made their way outside. Rocket stood in the shadows next to the building and addressed Nova. "Can you dim that glow while we're in flight? You're pretty bright and I don't want to give away our position before we've even begun."

"It's too bad your suit doesn't have a hood or cowl or something."

Amari looked at the man who nearly blended into the night with his dark skin and black suit. Amari felt ancient in the face of Gauss's youthful exuberance even though he was probably only a few years younger than her. "This isn't a comic book and I'm not a vigilante running around in the night. This suit is part of a matched set that belonged to my adoptive parents when they came to this planet decades ago."

He laughed quietly and held up a hand. "Chill out there, Nova. I don't need the run down on your *supersuit*. I was just wishful thinking."

Rocket interrupted their banter. "Have you flown formation with anyone else before?" Amari shook her head. "Since I'm the only one who knows where we're going, I'll take the lead. I want you on my wings, just like you see geese or those fighter planes flying. Watch my six, and I'll watch yours. Savvy?"

"Sure thing, Rocket. Dad says he trusts you more than anyone else but family so I do too."

Rocket turned to Nova and received a serious look in return. "I'll trust you, but I'm not nearly as worried about myself and Zen as I am about Steph. If anything happens to her..." She left the statement unfinished but Rocket didn't need further warning.

"Shovel talk noted. Let's go, and stay close!" She leaped into the air and was quickly followed by Gauss and Nova. The three dark-suited shapes hurled through the night directly west from their current position. What would normally take twenty minutes to drive by car was only about five with the uninterrupted speed of their flight. Rocket hovered in place about thirty yards directly above the warehouse when she reached it and the other two did the same.

"How do we get in? Do you still have the access codes? What if they've got people on the inside ready to ambush us?"

Rocket didn't answer him for a few seconds, instead looking at the layout below. The warehouse was surrounded by a tall fence topped with barbed wire. It was also well lit so that very few shadows existed around the building. She pointed down at the roof. "That looks like corrugated steel, can you confirm?"

Gauss focused on the surface below and nodded. "Yup, sure is. I can peel it back like a can opener if you want."

"I would imagine doing that would make a lot of noise, do we need a distraction?"

Rocket nodded, barely seen in the darkness. "Exactly what I was thinking. We do need a distraction and I've got just the thing." She thought of the distance she'd have to cover and the amount of time she'd need to get back to their location from downtown. "I'm going to need you two to stay here and I'll be back in five minutes." She pointed at Gauss. "Mark your chrono. At three minutes in, I want you to open up a ten by ten foot section then wait for me to return."

Nova looked at her with concern. "What are you going to do, and is it wise for you to go?"

"I'm going to blow a hole through the water tower that sits atop the CORP headquarters. That should cause some problems for them, at least temporarily. And I'm going because I know this city a lot better than either of you. I also know how my old team thinks well enough to evade them if necessary."

"Works for me."

Rocket looked back at the other CORP agent. "Mark your chrono." Then she took off like her namesake, blasting through the night toward downtown Chicago.

She stayed low enough not to interfere with local air traffic but high enough not to plow through most buildings. Once she reached the downtown area, Rocket was forced to fly around the taller skyscrapers. When the CORP building was within her sights, she increased her speed exponentially, aiming right for the water tower. For security purposes, the area around the CORP building was kept free from structures so she wasn't worried about debris fallout. Realistically the only thing that would happen was a whole lot of water raining down on the city block below. Exactly as planned, Rocket and her field of near-invulnerability crashed through the center of the rooftop water tower creating a four foot hole on the entrance and exit sides for water to pour out in a flood. Deed done, she quickly turned and blasted back toward the warehouse near Midway Airport. She was out of earshot before the sirens began going off downtown.

When she arrived at their target location minutes later, she was happy to see that Gauss had the roof opened exactly as promised and that both he and Nova stood by for further instruction. All three flew closer and peered into the darkened interior. "The next problem we face is that there is a laser grid inside that is meant to detect movement near the floor. Fortunately the system was designed by Lingua and I have the code to shut it off. Unfortunately the access panel is inside the main door. There are also sonar-driven sensors on all the doors."

Amari peered into the darkness below. "I don't see any lasers."

Gauss's voice rumbled quietly, a shadow of his father's deep tone. "That's a common myth perpetrated by TV shows. Laser security uses infrared which is invisible to the naked eye."

"Well that's just great. Do either of you have something to see these lasers with or another special power?"

Rocket shook her head. "No, but I helped Lingua set it up so I know where the laser, the photodetector, and all the mirrors are positioned, so I should be able to fly around them to get to the keypad by the door. When I bring the system down, we'll go through and fill a crate with supplies and that's where Gauss comes in." She looked at the young agent. "You'll be responsible for getting the steel crate of gear back to the school."

"And me?"

Rocket grinned at Nova. "You're the backup, our ace in the hole."

Nova thought for a second then grabbed Rocket's arm before the agent could fly down through the hole. "Won't the rogues be expecting this? I mean—someone is pulling the strings from the top and the ones on your team who knew you best would know that acquiring weapons would be a priority. I find it hard to believe that it could be this easy."

"No, I'm sure no one would have—shit! You're right."

"You've got a telepath on your team, don't you?" Gauss's voice was quiet, realizing exactly the problem that just occurred to their team leader.

"Minder knows. Ethical or not, I'm certain she's read every member of our team about anything concerning security or protocol. Plan B it is then. Let's do a little test. Gauss, that top crate closest to us is not in range of the lasers, try to lift it a few inches."

She pointed at the top of a tall stack of crates, barely illuminated by the full moon shining through the large opening.

Not even two seconds later, Gauss frowned. "I can't. Pretty sure they've got a barrier up."

"Isn't this just a bucket of fuck!"

The younger man laughed. "Now you sound like my dad."

Nova looked at the frustrated lead agent. "What if I carry you? Can we still make it around the lasers?"

Rocket sighed. "I suppose that's our only choice. Humiliating, but feasible."

Amari laughed but noticed her power was a little drained. "Before we head in, I spent a lot of power earlier with the energy blast—"

"What energy blast?" Rocket's eyes narrowed at learning new information about her unlikely teammate while they were in the middle of an operation.

"When we were fighting earlier, the Chromodec called Sonica was unwittingly funneling a lot of power into me. It was more instinct than anything but when I started to feel overly full, so to speak, I pointed my fist at her and some sort of energy beam hit her in the chest. It looked like what came out of Zen, er, T'ala and me in the park that night."

Mouth open, Rocket started to respond before thinking better of it and shaking her head instead. "We'll talk more about this back at the base. What do you need me to do?"

"Augur mentioned that you have enhanced strength and partial invulnerability in your flying but he also said you could do a kinetic punch too. I need you to hit me so I can juice up."

Gauss laughed quietly. "You sound like one of those 'roid ragers!"

Nova shrugged. "Yes, well, it's effective and fast." She turned to their leader. "On the chin please, not that it really matters where you hit me. The effect will be the same."

The youngest member of the trio flew back a few feet as Rocket cocked her fist and launched a "rocket punch" directly into Nova's face. Both CORP agents were left slack jawed to find Rocket's fist stopped abruptly at the corner of the alien woman's mouth. There was no jarring sensation, no bounce back. One second her fist was in motion and the next it wasn't. Rocket pulled her hand back and stared at Nova in amazement. "Hot damn, would you look at that!"

For Nova, she took a second to suck in a breath at the power of the kinetic hit. "Whew, you pack quite a punch but that was exactly what I needed." When neither of the other two agents could find words to speak, Nova elaborated. "Kinetic energy. Your molecular and mechanical frequency was instantly matched and absorbed by my cells the second your energy touched me. Absorbed and amplified."

"Impressive."

Nova rolled her eyes. "Noted. Now how do you want to do this? Should I carry you like a baby, or maybe piggyback?"

Rocket tried to remember the layout of the lasers and which way had more clearance between them, horizontal or vertical. "If I remember, they start low and crisscross the main space. They only cover about half the height of the warehouse. I think it would work best if you can remain horizontal and I ride on your back."

"Yee haw!" When the two women looked at Gauss he shrugged. "I may live in LA now but I grew up in Dallas. Still got my spurs and hat at Mom and Dad's house." He waved his hand at the two women. "Giddyup now. As Mom is fond of saying, time's a wastin!"

Nova turned in the air so she was horizontal facing down. Rocket flew over to her and situated herself in the dip at Nova's lower spine before the swell of her ass. "I'm ready."

"You're bareback." Gauss's quiet laughter had both women huffing in exasperation as Nova moved them forward into the warehouse.

It took fifteen minutes for Rocket to guide the other woman safely down to where the security pad was located next to the side door. The CORP agent knew where the mirrors were located in the walls and used those as a guide to the laser locations. There were times when they both had to huddle together in as tight a ball as possible to fit through an area with mirrors fairly close together. They probably would have been fine but it was better to be safe than sorry. Once they were on the ground, Rocket quickly typed in the ten-digit code and called out to Gauss. "We're ready for you."

"Is Nova going to come get me?"

Rocket quickly flew back up to the ceiling. "No, apparently the eloptic dampener is connected to the security system. Let's go."

On the ground, Rocket picked out an empty metal crate that was stacked off to the side of the warehouse. It was about six foot cubed in size and plenty big enough to hold what she was hoping to bring back, but not so large it was unwieldy for Gauss. She pointed. "Bring that and follow me. She walked with purpose down the aisles of tall metal shelving, seeming as though she knew the place by heart. When she got to the third row, she pointed to the left side of the main aisle. "Down there are helmets, communicators, bags, and MREs. The large field duffels are on the third shelf up right here on the end. I want you to start filling them with enough for the entire team. Bring spare suites in all sizes as well. I want gear for at least twenty." Nova nodded and flew up to start tossing giant duffel bags down to the floor.

Gauss followed Rocket farther into the warehouse until they came to another section of giant scaffolding. Instead of wood crates like the area where they left Nova, they found secured metal containers with electronic locks. "What's all this?"

Rocket walked over to one of the containers and placed her hand on the digital locking plate. The indicator light turned from red to green and the lid gave a hiss as it lifted up slightly, split down the middle, and slid open to each side. She reached inside and pulled out a single CORP tech explosive device, which was just a fancy-type of grenade with a remote detonator. There were hundreds in the crate nestled in motion-dampening packing layers. "This is victory."

The young agent looked worried. "I know that Mom and Dad trust you and all but even I know we can't win back our cities if we blow them up."

The lead agent shook her head. "I know you grew up in the country, Isaiah. Tell me, what did your parents do if there was a snake in the garden?"

He laughed. "Kill it, cut off the head, and throw it in the weeds for the other critters to have a nice meal."

"We're not going to take back our cities, Agent Bell. We're going after the snake in our garden. We may not have the organized manpower nor do we have the fancy security Oracle has down on that godforsaken island, but what we *do* have will make a nice dent."

He set the crate down as she moved along the row and opened another metal box. "Don't forget about our super-ladies. That asshole Maza isn't going to know what hit him."

Rocket waved for him to move the crate farther down the

line. "Set it here and start filling. I want rifles, pistols, ammunition, and body armor on the bottom. We'll throw some of those packing layers in and put the more delicate stuff on top."

"Hey, Rocket!"

The agent in charge was busy pulling the grenades out of the packing layer one by one, setting each carefully on the ground. She yelled back to Nova. "What's up?"

"I've got a crate over here labeled 'drones.' Is that something we can use? Doesn't Hatch need to see an area to teleport in?" Nova came around the corner carrying two duffle bags nearly the size of her own body in each hand.

Rocket smiled. "Yeah, I think those would be a good 'just in case' item. Grab a few, and check out Ten-B for overnight field kids. You'll see something that looks like loaded packs. Those have the things we'll need to stay at our new base." When Nova hesitated, she waved a hand near the big metal crate. "Just drop the duffels there and get the other stuff. I want to be out of here in the next quarter hour. It won't take long for that distraction to hold them, nor to start checking the city for anything unusual."

"Yes, ma'am!" Nova grinned, floated up in the air, and took off with speed back down the main aisle.

A FEW HAND grenades, some drones, and a selection of unappetizing military food doesn't sound like much when our heroes are trying to disrupt a plan that has been in the making for a decade. But while tech, gear, and weapons went a long way toward winning a war, a key deciding factor was heart. Our team of people, six CORP agents, two alien women from a distant star, and one normal human scientist may not have been the ideal team, but every single one of them had a passion to uphold truth, maintain justice, and fight for those who couldn't fight for themselves. And there wasn't a single one, including the lone human, who wouldn't lay down their own life if it meant saving millions of people all over the country.

"SET THE CRATE on the roof for now. There aren't any cameras up here that will tip off SIMoN or anyone else who may be looking for us. Nova and I will keep an eye on it. I want you to take the maintenance badge and go down and double-time Hatch up here to teleport this crate inside. On my mark—" She brought her wrist up to synchronize her chrono and Gauss did the same. "—I want the barrier brought down in eight minutes, and, go!" They both set their chronos and Gauss took off over the side of the building to get his mom. While he was gone, Nova took a seat on the edge of the building to stare north toward the Chicago skyline. She always found the twinkling lights beautiful at night. Rocket remained standing and alert though she too watched the same direction.

Both their thoughts were interrupted a few minutes later. "Someone looking to make a delivery?" Nova glanced back over her shoulder and saw Sinter carrying Hatch up to the top of the building on the adjacent side from where they were sitting. She stood and walked over to where they touched down near the giant crate.

Rocket frowned at Sinter. "What took you so long and where's your brother?"

The younger woman held up her wrist and smiled. "No worries, we synched before I came up. We've got—" she glanced at the small screen "—ninety-three seconds before the barrier comes down."

Her mother answered the second question. "We did a little rearranging when Isaiah explained the size of the crate. T'ala showed us a room where we can store some of the chairs and tables to make more room in the lab for essential gear." She patted her long-time friend's arm. "You worry too much, Rocky. We're all professionals and know our job here." When Rocket glanced at Nova, Hatch smiled. "There are no fools in our group. The ones that don't know will learn quickly."

Two minutes later they were all back in the lab with the crate and the barrier was safely in place. Augur, Gauss, Sinter, and Lingua got busy pulling bags and boxes from the large crate and organizing the items onto shelves for storage. Rocket called out before they could get too carried away. "I want the ammunition and explosives put back into the crate and sealed once the rest is pulled out. It should protect us a bit if something unfortunate happens."

"Aye aye, Captain!"

Rocket rolled her eyes at Lingua. "You're such a smart ass." She walked over to where Steph was organizing a stack of maps on the table. "Were any of you able to come up with usable intel?"

Steph looked startled at the question. "You're asking me?"

"Well, you were here and everyone else seems to be preoccupied. Not to mention the fact that you're smarter than most of the people in this lab and I trust you to know exactly what I'm talking about. So, yes."

The scientist blushed at the compliment. "Me, Zenda—um, T'ala, and Sinter were able to print maps of all the cities that have CORP teams. I believe Lingua printed another pile for the Guantanamo facility. And I'm not sure what Augur and Hatch were doing, looked like they were making a list. You do realize there are fifty-nine CORP cities don't you? How are we supposed to take them all back?"

A wry smile quirked the corners of Rocket's mouth. "Ah, but we don't have to take all of them back. The only ones that are an issue are the ones overrun by rogue agents. And even then, my plan isn't about winning back cities. It's about going after the person in charge of all those rogues."

"Maza? But that's..." Steph trailed off and shook her head with worry.

In an unusual show of physical affection, Agent Romy Danes put both hands on Steph's shoulders and looked her in the eyes. "Hey, we'll keep you as safe as we can though all of this, okay?"

Stephanie sighed and glanced off to the far side of the large lab where Zendara and Amari sat on the floor with their backs to the wall. Zen's right hand was gripped tightly in Amari's left and they appeared to be talking quietly between themselves. "What about them?"

Rather than the usual reassurance, Rocket snorted instead. "I have a feeling your friends will be the ones keeping *us* safe."

"I mean after all of this is settled." They locked eyes, both knowing how serious the discovery of the two alien women of such power really was.

"I'll do my best to mitigate the fallout *if* their true nature is discovered by the government higher up. I won't sell them out, if that's what you're asking."

Stephanie watched Romy's eyes and her breath caught as she remembered their time together the previous night. It seemed so far away after all that had happened in such a short period of time. "And what about you? Will I see you again when this is over?"

The agent's gaze softened and she nodded. "I'll do my best to make that happen as well. I know I bolted at an inopportune time but to answer your question from this morning — God, that seems like forever ago! But anyway, I look forward to seeing more of you when people aren't trying to kill me."

Understanding the image that the lead agent was trying to project, Steph stepped back out of Rocket's grip. "Good. Me too." She smiled, happy despite all that had happened over the last twenty-four hours. When Rocket was called back to the crate by Augur, Steph noticed a few duffel bags of MREs sitting on the floor and dragged one into the little kitchenette. She couldn't fly or hack computer networks so she may as well do something useful.

On the far side of the large lab, a much more private conversation was happening. "I'm worried for you, sirra."

"Me?" Zen pulled back to peer into Amari's dark eyes. "I'm not the one who keeps leaving and putting myself into danger."

"But that's my point! You don't know anything about your powers and I've been using mine for the past eight years. You barely know how to fly. What if something happens to you?"

Zen's pale brows drew down as she scowled. "I can take care of myself. If you want to start throwing numbers around, I've been doing *that* for thirteen years now — " Her words cut off when she felt Amari's grip tighten and she saw shimmering tears pool in the other woman's eyes. All the building tension abruptly drained from Zen's body. "I'm sorry. I worry too and I'll be as careful as I can. Besides, Rocket and Augur said we were going to head north tomorrow to train. You can show me more then."

Amari sighed and looked away. "There will never be enough time to prepare myself for the thought of you dying or being injured. I hate this!"

"Hey..." Zen waited for her Q'sirrahna to look at her again. "We'll get through this together, okay? I don't want to fight with you. It's almost as if I can feel it when you're upset and it hurts me here." She rubbed the center of her chest, much the way she used to do when she'd feel that familiar *pull*.

"I feel the same way. I think our soul mate connection affects us in ways that will take us a long while to fully grasp." She smiled. "In a way, I like being connected to you like that. It makes me feel..." She struggled to find the words.

"Less alone."

A brilliant smile washed across Amari's face and Zen's breath caught. "Yes! That's it exactly. And I don't want to fight either."

Zen leaned closer and whispered near Amari's ear. "What *would* you like to do then?"

The doctor of biochemistry spared a glance to where the rest of their group went about their business on the other side of the room. All the CORP members were busy pulling out, stacking, and creating an inventory of the retrieved weapons and gear. Satisfied that no one was paying them any mind, she leaned close enough for her word to whisper across Zen's lips. "This." Then she met her in a slow and sweet exploration. It was a much needed connection after all the upheaval they had experienced in the past few days. The kiss was languid and full of simmering heat though neither let it get too far out of control. It was the worst kind of torture knowing that they'd have to wait to fully connect again with circumstances the way they were. But with any luck they would be together again soon, completely, and forever.

Chapter Seventeen

IT HAS BEEN quite a whirlwind for our soul mates. Nay, a maelstrom of emotion and action. For the two women grown from babies created with love and matter in the rose light of Q'orre, they have yet to fully understand the level of their connection. And no, they haven't forgotten the passion that lurks below the surface at all times. But they know that trapped as they are among fellow heroes in a basement deep below the university campus, it is impossible to be as close as they'd like. The supplies that Rocket, Nova, and Gauss brought back from the warehouse included sleeping rolls and mats, which the group was forced to find nooks and corners in the large lab to lay them out. It seemed everyone wanted a small bit of privacy within the group. But it was hard, so very hard. Amari and Zendara needed to be close to each other in a way that eclipsed all others. It was a physical pull they each felt deep inside their chests. Amari surmised that the tightness would ease as their bodies got used to the newly deepened bond but in the meantime they had to accommodate it or be left uncomfortable and distracted. Both of which would not do in the fight to come.

FOLLOWING THE LEAD of Augur and Hatch, the married couple of the group, Amari and Zen zipped their sleeping bags together so they could hold each other as they slept. The passion remained simmering beneath the surface, tempered due to the circumstances and lack of privacy. To help assuage it a bit, they exchanged whispered kisses and sighs in the dark of the large lab. Those small sounds were covered easily by quiet murmuring between Romy and Steph, and by the slightly louder snores emanating from the two Bell men.

The next morning dawned much too early for a group that had stayed up way too late. Lingua spent the first hour tweaking the coms for each helmet to make sure they were on a separate and unbreakable network. The rest packed gear to be away for the entire day. It was decided the night before that Lingua and Steph would stay at the lab monitoring the CORP chatter on the channel that Lingua had tapped into. She had orders to continue searching for a way to find out which cities were compromised, and Steph was staying behind for her own safety.

"I don't get it, how will Hatch be able to teleport us to this Dubawnt Lake if she can't see the area? Aren't you worried about people, animals, or structures in the way?"

"Air drop."

Zen raised an eyebrow at Rocket's response. "What the fuck is that?"

Hatch laughed. "Simple. I open a portal high in the sky. There are no planes that cross that part of the country and if I go high enough we don't have to worry about birds. I open and Rocket goes through to scout for me. Now that we have helmets and they're synched to one another, it's nothing for her to push an image through to me so I can see the area.

Amari shrugged. "Makes sense. All right, I'm ready."

"Me too!" Zen's enthusiasm was almost incongruous in comparison with her sometimes recalcitrant demeanor.

Gauss grinned. "Look at y'all so eager to go learn to be heroes!"

Zen rolled her eyes, suddenly back to her normal self. "Whatever."

"Enough with the antics, time to get this show on the road. Augur, Hatch, Mag-twins, Nova, and T'ala, get ready. Once I confirm the coast clear, Hatch is going to bring the rest of you through. Lingua and Steph, keep at it until we return. I want to hear some good news."

"Geez, when she says all your names like that, I kind of wish I had a code name too!"

Lingua grinned at Steph. "Oh, I can think of a few things that Rocky would like to call you — "

"Zip it, King!"

No one had a chance to say more because Hatch quickly opened a portal to blue sky and Rocket dove through. Two minutes later her voice came over the com. "All clear."

Unlike the rest of the team, Nova and T'ala didn't have helmets. But along with the other gear cleared out of the warehouse, they also found the specialized communicators that the CORP used. Virtually invisible, they fit inside the ear canals and were extremely difficult to damage or dislodge in a fight. They were also given wrist comps, which strapped securely to the inside of the left wrists and looked like a cross between a smart watch and a smart phone. They were programmed along with the helmets when Lingua did a run down on all their gear.

The air was cool when they stepped through the portal, being fourteen hundred miles north of Chicago and two hundred miles east of Yellowknife, in Nunavut, not that Nova and T'ala felt much of it. And all of them were wearing suits that were thick enough to be more than just armor. T'ala was the first to speak. "So what do we do now?"

Rocket touched down. "Well first things first, flame on."

Nova's confusion matched that of her soul mate. "What?"

Sinter snorted at the bewildered looks sported by both women. "Don't y'all watch movies?"

Understanding washed over T'ala first so she explained it to Nova. "She means the superhero movie that came out when we were kids. The one with the guy made of fire."

Nova just shrugged. "Honestly when I wasn't studying back then, I was out hiking and taking pictures. I've never been one for television."

"Figures." T'ala grinned at her, understanding that her beloved had grown up as a bit of a nerd. "Anyway, they want us to make our head and faces glow with power."

"Ah, I see." She immediately complied but T'ala wore a pained look at her lack of skill, still in the dark as to how her powers worked. "You have to feel that spark inside you and touch it. I believe it's connected to that warmth we feel in our chest, focus on that warmth." T'ala closed her eyes and everyone stood waiting for something to happen. "Can you feel it, Q'sir-rahna?"

The other woman's voice was quiet in the windy Canadian north. "Yes."

"Just like when we flew to Maine...touch it, let it wash over you. Imagine yourself as something incredibly light, floating above the ground."

It seemed so simple to everyone else, though it probably didn't feel that way to T'ala. "Okay." As soon as she said the word, she rose into the air about a foot and her hair glowed like eerie black flame. "Now what?"

"Open your eyes, sirra."

She did and the black glowing depths of those eyes made Gauss take a step back. "Dayum!"

Suddenly realizing that she was no longer on the ground, T'ala's mouth dropped open. "Whoa, cool!" She shook her head.

"Seriously though, this is never gonna get old!"

Rocket chimed in before anyone else could comment. "Now that we've got 'float one-oh-one' covered, I want us to split into two teams. Sinter and Augur, I want you to work with T'ala on her flight capability." When the two alien women gave Rocket a questioning look, she elaborated. "Augur and Hatch have both trained more recruits than anyone else here and while he may not be able to fly, he knows the best training techniques. Sinter can be the flight back up to catch our new hero should something unpredictable happen."

Nova gazed back at her, trusting that the special agent in charge knew what she was talking about. "And the rest of us?"

The grin that split Agent Danes's lips was one that only Hatch had seen before. It promised an interesting few hours of training at the very least. "We're going to find out exactly what you're capable of." With those words she quickly shut the face shield of her helmet.

Before they began, Hatch teleported her husband, daughter, and T'ala about a mile into the distance so the newest hero's training wouldn't be affected by what was going on with the other group. Then she went back to perch on a tall outcropping of rock while Rocket, Gauss, and Nova took to the air. Out of curiosity, Nova addressed the younger man that floated next to her. "How is it you fly, anyway? Is it magnetic levitation, like the trains?"

Gauss shook his head. "Actually, my power allows me to manipulate and amplify the magnetic field around me. The stronger the field, the stronger I can be. So I'm not actually magnetic, superconductive, or diamagnetic. My sister and I are simply hosts for the scalar energy that allow us to work with magnetism specifically."

"Can you do anything besides fly or lift things that are susceptible to magnetism?"

He grinned. "Sure. Watch this." Nova watched as he withdrew a handful of marble-size ball bearings with his left hand. He picked one from his palm and tossed it up into the air and the metal sphere froze in place.

"And?" Both her and Rocket watched as the small metal object zipped away and was quickly lost from sight. A noise resembling a gunshot sounded a few seconds later as it broke the sound barrier and a shower of rock exploded in the distance, opposite the direction the others had gone to train. Nova's jaw dropped. "That's no different than a bullet, other than it doesn't have a sharp piercing end. You could kill someone with that!" The younger man's face turned deadly serious. "Yes, I can."

"What's the speed on that and what else can you do?" Rocket needed to see the full potential of her entire team, not just Nova. Since she'd never actually seen the twins in action, she was inspecting the mag-twins as much as she was the two alien women.

"It varies based on the size and shape of the object. It can be as slow as I want but the fastest one of my objects has been clocked is fifteen hundred miles per hour. The ball bearings are easiest to store and use, and the steel is hardened to make a good projectile. Now flying ourselves is a lot different. We're a lot bigger and so far both me and my sister have only hit a max speed of three hundred and fifty miles per hour."

Rocket gave him a look that was unreadable. "How is that possible? When I fly a little over Mach One, I have a nearly impenetrable scalar kinetic field that surrounds me so I can withstand the g-forces involved, as well as anything that may impact my person during flight."

He shrugged. "We don't have anything quite like that. I mean...I wouldn't want to fly through any buildings like you do. But when we fly it's like we're surrounded by a field of magnetic energy that protects us. On top of that we have specially reinforced suits that help mitigate the g-force pressure."

Rocket nodded. "I've got the same kind of suit. My top speed is about what Nova mentioned for her flight. I've hit eight hundred and fifty-six miles per during optimal conditions." She turned to look at Nova next. "Now you—you said that you can absorb any kind of energy?"

"Absorb and amplify. I don't know the exact amplification ratio, it seems to vary with each different kind of energy transference. But yes, kinetic, thermal, radioactive, electrical, soundwaves, I appear to absorb them all."

"So my kinetic punch, guns, Gauss's balls—"

"Seriously?" He leveled a look at her and grimaced.

Nova resisted the urge to snicker. Instead she nodded solemnly with only a hint of a smirk on her lips. "Yes. I can show you if you'd like..."

Rocket sighed. "Sure, but I want to run some aerial drills first."

They spent the next hour and a half running drills and during that time Rocket showed the two younger ones in her group some different tips and tricks while flying. Hatch had teleported to where Augur and Sinter were training with T'ala to help out there.

Once Rocket had an estimate of both Gauss and Nova's flying capabilities, she pulled the whole team. "What do you say we do some team simulations?"

"What do you have in mind, Rocky?" Hatch stood between her husband and son and while she was pretty tall for a woman, she was dwarfed by the men around her.

"Let's team up on Nova and T'ala." She addressed the two women in question directly. "You've told us about what you can do, let's see what your weaknesses are." She glanced around the gathered group. "Obviously we'll have to be more careful here since as a group we have the potential to do real harm."

Over the next hour they tried a variety of things to get the better of the two alien women. Hatch tried opening a portal right in front of T'ala while she was flying and have the exit facing the rocky ground. T'ala wasn't skilled enough yet to evade during flight but rather than do any damage to the younger woman, she simply stood up from the crater her impact left on the ground and ran superfast to Hatch before she teleport away. She left the agent with a big smudge of dirt on the face shield of her helmet before jumping into the air, albeit a little wobbly, and flying off to help out Nova.

Meanwhile, as Rocket was distracting Nova, the mag twins were busy with their own plan. Gauss pulled nearby iron up from the ground using brute force alone and crushed the pieces against one another. After that he spun the ore around using alternating polarity until all the non-magnetic rock was spun away and handed the metal mass off to his sister. Then as Nova paused nearby after leading Rocket into an outcropping of rock, Sinter bent and flattened the remaining ore and molded it into a crude mask around Nova's face. The results were instantaneous. Nova clawed at the steel but had no way to break free, nor to see either twin to force one to release the iron that had cut off both sight and air.

There wasn't even air for her to scream but her all-encompassing terror was answered by a panicked and pissed off T'ala. "Sirra!" She clumsily flew to her soul mate's side and attempted to help bend the plate away but it went all the way around Nova's head and had no points where either woman could get their fingers in to grab it. T'ala's heart clenched as her Q'sir-rahna's fear and panic beat at her from within. She spun around and dove in midair for the first twin she could reach. As soon as she hit him, they crashed to the ground. "She can't breathe, take it off!" While his helmet protected him from concussion, the impact still hurt and her grip on Gauss's arms was bruising even through the suit.

Sinter immediately realized the danger her brother was in while at the mercy of a panicking, untrained person of power and quickly removed the metal from Nova's face. "It's off! T'ala, you can let him go now, she's safe."

She was off him like a shot and ran over to where Nova was just touching down. Her concern was palpable to all who watched the glowing black disappear to leave spikey blond hair in its place. Her hands were gentle against Nova's cheeks and the others turned away from such a personal show of affection. Augur offered a hand up to his son and the younger Bell immediately accepted it. Gauss removed his helmet and rubbed the back of his head with his free hand as everyone else raised their faceplate. "Remind me never to piss either of them off again."

His sister raised her eyebrows at him. "Right?"

Before they could discuss it further, Rocket called out to the entire team. "Bring it in people." All seven of them took seats on a rocky outcropping and Rocket address the group. "I saw both good and bad just now. The good parts include Nova's use of the environment around her to help evade and hide during flight, T'ala's quick switch between powers to confuse whoever she is matched up against, and the twins' creative use of their power to nullify someone who is immune to nearly all offensive abilities. We also witnessed firsthand a few of Nova and T'ala's weaknesses."

Augur answered. "Passive air blockage. It was well done in that she couldn't use her strength to break free."

Sinter looked to the older agent, the woman who was practically a legend within the CORP. "You said a few, what was the other?"

It was her mother who answered. "Panic."

Rocket pointed at Hatch. "Exactly. Panic will get not just you killed, but can compromise everyone on your team." She focused on the two non-agents. "I know you don't have the training that we do, and things are even more difficult because you seem to be connected emotionally on some deeper level, but we really need to work on not panicking when fear takes control. Also, both of you should think of ways you can avoid situations like the one Nova was just in."

Nova sighed. "I saw it coming. I think if I would have put my hand up to block it from wrapping so tightly around my face I could have easily freed myself. But I didn't even think about that as an option before it was on me. I didn't have leverage to pry it off."

"Yes, and it's something you and T'ala really need to think about going forward. This may be our only time we can practice as a team and T'ala can learn about her abilities. So you'll both have to take what you've learned here and do your best to mitigate the negatives in a future confrontation with the rogues." After waiting a few seconds to really let the lesson sink in, Rocket moved on. "Let's split up again. Augur, Hatch, and Gauss, I want you to resume flight instruction with T'ala. I'll take Sinter with me and Nova since this twin is a little less beat up. I want to see a demonstration of Nova's absorption power now."

The four people mentioned teleported away into the distance. The lead agent looked at Nova expectantly and the younger woman nodded. "I'm going to head off about a click to the northeast. I want you two to take up equidistant positions from me and each other. Once in position, Sinter will shoot at you."

"Sounds good, boss."

A few minutes later everyone was in position and Sinter pulled her own steel ball bearing from a pouch at her waist. No sooner had it left her hand when a loud crack sounded as it reached top speed. Because she was used to tests, Nova knew exactly when the projectile hit her but there was no discomfort involved. Instead she got her usual power rush from the absorbed kinetic energy. Nova glanced down just in time to see the steel ball fall to the ground below her and roll into a crevasse between two large rocks. She called out over her com. "That was tasty, thanks, Sinter."

"All right, I want Nova to move up about two hundred feet and I want Sinter to take her old position."

The young Agent Bell responded first. "Roger that."

Once in position Rocket spoke again. "Now, Nova, I'm going to pour on the speed and head your way. I'm going to come in very hot and hit you head on. Agent Bell is going to be below to play catcher in case one of us falls."

Nova's voice had a worried quality. "Are you sure you want

to do that? I mean, if I absorb every bit of your forward momentum, you're going to plummet some two hundred feet to the ground. That's a good size drop for Sinter to catch you. You could pull her arms out of socket."

Rocket grinned unseen within the confines of her helmet. "We'll be fine. Worst case scenario, she can grab me using the trace amounts of metal within my suit. You can do that, right?"

Her voice came back to them both loud and clear over the coms. "Sure can. But remember, I've got the finesse and my brother has the brute strength that would probably be better for something like that."

"I trust you. On my mark. Ready?" They each chimed in.

"Ready."

"Ready, Rocket!"

She was off like a shot. Rocket flew outward in a wide circle, careful to avoid the other people training in the distance, and rapidly built up her speed. When she thought she was going fast enough, she turned back toward the two waiting people and aimed straight for Nova. There was no jarring impact, no rumbling of disturbance within Rocket's scalar field. One moment it was there and the next it was gone and she was falling through the air with no power. Three words could be heard by all over the com channel. "What the hell?"

Rocket was safe enough because as promised Sinter had grabbed her mid-air. But when they craned their heads to look back up at Nova, she was glowing like her namesake. Her mouth even had light spilling from between the minute crevasses separating her gritted teeth. Before anyone could ask what was wrong, she yelled over the com to her soul mate. "T'ala!"

The other woman stopped what she was doing and flew haltingly toward the glowing woman, shielding her eyes from the bright light. "Sirra, what is it?" No sooner had she gotten the words out when Nova pointed both fists at her and let loose with a bright beam of energy that took T'ala straight in the chest. T'ala's own black flame flared into a darkness that was the equal and opposite of Nova's light output. Understanding what was happening based on Nova's previous explanation of her powers, Rocket yelled over the com. "Nova, fly north and help T'ala get rid of that energy! I don't want Oracle to pick up an energy flare at our location when you two start amplifying this beyond what you can toss back and forth."

In the blink of an eye, Nova had T'ala wrapped in her arms

and took off as fast as possible, heading north and leaving the distinctive rumble of a sonic boom in their wake. After about ten seconds, the woman surrounded by the black glow could no longer hold the amplified power and she released it back to her Q'sirrahna. As Nova absorbed and amplified the power once again, it increased her speed faster than she'd ever gone before and the air roared around them. The various lakes and smaller bodies of water below became a blur as they traveled north overland toward the sea. Fifteen minutes later they broke over open water just off the coast of Nunavut and Nova held her soul mate even tighter. Face to face, Nova and T'ala, or the two refugee aliens known as Amari and Zendara, laced their hands together and pointed them upward. The power release was immediate and a great white beam shot into the sky above them. It was so massive that both women knew without a doubt that most major governments around the world would pick up on the energy signature. T'ala's words perfectly summed both their reactions. "Well shit. I think our training session is done."

"Yeah, probably. We need to get back as soon as possible. You okay to fly on your own?"

T'ala smiled. "I still wobble a bit."

Nova laced together the fingers of her left hand with T'ala's right hand. "I won't let go."

Despite letting off the pressure of amassed power, both women were plenty charged for the flight back. Holding Nova's hand to steady herself in flight, T'ala had no problems flying back under her own power. They didn't bother speaking on the return trip since the speed of their flight would have made it hard to hear even with their coms.

They found the rest of the group standing in a huddle. Rocket looked up at their arrival and the two glowing negative images touched down on the ground. "I've already alerted Lingua that our arrival is imminent. This place is going to be crawling with operatives soon so we have to bail." She touched a button on her watch and looked up at Hatch. "Ten seconds, on my mark...now."

Less than a minute later the entire team was standing in their lab hideout below the university. Professional agent persona set aside for the time being, Isaiah walked up to Zendara and punched her in the arm. "Well that was pretty badass y'all!"

The blonde punk standing in an alien ship suit couldn't help grinning in agreement. "Fuck yes it was! Did you see how fast we flew away? When Amari shot me with that first beam it was—I was..." Words failed her.

"Drunk on power."

Zen snapped her fingers and pointed at her soul mate. "Yeah, that's it exactly!"

The eldest Bell wasn't one to let his guard down so easy. Augur's voice rumbled with concern. "It was like a damn bomb went off. Where were you when it finally released?"

"We'd just made it to open water."

Rocket whistled. "That's about two hundred and fifty miles away, and definitely faster than your previously stated top speed."

The behemoth of an agent was still curious. He ran a hand over the smooth dark skin on top of his head. "Do you know what the energy output from that light show was?"

Amari shook her head. "I don't. I'm not even sure how I'd go about measuring something like that, or even what it could do to solid matter. Based on what happened to one of the rogue Chromodecs in my condo, I'd say it hits like solid matter. It certainly didn't burn them or catch the hallway on fire. As far as strength, we can guess the energy output based on what the input is and increasing that by about twenty percent to account for my average amplification."

Rocket shook her head slowly back and forth. "They thoroughly tested me back when I first joined Black Badge. They told me I could blow up the side of a mountain if I wanted to and left it at that. I'm sure my destructive capability is listed in megatons in the official records for me somewhere."

The lone human agent cocked her head and stared disconcertingly at the two women of Q'orre. "Can you imagine what would happen if one of them was hit by a nuke? I mean, would it kill them or destroy the world?"

Rocket's fine dark brows drew into a scowl. "I'd like to never find out, thanks!"

FINALLY, MUCH TO Amari and Zendara's dismay, we've seen a weakness in the women's seeming invulnerability. And it's a weakness that can be exploited by many more than just the young masters of magnetism. And concerning those young Agents Bell, it seems like Nova and T'ala aren't the only ones receiving supplemental training. With her decades of service, Rocket had been excellent at teaching the young agents more about situational flight than they picked up in their own compromised team. In the meantime, let's hope that our two heroes from the Q'orre system really understand that panic is as much a weakness as any of the more physical ones. And with a man like Oracle, he will surely exploit any he can find to its maximum potential.

Chapter Eighteen

"WHAT HAVE YOU got for me?" Rocket was the first to speak while they were gathered around the long central command table that originally began life as a standard lab bench. Her gaze was firmly pinned on Lingua and Stephanie. The entire team was in various stages of devouring their MREs.

Lingua answered in her typical snarky manner. "While you all were off playing cops and robbers in the great north, we stumbled upon some valuable intel. I discovered a signal emanating from nineteen different CORP facilities around the country. Doctor Young was the one who pointed out that all the cities broadcasting this signal had been listed on the news as being all clear and that Chicago was one of them. She hypothesized that it was a signal from the rogue Chromodecs to Oracle, to let him know the city had been successfully taken over."

The SAIC abruptly sat back in her chair. The news was a boon she hadn't expected. "So does that mean—?"

"After our conclusion I cross-checked the amount of cities that have reported themselves as stable, which is thirty-nine, and compared them to the ones with the signal, which is nineteen by the way. Now we have a list of loyal CORP controlled locations *and* rogue controlled locations."

The team leader ignored the way her friend spoke right over top of her question. Agent King lacked basic social curtesy ninety-eight percent of the time, whether by acclimation or by choice, Romy didn't know. Despite Lingua's abrasiveness, she was a fine leader when she *wanted* to be. Rocket hoped that going forward, her longtime friend would eventually mellow. "What's the closest loyal CORP city?"

Steph answered, shoving a printed sheet toward Rocket. "Milwaukee. Here is a list of all the CORP cities, separated into three columns. Ones that are loyal and secure, ones that have been taken over by rogues and have activated Oracle's signal, and the remaining cities where the Chromodecs are still fighting for control."

The deep voice of Augur broke the temporary quiet that took over the table after Stephanie's words. "We need to get Milwaukee on the horn ASAP." He glanced at his wife then focused his gaze on Rocket. "Lumos is the Special Agent in Charge of Milwaukee. He's on the list of safe contacts that Hatch and I put together, as is his twin sister, Ember, who is the SAIC of Minneapolis."

"Minneapolis is one of the cities that are under lockdown while the Chromodecs battle for control. According to the news they've had fourteen civilian casualties and more injuries than their hospitals can handle right now. The same for many of the other cities currently under siege." Steph's voice was solemn.

Rocket sighed and ran a hand through her hair. "We trained all day after a late night last night, we'll be no good to anyone without some solid REM. We should try to make contact in the morning."

"Rocky, even an hour could be the difference between life and death over there. You, me, Lingua, and Augy know Lumos better than most. He and Ember practically worshipped the ground we walked on back when we were in Black Badge. And I for one was so proud of him when they both got their SAIC commissions last year. We have to at least make contact." Hatch's voice was pleading and soft and her eyes shone with emotion.

The leader of their little team of loyalists growled under her breath as the skin between her eyes wrinkled with frustration. "You're right and I hate it because it's a risky plan. Fine, how should we do this? Lingua, can you pinpoint Lumos's location, or are we going to have to risk bringing down our eloptic shield so Augur can work his magic?"

Augur shook his head. "I'd be willing to bet that the Milwaukee facility is under lockdown themselves with the way everything is going. They won't know who to trust."

"Already on it." Lingua called out from across the lab. While cranky and abrupt most of the time, no one that had ever served with Lingua would doubt that she wasn't top notch at her job. She was out of her chair and seated at the computer nearly as soon as Rocket agreed that they needed to contact the CORP-MILWAUKEE team leader. "It looks like they have SIMoN locked out and no communications are coming in or out of the facility."

"Can you hack it?"

Lingua cursed. "Negative. They've probably cut the hard lines coming into the facility and are riding out whatever upset is happening."

Hatch frowned. "That doesn't sound like the Lumos I know.

Are we sure they're secure?"

Steph nodded. "He was the one on the news announcing that Milwaukee was safe."

Zen thought about the issue for a minute, considering the question at hand. Neither she nor Amari had much to contribute to the conversation in general, but they listened nonetheless. "What if they took a lot of casualties and there are only a few of them left to hold the CORP building? I mean, if it were me I wouldn't announce to the world that we were easy pickings. I'd say the facility was safe to waylay civilian concerns then I'd make sure no one could gain access to my building. You said the CORP facilities held a lot of data and control over the local region. Right?"

Rocket sat forward and knocked her knuckles against the tabletop in surprise. The hard table cracked as she forgot about her kinetically enhanced strength. "That's it exactly! They'd have their own eloptic fields up around the building so how the hell do we get in to tell him we're there to help? Nothing we have can penetrate the structure. CORP facility walls are a combination of steel and high density concrete, and at least three feet thick."

Zen raised her hand, slightly unsure of herself. "Um, couldn't we just knock? I mean, just because standard communications are cut to prevent hacks doesn't mean they wouldn't have some way of monitoring the news and the exterior of their facility, if only to see what happens next."

The entire table seemed to hold its breath while the three most experienced people of the group mulled over the suggestion. Hatch pinched her lips together between her right thumb and forefinger while her left arm rested across her ribs. Her eyes were distant with thought. Augur scratched behind his thickly muscled neck idly. Rocket glanced from one to the other. "What do you two think?"

"I think the idea has merit."

Hatch nodded. "I agree. I mean, worst case scenario we port to their front door and if they don't answer we port back before anyone thinks to track us."

"Lingua, can you rig a remote for the eloptic shield so we can leave without fear that any rogue agents can track us to this location and compromise our hiding place?"

The team tech guru continued typing away at her pirated keyboard. "Already ahead of you, boss. I'm just setting up the encrypted receiver to work with our coms. I just need a few more minutes here."

With those reassuring words Rocket slid her chair back and stood up. "Now that's settled, we're all going to take a little trip north."

Nova looked toward her best friend, then back at Rocket. "All of us? What about Steph?"

The agent nodded her head reassuringly. "All of us. Believe me when I say that Stephanie will be a lot safer in a secure CORP facility than some hacked and stacked old lab beneath the school you all work for."

Gauss spoke up then and for the first time his youthful cockiness was absent. "And if they don't let us in?"

Rocket grinned. "Then we come back, get some sleep, and plan some more."

With a flourish of keystrokes, Lingua finished her programming work and locked the computer console before shoving back and walking over to Stephanie. In a strange show of compassion, she took pity on the only other human in the lab. "Come along, Doctor Young, let's get you set up with a tactical jumpsuit so you've got some armor. You can never be too prepared."

IT WAS NEAR seven-thirty p.m. when the eloptic field dropped around the lab the little team had secured. First they ported up to the roof so Lingua could turn the field back on around the room far below them. Seconds later another portal opened and they stepped through to find themselves right outside the front door of the Milwaukee CORP facility. Rocket wasn't surprised to see the steel security doors firmly in place over what used to be a stylish aluminum and glass entrance. That was standard protocol for any emergency situation that had the potential of compromising the facility's security. She strode right up to the heavy door and with a kinetically boosted fist, gave three loud knocks.

The booming sound echoed and the entire team looked around warily, despite the fact that the streets were practically empty in the aftermath of the battle that had taken place in recent days. "This place feels spooky as shit! Where is everyone?"

T'ala looked at Sinter and felt a sort of kinship to the young woman that was nearly her own age. "Right? I don't know that I've ever been in a city this size and not heard the constant drone of traffic or sirens. It's weird."

Lingua was quick to pull them back on task. "Weird or not, keep your eyes on our surroundings. Best case, they open up and let us in."

Stephanie cocked her head to the side. "What's the worst case, they attack us?"

Hatch hijacked Lingua's answer. "Worst case scenario, they attack *and* the rogues attack while we're standing here out in the open."

"Jesus, Mom, way to be a harbinger of doom!" Sinter made a face.

All eyes turned toward the big door as a series of muffled clicks sounded behind the surface. "Look sharp people, locks are disengaging. Nova and T'ala, take positions in front of Stephanie and Lingua. Mag twins, take the wings where you won't be in the direct line of fire."

Nova moved in front of Stephanie while her Q'sirrahna did the same in front of Lingua. "What about you three?"

Augur responded as he held himself ready. "First of all, as Chromodecs, we can take a little more damage than the average human. Second, we're the ones that Lumos will most likely recognize."

"Hey asshole, I practically raised that kid!"

Hatch laughed at the familiarity of Lingua's bitching. "Yeah, but he hasn't seen you in probably ten years. That's three hair styles, and two dye jobs ago."

Before anyone else could respond, a loud clank echoed through the door and it swung open. A man in his early thirties stood just inside sporting the scruffy beginnings of a deep red beard, a cut above his right eye, and a bandage around his upper left thigh. Clearly he'd seen better days. "Look what the cat dragged all the way to Milwaukee!"

Rocket grinned and eyed the man up and down. "Looks like the cat got to you first, my friend."

Despite the man's obvious relief, he glanced around nervously and quickly limped out of the way to wave them in. Once everyone was inside, Augur helped him shut and lock the big door then the man punched in a passcode next to the door and the keypad flashed green. He turned to the big African American man and pulled him into a hearty embrace with a few back slaps. "It's really good to see you, pops. I'm not sure what the hell is going on right now but I lost contact with Ember yesterday and I'm in no condition to help her out. At least not on my own."

Rocket, Lingua, and Hatch all moved forward and took their own turns pulling the man that could only be Lumos into quick embraces. Rocket was last but rather than a hug, she clasped his arm in a show of solidarity. She more than the rest of the group knew what it was like for the leader to be betrayed and lose part of their team. "Well, that's what we're here for."

Lumos looked around at the ragtag group before him, then back at Rocket. "Chicago?"

She shook her head. "Compromised. This is it."

He narrowed his eyes as he took in the two women in strange deep black suits and the person wearing a CORP suit who was obviously *not* a CORP agent. He nodded their way. "And those three?"

"Allies. It's—" Rocket sighed and took off her helmet. "We can explain better when everyone is all together. Your team?"

He shrugged and waved the group toward another door a little farther down the entryway. The group followed as he spoke. His limp was obvious but he didn't let the pain slow him down. "Howler has a bruised larynx so is out of commission for probably a few days, maybe longer. Kreskin took a blow to the head and remains unconscious in the med lab. Fist and Flux are in relatively good shape, better than me at any rate. The rest were all rogue agents. Damos is dead and the other two are locked up until we figure out what's going on."

All of the Chromodec Office of Restraint and Protection headquarters were set up exactly the same with no details changed from the master layout, so the majority of the group was unfazed by their little tour. But for the two alien women and lone human scientist, it was like touring one of the most mysterious modern facilities in the world. No one was allowed inside a CORP facility unless they were a CORP agent. The group eventually found their way to a large control room, with three out of four walls sporting screens of various sizes. All were tuned to either the streets around the facility or news broadcasts from around the country. As soon as the entire group cleared the door, two female agents at the far end abruptly stood and pulled weapons. The shorter one with medium-length auburn hair spoke up. "Who the hell are they?" As if the aggressive gun draw weren't enough, the room grew noticeably cooler.

"Flux, that's enough. You and Fist put your guns away, everyone here is an ally or friend."

The other woman, Fist, had short-cropped black hair and

dark skin and appeared to be of Pacific Islander decent. She snorted and when she spoke her voice had a distinct British accent. "Well, that's certainly a change of pace, isn't it?"

Zendara whispered to Amari. "I thought all Chromodecs were US citizens?"

"Duel citizenship, love. Oh, and because I spent many years legally deaf I'm fluent in sign language *and* I can read your lips."

Lumos pinched the bridge of his nose. "Fist, please." The taller of the two Milwaukee female agents quieted but didn't lose her suspicious look. He turned to Rocket. "Look, I'm gonna be frank with you. The only thing that's keeping us from going to aid my sister right now is numbers. We've got an X3 chopper in the topside bay and Fist can have us there in less than an hour and a half."

Rocket gripped his shoulder firmly. "Well, you've got numbers now, and Hatch can have everyone there in a matter of minutes. How ready is your team? Should we start in the morning?"

The two women spoke almost simultaneously. "Ready."

Lumos shook his head and grimaced. "Now. It has to be now." He paused then went on. "I can't explain it, but something tells me we have to get to her as soon as possible."

"It's twin—"

"Intuition." The younger agents, Sinter and Gauss, grinned at each other.

The de facto leader of the Chicago group raised a dark eyebrow. "What do you think? You all have enough in you for a full-on fight against rogues?"

Zendara looked fearfully toward her Q'sirrahna.

LET'S PAUSE FOR a moment and think about what this young woman must be going through. Things have happened kind of fast for Zendara Inyri Baen-Tor. It's not like she had the easiest life, and to spend half of it searching for something or someone she wasn't sure was even real, well that is a lot to deal with. Then she finds out she has powers, finds out she isn't even human or from this planet at all, and all of it is told to her by that one she felt inside her heart for years. Forever.

Every one of those things would have made a bad day even more difficult. But after all the changes thrust upon Zendara's life, the country then goes nuts and she

finds herself on a team of rebels fighting against
traitors and enemy agents that have more power than
most dream of. Zen grew up fast and she grew up tough,
but there are things that even a hard life can't prepare you for. However, one thing she knew a little too
well was what it felt like to lose someone. She was
bereft when her parents died and left her a victim of
the system. But Zen knew with certainty that their
death could never compare to that of her soul mate.
There was no doubt in Zendara's mind that Amari was now
a permanent part of her and to lose her Q'sirrahna
would mean losing her own life. Even if it didn't kill
her, Zen would never survive. So she was afraid of the
entire situation, though she does a good job showing
contrary. But you can't hide your heart from someone
who is inside it.

AMARI LOSIRA DEL Rey looked fearfully toward her Q'sirrahna. It was as if time stood still when their eyes met, both pale
and dark. She feared for the other half of her soul. While Amari
had been exploring her powers for a third of her life, Zen had no
such safety. She spoke quietly but directly to Zendara. "Sirra, it's
your call. I will do whatever you want me to do."

The young punk that had lived life not caring about anyone
but herself looked around the room full of strangers and recent
acquaintances. She suddenly found herself caring a little too
much. The full power of her gaze met Rocket's. "We're in."
Everyone else nodded and declared their own agreement. It was
time for them to be the heroes they were meant to be.

"Because I'm injured and not senior agent, I think we should
agree that Rocket take the lead here."

Rocket looked at the man she first met when he was naught
but a boy. Rather than acknowledge his deferment she got right
down to business. "We need two people to stay here on coms to
look up information real time and help us navigate the city and
rogues within. Lingua, can you get their satellite systems back up
without bringing SIMoN online?"

The Asian-American woman shrugged. "Depends on what
the kids here did to cut the lines."

Fist was the one who answered. "Didn't cut anything, ye
plonker. What do ye take us for? Simply unplugged the external
facility circuits and rerouted outside cameras to the console in
here."

Lingua rolled her eyes, looking more like a youth than the two Milwaukee CORP agents. "Fine. Show me the switch room and I'll see what I can do."

Rocket's voice caught Fist and Lingua's attention before they could leave the room. "Don't take all her time, King. I want Fist back here in fifteen, fully suited and armed." She turned to Lumos and gestured to the duffle bag that the team had brought with them from Chicago. "We've got all the gear we need. Let's you and I confer with Augur and Hatch to see what our best entrance should be."

They moved off to the edge of the room, leaving Stephanie, Nova, and T'ala with Flux after the twins announced they were going to raid the kitchen. The auburn-haired woman made no secret of her scorn of the three non-agents. "And why are you three here? Regulations state that civs don't belong in a CORP facility."

Zen's fear easily turned to anger and she was quick to respond. "Yeah, well do regulations also state that fucking agents shouldn't take over the goddamn world? If you all followed your precious regulations we wouldn't be standing in your piece of shit facility!"

Amari placed a soothing hand over Zen's arm while at the same time she attempted to defuse Flux's anger. Stephanie just stepped back and watched it all with wide eyes. "Easy, sirra. Everyone is on edge right now and I'm guessing their entire team has been going steady since yesterday morning." She looked at the Milwaukee agent and took note of the dark circles under the young woman's eyes. She couldn't have been much older than the Bell twins. "Am I right?"

Everyone held their breath until Flux answered. "You're right, we have. And I'm sorry, it's just everything is so crazy right now. I mean, they didn't train us for anything like this down at Guantanamo."

Zen snorted. "Obviously they wouldn't."

"What do you mean?" Flux looked at her, totally confused.

Amari ran a hand through her hair. "We've discovered that the entire uprising was planned and implemented by none other than Colonel Marek Maza, better known as Oracle."

Suddenly Flux's eyes showed something greater than the ever-present worry. Fear drew her eyebrows up and together at the same time wide lips turned down. "Well, isn't that just a bucket of fuck!"

Steph snorted at one of her favorite exclamations coming from some strange Chromodec's mouth. "Right?" She decided to fill in the agent with who they were. "Long story short is that Romy, uh, Agent Danes was with me when she found out about the attacks and later took shelter at my apartment." She pointed at Amari. "This is my best friend, and she's a powerful alien from another planet. And that is her soul mate, another powerful alien, but not from the same planet."

Flux's mouth dropped open as she followed Steph's words and her pointing finger. "You have got to be shitting me."

Amari smiled. "I'm afraid not. My name is Doctor Amari Losira Del Rey. Once Agent Danes realized the potential of our power, she brought us into her little band of misfits and gave both me and Zendara code names. I'm Nova and my soul mate, Zendara Inyri Baen-Tor, is called T'ala. Steph is just Steph." The human biologist gave a little wiggle of her fingers.

"So what's your power, Flux? Do you make ice like that comic book character, is that why it got so cold when we walked in?"

Still reeling from all the information that had just bombarded her, Flux shook her head. "Uh, not exactly. I'm Agent Jordyn Fitz and I can supercool or superheat the air within a matter of seconds."

"Cool! I would have loved that when my apartment's AC went out last year."

Flux shrugged at Steph's comment. "It has its uses though I usually just put my power to work for the CORP. I've only been out of training for three months. This—" she circled her pointer finger around to indicate their surroundings "—was not exactly what I was expecting. You know?"

Zendara burst out laughing. "Oh man, I hear you there. This whole thing has been one shock after another."

They chatted for a few more minutes before Rocket clapped her hands and called everyone in. "All right people, bonding time is over. Lumos is now up to speed on the state of everything and we've all agreed that Augur and Hatch will do a sight and send to locate Ember. Two minutes to go time. Check your gear and be prepared for anything the minute we step through the portal."

"Hey, Rocket?"

"Yeah?" The SAIC of their motley group turned toward T'ala.

"Do you think we can see a picture of this Ember so we know who we're fighting for?"

Lumos began laughing and pointed at his own head. "You see this face and flaming hair? Take off the stubble and slim it down and you'll have my sister. Protect her or anyone that looks like they have her back."

The rest nodded. "Gotcha."

Rocket pointed to Lingua where she and Stephanie stood off to the side. "Field back on and lock it tight when we're gone. And protect that civ!"

Lingua saluted her boss with a middle finger. "Aye aye, Captain!"

Lumos snorted. "Some things certainly never change." Those were the last words spoken before they walked through a portal into hell.

Chapter Nineteen

CHAOS WAS AN understatement when they all stepped through Hatch's portal. She began closing it once everyone was through but when it had shrunk down to a mere eight feet in diameter, a huge flash from the back side startled everyone. "What the hell was that?" Zen looked around, eyes wide, at the flashing lights and sound of gunfire that erupted sporadically around them.

"That was you all saving our lives."

"Ember!" Lumos rushed to what could only be his sister. The entire group realized immediately that he hadn't been lying about how much they looked alike when she lifted her face shield. Even the bandages they sported were similar. On the ground behind Ember was another agent in black with an obviously broken arm, cradling the un-helmeted and unconscious form of another agent. One more agent stood at attention with their back to the rest of the group, scanning the surroundings. Rocket took it all in with a critical eye. The small group was hunkered down behind a car that had been flipped onto its side. They had the reinforced wall of the CORP building at their backs but that still left two other sides wide open to defend. Hatch's portal had blocked one of the vulnerable points and most likely took fire that was meant for the small group of CORP agents on the ground.

"What's the status here? Is this all that's left of your team?" Ember nodded and Rocket turned to the rest of her team. "We're abandoning the city then. I want Gauss and Sinter to form a metal shield around us then Hatch is going to take us back to Milwaukee. Do you copy, Lingua?" Rocket yelled over the sound of gunfire and random energy blasts.

The genius agent's voice was clear over their coms. "Got it. Give me ninety seconds to bring down the field, on my mark."

"Copy that."

"Mark!"

It took less than a minute for the twins to have a stable shield fabricated from burnt out cars and girders of at least two demolished buildings. As they were building it, Augur, Hatch, Fist,

Flux, and the standing Minneapolis agent returned gunfire while Nova and T'ala used their own bodies to protect the injured people on the ground. None of the uninjured agents had offensive powers that could affect the attacking rogues. Ninety seconds later a portal opened in one wall of the metal shield and all able bodies helped the injured through to the other side.

Once there, Lumos directed Fist and Flux to help the two injured agents to the infirmary. Everyone breathed a sigh of relief. "You cut it a little close there." The SAIC of Minneapolis sounded tired.

"Sorry sis, we did the best we could. Wouldn't have made it at all if Rocket and her crew hadn't ridden in to save the day."

Ember glanced at Rocket, then back toward Lumos. "Milwaukee?"

He gave an exhausted grin. "Ours."

She looked to Rocket. "Chicago?" The older agent pursed her lips and shook her head.

"Dallas and LA are under rogue control as well, but plenty of cities are still fighting." Rocket thought for a few seconds before addressing their newest SAIC to the little group. "How many rogues would you say were left in Minneapolis?"

"Hmm, only three. Unfortunately they all have offensive capability and our primary focus was to protect Pharma and Frost. With Pharma unconscious there was no way to heal our injuries and we were nearly out of ammo."

"Who are the three rogues?"

"Lazor, Blaster, and Shriek."

Rocket smiled, confusing the agents from both Milwaukee and Minneapolis. "So light, energy, and sound? Oh, this is going to be fun." She looked over to where Nova and T'ala were watching intently. "Feel like making a test run?"

Nova looked around the room at the assembled agents, taking note of the assorted injuries on most of the new acquaintances. T'ala looked at Nova. "We're ready whenever you are."

"Hatch, I need a portal back to Minneapolis. I'll contact you for the return."

Both Ember and Lumos looked alarmed, but it was Ember who spoke up. Being her city in question, she felt most responsible for any risks incurred by taking it back. "What exactly are you doing, Rocky?"

Rocket laughed and waved at Hatch to begin. "We're going to take back your city. We'll return in a few, don't wait up kids."

The portal opened and Rocket looked over her shoulder. "Let's go, ladies, we're going to put your absorption powers to the test." Then seconds later, the three women flew through the portal and disappeared.

Ember looked at Lumos, and Lumos looked over at Augur and Hatch. "What the Sam Hill just happened? And who were those civs? *Are* they even civs?"

Augur's deep laugh cut through the room. "You got any whiskey in this place? This story needs a drink."

ALL THREE WOMEN split apart as soon as they crossed back into Minneapolis and the rogue Chromodecs were immediately on them. A concentrated beam of light hit Rocket the second she cleared the portal but since she was flying, her field of near-invulnerability kept her from harm. She merely powered through it and aimed strait for the shooter, which was the agent known as Lazor. She couldn't see his face but she watched him pause his laser fire and raise his head as soon as he realized who she was. Rather than face the legendary senior agent, the rogue ran into an abandoned storefront where he knew she couldn't enter while flying. It also meant she wouldn't have her invulnerability if she followed him on foot. The man may have been morally corrupt but he wasn't stupid. "T'ala!"

T'ala's voice came back through the com in her helmet. "S'up boss?"

Rocky pointed toward the storefront. "Trade you Lazor for Shriek? I can't fly in that damn store."

T'ala grinned and her glowing black hair and eyes made the gesture seem especially creepy in the agent's magnified helmet HUD screen. "Sure thing, Rocket." She flew down and walked straight through the front doors of the store while Rocket made a beeline for the sonic powered Chromodec. The rogue had a modified field helmet that left the lower half of her face uncovered. Rocket knew that Shriek's sonic scream would still hurt her, not being fully stopped by her blast field, but Rocket wanted to take the woman down as soon as possible.

Much like Lazor, Blaster was not flight capable. And seeing flight capable opponents, he ran to take cover behind a burned out truck. His first shot missed Nova due to her speed but as she zeroed in on his location, the second one was a direct hit. She hovered in the air as the energy was absorbed and amplified and she was left feeling incredibly juiced. Seeing her pause, the rogue Chromodec fired again. Nova felt the now familiar pressure of power build-up and pointed her fist at the man as the energy coursed back out of her in a straight line. Not knowing what to expect, he made a last second dive from behind his makeshift cover just as her own beam struck the truck. The concussive force of her directed power echoed between the tall buildings and the wreck flew down the street nearly two blocks before screeching to a halt in a shower of sparks.

"Holy fuck! Who are you?"

The glowing white head and eyes turned to look at the rogue. "I'm one of the good guys." Before he could run or respond with another blast, she flew at high speed to his location and ripped the helmet off his head before knocking him out with a well-placed fist. She was careful enough to temper her strength but realistically knew she probably broke his jaw.

Less than a minute later, T'ala emerged from the shopping center dragging another black-suited Chromodec by his collar. She grinned at her soul mate. "This city sure has some big fish!"

"Hey, Nova, catch!"

Nova looked up in time to grab the falling body. She placed the dazed last rogue on the ground as Rocket touched down near them and lifted the face shield on her helmet. Looking at the three apprehended Chromodecs, Rocket placed her fists on her hips. "Well done, ladies."

A groan sounded from between Shriek's lips. Rocket had stunned the woman enough that she couldn't use her powers but she was still conscious. "Who the *hell* are you people? We were told this city would be easy!"

T'ala smirked. "Cities are easy, it's the people who make it tough."

Not able to resist the gibe, Rocket chimed in. "Doesn't she make you want to scream?" Everyone laughed at the remark, except the rogue. Seeing their work was done for the time being, Rocket crouched down and searched the pouches of the rogues' uniforms, coming up with three eloptic collars. She held them up in triumph. "Not that we'll necessarily need them for this trio but protocol dictates we don't transfer prisoners without negating their powers."

"Oh yes, we wouldn't want to break protocol now." T'ala rolled her eyes.

Nova watched Rocket lock the collar in place with a thumbprint. "How do those lock? Won't they be able to get their own collars back off again?"

"All the collars have a quick lock that is fingerprint activated. The only person who can remove the collar is the one who locked it, unless they are logged into the security system and deactivated with the proper passcode."

Nova nodded. "Well, that bit of tech is advantageous."

"Are you two just going to ignore how fucking awesome that was? Did you see how we just brought these three down? We can really do this, right—I mean, save the country and people?" She looked at Rocket for confirmation.

The SAIC smiled at the younger woman's enthusiasm. It was worth seeing after experiencing Zendara's initial skepticism and dislike of authority. "Despite the odds, I think we really do stand a chance. Thank you both for all that you've done to help."

Hero persona momentarily lost, Amari's white glow extinguished and she smiled back at Agent Danes. "You're welcome, I'm glad we could help." Her smile quickly disappeared though as she took a slow look around at the devastation wrought on downtown Minneapolis. "I have a feeling we still have a long way to go before the world is back to normal though."

Rocket sighed and pinched the bridge of her nose through the open faceplate. "Unfortunately that's true." Waiting a beat, she touched the communicator under the edge of her helmet. "Lingua, tell Hatch that we're ready for a door home. The street has a ten foot clearing about...hmm, fifteen feet southeast of my location. We've got three prisoners."

"Roger that. Please standby."

Thirty seconds later a large portal opened in the area Rocket described and the three women wasted no time in dragging the rogues through to the CORP control room on the other side. Lumos went into action immediately. "Fist, Flux, and..." He looked around, spotting the uninjured member of his sister's team. "Candor, use the rolling chairs and take these three to the holding cells." Everyone helped the three agents load the rogues into office chairs for easy rolling around the facility.

"And bring back those Eloptic collars." Rocket called out. She looked around. "The chairs too!"

"Yes, sir!"

Rocket's gaze moved across the experienced agents. She nodded her head toward the door of a conference room. "We need a plan." With that, Augur, Hatch, Lumos, Ember, and Lingua made their way into the room one-by-one. Before Lingua disappeared completely, she paused. "Hey, Steph!" The civilian woman looked up from where she was watching the monitors. She had been given the task by Lingua while Zen and Amari were gone and happily complied. She was a little too aware of her vulnerability in the group of loyal CORP agents and wanted to help any way she could. "If you see *any* black suits on those screens, come get me ASAP!"

Steph smiled and gave an awkward thumbs-up. "Sure thing!"

Meanwhile the two youngest agents of the group mobbed Zen and Amari. Isaiah was first one to ask. "So? How was your first fight?"

Zen's pale eyes were bright with exhilaration. "Dude, it was sick! Seriously, their shit was weak!"

Isaiah laughed and his sister followed suit, both remembering their first fight, which wasn't very long ago. "Yeah, it was a pretty good idea Rocket had pulling you two with her. Mom and Dad say she's the best when it comes to reading people's strengths and weaknesses."

Imani smiled but was quick to temper her brother's encouragement. "Isa's right but don't forget that you *do* both have weaknesses. Y'all don't want to get too cocky out there. It's one of the first lessons we learn as agents."

Wrinkles appeared between Amari's dark brows as she frowned. "Believe me, I'm well aware of how devastating our weaknesses can be. I'm definitely not taking chances out there." She glanced toward the conference room door. "I just wish I knew what our next move was going to be. I can't imagine we'll be staying here too long."

Isa shrugged. "We'll find out as soon as the senior agents come up with something. Until then, not much we can do besides wait. And grab a snack."

"Always thinking with your stomach!"

The younger Bell man grinned. "Well, that and my—"

Imani swatted the back of Isaiah's head to still her brother's words. "Nuh-uh, eww! I never want to hear you finish that sentence, got it?"

"Ouch, damn it all! I was just gonna say—"

She held up a hand as she turned and walked away. "Nooooope!"

The remaining three started laughing and Isaiah continued. "I was just going to say my heart."

Children of the Stars

Zendara rolled her eyes. "Sure you were. But while we're on the subject, I'm hungry too. What kind of food do you suppose they have in the joint?"

The young agent shrugged. "I don't know, let's go find out." She turned to her Q'sirrahna. "You coming?"

Amari shook her head. "I'm going to go keep Steph company since she's been stuck here with a bunch of people she doesn't know. Bring us something?"

Zen gave Amari a fond smile. "Will do."

When everyone else was gone from the room, Amari walked over to stand next to her best friend. "How are you doing?"

The elder of the two scientists only glanced away from the screen for a second to acknowledge Amari's words. She took her duty very seriously because she knew what kind of people they were dealing with. That and she was a little afraid of the recalcitrant human agent. "Shouldn't I be asking *you* that? After all, you and Zen are the ones out there fighting rogue Chromodecs. You know, the people of power that we all grew up somewhat terrified by?"

Amari shrugged. "I don't know, it's okay I guess. I mean, it's nice to finally use my powers to their full potential. And I have to admit there is something extremely satisfying to help bring down the 'bad guys.'"

Knowing her best friend better than anyone else, save Amari's adoptive parents, Steph prodded. "But?"

The younger woman scrubbed her face with her hands. "But I'm worried about what will happen after. Let's say we beat this Oracle and round up all the rogue Chromodecs, what happens to us?"

"You and Zendara?"

"All three of us, you included." Steph cocked her head to the side in confusion. "You've seen their precious inner sanctum. Not only that but if the uncompromised CORP top brass press for answers about me and Zen, they're going to start asking questions and they'll probably start with you since you're here with us."

With another quick scan of the screens, Steph turned her chair to face Amari in full. "Hey, listen to me. I knew the risk when I said yes, same as you. I don't regret it and I don't want you to worry about me in the scheme of things. Besides, I really think that Romy is going to come through for us."

"How? Nearly a dozen people know we're aliens now. That's

too many considering I've lived my entire life until now guarding this secret!"

Stephanie pulled her into a hug. "Hey, it's gonna be okay. I just know it. Besides, you and Zen finally found each other. I mean, holy shit! This is the woman you've been talking about for as long as I've known you. You ladies have to have your happy ending, you know?"

Amari snorted and pulled free from her best friend's embrace, feeling better. "Life isn't a fairytale."

"No, but it sure reads like a comic book right now, doesn't it?"

"What do you mean?"

Steph glanced at the screens again to make sure no rogues had shown up within the view of any of the cameras. Then she gestured with her hands. "Think about it. A small ragtag band of heroes with powers, facing insurmountable odds to save the world? Classic storyline right there!"

The younger woman burst into laughter. "You are such a nerd! How are you still single?"

The door to the conference room opened and Agent Romy Danes led their group of senior agents back into the control room. Steph met her eye from three yards away. "I don't know but I'm going to work on that after we take care of this little Chromodec problem."

Amari followed her friend's gaze and smirked. "Good luck with Agent Danes, she seems married to her job."

Steph feigned nonchalance. "Well, even if it doesn't work out, think of the fun we can have in the meantime." She winked at Amari then turned back to watch the security screens.

Despite her friend's casual words, Amari knew Steph better than that. Her best friend had a real chance of getting her heart broken. But after noticing the way Romy watched Steph when her friend wasn't aware, Amari conceded that perhaps there was a chance between them.

SO OUR LITTLE band of heroes has grown into a force to be reckoned with, but what will the leadership decide to do with that force? Too many cities were still locked in a battle for control to realistically take them all back at once. Minneapolis had been fairly easy but not all would be the same. The team simply didn't have the manpower to achieve such a lofty goal.

And it would take much too long to travel from city to
city with their large group. No, they needed a better
plan of action before the entire country fell to chaos
and too much basic infrastructure was damaged in the
fighting. Too many people had already died and the
senior agents knew they would have to act fast to prevent further loss of life. They had determination, now
they just needed some direction. Lucky for them, Agent
Romy Danes was an amazing strategist. Unlucky for the
citizens of the United States of America, there was
another strategist sitting at the table.

ANOTHER GROUP OF Chromodecs located in a bunker far
to the south watched as three more beacons blipped out and disappeared from the screen. The man monitoring that particular
screen turned to face his commanding officer. "Sir, three more
have disappeared from Minneapolis. It's the same circumstance
as the others in Milwaukee. Vitals of our agents are all green then
they suddenly disappear from the tracking system like they're
being shielded."

Marek Maza gritted his teeth in frustration. "That's because
they are. And the only place with shielding from our bio-tracker
is in a Chromodec containment cell."

The man squinted with confusion. "Perhaps they're moving
prisoners into the cells?"

Oracle rubbed his temples, frustration and stress having
given him a headache sometime within the past hour. "No..." he
ground out. "They aren't moving prisoners into the cells. They *are*
the prisoners you idiot!"

"But sir—" Pressure filled the unfortunate junior agent's
head and he reached up to grip his skull as he met his colonel's
ire-filled gaze. Blood trickled from the young agent's nose.

"Never. Question. My. Authority!" Then as if to punctuate
Oracle's words, the poor agent in question gave a hoarse cry and
slumped out of his chair onto the ground. Dead eyes remained
open and unseeing while blood flowing freely from his nose and
ears. Holding the powers of telepathy, clairvoyance, prescience,
and telesthesia, the grandson of Doctor Brian Daggett had certainly earned the fear others felt in his presence.

He turned to the agent sitting at the next console over. The
man stared back with a pale face and wide eyes. "Sir?"

The colonel waved toward the dead Chromodec. "Call someone to deal with that." Oracle continued rubbing his temples as he thought about the problem at hand. He knew exactly who was responsible for his missing sleeper agents, the very same person who had been reported MIA in Chicago. Not only was Agent Danes and her human computer jockey, Agent King, still on the loose, but both Dallas and LA facilities had reported losing all visual contact with the Bell family as well. Every single one had been a thorn in his side over the years, with the senior agents' Black Badge training and seemingly impenetrable mental fortitude. Those things alone wouldn't have been so bad if even one of them had been the slightest bit morally corruptible. But no, they were all disgustingly loyal.

He was only vaguely paying attention as a team of agents came in to take the body away, leaving one behind to scrub the blood and urine from the floor. He muttered to himself while he considered what Rocket's next move might be. "Think, Marek, think..." He studied the large map on the center screen. "Where will she go next?" He studied the map, taking note of the cities where his agents still battled for control.

"Sir?" The agent that had taken over for the dead man looked at Oracle with concern. "Do you need something more?"

"No!" he growled out without looking at the worried man. Then the answer came to him and he pointed. "Yes! I want you to get Shockwave on the line for me."

The man spun in his chair and quickly brought up the requested connect. "Sir, yes, sir!"

Oracle smiled for the first time in hours. "You and your allies are going down, Rocket."

NOVA, T'ALA, AND their new friends and allies were *not* going down without a fight. The small group of senior agents received notice over the intercom that Pharma was not only awake in the medical bay, but had already begun healing the other wounded agents. Knowing they had that much more firepower at their disposal, Rocket suggested splitting into two teams. The idea was to simultaneously deal with the cities that needed help and go after Oracle. The rest of the agents quickly agreed. All the flight based heavy-hitters would ride the Eurocopter X3 to Guantanamo while the rest would teleport to Indianapolis. Once Indianapolis was secured they'd move on to the next city on their list. Indianapolis, Columbus, Louisville, and

Memphis were all close geographically and still fighting for control. With a major influx of loyal agents, they would be sure to turn the tide against the rogue Chromodecs.

Augur was chosen to lead the group that would liberate the cities. Rocket was going to head up the fighters selected to take on Oracle. The Guantanamo group was flying because the high-speed helicopter had firepower on board they might need in the fight to come.

After the meeting broke up, they announced to the entire group of agents and civilians alike that they were being given a mandatory ten hours of downtown to get some rest. Lingua would stay awake and man security feeds while the rest slept, knowing she'd have help watching the next day.

The next morning the news of the team split didn't go over well, especially for the twins and Amari and Zendara. Since Rocket was the one addressing the entire group, she was the one who faced the backlash. "Lingua, Pharma, Steph, and Hatch will remain in Milwaukee to facilitate coms, health, and movement. Augur will take Lumos, Fist, Flux, Kreskin, Candor, T'ala, and Sinter. And I will lead the X3 crew that's heading down to Guantanamo to take on Oracle. Frost, Ember, Howler, Gauss, and Nova are with me."

"No!" Zen's shout startled everyone and her grip was like iron around Amari's hand. Her voice lowered with equal parts anger and fear as she leveled her gaze at Rocket. "I'm not going anywhere without Amari." Never having served apart, the twins were of the exact same thought but they decided to see how Zen's protest played out rather than say anything.

For her part, Rocket didn't react to Zen's outburst. Truthfully she had been expecting it. The young woman was certainly a wildcard, much more volatile than Steph's best friend. Special Agent Danes knew the rest of the team was looking to her for more than leadership. They were looking for some semblance of hope and Rocket felt the weight of numerous pairs of eyes as she thought about how to respond. Finally she sighed and ran a hand through her hair, tucking it to the side behind her ear out of habit. "Look around you." When Zen hesitated, she waved her hand through the air with impatience. "Do it. Which one of them are you willing to sacrifice?"

"What?"

"What would you do if you needed to put together two teams of people, with two different objectives? You'd want those teams to have the best mix of powers. You'd want both teams to succeed without loss of life. Now you have two individuals with identical, amazing amounts of power, do you stack one team and leave the other at risk of failure? No, you spread out your talent to ensure the greatest chance of success for both. *That's* why you and your partner there were split up, and that's why the mag twins were also split. No one is being cruel here. Everyone is afraid. But you don't fight against insurmountable odds with fear at your back. You fight with determination. And I'm gonna be honest, without the two of you we wouldn't stand half a chance against Oracle and his rogue agents. I know you aren't a trained agent and all of this is frightening and unfamiliar. It is for me too because I'm asking a civilian to go to war with trained soldiers. But we need you onboard with the plan one hundred percent or it's going to fail and even more lives will be lost. I'm sorry but that's the honest to God truth."

Zendara looked around the room and saw worry on everyone's face, the people she didn't know, and the ones she had come to respect over the past few days. Then she looked at her Q'sirrahna and was struck by the love and determination on Amari's face. *That* was who she wanted to be. Not the angry orphan who felt abandoned for years and took her fears out on all those around her. She sighed. Unsure where the words came from, she released Amari's hand and took a step toward Agent Romy Danes and glanced around the room. "My name is Zendara Inyri Baen-Tor, and apparently I'm the lost Princess of Tora. I didn't have a home or family for half my life because they were taken from me. I wasn't in a good place for a long time…" She glanced back at Amari. "But I finally found my heart and family again with Amari. The thought of losing her terrifies me but I don't want some other kid to go through what I did. I'm ready to help take these fuckers down."

Imani and Isaiah glanced at each other, communicating on a level that only twins could understand. Nodding slightly, they abruptly separated and each walked over to where their groups had already formed. With one last look at Amari, Zen smiled and walked over to stand next to Imani. Augur grinned at his children, proud of the agents they had become. But he also directed a fond look at the two special young women they had come to know over the last few days. His deep and confident voice eased the remaining tension in the room. "Ready to roll, Rocket. Let's nail those sons-a-bitches' balls to the wall!"

"Are we ready then?" Rocket looked around the room at the ragtag assembly of heroes.

"Aren't you forgetting something, Rocky?" The speaker was Lumos.

The Special Agent in Charge of Chicago looked at her counterpart and rolled her eyes. "Bring it in everyone! Give me three on three." Rocket called to the assembly of nineteen. The group moved forward into a tight circle with everyone's right hand stretching toward the middle. Steph, Amari, and Zen followed suit, confused at first until Amari got both their attention and nodded toward the CORP seal that was painted on the one solid wall. The motto was a simple three words along the top arch of the circle. "One, two, three—"

The entire group yelled out in a chorus of strength and purpose. "Peace, prosperity, protection!"

Now they were ready.

Chapter Twenty

SEPARATION HAS MULTIPLE meanings, doesn't it? It could be something as simple as two pieces coming apart, or as heart wrenching as a married couple taking a temporary break from their relationship. Separation is a place, line, or point of parting. It is a gap or hole found within something that was once a single entity. The separation of soul mates wasn't as innocuous as two pieces coming apart, or a small gap of space. But it wasn't quite as extreme as the temporary breakdown or pausing of a marriage either. For Amari Losira Del Rey and Zendara Inyri Baen-Tor, it was a hole left inside each of them. It was a line pulled tight between each heart until discomfort rode their bodies like a parasite. And fear was an ache that traveled up and down that line. But the two improbable protectors hailing from the Q'orre system had no idea what to expect from their separation. They only knew that the simple *thought* of it left them feeling more than a little fragile and bereft.

Despite the difference of their biology and origin, and ignoring the mundane hardships that young Zendara had to face growing up without parents, the two women had led fairly sheltered lives. Neither had been exposed to the violence of conflict, nor had they been subjected to the mental anguish associated with being attacked or hurting someone else. They were not trained soldiers like the CORP teams. They were two women trying to live life the best way they knew how with only half their soul. And while the coming events may not have worried them quite as much had they not found their way into each other's lives yet, everything changed the night their eyes met on that train platform. Because no matter what *could* have occurred had the past been different, they were together *now*. Amari and Zendara had so much more to lose.

WITH THE TEAMS set, everyone went through their supply packs to make sure everything was in order for their individual missions. Rocket also recognized that many people had been put into groups they were unfamiliar with, some of them split from their normal teams and families for the coming operation. In order to get their gear in order and say goodbyes, she gave everyone thirty minutes before meeting back in the control room. It didn't take long at all for the three civilians to get their own things ready. Steph wasn't leaving the CORP facility, and Amari and Zen didn't have weapons or tech they needed to pack, just food. Stephanie pulled her best friend into a strong hug. Then a few seconds later she surprised Zen when she did the same with her. The older scientist's eyes watered as she stepped back from the women in black suits. She drew in a deep breath. "You two be safe, and don't forget to save the world while you're out flying around."

"You know we'll be as safe as possible. I'm also really glad you're staying here." Amari sighed and spared a glance toward the Bell family before refocusing on Steph. "If things go bad, if we can't beat this Oracle guy, listen to Lingua and Hatch. I know they'll keep you safe and get you to a place where you won't be in danger."

Steph began to protest. "But—"

"No, listen to Amari, please!" The two friends were surprised by Zen's outburst and Zen immediately blushed. "I mean, we can take care of ourselves but you're Amari's best friend and...well, I don't have many friends but I kinda feel like you're my friend now too. I'd want you to be safe."

"Aww!" Steph gave Amari a shove against her shoulder. "She's a keeper!"

Zen just rolled her eyes. "Technically, I don't think she has much of a choice."

Amari grinned and the happiness of it showed at the crinkles at the corners of her eyes. "That's a pleasure, not a burden. No choice is necessary, sirra."

Amari met Zen's eyes after the sweet words fell from her mouth and the rest of the room faded away around them. Seeing the beginning of a private goodbye, Steph elected to head back to the console where she'd been sitting.

"I'm—" Zen's voice cracked so she cleared her throat and tried again. She hated admitting weakness of any kind but fear for Amari's safety had made her weak. "I'm scared."

Misunderstanding, Amari tried to sooth her lover. "Just listen to Augur and Lumos. They know you're not a trained soldier and I have no doubts that they'll keep an eye on you and keep you safe to the best of their abilities."

"No…" Zen shook her head then drew Amari into an abrupt embrace. She whispered her real fear quietly into Amari's ear. "I'm afraid for *you*. I can't lose you. I loved having the feel of you in my heart for so long and now that we're finally together I just—" She sucked in a breath but didn't continue.

Amari squeezed her as tight as she could. "You're not going to lose me."

"I lose everyone." The words were so quiet that Amari almost didn't hear them.

With supreme effort, the two women pulled back from each other. Amari cradled Zen's face between her palms. "I'm not everyone. I'm your Q'sirrahna and you'll *never* lose me."

Zen sighed again. "I just found you."

"Then you best be careful because when this is all over, you and I have a date to watch the videos from your pod. I'll do everything I can to make sure that happens, you just need to do the same. Savvy?"

Zen snorted and discretely wiped a tear from her eyelash. "Now you sound like Hatch."

"No, I sound like Nova, one of the people that's going to go down and kick Oracle's ass—"

The intense and deep kiss cut off whatever else Amari was going to say. Both women moaned with the desperately missed connection. When Zen reluctantly pulled back again, she winked at her. "I love it when you talk tough." Seeing more and more agents now coming back into the control room, Zendara reluctantly let go of Amari and stepped back. "Be safe, Nova."

Amari delivered a mock salute. "Be safe, T'ala. May the light of Q'orre shine on the path to your victory."

Zen gave a little nod, grabbed her duffel bag, and spun on her heel to go join her mission team.

Five minutes later, Hatch opened a portal to the inside of a warehouse in Indianapolis and seven CORP agents, and one powerful woman from a planet called Tora, rushed through. Rocket exchanged a few more private words with Lingua and Hatch before leading the rest of the group up the elevator and to the rooftop bay that was built to house the X3. Even though Rocket was the team leader and trained to fly a variety of aircraft, Howler took the pilot seat because he had the most experience with the Milwaukee team's speedy, long-range helicopter. Everyone kept their helmets on since they were just as safe as the normal chopper helmets, and they would allow the team to communicate along normal channels, though all of them chose to leave the face shields up so they could see each other better. The duffle bags were also within easy reach. A rough voice came through the com. "Everyone buckle up and ready yourselves for takeoff. We're going full throttle all the way down."

Gauss voiced the same question that popped into Nova's head. "Can this thing handle that without overheating?"

Howler was a gruff dude and not particularly social and it showed in the way he addressed the youngest Bell man. "Sweetheart, this bitch can have us there in seven hours without breaking a sweat or needing to refuel. I hope everyone used the lav before we left."

Rocket held up a hand and cut in before anyone could complain. "There is a head through the small door in the back. Once we reach cruising speed, you can unbuckle your harness and use it as needed." She glanced at the difficult pilot. "And can the attitude, Howler."

Rocket moved to sit in the co-pilot's seat as the next question came across the com. "So why didn't we just have Hatch teleport us down and save the long trip?"

Howler answered. "We're also fully loaded with munitions in case the fuckers on the base in Guantanamo want to bring out the big guns before we even hit the ground."

Everyone got quiet after that as the machine took off and climbed to a higher altitude. Ten minutes later Rocket unbuckled and stood to address the rest of the X3 team. She grabbed a tablet from her duffel bag on the way toward the back and brought up a map of the facility and surrounding land. "Here's the game plan. Howler is going to set the X3 down in the foothills just northeast of the fenced off detention center grounds. To prevent Oracle from getting suspicious, we had Lingua file a standard civilian flight plan with the Mariana Grajales Airport so our approach to the big island won't be suspicious. Lingua has also taken the X3 off the CORP network. Savvy?" A chorus of helmets nodded, along with the single bare head of Nova. "Before we veer off course to approach the foothills, Howler is going to drop us down and depressurize the cabin so Nova and I can exit mid-flight. It will be our job to take out the radar and satellite receiving station within the Guantanamo Detention Center."

Nova looked closely at the map where Rocket had her gloved finger. "Is that the intel that Lingua pulled from the system while we were still in Chicago?"

"Yes. Now, once we take out their advance warning systems, I'll give Howler the all clear then we proceed to phase two."

Ember stood from her own harness. Lumos's twin sister had been fairly quiet since coming into the group, at least compared to the rest. To Nova's eyes, she seemed as capable as any of the other agents she'd encountered, it was just that the SAIC of Minneapolis was significantly more reserved. There was a way that Ember held herself, a wariness in her eyes that reminded Nova of one of her friends in college. It seemed incongruous from a powerful Chromodec that was responsible for a team of other powerful Chromodecs. Ember's words interrupted the rest of Nova's thoughts on the subject. "Once we've got cover, Nova and Rocket will continue on toward the US airstrip and take out as many fighters and heavy munitions machines as they can. They'll also disable ground support as they are able. Once the X3 touches down, we'll have one flight capable agent and three on the ground. It will be up to Gauss to fly us all to the nearest access tunnel that will take us inside the underground bunker network. It's a fairly good distance away but fully within his range."

Nova looked at her curiously. "That has to have some pretty serious security, all things considered. Will you be able to get inside?"

Lumos's twin sister smiled back at her. "With a team comprised of a magnekinetic, a cryokinetic, a pyrokinetic, and sonic voluminizer, we can get through just about anything. I wouldn't worry about us, you just keep the birds busy in the sky."

Nova grinned back. "I think I can do that."

Rocket picked up the speech again from there, giving a more detailed description of their attack plan. They didn't know exactly where Oracle would be located but Rocket was counting on a report from Augur when the right time came. She made sure the map was pushed to everyone's helmet so it could be seen with their heads-up display. Nova had hers on the wrist comp. When Rocket was finished with the briefing, she went back to her seat. It was Howler's gruff voice that came over the com a minute later, more subdued due to the senior agent's earlier warning. "Settle in folks, bus is gonna be in the air for another six and a half hours. Nap if you can."

While the seats were built for long flights, they weren't *that* comfortable. Frost grimaced. He was the male agent from Minneapolis that had a broken arm when they initially found him. "Yeah right."

Gauss chimed in too. "Anyone have a magazine?" Laughter was the only response.

THE INDIANAPOLIS TEAM teleported into an old high-security storage warehouse on the outskirts of the city. Hatch had a visual lock on the space because Lingua brought up live images using remote cameras placed around the inside and outside of the building. Indianapolis was still caught in the middle of the battle for control between the rogues and the loyal CORP agents. None of the local agents were on Augur and Hatch's list of trusted individuals and Augur felt it safer to remain inconspicuous until they could suss out who were the good guys and who were the bad. The brawny agent was surprised to be leading the team, considering Lumos was of a higher rank, being SAIC of Milwaukee. But the younger Special Agent in Charge deferred leadership of the small force to the man who had been like a father figure in Lumos's first days as a CORP agent. Augur had a cool head and a lot of experience during emergency situations with his years spent in Black Badge.

Despite the early hour, the sound of gunfire could be heard clearly by the newly arrived team. There wasn't much of a solid plan, other than identifying the rogues and taking them out. T'ala jumped when an explosion rattled the wall near her shoulder and Augur called the team to attention. "When we get outside, Kreskin and I will use telepathy to figure out which combatants are the rogues. I want Lumos, Sinter, and T'ala to stay at our backs and cover us while Fist, Flux, and Candor find high vantage points and set up the riot rifles."

Everyone but T'ala checked their weapons and spare clips one more time, and the last three agents mentioned picked up the duffle bags they'd arrived with. Standard protocol for all CORP agents meant those without range-oriented offensive powers or flight capability were required to become excellent marksmen to help cover the other powered members of the team.

Kreskin shut his eyes and reached through the open face shield to press the first two fingers of each hand over his temples and T'ala had to stifle a snicker at the classic "telepath" pose. He was like an old movie caricature. "I've got two in the sky, both rogues. And I'm picking up two more about four blocks northwest. They're all pretty far off still. I suspect the explosion we felt a minute ago was someone's stray munition. Probably one of the flyers."

Augur's face shield was closed so it was hard to tell if his eyes were open or shut. "I can confirm the nearby Chromodecs. We also have five fighting on the ground but not all are enemy agents." He held up a hand for a second of silence then spoke again. "I'm getting the names Mads and Digg...Colt, Memno and Gallos — damnit! I lost the flyers."

"Hawk, and Levosa." Kreskin was focused on nothing but the task at hand and it showed with his nearly instant lock on the remaining two rogues' names.

"You copy, Lingua?" Lucky for both teams, they had full support and coms back to the Milwaukee office. Though the two missions weren't on the same channel.

"Roger that, Auggy. I'm pushing their bios to everyone's HUD so everyone knows who to look for based on power signature. I also wrote an algorithm that will track their helmet beacons so you have a better visual on who's who out there. I mean...all us 'Decs look the same, am I right?"

T'ala winced and spoke before she really put any thought into it. "Jesus, Lingua. That's a dick thing to say!" She checked her wrist computer to see the bios that the human agent sent.

"Sure, civ, pretend like you didn't think the same way before you tumbled into this little operation."

"Focus on the mission and shut y'all's clap traps! Lingua, give me a four block city grid on my HUD." Augur was used to Lingua's chatter but the rest weren't so he needed to reign her in early or she was bound to rattle and distract the group. However, he didn't read her the riot act because he knew what few others did. Lingua's mouth got worse the more nervous she became. It usually happened when she wasn't able to join the team. She felt left out and useless. Even though she was one of the minority human CORP agents, she had more drive and dedication than almost anyone else he'd met.

Lumos added one last bit of advice to the team before the snipers could break away. "Remember, as you get each rogue incapacitated with a collar, catch the base on coms so we can get these assholes teleported back to Milwaukee for incarceration. We don't want to leave anyone lying around for other rogues to rescue."

"Yes, sir!" The team as a whole responded to his direct order.

Three agents broke from their group, each heading for a tall building nearby at a fast clip. The rest started forward on foot, edging along the side of the street, using the buildings as cover.

They hadn't gone more than twenty feet when two black-suited agents pelted around the corner in their direction. Augur, Lumos, and Kreskin took cover behind a parked delivery van while T'ala and Sinter ducked into a doorway. An explosion sounded from the next block over, much too close for the group's comfort. HUD screens didn't light up to indicate they were rogues so Augur yelled through the com. "Friendlies, don't fire!" Seconds later two more agents rounded the corner at a dead run. HUDs on every helmet lit up with their identities, Mads and Digg. They had their sidearms pointed at the loyal agents and the *pop pop* of gunfire sounded loud between the buildings. One of the loyal agents cried out as their arm was clipped but they didn't stop running. Suddenly the rogue on the left switched hands with his gun and pulled something from a pocket of his suit. He lobbed the object far ahead and it landed about ten feet in front of the fleeing Indianapolis agents, thirty feet in front of the group of loyalists from Milwaukee. Augur knew they only had seconds. "T'ala!"

T'ala wasn't an idiot. She'd watched enough movies and TV shows that she knew a grenade when she saw one. There was no time to speed to it and attempt to fly it away. Instead she ran from the doorway in hyper-mode and snatched it up, wrapping the core of her body around the small object as best she could. Much to the shock of most everyone watching, there was no explosion, only a muffled *boom* with some smoke leaking from around T'ala's hands and torso. The young woman was so juiced from the blast that her eyes glowed inky black along with her hair, trailing away from her head a good two feet as she rose into the air. Just like in their day of training, it was too much power and she panicked for a second. "Augur!"

Sensing her predicament, he gave advice as best he could. "Remember what Nova said, point and shoot!"

"Yes, sir!" Following his instruction she aimed in front of Mads and Digg, the identified rogues, and relaxed her hold on the energy coursing through her. They had paused to watch her actions, as did everyone else. Just like in Canada, the beam shot away from her. It hit the pavement a few feet in front of the two men that had turned to fire on her when they realized she was a bigger threat than the ones running away. Concrete, patched asphalt, and water shot into the air from the resulting explosion. The two men were thrown back, which proved to be lucky for them since another explosion happened right after T'ala's release of power. Everyone in the vicinity could feel the heat from the unceasing column of flame.

"Gas line was hit. Lumos, can you control that flame? Sinter, push the vehicles away so the fuel tanks don't catch. And Lingua, hack the digital shutoffs for the city and lock that down." Once he was sure Lumos and Lingua were handling the fire, he walked up to the two agents who had been fleeing the rogues minutes before. The woman held her hand to her wounded arm in an attempt to staunch the bleeding. They both gave the new group a wary look and Augur sighed. "I see y'all got a rogue problem down here in Naptown too. They're everywhere nowadays."

"Who the *fuck* are you people?" The injured woman's voice was harsh with pain. Based on the inception number below their badges, both agents were younger, too young for Augur or Lumos to be familiar with them.

The twenty-foot spout of flame was just beginning to die down so Augur raised his face shield. "Agent Jaxon Bell, but you can call me Augur. We're the good guys who are here to help you take your city back from the rogues." Sinter walked up to stand behind her dad.

"Holy shit, you're a legend!" The man raised his own face shield and his fellow agent let go of her arm to followed suit. The action left a smear of blood on the side of her helmet. They both looked pale and exhausted. "I'm Demos, and this is Shackle. But what are rogues? *Who* are they?" They watched as Kreskin and Lumos jogged up the block to where the two enemy agents lay unmoving while T'ala hovered protectively.

Before Augur could answer, Fist came over the com. "We've got movement five blocks northeast."

"Could they be civ?"

"Negative. They're in a CORP transport, with one flight capable trailing behind."

Augur shut his face shield again and addressed the newcomers. "Any more allies with you?"

Shackle spared Demos a worried glance before answering. "No. We had two more but we split up a half hour ago. I don't know what happened to Reaver and Sensen."

"Give me five and I'll answer your questions." He caught a flash as a portal opened near Kreskin and Lumos. Thinking fast, Augur waved his daughter forward. "See if there's something in that duffle to wrap around Shackle's arm." Then he looked up and yelled to their other flight capable team member, their ace in the hole. "T'ala, you're the quickest of us. Do you think you can stop the transport?"

Still a good twenty feet in the air, T'ala turned so her eerie black glowing eyes were facing him. "Hell yeah."

"Do it then. Fist, point her in the right direction."

Candor's voice came over the com next. "They've just passed my corner. I'm three blocks from your location, directly north and over one. You want me to take a shot on the flier? I think it's Hawk."

Augur cursed under his breath and queued the com again. "No visual on Levosa?"

"No, sir."

He looked up to where T'ala hung in the air and pointed to the north. "T'ala, go!" While T'ala seemed to levitate with ease, flying still proved difficult. Her directional movement was halting and shaky at best. So instead of flying she dropped down to the ground and took off at a hyper-fast run. The agents on the ground nearest to her path did a double take as she disappeared in a black blur. "Candor, wait 'til T'ala hits that transport then take out the one in the air." Seeing everything else squared away in the immediate vicinity, Augur directed the rest of the agents on the ground. "Let's go. Double team north to join T'ala. With any luck the transport will be the last of them in the city."

They took off at a run in the direction that T'ala had disappeared and Sinter flew ahead of them. Seconds later the sound of rending metal hit their ears, then automatic gunfire erupted, killing the remaining silence. They rounded the last corner in time to see the smoking remains of the CORP transport. The entire front center of the hulking vehicle was crushed in and smoking. It looked as if the driver had run into a tree. Maybe a better description would be if the tree had run into the vehicle. Augur blinked at the sheer destruction then his training kicked back into gear as T'ala ripped the gun from the hands of one agent while another blasted her with some sort of energy beam. Rather than slow her down, she sped to the next attacker knowing the agents behind her would take care of the unarmed rogue. For being completely untrained, she was doing remarkably well.

A piercing *screech* filled the air from the recently disarmed woman. Sinter was first on the scene and used a piece of metal she'd stripped from the transport to muzzle and incapacitate the sonic rogue. Then the young agent pulled the eloptic collar from her cargo pocket and clicked it around the woman's neck, securing it with a thumbprint. T'ala had no way to carry one of the power-dampening collars, nor did she want to. While she and her ultra-black ship suit could absorb energy beams and the concussive force of a grenade, the collar was a lot more sensitive and would not have fared so well.

"Sir, I've got the flyer on the ground, one block east of your location. He needs a collar." Lumos shot a low-level laser beam at the second man T'ala disarmed while Augur tackled one that had stepped out from behind the wrecked vehicle to take aim at Lumos.

"Fist here, I'm positioned with the downed flyer but my collar got damaged and he's not carrying one."

"Sinter!" Kreskin tossed her the extra collar he had stashed in his side pouch and she took off to assist Fist. She let the Milwaukee agent know she was coming. "Keep Hawk down for a minute longer, I'm on my way with another collar now."

Augur was in the middle of subduing his opponent so Lumos directed the other two high vantage point agents. "Candor, take the northeast one-eighty, Flux take the southwest. Let us know if that last flyer shows up—"

"Incoming! Southwest side, too fast for me to get a shot in."

"I've got them!" With all but Augur's rogue rendered non-threatening, T'ala was free to help stop the last one and excited to do it. She quickly rose straight into the air. Seeing T'ala, Levosa adjusted direction to head straight for her. That proved to be Levosa's first and last mistake of the day. By nine-fifteen a.m. Eastern Standard Time, all the rogue agents in Indianapolis had been defeated and taken to Milwaukee for incarceration. Once everyone but the outlying agents were back on the ground in one place, Augur raised his face shield and breathed a sigh of relief.

"Booyah!" T'ala high-fived Sinter as the reality of their relatively easy success sank in.

The young Bell woman smiled and shook her head. "Hell yeah, we're getting shit done right here."

They sobered quickly when Flux's voice came over the com. Both she and Candor were slowly making their way toward the group from their previous vantage points. "Sir, I've got two downed agents, three blocks west of your position."

Augur swallowed. "Alive?"

"No, sir. Idents are oh-seven-two-three and oh-two-four-one. With our HUDs on a limited network I can't bring up their IDs."

Lingua had been listening and seconds later had the Agents'

names. "Agent David Pleschett and Agent Shelly Smith. Code names, Reaver and Sensen." Augur repeated the news for the two Indianapolis agents since they weren't on the same com channel as the rest of the group.

"No!" It took only a second for Demos to rip off his helmet and throw it away from him. It bounced and clattered and everyone on Augur's team stilled. The twenty-something man crumpled before their eyes as he dropped to his knees in the street.

Shackle put her good hand on her teammate's shoulder to comfort him as he broke down. Her face was solemn when she met Augur's eyes. "Reaver and Demos were engaged to be married. They just celebrated their three year anniversary together last week."

T'ala closed her eyes at the agent's words. Her thoughts immediately turned to Amari, wondering how she was doing, worrying that she'd never see her own love again.

EVERYONE HAD BEEN aware of the casualties occurring around the country, after all, that's why they were fighting to make things right. But knowing of loss and experiencing that loss first hand were two very different things. Discovering the death of two agents that none of the original heroes had even known was saddening. But it was nothing compared to witnessing the intense grief of those that loved them best. It highlighted the reality of the danger they faced, and the permanence of death hit home for more than one of the assembled men and women. Some had never suffered through the death of someone they loved and the concept of it was foreign to them. But there were a few like T'ala, who had lost everything and feared losing more. In a matter of seconds, Demos's grief stripped them bare.

Chapter Twenty-one

ROCKET LISTENED INTENTLY in a three-way communication between herself, Augur, and Lingua. While part of her rejoiced at the other team's victory in taking back Indianapolis, she also mourned to discover that only two loyal agents were left alive. She knew that if things ever returned to normal, every member of CORP would need extensive counselling to help them heal mentally and physically from the events of the past few days. The very nature of the Chromodec uprising was such an aggressive breach of trust from their former teammates, she knew it would be years before some fully recovered, if ever.

The X3 had covered about half the distance between Milwaukee and Cuba and with Oracle's loss of Naptown, she knew that the man would be even more dangerous and determined. He was sure to send additional agents to the Midwest to confront Augur's group and Rocket feared for her friends. When she passed on the news of Augur's victory to her own team, a whoop went through the inside of the chopper. She quietly celebrated with them for a few seconds until she looked at Nova. The young woman's clenched jaw and tightly shut eyes were proof that their lone civilian, the genius scientist who had been born on another planet, had figured it out that Oracle would be sure to retaliate. Since he didn't know about their little group in the sky, his target would be the loyal agents that Nova's soul mate was currently helping. Rocket glanced at the chrono in the upper left of her HUD screen. Augur would be taking the team on to Columbus in less than twenty minutes. They'd know soon enough if there was fall-out from Augur and crew's productive morning.

AUGUR STOOD IN the middle of the street, fighting back-to-back with Lumos. Kreskin lay on the ground nearly ten yards away. His fellow telepath had taken another blow to the head hard enough to crack the helmet. Augur was using his mental abilities at maximum capacity to dodge blows and random energy beams. Kreskin had been doing the same but got distracted and was incapacitated by an attack from behind. Sinter worked fever-

ishly, pulling pieces of metal together to shield their little group
as rogue after rogue fired upon them. Fist was in the melee doing
her best to punch her way out of a barrier that a telekinetic had
erected around her. Unfortunately the barrier wasn't metal so
there was no way Sinter could help her out.

Despite the addition of five loyal agents from the Columbus
CORP team, their own original group was down a few. Besides
Kreskin, Flux had taken a bullet to her upper thigh and nearly
half of Candor's left side was scorched. Augur sent them through
a quick portal back to Milwaukee for healing. But the way the rest
of the group was pinned down meant there was no way any of
them could reach Kreskin to drag him to safety, let alone get him
through a portal without enemy agents following.

The city had started out fairly easy. There were only two
rogues left fighting the five loyalists by the time the liberating
team had arrived. That all changed in the first fifteen minutes
when a massive portal opened up on the roof of the Columbus
CORP building and a score of Chromodecs poured out. It was in
that moment that Augur knew Oracle was aware of their plan.
Colonel Maza clearly didn't want to lose any more of his corrupt
agents so he sent a massive team to quell the resistance. Some of
the rogues he recognized as their powers made themselves
known. The ground shook beneath his feet, knocking more than
one person from both sides to the street. A nearby apartment
building collapsed with a slow groan, a testament to Shockwave's
power.

His com screeched to life. "Fucking hell, Auggy! I've got city
alerts screaming all over my coms here! You need to take out that
shaky bastard ASAP!" Lingua wasn't subtle, nor was she stupid.
Both of them were familiar with the cocky SAIC of Los Angeles.
The man had graduated CORP training about ten years after they
switched from Black Badge to the more public government organization. He was handsome, powerful, and charismatic, but
they'd heard enough stories along the back channels to know that
Agent Collin Bremmer was trouble, not that they needed the back
channel rumors after what he did to Ember. Augur glanced over
to Lumos. He could feel the rage emanating from the younger
man. Lumos hated Shockwave with a passion and it was obvious
by the way he spun to his left and shot a solid beam toward the
rogue. While light is fast, nothing is faster than precognition,
which was how Shockwave must have known to have a reflective
chest plate strapped to the front of his uniform. Oracle. Shock-

wave grinned at them and didn't even flinch as lightening rained down from the sky to strike the pavement at their feet.

Good and bad agents flew through the air at the resounding explosion. T'ala was all but salivating for a hit of that lightning because she was near empty, barely staying afloat high above. She had lifted a bus of civilians to safety ten minutes before. The Columbus agents had assured everyone that the area was evacuated so she had no idea why there was a bus full of travelers so close to the fighting. But between the lift and the halting flight, she had drained her reserves. T'ala was about to take a page out of Nova's book and slam straight into the ground for the energy kick when she suddenly found herself caught and held by some invisible force. She had no energy to break free and as she was lifted higher into the air, T'ala realized that she was no longer flying under her own power. Her eyes scanned the horizon and spotted someone floating maybe twenty yards from her position. It was a woman if the cut of the suit meant anything. The pressure increased, making it harder and harder to drawn in breath and she panicked. "Sinter!"

The youngest Bell woman quickly saw the problem and began to ascend to T'ala's position. At that moment another bolt of lightning arched across the sky from the hands of a rogue on the ground. It struck Sinter, a woman whose greatest affinity was with iron, and her entire body went into a near-epileptic spasm before dropping ten feet to the ground where she lay unmoving on the cement. T'ala saw what happened to her friend but she had no more breath to cry out. She had no breath for anything and her lungs burned from lack of oxygen. Just before she slipped into darkness, she saw the flash of another portal opening and hoped that Hatch got to her daughter in time.

The portal didn't belong to Hatch. It belonged to Portis, one of the LA rogues that had come in with Shockwave. The good news was that when Shockwave and Portis teleported out of Columbus, they took all but five other agents with them, which meant fairly easy cleanup for the rest of the liberating team. The rogues left behind the weakest members so they were quickly taken out. Sinter rose, much to Augur's relief, and used the rest of her reserve power to corral in the remaining corrupt agents with sheets of metal and rebar she found on a semi that had been abandoned nearby. The bad news was that despite their success in taking back Columbus, Augur had to be the one to tell Rocket that one of their aces had been captured. While he didn't know for certain, he had a guess as to how Nova would react to that news.

"SIR, WE'RE FIFTEEN minutes out from Cuban airspace. Permission to drop down and depressurize?" Rocket glanced back at Nova, taking note of the young woman's sudden unease. It was easier to follow the emotions on her face since she was the only member of the team not wearing a helmet.

"Drop us down, Howler." Rocket spun her seat around to observe the young woman more closely. She was about to say something when her com sounded with the tones of a private communication. The team leader quickly shut her face shield and responded. "Go ahead."

She'd heard Augur's deep voice in just about every situation a person could find themselves in, and Rocket worried at the tone of it before the meaning of his words even registered. "We have a situation."

"Columbus?"

"The city is secure."

She sighed, knowing he had more to say. She wasn't in the mood for Augur's reticence. "And? Casualties?"

"Two rogues and multiple wounded on both sides. That's not the problem. Oracle knows about our efforts and sent more than twenty additional rogues to our location as we were mopping up the last few. Shockwave was leading the group."

Rocket's eyes darted to Ember then back to watch Nova. "Go ahead. If you've got a point here, Auggy, get to it fast because we're about to drop down so Nova and I can jump ship."

"They have T'ala."

Augur's point could potentially be disastrous. "Fuck!" Some sound must have carried through her helmet because more than one agent, along with Nova, looked in her direction. She spun the seat to face forward where the only person that could see her body language was Howler. "Tell me."

Augur sighed and Rocket could picture the big man scrubbing his hand across the top of his bald head. "They brought in too many high powered agents and we were quickly overrun. I had multiple people down and the last I saw T'ala, she was carrying a busload of civs away from the engagement zone. Sinter told me after that T'ala must have been depleted. Before she could power up the way Nova showed her, Shockwave's pet TK snatched her up."

"Let me guess, Python?"

"Bingo. Anyway, some fuckwit throwing lightning bolts around hit Sinter as she was flying up to help and before we could even think of responding, Portis took the lot of them out of here, including T'ala. My guess is they'll be waiting for you down in Guantanamo."

Rocket groaned. "Jesus, Aug. This shit's fucked seven ways to Sunday. Do I tell her or don't I tell her?"

"Not my call, boss."

"I knew you'd say that. Thanks for the heads up. We'll do our best down here, and you continue to be safe. Savvy?"

"Copy that. We're headin' on back to Milwaukee now to recover and get some rest. Probably won't hit the next city until tomorrow. Augur out."

Her thoughts clamored amidst the noise of worry. Rocket did what she was best at and made the call. She queued the general com. "Howler, increase descent speed and level it off. We're bailing out five minutes early."

Every part of the plan had been thought out and calculated as far as the timing of their approach. And leaving the X3 earlier wasn't part of that plan. "Sir, I don't thi—"

"Do it." Without any more second-guesses, Rocket stood and took the few steps into the main cabin. "Nova, new intel means we're jumping ship five minutes early."

The younger woman stood as well and her face grew pale. "T'ala..." She didn't even know what her unease could be about other than her soul mate. But the shiny black surface of Rocket's face shield gave nothing away.

The X3 continued to drop then Howler's voice came back over the com. "Anyone that doesn't want to practice skydiving without a chute better buckle up! Twenty seconds to drop." The remaining agents scrambled to make sure their belts were secure.

Both Rocket and Nova counted off the time in their head and when the cargo door opened, they flew out into a clear sky. They were immediately buffeted by wind from the rotors but made it safely clear. For a second Nova looked down at the glittering blue of the Caribbean Sea and marveled at its beauty. Then she remembered Rocket's last words and turned to where the agent hovered nearby. "You said something about new intel?"

The agent's voice was clearly heard through the com in Nova's ear. "First I need to know you're with us, that you'll follow orders."

Nova's eyes and hair glowed bright white, nearly blinding in the bright sun of the tropics. "Of course I'm with you. I thought T'ala and I made that abundantly clear when we started all this. What's going on?"

"Augur's group got hit by a large team of rogues. Oracle knows what they've been doing in each city and he sent his dirty agents in to stop it."

It was much harder to read expression on Nova's face with the power glow. "T'ala, the team? Are they okay? Don't fuck with me, I know something is wrong!"

"Everyone is fine but..."

Nova's body suddenly straightened in midair with her hands down to her sides in tight fists. "Just tell me already!"

"They took T'ala. Most of the surprise rogue force teleported out and they took her with them. I'm sure they'll be waiting for us at the base."

"No." The word was nearly a whisper over the com.

Rocket glanced at the HUD chrono to check time and she knew they had to get this sorted soon. "We'll get her back or die trying." She flew closer, right next to the stiff woman, and put a hand on the clenched fist. "We'll get her back." The white glow where Nova's eyes were located suddenly winked out as she squeezed her eyes tightly shut.

"I can't feel her, which I've been able to do since our bond was completed. Wherever they have her or whatever they've done, I can't feel her."

"Can you feel her when she's unconscious?" Rocket tried to think of an answer that would keep Nova calm.

Nova blew out a breath and fell back into logic to prevent panicking. The agent had a point. "I don't know, I guess I've never tried."

"You need to hold on hope that she's fine, just incapacitated. I don't see Oracle throwing away a potential resource."

"No, you're right. I'm just—" Nova clenched her jaw and her posture got even stiffer as they floated high above the water.

Rocket let her process for about thirty seconds before prompting the younger woman. "Tell me what you need."

Glowing eyes opened again and despite the strange effect of the seeping energy, the anger on Nova's face was plain as day. It was a strange emotion to see on a woman she'd only known as calm and mild-mannered. "Hit me."

"Are you—?"

"I want to be as juiced as possible going in. Hit me *now*, Agent Danes!" The kinetic punch was everything Nova remembered and she sucked in a breath at the increase in power.

Rocket's helmet tilted to the side as if in question. Like a dog. "You ready?" She got an angry nod but that was all she needed. "Stay on my tail, we're going in low and fast so they don't pick us up on the scanners until the last second."

The first thing Nova noticed was the rocky shore. Then as they got closer the green rolling hills became obvious. They were flying so low to the water that their fast passage kicked up a line of spray behind them. Her observations were interrupted by Rocket's voice in her ear.

"After we take out the radar and satellites that are sitting on the coast, we'll hit Leeward Point Field since that's the active military airfield. Fly straight through the aircrafts, I don't care about the damage."

"I bet your bosses might."

"I think my *real* bosses want this problem handled as soon as possible. McCalla Field was designated as the auxiliary landing field, we can head there second to make sure they don't have any backup planes there. After that we'll move off to the base proper."

They were coming around the coastline fast so Nova didn't have long to think on the plan. "How careful?"

Rocket knew exactly what she meant. "They don't have much in the way of personnel, most security on the base is automated. They count on collars and locked rooms for the prisoners. I'm going to assume that anyone still stationed there has been complicit with Oracle's plans. That being said, try not to kill anyone. Chromodecs are pretty hardy, we'll take care of the aftermath...well, after."

Nova's response was quiet and the com barely picked it up at the speed they were flying. "Okay."

They had circled slightly south so they could approach the island in a northerly direction. They made short work of the communications station and continued on toward the airfield. The Leeward Point Field was situated on the left entrance to the big bay, its two long concrete runways looked like the sides of a ladder on the ground with connecting strips evenly spaced along its length. There was a line of fighter jets in one area and half a dozen helicopters at the other end of the airfield. Rocket debated for a second. "You blast through the landing gear on the jets, which will prevent them from taking off. I'll hit the rotors on the choppers. That should keep the damage minimal but still sufficient to keep them on the ground."

Less than a minute later the two flyers split and rose high enough to clear the fence along the shoreline. Carnage ensued. Rocket's plan went exactly as she imagined, though her thought of keeping damage to a minimum was a little overly ambitions considering the size of her scalar-powered levikinetic field when she's flying. It's not an exact science and the actual shape of it changes while she's midair. More than one of the choppers had the entire top crushed and ripped open as she rocketed through.

Being impervious to impact without having a field of protection, Nova had a lot more luck with the jets. She precisely clipped the nose gear from each plane, flying low to the ground. Of course there was damage as each one dropped nose to the cement, but it would be a lot easier to repair than the scrapped out helicopters. After all the obvious fight capable vehicles were rendered inoperable, Rocket took off across the bay with Nova hot on her heels. They did the same on the opposite side and by the time they flew up to recon a few hundred yards directly above the water, sirens and alarm claxons sounded all around the base. Rocket checked the chrono of her HUD. "The X3 should be landing right now, it's time we went down and started our distraction."

Nova laughed. "You mean *that* wasn't distraction enough?" Her laughed cut off abruptly when gunfire sounded from below. Whatever they were shooting was big and Nova felt the impact though they didn't hurt. The bullets themselves were about half an inch in diameter and nearly four inches long. Nova had never seen anything like them but wasn't impressed enough to do more than watch dispassionately while they hit her and simply fell away to the water below. Every bit of their kinetic energy absorbed and amplified.

"Nova, take out that M2! While you're lily skin is protected, I'm not quite so invulnerable over here and those shells are taxing my scalar field."

"I'm on it!" All the absorbed energy from the large caliber machine gun rounds was put to good use when Nova pointed back toward the ground and released a burst of energy. She let the first shot hit the ground near the gun to scatter the operators. When she saw the soldiers running away, she fired another shot destroying the weapon.

"There are two more on the other side, take those out as well."

Nova turned and did the same on the opposite side of the bay, right down to the warning shots. A blast of lightning arched across the sky and hit her, giving the alien woman an instant recharge. "Whoa! What the hell was that?"

Rocket increased magnification on her helmet and searched below as another bolt of lightning moved from the ground upward. One of the smaller branches skimmed her TK field. "Well that feels familiar. If I were a betting woman I'd say it was the same douchebag we nabbed in Chicago a few years ago. Went by the name Zeusifer."

"It looks like your *Zeusifer* is now one of Oracle's rogues. I'll take care of him—shit! Rocket!" Nova found herself immobilized in an invisible squeezing force. "I. Can't. Move."

Rocket quickly scanned the surrounding space and found who she was looking for a hundred yards away. She took off full speed toward the floating Chromodec. Python could withstand blasts similar to Rocket, but speed wasn't her specialty. And she certainly couldn't project her telekinesis onto another person while levitating and protecting herself. Seeing Rocket's rapid approach the rogue was forced to release Nova and defend herself. "Go now, take out the guy on the ground and any others you see."

Ember's voice came over their coms. "We're in the tunnels below the base but I have no idea where Oracle is located. We encountered some resistance, basic soldiers on the ground. Nearly all are low powered and easily contained with their own collars. Orders?"

Rocket dodged a telekinetic hit and responded. "Two priorities. Find Oracle and find T'ala. They took her from Columbus and came down here. And Ember..." She paused and Python flew down toward a small group of rogues on the ground.

"Yeah, Rock?"

"Shockwave is one of the leaders below Oracle. He's here so be careful, especially in the tunnels. His power would be disastrous." Rocket didn't provide any more warning and didn't try to figure out Ember's mental state with the news. She already knew what the woman would be feeling. Ember would stay on task.

"Yes, sir."

Nova flew back toward Rocket as more rogues fired from the ground. Machine guns, side arms, sometimes blasts of fire or ice, whatever they had available. "What's next, boss?"

"We need to grab someone down there, find out who may know where T'ala and Oracle are located. Python would be my best bet but she's a hard one to hold. Let's see if—ngguh!" Rocket grabbed the sides of her helmet, nearly clawing at the shiny black surface and began to fall. Nova quickly flew down and caught her.

"What's wrong? What is it?"

"T—telep—path. Trying to...ugh, get in...my head!"

Nova held Rocket in one arm while she scanned the group below. Nova was almost invulnerable to everything they were throwing at her, but Rocket no longer had such protection while she wasn't blasting in her field. Without caring what kind of damage she inflicted, Nova pointed her fist toward the center of the group and fired one of her white blasts, releasing more than she'd ever done before. Bodies flew through the air and Rocket immediately roused from her stupor.

"Uh, shit! I fucking hate telepaths. Give me a second." Sure enough, within a few seconds Rocket was blasting up and out of Nova's arms. They both turned to see a few people standing up from the ground while the rest stayed down. Rocket didn't feel bad at all. "Nice job. Now, let's go fishing." Nova followed closely behind Rocket as the SAIC blasted toward the ground. A few of the agents left standing tried to bolt away but Rocket zig-zagged between them, cracking helmets with her fist, her scalar field providing protection and an added impact that was enough to render the rogues unconscious. "Nova, check out a few and snag some collars if they've got them." Rocket landed on the ground and scanned the various bodies around her as Nova did the same.

"Aha!" The younger woman held an eloptic collar aloft and trotted over to where Rocket was standing. Just before she reached the agents location, an explosion sounded somewhere to the northwest.

Both women stumbled and Rocket's voice was grim over the com. "Team Two, what's your status?" While waiting for a response, Rocket saw the one person she was looking for sit up a short distance away. The woman removed her helmet and seemed disoriented. Before she could become fully aware, the SAIC snatched the collar out of Nova's hand and bolted for Python. She had the eloptic collar around the woman's neck and engaged before Python had even fully roused.

"The fuck!" Python was livid.

Rocket quickly spun the woman onto her stomach and grabbed a pair of flex cuffs from the thigh pocket of her uniform. The flex cuffs didn't take up much room, unlike the collars, so each agent was able to carry multiple pairs. Python was quickly cuffed and jerked upright as another tremor shook the ground. A few seconds later Python became fully aware of her situation and Rocket struggled to hold her. While the lead agent was strong, she was at least six inches shorter than the other woman. "A little help here, Nova."

Nova had collected a few more collars and had them hanging from her left wrist like bangle bracelets. She grabbed the fractious woman in a bear hug from behind to hold her still. "Now what?"

"Base, do you copy?"

"Uh, roger um, Rocket. This is Steph."

A look of surprise crossed Nova's face but she shrugged. Steph was supposed to be helping. Rocket patted Python's cheek lightly. "I've got a package for you. I need a quick portal and a mind scan. See if she knows the location of our two targets."

"Hey Rocky, Hatch here. Who do you have for us? Kreskin is in with the healer but Augur's on his way. Give me a lock."

"We've got Python." She looked around. "Two meters north of my location, in twenty."

Twenty seconds later a portal opened up exactly where Rocket requested and she wasted no time shoving Python through. Then the portal shut again as if it had never existed. Rocket looked back to where Nova was staring at the unmoving bodies. "Let's put those collars to work and go see if we can help out Team Two, shall we?"

"Okay."

The com came to life again with Augur's deep voice. "Python's gonna take a little bit to crack. I'll do my best here, but you know she was specially trained by Oracle to resist telepathic tampering."

"Do what you can. I need that intel yesterday!"

The two women made their way around the agents on the ground, removing helmets and putting collars on them. Much to Nova's dismay, two people had died from the impact of her white energy blast, having been nearest to the center of it. Rocket merely put her hand on the younger woman's shoulder and gave the same advice she always gave. "Work now, grieve later. We need to get to T'ala and Oracle. Okay?" Nova didn't say anything at first. She shut her eyes to the gruesome site and drew in a deep breath. When Rocket's hand gave a little shake, Nova's eyes popped open and she nodded. "Good. Now, let's see if we can—"

"Rocket...can ...ou... ead m...?"

"Ember, you're breaking up. What's your status?"

"Tr...ped ...ow qua...nt four. Reqest ex...action."

Rocket groaned. "Fuck me running. They're too far underground. They've made it quite a ways if they're in quadrant four."

Nova cocked her head. "Where is quadrant four?"

Rocket checked the map on her HUD then spun and pointed east. "There's another bunker entrance that will lead into quadrant four. It's in the foothills, just north of Blue Beach. "Let's go!"

It took mere seconds for Rocket to find the spot she was looking for. All the pertinent map information had been programmed into her HUD, including bunker locations. There was a solid steel door set into the side of one of the larger hills. They hovered about fifty feet away and Nova gave the unassuming door a skeptical look. "This is it?"

"Yup, and you're up. You can take out the door and juice up all at once. Try to make sure the tunnel on the other side remains clear."

"Yes, sir!" While physics had been a breeze for Amari Losira del Rey, she wasn't trained as a physicist or a structural engineer. She had no idea how much force she'd need to go through what was probably a thick steel door embedded in concrete. The first hit wasn't hard enough and she found herself stopped abruptly. Though the massive hit did bend the entire door inward and rained concrete and other debris down around the edges. Because of the amount of kinetic energy she absorbed with the impact, one punch was all Nova needed to complete the job. The door *shrieked* as it was ripped from its hinges and flew down the corridor on the other side. Another tremor shook the ground as she stepped inside and the lights flickered above. Rocket flew in and landed next to her a few seconds later.

"Well done." She called up her HUD map of the underground complex and took off at a fast jog farther inside. Nova had no choice but to follow. "Mil Base, anyone copy?"

"Lingua here. What do you need?"

"Can you hack in and check the sensors to see which sectors have been damaged in quadrant four?"

Lingua's voice came over the com a few seconds later.

"Working on it now, give me a minute."

Another tremor shook the walls and floor and the lights went out in the hall. Rocket cursed and quickly switched her HUD to infrared. "Nova, kill the glow!" Nova's white flames winked out just as a group of soldiers rounded the corner ahead. Rocket knew she was vulnerable in the tunnels without her blast field and had no problem letting the young alien woman take the lead. She also knew Nova didn't have night sight. "Four Chromodecs, about fifty feet straight ahead. Ready to go bowling?"

Nova snorted and flew down the corridor in the direction indicated. As soon as she hit the first Chromodec, she spun her body horizontally, taking the rogues out with feet and fists alike. All went down from the strength of her blows. Both she and Rocket made short work of removing helmets and putting the corrupt agents own collars on them. "Rocket, I've got your intel. Looks like three sections have suffered a collapse. One is fairly near you in ZG forty-eight. The other two are BL thirty and M twenty-seven. Gonna warn you though, you're probably at the limit of our sat transmissions right now so you're going to lose connection with us in another twenty feet or so."

"Good to know, thanks, Lingua. Keep Hatch on standby."

"Will do."

Rocket pulled a small glow stick from one of her many pockets. She snapped and shook it, causing a bright glow to start. After that she pulled out a tactical knife and carefully cut the stick in half, flinging glowing liquid all over the floor and walls, thoroughly marking the area.

"What is that for?"

"If the team we're extracting has injuries, I know we need to get them back to this point in order to make contact with Base and request a teleport. I'm not leaving anyone down here!" Nova didn't say anything to that. She tailed Rocket as the agent jogged down the corridor, following her HUD map in the darkness. For safety purposes, Nova floated behind the senior agent with a slight grasp on Rocket's gear harness to use as a guide. It wasn't long before they came to one of the collapsed sections, completely blocked by stone and fallen beams. "Son of a bitch!"

"Wait, I can clear this out. I've got lots of energy from the door still. Can you light it up?" Rocket pulled a small high-intensity flashlight from her utility belt and stood back. Nova went into hyper mode, moving the large chunks of concrete and steel girders to the edges of the corridor along each side.

It took five minutes to have a clear walkway and they started off again, though Rocket eyed the space above warily as more debris rained down. "You may have to make another path on our way back."

Once completely clear of that section, they picked up the pace again. Another tremor shook the hallway and Rocket nearly fell. She would have if the floating Nova hadn't grabbed the agent's harness to keep her upright.

"That son of a bitch is going to bring the entire complex down around our ears!" Urgency now even greater with Shock-wave's continued assaults, Rocket relied on the HUD map that was downloaded to her helmet and broke into a sprint. "You better not plow me over if I stop on a dime, savvy?" She was huffing as she spoke. Running in full gear was no joke, even for someone in top condition.

"Gotcha." Nova wasn't tired but worry had her running on autopilot as much as anything. Rocket suddenly skidded to a stop as another group of figures rounded the next corner. A fireball came down the corridor ahead of the group and Nova jumped in front of Rocket, taking it full in the chest, though some flame leaked around her and singed the elbow of Rocket's suit.

"Shit!" The senior agent called out over the com. "Together, now. You take left!" She blasted down the right side of the hallway as Nova flew down the left. With both near invulnerable, there wasn't much the rogues could do to defend themselves and the group was left tied and collared like the rest. When they reached the next collapsed section, Nova cleared it out just as she'd done before. It was a good thing the alien woman was first to show her face through the cleared area because she took a fireball right to the head. It was a lucky thing really, because she was starting to feel drained from the earlier activities. Ember's flame was just the kick she needed.

The leader of Team Two immediately stepped back when she realized who she'd fired on. "Jesus, are we glad to see you two!"

Rocket played her flashlight around and quickly took in the scene. Frost was missing his helmet and sported a large cut above his left eye. Rocket assumed he was concussed based on the dazed look on his face. Howler was holding his left arm and she was unsure if it was broken or just dislocated. Gauss appeared fine, as did Ember. She mentally cursed that their small group was down by two. "Let's get everyone top side and see if Lingua has the intel I requested. Frost and Howler are going back as soon as I get a portal from Hatch."

"But sir—"

She cut the pilot off. "No, I need everyone healthy for this mission. We're close, I can feel it. Let's go, fill me in on what happened with Shockwave while we head back to the extraction point."

Ember floated a fireball in front of the group as they set a fast pace back the way Rocket and Nova had come in from. The trip back to the marked section of the hallway took about thirty minutes and Gauss was carrying Frost by his metal-laced harness by the time they arrived. Lingua's voice came over the coms as soon as the group was within range and her news gave them hope. "We've got a lock on T'ala's location. She's in Section Eight, which is about a mile north from Camp America. It's what is commonly referred to as Camp No. It's a black site. Your best bet is to head topside and go in through another entrance."

"Probably a solid idea since Shockwave is sitting up there somewhere trying to shake us out like moles in a field. Any lock on Oracle's location yet?"

"No. And not to make bad news worse but I was finally able to hack into the CORP system and I tried checking on Vision and Voda back in Chicago. As far as I can tell they're in security cells in our CORP facility but it looks like Shyft teleported Minder and Chinook out of the city, my guess is that they're also down there with you."

"Well if there is a telepath that can track our location, it's certainly Minder. She's got the range for it. That explains how Shockwave was able to target us so well while we were underground. Get a visual on the tunnel with my helmet cam. I need a portal opened now because I'm sending two wounded your way."

A minute passed without response, then Lingua's voice came back over the com. "Give us three minutes to prepare."

Rocket's eyebrows went up, unseen within her helmet. "Three minutes? What the fuck do you need to prep—?"

"Three minutes, Rock! Lingua out."

Despite the gravity of the situation, Ember couldn't help laughing. "She's just as bitchy as I remember. Doesn't she like the weather down there in the Windy City, Rocket?"

Howler was less polite. "Served with that woman for years. Pretty sure she was born with a stick up her ass."

Before the SAIC could respond, her com came to life again.

"Screw you, Howler! Ready for portal, three yards down the corridor, toward the exit."

"Ready."

The portal suddenly opened and the entire team did their best to assist the two injured agents through to the other side. Once they were handed off, Augur stepped through to Rocket's side, armed to the teeth. He flipped up his dark face shield and gave Rocket a grin. "We couldn't let you have all the fun, now could we?"

"We?"

Three more black-clad agents stepped through the open portal before it spiraled shut again. Lumos, Sinter, and Hatch rounded out the additions to their group. Hatch's voice held a hint of mirth. "Y'all want a ride topside? I've got the current satellite feed map on my HUD so I can see anyplace that's not underground."

Gauss had embraced his sister but turned to look toward his mom. "You serious?"

Hatch tapped her helmet. "Courtesy of Lingua. She moved the satellite earlier today and patched me in. Now we all have eyes on the ground thanks to what used to be a Google tech."

"Baddass!" Gauss again.

Rocket shook her head. "Fine, let's go."

Augur dropped the face shield back into place and Hatch opened another large portal a little farther down the corridor. When they came through on the other side, the group found themselves near another access door in the middle of a clearing. The sun was just setting over the ocean in the west and the entire team took a moment to orient their HUD maps. Everyone but Nova had the location of T'ala clearly marked on their map of the underground area inside their helmet. Nova's was on her wrist comp. Suddenly the ground shook, harder than it previously had. Ember's voice was grim. "That's Shockwave and he's close."

A small group came through the trees near the edge of the cleared area around the entrance. Rocket blasted up about ten feet. "I'll take care of them. You need to get inside and get T'ala!"

"Rocky!" Augur called out to her and the agent paused before taking off.

"I can handle it. Get her back. That's an order, Agent Bell."

Both Sinter and Gauss were working on the lock to the door and Nova moved her gaze back and forth between them and Rocket. She wanted to get her soul mate but she also didn't want to leave Rocket to face the enemy agents by herself. The door suddenly swung open and Nova watched as Rocket blasted away from them. She quickly announced her intentions. "I'm going to help Rocket!" She then flew off after the determined agent. She didn't see Augur's discreet motion that sent Gauss after Rocket too.

Rogue agents dove left and right to avoid Rocket's charge. The responding lightning and energy blast missed her but scored a direct hit on Nova as she flew right behind. Even as the two of them spun in midair to reengage, Lingua's voice came over the com again. "Rocket, Tomahawk missile launched from the bay. Must have been a sub underwater that the initial scans didn't pick up. I can't break the tracking on it and it's headed right for Section Eight."

Rocket's heart thundered. "Payload?"

"Unclear. I'll keep digging into the specs but the standard would be enough to take out a house but hard to tell what's on this one"

There was only one option. "Nova, go!"

Nova took off into the sky in search of a lone missile, panic speeding her flight. She wasn't sure what to do with a missile but she knew she couldn't let it hit the ground. She could hear Lingua's voice in her ear.

"Oracle must not be in the same section as T'ala if he's not worried about the damage from that blast. My scanner is still running, we'll find him soon enough."

YOU MAY ASK yourself, how brave can someone be when they're invulnerable to nearly every type of energy? Think about the situation our new hero has suddenly found herself in. Logically she knows that she can absorb any type of energy. But she's also a genius who is intimately aware of her own weaknesses as well. An explosion is nothing more than a rapid increase in volume and release of energy in an extreme manner. Sometimes it generates high temperatures and the release of gases. It was one thing getting hit by Rocket at top speed. That was an impact that *simulated* explosive energy, but it wasn't a real explosion. Nova still needed to breath and how could a person do that if they were enveloped by supersonic or subsonic shockwaves? How much oxygen would be left around her? But more importantly, Nova had no idea how much she could absorb before it became *too* much. Bravery meant facing the unknown, pitting herself against something that was potentially dangerous, difficult, and painful, despite fear. Yes, Nova certainly wasn't going to back down from this new challenge. She was going to try as a hero, or die as a hero. There was no in between.

Chapter Twenty-two

NOVA YELLED INTO her com to be heard over the rush of wind, hoping someone could give her a suggestion. "What do I do with it?"

"Lingua, help her out. Gauss just got here and we're a little busy with Shockwave and his — ugh" Rocket was shook as her kinetic blast field absorbed another massive hit of Shockwave's seismic energy. " — crew right now."

"Fine. You have to catch it first, Nova. Environmentalists will scream if you dump it into the ocean. How high can you fly?"

Nova didn't have to go far to see the incoming missile. It was coming up on her position fast. "I can fly pretty high but I still need to breathe. How stable is it?"

Lingua had pulled up the military missile manual and was skimming as fast as possible. "I think you should be able to alter its flight path. Right now it's set to arch down and impact the area very near the access door the rest of the team entered. Looks like the USS Olympia is carrying a payload of tandem warheads. There will be a smaller leading charge that will explode on impact to allow the missile to become entrenched, then the main warhead will go off. They're called bunker busters. Just grab it and fly it upward if you can. It won't explode unless it impacts something."

Nova grabbed the missile and grunted at the amount of thrust it had. Using all her power, she was able to turn the nose so that it was flying straight up and slowed it down as much as possible. "Lingua, where do I go with it?"

"Good, you've got it at about half speed. Keep it pointed up, I'm trying to break the code so I can guide it from here."

Forty-five seconds in, oxygen began to thin and Nova knew she wouldn't be able to hold on much longer. "Lingua…"

"Got it, turn it loose!"

Nova let the rocket go and watched as it continued to climb upward. She herself was near the edge of her limit for oxygen density, which was greater than that of a human at about five miles up. She nearly lost the missile from her sight when it turned into a blinding flash and about ten seconds later she heard the rumble of the explosion. "That was way too close!"

"Yeah, not to mention that was significantly more than a standard payload. And you better hope they don't launch another because I have to break the codes individually to get control and they're all going to be that close."

Nova began a quick decent to aid Rocket and Gauss with their fight against the group of rogues. Though the battle had started in the trees near Section Eight, it had quickly moved nearly half a mile east by the time she caught up with them. When Nova arrived on the scene, the youngest Bell man was flinging ball bearings like bullets. Every so often she'd hear the crack of one hitting a tree trunk. Rocket was trying to battle against both Shockwave's powerful seismic energy and another agent with telekinetic grip similar to Python's. Three agents were on the ground unconscious and another was coming up behind Gauss with a pistol. That was the one she targeted. She was a little better at her controlled hits now that they'd been fighting so much so she was hoping to knock the person out. However, the agent turned at the last second and ducked below Nova's pass. Startled by the commotion behind him, Gauss spun around. "Watch your six. Minder is a telepath and empath."

Sure enough, the corrupt Chicago agent easily sidestepped Gauss's swing and delivered a solid kick to his torso. Gauss lifted into the air to avoid her next blow and she re-aimed the pistol. Rather than attack, Nova flew in to block Minder's shot then slowly floated closer to the woman. "Minder...you're one of Rocket's old team."

Nova couldn't see the agent's face behind the dark helmet but she could definitely hear the smirk in the tone of her voice. "Ah, my little secret. You see, I've only ever been on Oracle's team, even when I was in her bed." Shock hit Nova in the gut. She knew that Rocket was stung beyond belief by her team's betrayal. But to find out that the woman had betrayed the SAIC long before Chicago seemed especially diabolical. "Too bad I was never able to turn her. Oracle gave me a second chance in Chicago and I'd like to think that our takeover of the CORP facility was a rousing success."

At first, Gauss's words made Nova think that Minder would be difficult to beat because she knew that Nova was coming up behind her. But her first meeting with Augur tickled the younger woman's memory. She *couldn't* be read by Chromodec telepaths. It must have been Minder's HUD proximity sensors that tipped the agent off. That was an easy enough problem to fix. She sped down to the ground, right in front of Minder as Gauss called out a warning. "Careful there!"

Nova's grin looked ominous with the white glowing eyes and hair. "Oh, but I don't have to be careful. Because here is *my* little secret, she can't read my mind."

Minder took a step back out of range and brought her pistol up to aim at Nova. "I can read anyone's mind, no matter how strong the Chromodec!" She fired three times and watched in dismay as each bullet hit Nova and fell harmlessly to the ground. "What the fuck?"

"Oh, did I forget to tell you? I'm not a Chromodec, bitch!" With those words Nova swung her fist around to knock the pistol from Minder's hand. The hit was so hard that it broke both bones in the woman's lower arm and she screamed in agony. While she was distracted, Nova ripped the helmet from her head.

"Hey, Nova, catch!"

Nova looked up and snagged the eloptic collar that her friend dropped down to her. "Thanks." It took less than five seconds to have it securely fastened around the rogue agent's neck.

Gauss dropped down and grabbed a set of flex cuffs from his uniform pocket. "I've got her, go check on Rocket." Minder screamed in agony as the flex cuffs were fastened around the wrist of her broken arm. Gauss felt no sympathy for her.

The SAIC's voice was breathless over the com. "Rocket wouldn't mind a little help right about now."

Nova sped over in time to take a full blast of Shockwave's seismic power. His entire body language radiated surprise when she didn't go down. Instead her glow strengthened with absorbed power and anger. "You're the one who took my Q'sirrahna."

The man's helmet looked to the right then to the left, as if he were searching for an escape. But there was no escape. She snatched the rogue agent right off the ground and flew him straight up. The cocky man had lost all his bravado and his voice came out high and frightened. "What are you doing?" Higher and higher they flew until the air turned cold and started to thin. The helmets didn't help an agent breathe, they merely provided tech and protection. Shockwave's breathing grew labored as he struggled for oxygen.

"What's the matter? Can't you breathe, d'eeshek? How does it feel to be helpless with your consciousness failing you? How does it feel to be afraid?"

"Nova! Bring him back alive. That's an order."

The young woman from Reyna went a little bit higher until Shockwave's head lolled forward as he lost consciousness, then she immediately began her decent again. When she got back to the clearing, she dumped him onto the ground, none too gently. The rest had been taken care of and she took great pleasure in removing the collar from Shockwave's suit pocket and placing it around his neck.

"Rocket, this is Augur. We've found T'ala. She's..."

Rocket looked over at Nova who suddenly stiffened. "Just say it, no private coms now, Aug."

"They were holding her in a sensory deprivation tank. Her only air was an oxygen mask set low enough to keep her in a stupor. There are cuts all over her body. Ember thinks they were testing her powers."

Nova spun in place and Rocket quickly blasted ten feet over to block her path. "No! There's no one left down there, let them bring her out. Save your anger, okay?"

White eyes were fierce with the force of her energy. "They hurt her."

"They'll all pay. I made a promise to you, and you made a promise to me. Work now and grieve later." When Nova remained frozen, her gaze locked on the far entrance, Rocket grabbed her shoulder. "Say it!"

In a move that immediately reminded Rocket of the volatile T'ala, Nova ripped her shoulder out of Rocket's grasp and stepped away from the SAIC. "We should probably—"

"Rocket, another Tomahawk is headed your way!"

"Fucking hell, can't we catch a break? She turned to the brooding young woman. Nova's flame had gone out as she stood alone next to a tree. "I'm sorry, Nova, but we need you again." Nova gave her an unreadable look.

"I'm working on this one, kids, but someone altered the code before launch and added an extra layer of security. It's gonna be close."

Nova lit up as she jumped into the air to intercept the newest missile and Steph's voice suddenly came over the com. "Hey, we just got a lock on Oracle's position! It's some kind of underground bunker a half mile east of your location. I'll send it to everyone's HUD while Lingua is busy." The wrist comp vibrated and Nova looked down to see Oracle's location pop up on her map. He was close. Her smile was grim as she flew up toward the stars to intercept one last bomb.

"Just like last time, Nova. Try to slow it down and fly straight up to buy me some time."

UNTIL THE CHROMODEC uprising, Amari Losira Del Rey had led a fairly charmed life. She'd never known the heartache of intimate loss. She had never suffered from poverty, prejudice, or hardship. As a result, Amari was a well-adjusted and overall happy woman. She was serious, sure, but she also smiled easily and was rarely prone to anger. But they say the deepest loss can only stem from the deepest love. The same can be true about true hatred coming from a place of fear. For Amari, anger was an unfamiliar emotion and she had no tools to properly deal with it. Hearing of her beloved's abduction had lit the fires of anger in Amari's gut. But it was knowing of their treatment of her Q'sirrahna that fully pushed her into rage. She was tired of fighting, and tired of fear. A wry thought passed through her head for just a split second that maybe her history records were wrong, that it was really Reyna that had been the more warring of the two planets, because Amari's plan was not going to be tender in the least.

Nova grabbed the rocket as it reached its very short apex but instead of turning it toward the upper atmosphere, she held on and gave it a new heading. Her com sounded faint in the rushing wind. "Nova, what are you doing? You're supposed to push it up."

She flew high above into the inky blackness of night, with the stars as her backdrop. Nova ignored Lingua's question. "Is T'ala out yet?"

"Hatch here. We've got a few more feet to go before I can get satellite visual on a clear point—"

Nova's voice was firm but resolute. "Get out now. Go to Milwaukee if you have to." Maybe it was the tone of her voice, or some sort of agent intuition, but Hatch listened. A blink later Nova felt her soul mate connection stretch like a great distance had suddenly come between them. She knew her Q'sirrahna was safe.

Rocket had no clue what was going on. "What are you—?"

"Oh fuck me running. Guys? You better take cover because

she's gonna run that missile right up Oracle's ass! And we have at least four missile arrays sitting top side at his location that will go off with it." Lingua was succinct as ever.

"Christ! Nova, don't do that. You have no idea if you can withstand that much energy." Nova didn't answer and Rocket knew there were only seconds left. She assumed Hatch would get everyone else out. "Please, Nova. We need him alive to stand trial."

Three words came back, right before the world trembled and roared beneath their feet. "He's already dead."

Their fight with the rogues had unknowingly taken them within a quarter mile of Oracle's location. They weren't worried as much about the missile, the blast range of the Tomahawk was small enough that they could fly beyond it without taking damage. But a combination of the bunker buster missile *and* a full array of others? That would be a big *boom.* Rocket and Gauss flew as fast as they were able, attempting to outrun the explosive wave of fire, shrapnel, and debris. But Gauss wasn't nearly as fast as the "human rocket." And the SAIC wasn't going to leave the young agent behind. Just when they thought they'd be caught, a portal opened in front of them and they flew through into the night sky of another city. They both stopped and floated in place, high above what they recognized as Milwaukee. Gauss flipped up his face shield and leveled a look of panic at Rocket. "Nova!"

They took off toward the CORP building but Rocket couldn't wait. "Hatch, give me a portal inside, now!"

Two seconds was all it took between where they were and the marked out teleportation corner inside of the control room. Rocket raced to the main console as Lingua's fingers flew over the keyboard. "Coms?"

"Down."

Rocket ripped off her helmet and flung it across the room. It crushed against the steel wall from the force of her kinetically-powered throw. "Of course they are. Nothing could withstand that. Get me a satellite feed then."

An image flickered to life showing the whole of Cuba, a massive plume of smoke rising above the southern coast. Lingua hit a few more keys as agents gathered around to see the large screen. "Magnifying now."

A tired voice sounded from the back of the crowd of agents. "She let it go."

Rocket took her eyes off the too-slow magnification. "Let her through!" T'ala was wrapped in a blanket looking just as bad as the SAIC imagined she would. "What did you say?"

"I said, she let go. She let the missile go before it hit. If she hadn't there wouldn't have been such a big explosion. She must have wanted it to blow up. That means she wouldn't have absorbed the full amount of energy."

"At ground zero she may as well have absorbed it all."

Ember spoke up from the other side of Lingua. "She wanted him dead."

Rocket cut a sharp glance at her. "We needed him alive."

The younger SAIC shook her head and clenched her jaw. It was almost enough to prevent the words from escaping. "She wanted him dead and I can understand that." Her own thoughts turned to the rogue agents she knew were left on the ground when Rocket and Gauss fled the area. Shockwave and his crew. Hatch was supposed to open a portal so the prisoners could be retrieved but they never got a chance. Ember's memory turned dark. She knew what it was like to want someone dead so bad you'd be willing to go down with them.

Augur clapped a big hand on Rocket's shoulder. "I've been on the line with President Lee twice and she was well aware that this could be a potential outcome. We knew he wasn't going to come quietly."

Rocket pinched the bridge of her nose and ignored the fact that Steph had moved up to hold T'ala's hand. She had to keep it together, she had to be their leader. "I know, it's just—where the fuck is the image, Lingua?" The words exploded out of her with pent up frustration. Most in the room were shocked. Hatch and Augur shared a look because they knew Romy better than most. She was worried and she felt guilty.

"Got it. There!"

The room stilled as a lone figure remained immobile with one knee on the ground. Nova glowed as brightly as her namesake and Lingua quickly applied a filter to the image so they could watch the screen without half blinding themselves. They all waited with baited breath to see what Nova would do with so much power. Despite the lack of sound their hijacked satellite provided, the image was quite clear. Nova's mouth opened wide as she appeared to scream into the night sky. Then as suddenly as the scream came, it ended and Nova thrust both fists above her head. It looked a lot like she was pointing right at the people watching. "Is she pointing toward the satellite?"

"Oh hell, I think she is." A massive flare of white covered the entire screen then the image blinked out completely, leaving behind nothing but the blackness of a lost signal.

It was Sinter who found the perfect words. "Dayum, son."

But T'ala had the best ones. "She's alive." Not that she really doubted that fact. She could feel Amari deep within her heart and knew that her Q'sirrahna had not left her. Voices continued around her but Zendara Inyri Baen-Tor tuned them out. Amari was safe. She was alive.

"Damn it. I liked that satellite too!"

"Lingua, you *stole* it!"

"Thanks for the info, *genius*. Finder's keeper though, am I right guys? Guys?"

Someone laughed and Zen sank into the nearest chair. It was over and Amari was alive.

IT TOOK TWO weeks for the rest of the rogue Chromodec agents to be rounded up and the cities put back to some semblance of order. The gathered loyal agents all went back to their own cities with a few exceptions. Because so many places were left severely bereft of CORP agents, some rebalancing needed to happen. With the CORP team in Los Angeles completely wiped out, Augur and Hatch were temporarily reassigned there with Sinter and Gauss to keep an eye on the second largest city in the country. Augur was made interim SAIC since he had two years seniority on Hatch. Lingua was also made temporary SAIC of Chicago while Rocket was stuck in Washington DC in meetings with the Security Council and President Lee herself. Unfortunately for Agent Danes, once the Security Council was finished with her, she was ordered to appear for a full Senate hearing where their harsh questions and attitude made it seem as though Rocket were the mastermind behind it all, rather than a man that was already dead. They wanted a fall guy and were using her reluctance to release the names of her allies as an excuse to punish the highly-decorated agent.

The reason the names weren't available was actually due to Lingua. Per Rocket's request, the other agent had scrubbed the various CORP systems of any reports or images of the three non-agents. Rocket promised to keep them safe and everyone was on board with helping Nova and T'ala stay off the government's radar.

Fear and anger at the Chromodecs ran hot across the nation and the Senators were merely reacting along with their constituents. When everything was tallied in the end, Oracle's uprising had cost more than a trillion dollars in damages. But worse than that was a loss of life that was unforgivable. President Lee led the placement of a memorial for all the people who died in the uprising. She declared the date that the uprising started as a National Day of Mourning. Then she ordered flags around the nation to fly at half-staff for a week.

Three hundred and seventy-eight deaths, and more than twelve hundred people were wounded before the last rogue Chromodec was rounded up and remanded to a military prison in Wyoming. Blame, motive, and reparations had to be made before they could begin to deal with the fate of the Chromodec prisoners. For the safety of everyone, all wore an eloptic collar that required the president's own override code to unlock. She would only provide the code when she was sure the broken and battered CORP division had a better way to contain them.

A week after Oracle's death, most of the CORP cities had been taken off the uprising watch list, one of which was Chicago. Steph returned to her job at the university but after everything that had happened, and what she herself had done at the end, Amari couldn't bear to go back. She took a leave of absence and flew her and Zendara out to stay with Amari's parents. James and Michelle Bennett were understandably worried but were happy to welcome Zendara into the family. But even with spending their nights reveling in their bond and their days roaming the mountains near Amari's childhood home, watching the histories from their planets and learning the common language of the Q'orre system, the two women still couldn't relax.

"Why are they doing this?" Zen gripped her knees tightly as the four of them watched the Senate hearings on TV. "She saved the fucking country! Why are they making her out to be the bad guy?"

Amari's dad answered. "Humans are curious creatures. They are quick to blame, slow to believe. One of the problems I see is that they know your Agent Danes is innocent. But they don't have the guilty party in hand to show the country that everything is okay. People want proof that the bad men can't hurt them anymore."

"This is my fault. If only I'd listened to Rocket then she wouldn't be in this position right now!"

Zen glanced at her Q'sirrahna who practically radiated guilt and self-castigation, then looked back at James. "You said one of the problems?"

Michelle Bennett sat down next to her mate and placed a digital tablet on the coffee table. "You are the other problem."

A pale eyebrow went up and worry churned Zen's gut. "Me?"

James smiled. "No, both of you. The world was fairly traumatized by what two hundred super-powered rogue agents could do. Then videos show up on YouTube, Facebook, and Twitter of two people fighting that *weren't* wearing the uniform of CORP agents. Two people who appeared to be significantly more powerful than the very agents the citizens are frightened of."

Amari continued to watch the hearing. "They keep asking her how the missile was able to target Oracle's exact location. They seized all the logs from the Milwaukee CORP facility's database so they know that it wasn't Lingua. Rocket is protecting me."

Zen reached over to take Amari's hand. "Sirra, she's protecting *us*." James and Michelle Bennett exchanged a glance, one that spoke so much more than words. They knew their Reynan daughter very well.

Suddenly, Amari's head jerked up. "Does she even have to?"

"Protect us?" Zen was confused.

"Yes. Does she even have to protect us?"

A commotion on the TV drew all their attention and Zen quickly turned up the volume.

AGENT ROMY DANES'S voice had turned raw from hours of questioning and her patience was just about spent. It had been a week of the same thing day in and day out. The presiding officer of the Senate was usually the vice president, though sometimes it would change if he wasn't in attendance. Whoever presided over the hearing was always referred to as Mister President, or Madam President. While Vice President Kester did his best to keep the chamber from devolving into chaos, people were afraid and the days grew long.

Rocket found it strange to address her Vice President as "Mister President" whenever she had to answer one of his questions but that was simply the way things were done. Even after hundreds of years, the United States government was still very much entrenched in the rituals of pomp and ceremony.

But even Vice President Kester couldn't fully hold the reigns of such a runaway wagon. The conservative Senators were particularly vicious, seeming to have two purposes to their attacks, the first being to root out who the mysterious allies were that helped quell the Chromodec rebellion. And as she refused over and over to give up names, they moved their attacks to that of Romy's character. After one particularly harsh round of questioning ranging from her confidential work with Black Badge to her own sexual history, Romy finally broke. She abruptly stood from her hard wooden chair and everyone unconsciously leaned back. Not that there was cause for concern. The SAIC may not have been wearing an eloptic collar, but the entire Senate Chamber was wired to prevent Chromodec powers from working, similar to the holding cells in every CORP facility across the country. It was a renovation that happened soon after the technology was discovered.

The current presiding officer just so happened to be Vice President Kester. "Do you have something to say, Agent Danes?"

"My apologies, Mister President, but the people you seek have done no harm. On the contrary, they prevented a loss of life the likes this country hasn't seen since the last World War. No one is in danger from them and I am fed *up* with this dog and pony show!" Gasps sounded throughout the hallowed chamber.

Another particularly vociferous senator yelled back. "Untrained rogue Chromodecs will always be a danger to the public and it is our duty to see them contained! That is one of your duties, Agent Danes...or have you become a traitor to this country too?"

Romy's face flushed with barely restrained fury. "As I have stated each day of this hearing, every single CORP agent that helped take down Oracle and end his uprising are dedicated and loyal to this nation. That's our *job*. We are trained for years to do exactly what we did in service of our country. Peace, prosperity, protection—it's not our motto by accident, sir. But we don't need your praise. The real heroes are those allies that helped us. They were regular citizens who went above and beyond expectation to help protect this nation. I'm telling you here and now that they are NOT A DANGER to you or anyone else. They don't deserve this witch hunt and I will go to hell before I tell any of you their names!"

The room exploded in a cacophony of voices and the distinctive ivory gavel slammed repeatedly into the base. "Order!" The Vice President rubbed his forehead tiredly and glanced off to the side where he knew the president of the United States watched in secret from behind a decorative panel. Then he looked at his watch. "As it is going on noon, I'd like to suggest a recess for lunch. We'll adjourn here until two p.m."

Senators and aides shuffled out as fast as their feet could take them, muttering and angry. The party secretaries in the desks in front of Romy were next to go, and lastly the clerks that sat at the long marble in front of the presiding officer filed out. They left behind a few marines and one lonely CORP agent. Romy was so in her head that she didn't notice a handful of Secret Service agents slip in the side door, followed by a tall woman with sleek black hair. The woman was perhaps in her mid-fifties and wore the dark navy suit like it was a natural extension of her body. Perhaps it was. Romy was startled when President Lee took the seat next to her. The agent shot to her feet and delivered a crisp salute. "Madam President!"

President Catherine Lee quirked her lips into a smile. "At ease, Agent Danes." She patted Romy's chair. "Please, have a seat. I don't want to get a crick in my neck staring up at you, no matter how little height you seem to have."

Romy scowled but relaxed and resumed her seat. "Yes, ma'am."

The president didn't beat around the bush about her feelings. "I'm sorry. I would prevent all of this if I could but even I'm not immune to protocol. I can't interfere with government procedure."

"I understand." Romy sighed.

President Lee paused, as if her next words were delicate. "And these allies...is protecting them worth your career?" She got a hard look from the woman known in the CORP as "Rocket."

"They saved our lives. ALL of our lives, Madam President."

"Very well then. Can you at least tell me what planet they're from?" She smiled at Romy's surprised look. "I know they're not Chromodecs."

"How do you know that?" Romy's look went from surprised to suspicious. And she suddenly wondered at all those secrets Amari didn't share.

The president seemed to ignore her question. "How about this, I will give all allies a full presidential pardon, as well as immunity. Can we work out a deal under those circumstances?"

Romy thought for a few minutes before slowly shaking her head. "I'm sorry, Madam President. But their identities are secret, and it's not my secret to tell. I gave my word of honor to protect them at all costs."

President Lee cocked her head and the lights of the Senate floor cast a shine on her perfectly styled glossy black hair. "That is very noble of you. Perhaps you could ask them?"

A surprised laugh bubbled between Romy's teeth. "And have my call traced back to their location?"

A shrug. "I had to try."

"I suppose you did."

The president stood to leave but turned back to the resigned agent. "Thank you for your service, Agent Danes." She looked around the empty room. "Will you stay here until the hearing resumes?"

Romy shrugged. "May as well. I can contemplate the end of my career here as well as any place else. Besides, I'm not very interested in sight seeing in a city of failed promises." The president frowned and turned away but Romy's voice caught her attention again. "How did you know they weren't Chromodecs?"

President Lee paused to look back at her, then gave a secretive kind of smile. "I watch the world around me. I observe. How else would one know?" Then she gave Romy a wink and walked away, Secret Service agents bracketing her on all sides.

Agent Romy Danes sat in shock, her body buzzing with sudden energy as she remembered what little Amari did tell them about the mysteries of her world. About *their* world.

"...there are thousands of Watchers all over the world, from the lowest of maintenance workers, all the way up to high level government positions."

She closed her eyes and wished very hard she could talk to Augur, Hatch, and Lingua. "No fucking way." Maybe even Amari. But she couldn't because her phone had been confiscated in the investigation. Instead she looked at her watch and gave a sigh. Just an hour and a half until session resumed.

Chapter Twenty-three

SECONDS AFTER THE hearing adjourned for lunch, Amari turned off the TV and stood from the couch. "I can't let her do this. I'm the one who killed Oracle and I can't let her take the fall for me."

"Um, technically Oracle killed himself since he's the one that ordered the launch of the missile."

His position as a Watcher was the most significant duty in James Bennett's life, but being a dad was the most important. And he worried for his adopted daughter. But despite the seriousness of the situation, he gave a low laugh at Zen's blithe response. "I like the way you think, Zendara! You're a great match for my baby girl here."

Zen's eyebrows rose and she looked up at Amari. "Your alien dad calls you 'baby girl'?"

Their attempt at humor failed. Amari would not be dissuaded. "I need to get to Washington DC. Right now!"

James suddenly sobered. "You're willing to risk the life you've built here?"

Amari loved her life. She loved her job, her best friend, and she had finally found the missing piece of her puzzle with Zendara. Amari's eyes filled with glittery tears. "It's the right thing to do. I have to help her!"

Zendara stood and slipped her hand into Amari's grasp. When Amari met her eyes, Zen smiled. "You're right, it is the right thing to do, which is why *we* have to help her, sirra. I'm with you all the way."

Amari squeeze her hand. "Thank you. Now we have to get there."

Michelle had another sobering reminder. "You also have to get into the hearing. You'll need a pass. It's easy enough to get one from your senator."

Amari looked at her mom and sighed. "I'm not exactly tight with the Illinois Senators right now. Do either of you have a connection we can use?"

James chuckled. "Actually, Senator Colbert of Washington is an *associate* of ours. He's in DC now but I can call his office and see if you can get passes for the afternoon session."

Zen's pale brow rose with the mention of an *associate* but she didn't remark on that particular detail. Amari continued on full speed ahead. "So that gets us inside, but we still need to get there before the session starts back up. DC is nearly three thousand miles away and even flying at top speed it would still take hours."

A blonde head tilted slightly, then Zen gave her wide smile. "It may be thousands of miles to DC but it's a short trip down to LA."

"At the risk of stating the obvious, you're a genius!" Amari turned and planted an overzealous kiss on Zen's lips. "Let's go." She started to drag Zen toward the front door but her soul mate pulled her to a stop.

"We should wear our suits for the flight to LA and pack a bag with things to change into. I mean, if things go really wrong down in DC, I'd like to have a good escape plan."

Amari frowned and sighed. "You're right, of course."

After speeding to Amari's bedroom to change, they came back into the living room to say their goodbyes. They each wore their slim backpacks beneath their uniform since the suits were flexible enough and it would help reduce drag on the backpack for the flight down to Los Angeles. They needed a speedy trip across the country and knew just the woman who could help.

FOR THE WATCHERS that had inadvertently become parents twenty-five years before, it was a worrying day. They knew their adopted daughter and trusted her, but they also knew the government and feared that nothing the two young women could do or say would assuage the citizen's fears. But someone had to try. As Watchers, they were forbidden to act. They could only observe and record. Neither Amari nor Zen were Watchers and consequently had a lot more freedom where human society was concerned under the guidelines of the Sol-Ceti Pact. After all, revealing themselves to the world wouldn't advance the human race. All the Bennetts could do was turn the TV back on and watch the hearing while sipping their tea. Humanity would either succeed or flounder, and only humans could control which way they would be recorded in the Official Tomes. And perhaps maybe it wouldn't be so bad if a couple aliens from the Q'orre system gave them a hand.

THE BELL FAMILY was a frightening force of anger and worry, for both Rocket and for Amari and Zen. The layout for LA was especially familiar. After all, they were told that all CORP facilities were built to the same specifications. The two women of Q'orre laid out their plan as soon as they reached the main control room. At first Hatch refused to create a portal, knowing that Rocket had chosen to protect the young women who helped them win against rogues in the uprising. But Amari assured her that they didn't need anyone sacrificing themselves. If they were willing to accept the risks then Hatch knew she couldn't interfere. "The problem as I see it is that I can get you to DC but how will you gain access to the chamber?"

Zendara smirked. "Amari's parents made a call and Senator Colbert's office will be holding two passes for us."

Augur shook his head and his voice was a soothing rumble that both Amari and Zen had missed. "Just keep in mind that right now nobody but a few of us knows that you're not Chromodecs. If you use your powers in that Senate chamber the entire world will know."

His wife frowned and nodded. "He's right. The entire room is on a dedicated circuit that's not connected to an outside network. Un-hackable."

Amari put her hand on the older woman's forearm. "We are fully aware of the consequences should we 'out' ourselves. It's okay."

"You use y'all's powers, that whole place is gonna flip their shit!" Gauss flinched when his sister punched his arm.

"You're not helping the situation, ya tumbleweed."

He glanced back to Amari and Zen. "Sorry."

Zen looked worried with his words but Amari was resolute. "We'll be fine." She pulled out her cell phone to check the time then turned back to Augur and Hatch. "Now do you think you can do your thing and get us to a discrete location that's close to the Capitol building? We don't want to be seen."

Hatch looked offended and held up her hand. "Girl please, I've been making portals as long as you've been alive. I think I know just the place."

Augur grinned at her. "Marcus?"

"You know it."

"Isn't it breaking the rules to bring non-agents into the CORP building?

Hatch winked at Zen and continued her explanation. "Marcus is my cousin on Mama's side. He's a reporter for the DC Sentinel, I'm sure he can help us out." She stepped close to Augur. "Can you get me a visual, darlin'?"

Even though Hatch was only a few inches shy of six feet tall, her husband had at a good seven inches on her. They stood facing one another with fingers on each other's temples, trying to get a lock strong enough for a sight and send. A few seconds later a portal opened and a thirty-something African American man stepped through to their side. "Shawna, I knew that was you!" He grinned when he saw the twins. "Jesus, you two get taller every time I see you. So what's up? I bet you want to check in on your girl, Rocket. I hear nearly the entire government is up in arms about her mysterious allies—" He stopped and gave Hatch a questioning look when he caught sight of the two new faces in the group.

She threw her arm around Zen's shoulders and Augur did the same for Amari. "Marcus, these are two friends of ours that need a place to land in DC. They need to get to Senator Colbert's office to pick up passes then they're headed to the hearing for the afternoon session. Do you think you could play tour guide for a little bit?"

Gauss snickered. "More like 'Uber' for them."

Marcus narrowed his eyes. "You're them, aren't you? The ones that everyone is looking for?"

Zen and Amari exchanged glances. The fact that he was a reporter gave them pause but both trusted Hatch and Augur. "Yes. We are the allies that Rocket is protecting."

He tilted his head, brain working fast to put together the puzzle pieces. "I don't get it. What's the big deal about a couple more Chromodecs? Unless…" His gaze moved across the four members of his family, then alit on the two women again. "Unless you're not Chromodecs at all. Holy shit, this is the scoop of the century!"

"Marcus…" Augur's tone was a warning.

A sigh. "Let me guess, off the record, right?"

Amari smiled at him. "If we're forced to disclose that particular detail to the world, I promise you the first interview." Zen nodded in agreement.

Hopes suddenly raised, Marcus shrugged and gave them a boyish grin. "Fair enough. What do I call you?"

Zen smiled. "Zen and Amari is fine. You'll get our details if we give you an interview."

"Sounds good." He glanced down at his watch. "All right,

we've got about fifty minutes until the lunch break ends. Let's go get your passes, then I'll get you over to the Senate hearing in time for the afternoon session to begin."

Hatch raised a single dark brow. "You have a safe place?"

"Well, I was actually in my apartment eating lunch, so we can go back there. No one will see them arrive that way."

She smiled and clasped his shoulder. "Done. And thanks, we owe you one."

Marcus shrugged and smiled back at her. "Naw. The way I see it, the entire world owes you all. This one's a wash." A few minutes later a new portal opened up and Marcus, Amari, and Zen stepped through. It was time to set things right.

As soon as they were away, Hatch gave her husband a worried look. "Should we be there?"

Augur scrubbed the top of his head with a meaty hand. "It could make things worse."

Sinter wasn't so reticent. "But it could make things better if they have backup. We need to show them that the *loyal* CORP agents are behind them one hundred percent."

Gauss shrugged and pointed at his sister. "Yeah, what she said."

Hatch pinched her bottom lip in thought, then immediately brightened. "What if we have a crew on standby?"

The Bells had been married a long time and Augur knew exactly what his wife wanted. "I think that could work. Maybe just the seven of us? We need to call Lingua, Ember, and Lumos. I'm sure they'll come with us if the need arises."

"That's exactly what I was thinking." Hatch walked over to the main console and punched in the code for Chicago CORP.

Lingua answered with an uncharacteristic smile on her face and her hair had been dyed deep fuchsia. "*Hola, ¿cómo estás?*"

Gauss snorted. "Dude, you're not even a little bit Spanish!"

Lingua sniffed. "I could be. I mean, just because both my mother and father were Korean American doesn't mean I don't have any Latin American in me too."

Sinter burst out laughing. "You're the most Asian American, American Asian I have ever met!"

The other three in the control room turned to give Sinter a perplexed look and Lingua huffed. "What the fuck does that even mean? Like you grew up seeing a lot of Asians in 'Whitesville, Texas,' you little tumbleweed!"

Both Sinter and Gauss cracked up laughing that she used the

same name Sinter had used earlier. "Well, it certainly wasn't so white with us there. And for your information, we had plenty of Latin Americans down by the border." She looked at her parents. "I think I should probably visit the med center. Clearly there's something wrong with me because I actually miss that cranky woman."

"Damn right you miss me. Now what can the great and powerful Lingua do for you? You want me to hack every senator at that hearing and re-route their paychecks to orphanages and homeless shelters? I can do that, you know."

Hatch rolled her eyes, always amused by her old friend. "Uh, no. Tempting...but no. T'ala and Nova are in DC right now. They're going to the hearing to support Rocket."

Lingua looked surprised. "And what exactly are they going to do? Out themselves to the world? Bust Rocket out of there?"

The older Bell woman shook her head and smiled. "Hopefully it won't come to that. But they are down there to ride to her rescue. It's real sweet for Rocket to take the fall but those young ladies have had enough. In the meantime, we need a team of people we can count on in case things go south."

There was silence as Lingua processed Hatch's words, then she gave the group a smile that few others had seen before. "Good on them. And yeah, I've always got your six. I'll keep an eye on the hearing and expect a call if it starts to sour." She looked away from the camera in thought, then glanced back. "You should ring the flame-twins. I bet they'd help too."

Gauss and Sinter had matching snorts but Augur laughed outright. "Lumos and Ember were actually our next call."

Lingua rolled her eyes. "Fine, get to it then and leave me be. I'm a real busy Special Agent in Charge now and I don't have time for this idle chitchat." She waved them away with her fingers but smiled and added, "Keep me posted."

"Will do." Then Hatch cut the connection. "I think it's safe to say we've got a team if we need it. What do you think?"

Augur wrapped a muscular arm around her shoulders, enjoying their closeness. "Darlin', I'm about as sure as a tick on a friendly dog." The twins both rolled their eyes and Hatch just looked up at him fondly. They'd made the right call, now they had two more.

THE GALLERY WAS only half full when Amari and Zendara

arrived and took their seats. They were a little early since it didn't take long at all to make their way from Marcus's apartment to Congressman Colbert's office, and then to the Senate chambers. There were a series of underground tunnels with security on each end that made the trip significantly easier. When Marcus completed his guide duties, he left them with his business card, a wink, and a firm "good luck."

The second floor gallery surrounded the chamber on all four sides. The back of the gallery had the best view since it faced the presiding officer but its popularity also meant it was the only section at capacity. Amari and Zendara found seats on one of the sides in the front row, within easy view of where Rocket sat below. Their friend and compatriot sat dejectedly in her seat and while they wanted to call out to her, they weren't quite ready to make a scene. Amari cautioned against announcing their presence too early and Zen agreed with her.

Unfortunately for everyone in attendance, the tone was no less hostile when the Senators returned from lunch. Senator Grassley became the newest one to sling barbs and arrows. His frustration quickly became evident. "Agent Danes, why are you incapable of answering the simplest of questions? Is there an invocation of executive privilege by the president of the United States that we have not been informed of?" She remained mute. "Is there or not?"

Rocket gritted her teeth. "Not that I'm aware."

"Then why are you not answering our questions?"

"Because I feel that they are inappropriate, sir."

Grassley's face clouded with anger. "What you feel isn't relevant, Agent Danes."

Voices rumbled through the gallery and the presiding officer was forced to intervene yet again. Kester regretted his next words but they needed to be said. "I'm afraid that without the invocation of executive privilege, you are required to answer the questions laid before you by the sitting Senators in this chamber. To do otherwise will incur consequences."

Rocket didn't even hesitate. "I decline to answer, Mister President."

"You realize that if you stand by that statement I will have no choice but to find you guilty of inherent contempt. By the statutory power of 2 USC 192 you will be fined no more than one thousand dollars nor less than one hundred dollars, and imprisoned in a common jail for not less than one month nor more than twelve months. Not to mention, it will surely mean the end of your career. Are you *sure* this is the way you want things to go, Agent Danes?"

Before Rocket could answer, Amari gripped Zen's hand tightly and as one they stood from their seats in the gallery. Amari's voice was loud in the hushed chamber and as soon as it carried across the space all eyes turned to them. "Pardon me, Vice President Kester, but I don't believe that will be necessary. It's our secret Agent Danes has been holding so tightly. It was a promise to keep us safe." Amari looked around the rapt chamber. "No different than the promises she has made to keep the rest of the nation safe."

Zen finally spoke up, with a small amount of anger tinging her words. "She doesn't deserve your disrespect, nor your contempt. Agent Danes is a hero and it was an honor helping her defend the country against a man like Oracle."

Guards discretely filed into the chamber below and the upper gallery. With their attention riveted on the two women standing in the balcony, no one noticed President Lee slip in from the side door to take a seat below. Senator Kendall, a contemporary and fellow party member of Senator Grassley's, sneered up at them. "And who exactly are you?"

Amari glanced around the room and noted the added security. She addressed the president of the Senate who just happened to be Vice President Kester. "May we come down?"

Sam Kester had spent nearly the entire break in a private room with President Lee. He wasn't shocked by their appearance because the president told him they'd probably show up. She said that if they were half the people she thought they were, the allies would not let Agent Danes put herself into contempt. She was right, as usual. "Protocol be damned, why not?" He gestured up to some of the guards near Amari and Zen. "Can you clear a path to the stairs so they can come down?"

"I don't think there will be a need for that." It was almost as if they'd choreographed the move. Amari and Zendara both lit with their distinctive glow as they floated up and out, then slowly flew down to stand next to Rocket's table. Panic ensued. All those senators in attendance that sat secure in their knowledge that the Chromodec freaks couldn't hurt them grew terrified in a matter of seconds. Rocket smirked.

The president of the Senate slammed his ivory gavel repeatedly until some semblance of calm returned. "Take your seats!"

Amari spoke again. "We give our word that we mean no harm. Please, we only ask to be heard."

It was as if a damn broke. Senators yelled questions faster than even they could answer.

"Who are they?"

"How are they using their powers?"

"This is unacceptable!"

"Someone have security check the eloptic field!"

Vice President Kester was forced to use the gavel again. He sighed and waved toward the seats to the left of Special Agent Romy Danes. "Please, have a seat. Let's start with the basics. Who are you?"

"My name is Doctor Amari Del Rey."

"And my name is Zendara Baen-Tor."

Senator Grassley called out. "Why are you here?"

"I believe you asked for us." The unspoken "duh" was left off Zen's response but snickers throughout the crowd confirmed that the implication was understood well enough.

Senator Bean attempted to clarify with a gentler tone. "Perhaps Senator Grassley meant to ask why you both volunteered to help Agent Danes and the rest of loyal CORP division with such a terrifying and monumental endeavor."

Zen's voice was firm. "This is our home. We were both sent to the United States as babies. I grew up in this country and watched as the government struggled with the Chromodecs. People aren't scared of Chromodecs because they're different, they're scared because Chromodecs are powerful, and they've proven to be just as emotionally human as anyone else. As Lord Acton is famous for saying, 'power corrupts and absolute power corrupts absolutely.'"

Grassley smiled in a way that wasn't friendly or welcoming. "By your very words, Ms Baen-Tor, are the two of you not highly corruptible?"

Amari placed a comforting hand on Zen's when she saw the scowl appear on her soul mate's face. She could sense Zendara's anger and didn't want it to escalate. She also answered the senator's question. "Everyone is corruptible, Senator. From the president of the United States down to the person who cleans this room at night when everyone else is asleep. What Lord Acton got wrong was the assumption that the most powerful people couldn't or wouldn't be held accountable for their actions. I believe that no one is born inherently evil. But rather it is circumstances, time, and lack of mental fortitude that allow someone to become twisted and dark."

"That is ludicrous!" Senator Grassley blustered.

Amari ran out of words and Zen took over again. She observed Grassley's cross cufflinks and his wedding ring and gave the sweating man a piercing look. "Despite what you may think, Senators, even the best among us is capable of poor choices and corruptible offenses. We all have a line that we wouldn't cross under normal circumstances. But there are events that could tax the most pious man. Take Senator Grassley for instance. Would you shoot a man point blank in the face, sir?"

"Of course not! That question is out of line."

"I believe that you mean that. But what if they have a gun to your wife's head, or your child's. Given the ultimatum that you either shoot a man in the head, or your family would be killed in front of your eyes, what would you do?"

"I—" He paused and looked down at his hands. Then with deliberate focus he twisted the ring on his finger and looked back up to meet Zen's pale eyes. "I don't know. God help me, but I don't know."

Murmuring went through the crowd and the president of the Senate noticed President Lee off to the side. She had shared some information with him, but not all. There were things that she wasn't at liberty to discuss, enforced by a much higher power than even she held. One thing Kester did know, it was time. "Miss Baen-Tor, Doctor Del Rey, please...why did you come forward now? Are you a legal citizen of this country?"

Amari smiled because it was time. "Vice President Kester, we have both lived in the United States since infancy. We came forward now for a few reasons. First and foremost to protect a woman who has done nothing but serve this country. Special Agent Romy Danes is a hero in every sense of the word."

Kester tilted his head curiously and everyone else leaned forward in their seat. President Lee had a self-satisfied smile on her face. "And the other reason?"

"We need something that only the government can provide." Senators began talking amongst themselves and even Vice President Kester covered the microphone and whispered to the senator to his left.

Rocket merely sat back in her chair, curious as to how this was all going to play out. She didn't know what game Amari was playing at, but she had a clue. She tried to gauge the receptiveness of the room, and her eyes were drawn to those of President Lee. The woman looked nearly predatory with pleasure. The vice president's voice brought her back from her wandering thoughts. "What exactly is it you need from the United States government, Doctor Del Rey?"

"Amnesty."

The room exploded in a cacophony of mutterings, questions, and comments and immediately quieted again when President Lee herself stood. She handed two packets of paper to the nearest aide and instructed them to be taken to the president of the Senate. As soon as they were in Vice President Kester's hands the room hushed again. His eyes widened when he read the paperwork of Presidential Pardon. All that was needed for the amnesty to be legal were the names and signatures of the two women before him. He looked up at his president with something akin to shock and she smiled. All eyes in the room were on her when she spoke.

"Like Agent Danes, I too am sick of this dog and pony show. I have signed paperwork providing amnesty to both allies involved with quelling the Chromodec Rebellion. Now if our citizen heroes can simply sign on the dotted line, perhaps we can finally close out this Senate hearing."

Vice President Kester looked down at his digital tally sheet and nodded. He handed the paperwork to the clerk who delivered it to Amari and Zen's table. Each woman read through the documents in quick order and signed their names. Once the official paperwork was signed and back in the Senate president's hands, he made his motion. "Now that this is taken care of, I'd like to call a vote to declare this hearing official closed. The only questions this hearing truly had for Special Agent Danes concerned the identity of the two allies during the quelled rebellion. Those questions have been answered."

Senator Kendall's face was red with anger. "We still have questions!"

Kester waved out to the gathered assembly. "Then by all means, vote to prolong the hearing." He knew that the only reason Kendall was so angry was because Kester's party had a strong majority and were sure to vote the hearing complete. And they did. "In light of the vote and information imparted today, I'd like to declare today's session complete. Regular business will reconvene tomorrow." He pounded his gavel to end their day early.

People milled around the room, many giving the table where

Rocket, Amari, and Zendara sat a wide berth. It was strange how all of them seemed to have forgotten about the display of powers in a supposedly safe room. Rocket shook both their hands then gave each a hearty back slap. "You didn't have to do that you know."

Zen made a face. "Are you kidding me? And let those blow-hards continue to rake you over the coals? Nope, not gonna happen."

Rocket grinned as she took in Zen's professional clothes. They looked like something Amari would wear. "What happened to that young punk I met in Chicago?"

The self-proclaimed punk woman scowled but Amari quickly came to her defense. "Agent Danes, everyone knows that being punk is merely a form of social armor to protect oneself against the simultaneous fear of being an outcast *and* of fitting in. It is a purposeful rebellious cultural affection."

"Uh huh."

Zen finally rolled her eyes. "Leather makes me look tough and I wanted to seem especially harmless today, okay?"

Laughter met her words and the trio nearly swallowed their tongues when they realized some of that laughter came from their president. All three of them stood but only Romy snapped a crisp salute. "Madam President."

"At ease, Agent Danes. If you all are staying for a bit, I have some things I'd like to discuss with you at your earliest convenience."

Romy looked around the chamber that had mostly cleared out. "Apparently I have an open calendar all of the sudden."

Amari and Zen exchanged glances. "We're free too."

President Lee clapped her hands together. "Good! I believe Vice President Kester will let us use his private office for the sensitive matter I'd like to broach with you."

After a week of grueling testimony and government disparagement, Romy Danes was understandably leery. "Excuse me, Madam President...but what is this all about?"

The president glanced around to make sure no one was within earshot. "It's about national security. And I have a proposition for the three of you that I think you'll like. Now if you'll follow the nice agents, they'll lead us to the correct office."

After a moment's hesitation, Romy gave a quick nod and turned to follow the men dressed in black. Amari grabbed Zen's hand in a tight grasp. The day had turned out much better than anticipated, hopefully the pattern would hold.

COMING OUT. IT'S such a human concept, isn't it?
The notion can be good or bad, it can be fraught with
danger and heartache, and because of all the negative
associated with the phrase, it is often hard to do. But
it doesn't have to be a revelation of sexuality. Based
on the dangers and repercussions, it perfectly fits
what our heroes have done. But one thing to take notice
of is the way that Amari Losira Del Rey and Zendara
Inyri Baen-Tor never revealed that they weren't actually from the Planet Earth. No, Zendara sidestepped
that question quite nicely. And the president, with all
her foresight and connections, was quick when the
moment arose. While their actions would in no way garner repercussions in regards to the Tau Ceti Act, the
Tau were certainly aware of what was going on. By holding onto the remaining secret of their true origin,
Amari and Zen had made everyone's lives just a little
bit easier. At least for those holding the secret of
that pact.

Sure, there were those humans out there who thought
they knew the truth, but most were easily written off
as conspiracy theorists. They were the same type of
people who had crazy hair and crazier shows on TV.
Alien fanboys were no one of consequence and barely
deserved mention in the Watcher's reports. The real
fear during the Senate hearings was that a disclosure
of Amari and Zendara's true origins would prompt further examination and investigation. And with the full
power of the US government at the ready, humans would
surely discover not just the existence of the Tau Ceti,
but the extent of their control over human society. And
that would be a disaster for all. The president was a
good ally to have, most certainly.

Chapter Twenty-four

"ARE YOU NERVOUS?"

"To be honest, it seems a little surreal. I mean, seven years ago I was working in a strip club barely making enough to feed myself. If someone had told me years ago that I'd find out that I was a rich alien, meet my soul mate, help quell a Chromodec uprising, and become an infamous CORP agent, I would have asked them what they were smoking."

Amari smiled. "But you have accomplished all that and now one more thing."

"It's been amazing." Zen sighed. "And I thought nothing could top our badge ceremony last year. You know I wouldn't have joined if they made us go off to the middle of the desert for training, right? I hate the desert. I grew up with trees and I don't know what I'd do without regular access to water." She shook her head. "I really don't know how Augur and Hatch stand it." Zen was babbling, as she was prone to do when nervous, just one of the many small details that Amari had learned about her as they grew into their relationship over the past two and a half years. They were twenty-seven now, ten years past the age when Amari first discovered her powers by falling off a cliff near her parents' home in Washington.

"I know, sirra. Honestly, I wouldn't have either. But it's not like they were *forced* to take over the Area 51 base. At least they didn't try to re-open Guantanamo. That would have been worse I think. And I'm really glad Rocket wasn't the one the president tapped to take over the CORP training program. If only for Steph's sake. I think Romy's been good for her."

Zen snorted. "I think Steph has been good for Romy. Our SAIC is way too uptight for her own good."

"She's loyal."

"She's a pain in my ass."

Amari pulled Zen into a hug. "She's trained you into a great agent and you'll be an even better leader for it." Over the past two years Rocket had taken on the heroes, known throughout the country as Nova and T'ala, as personal trainees. She bypassed the training program in a breach of protocol that was approved by both President Lee, and the newly-made Executive Assistant Director of Training and Rehabilitation, Agent Shawna Bell.

A lot of things changed after the Chromodec uprising. The CORP had essentially been stripped down and built back up from scratch after loyalties were verified. Much to Special Agent Romy Danes's bemusement, President Lee had made her Director of the Chromodec Office of Restraint and Protection. She begrudgingly agreed only if Agent Jaxon Bell were made Assistant CORP Director. She trusted him and knew he'd handle the responsibility well.

Two years after the greatest threat the country had ever faced, the United States was still in a period of reconstruction. The president held ceremonies to honor the people that lost their lives during the uprising and to honor those heroes that did everything they could to protect the citizens. The populace was extremely frightened of the people of power at first, but Rocket instituted a program that had CORP agents volunteering in every city to help with the rebuilding efforts. Seeing the powers used for creation and construction and not to attack helped many with their fears. After a year, the furor over the two allies died down. It was mostly due to everyone assuming the two women were simply Chromodecs that had been hiding all their life. The story was further nudged toward truth by documents and false accounts propagated by Watchers across the country. It didn't affect the biological or technological development of the human race and they were doing it as a favor to two of their own — Amari's parents.

As for the two soul mates that had been born in a far off galaxy, they had been extremely busy but fulfilled. While Zen had devoted all her extra time to schooling, Amari was hired by the government as a scientist to work on a biological and non-lethal way of dealing with criminal Chromodecs. She worked closely with another CORP scientist that specialized in nanotechnology and they had already begun the testing of eloptic implant prototypes. It was meant to be a more humane form of restraint than an uncomfortable physical collar. It was also significantly cheaper than outfitting entire detention centers with complicated eloptic grids. With all the rebuilding going on around the country, the government could ill afford to throw money around.

Amari glanced at the stage when she pulled back from their embrace. "This was the last piece you needed to be fully accepted into the CORP officer track."

A shrug met her words. "It's not that big a deal." Zen didn't notice the group of three women walk up behind her.

"Are you kidding me, kid? You completed your bachelor's degree in two years, with a double major in criminal justice *and* psychology! You're making me look bad. Keep it up and people won't think I'm the smartest cat in the room anymore."

Steph laughed at Lingua's words. She made an exaggerated motion of looking back and forth between Amari and Zen. "Uh, you're *not* the smartest with these two around. So you better get used to it, *Special Agent in Charge* King."

Lingua rolled her eyes and Zen laughed as she responded to the title Steph used. "Jesus. It trips me out every time I hear them call you that. I can't believe they put *you* in charge of the LA facility." Lingua flipped her off.

Rocket poked Zen in the chest. "As fun as this is, you need to go get your cap and gown on."

Zen huffed. "You're not the boss of me."

Steph put a finger up. "Well technically, she *is* the boss of you in some areas of your life."

Amari smiled and defended her soul mate to her best friend. "Well technically, we could say the same about you." The entire group laughed at her quip and Steph's cheeks flushed. Amari turned to Zendara. "But seriously, you need to get your stuff on and meet your group. I want to watch you walk." She gave the blonde a kiss and shoved her toward the group of University of Chicago grads.

Zen stole another kiss then waved her fingers in the air as she jogged down the aisle. "Catch you later."

Romy Danes squinted at her protégé of the past two years. "Is she...is she wearing combat boots with those skinny-legged dress pants?"

Amari smiled fondly as her Q'sirrahna met with her fellow graduates and donned the cap and gown that she'd left on her seat. "I did get her to leave the leather jacket in the car at least."

Lingua snorted. "You can take the kid out of the punk, but you can't take the punk out of the kid."

Amari nodded acknowledging the truth of Lingua's words, though she wouldn't exactly consider themselves kids at twenty-seven. She pulled her gaze away from where Zendara was standing. "Do you know if anyone else can make it?"

"I've got the weekend off but the twins are on duty. LA is still short-handed with personnel and it was a miracle all of us could be here when you two got your CORP badges. I'm not sure about Hatch and Augur. You hear anything, Rocky?"

"They'll be here for the ceremony and a little bit after but then they have to get back. They've got a huge group of recruits coming back from rehabilitation."

Lingua sighed. "Must be nice having a teleporter in the family. I had to take a damn transport here."

Amari gently squeezed her shoulder. "I appreciate it, and I know she does too. Her friend Cin is supposed to be here soon, as are my parents. I know stuff like this is hard for Zendara because she doesn't really have anyone outside us and Cin. So everyone that shows up for her helps. She'd never admit it, but it means the world."

"Yeah, well, the kid is going places. Who knew that punk I met a few years ago would be such a damn good tactician?"

Rocket laughed. "I knew. Why do you think I begged to make an exception with their training?"

"Because you knew I'd be sad without my best friend?" Steph smiled at Romy and they were lost for a moment in each other.

"Oh God, kill me now. Rocket's gone completely soft and squishy!" Lingua got a threatening fist shaken in her general direction. The quirky agent with newly-dyed electric blue hair laughed at the empty "Rocket punch" threat. "What? Are you denying that you're completely love addled? I'm surprised you two aren't living together yet."

"Well..."

"Actually —"

Lingua rolled her eyes. "Jesus Christ, tell me you didn't!"

Romy narrowed her eyes at her longtime friend. "You know...I understand that Los Angeles is a pretty sweet gig for a SAIC. But you may not be aware that Anchorage is also short a Special Agent in Charge. It would be a shame if you were to be transferred to such a cold and inhospitable climate..."

Lingua had opened her mouth to retort but quickly shut it again at the transfer threat. "I hate you. That's a pretty low blow."

Steph covered her mouth so she didn't blurt out a laugh. Amari smiled. "It was pretty *cold*, wasn't it?" Everyone groaned at her bad pun.

Romy wasn't finished. "You love me and you know it."

"Of course I do but you're an asshole, Director Danes."

Romy narrowed her eyes. "What was that?"

Lingua held out her hand with a closed fist, with the exception of her middle finger pointing to the ground. "Hard of hearing? Here, let me turn this up for you!" She rotated her wrist and flipped her boss the bird then stalked down the aisle. "I'm going to find my seat, losers."

Steph shook her head. "The more I get to know her, the weirder she gets. I'm pretty sure she was socially stunted as a teenager."

Romy laughed at Lingua's antics. "Weren't we all?"

Finding a moment to jump in, Amari pinched Stephanie's arm. "When did you two move in together? And why didn't you tell me?"

"We're not living together yet, but we've been looking for something in our general neighborhood. We'd both like a slightly bigger place than either of us have." She threw her arm around her best friend. "You can be sure that you and Zen will be the first I call when it comes time to move."

Rocket started laughing. "For someone so smart, you sure are short-sighted. You don't call the strong people when you want to move. If you're going to recruit people with powers to be your moving crew, you find someone that can teleport. No moving truck needed!"

"Sound advice. I guess that's why you sit in the tall chair, *Director* Danes." Augur's deep voice startled all of them. Amari checked her watch as Jaxon and Shawna Bell joined their little group. Now all that was left was for her parents and Cin to arrive.

"It's quarter to, should we find our seats?" Hatch's lyrical voice was a soothing counterpoint to her husband's deep bass.

Amari nodded toward the double doors ten feet away. "I'm waiting for my parents to get here, but you all can go down if you want." As if her words conjured the Bennetts from thin air, they pushed through the door right after she finished speaking.

Her dad's face lit up upon seeing her. "Hey, there's my baby girl!"

Rocket turned to stare at the woman she had watched absorb the concussive blast of a missile. "Your dad calls you baby girl?"

Amari sighed but ignored the question. "Mom, Dad, these are my friends. Steph, Romy, Jaxon, and Shawna. Guys, these are my parents, James and Michelle Bennett."

Michelle stepped forward first to shake their hands. "Very nice to meet you, Doctor Young, Director Danes, Deputy Director

Bell, and Executive Assistant Director Bell."

At the CORP agent's surprised looks, James spoke up. "We've been following all your careers for years and I'm glad to see the government finally gave you all the recognition you deserve. Every one of you has been recorded into our records as Terran Defenders. I know we're supposed to remain impartial but I have to say that it's an honor to finally meet you."

Romy shook his hand. "The honor's all mine, sir."

Amari was touched that her family and friends were getting along so well but the ceremony was about to start. "Let's go find our seats. We're having lunch at our place when we get done here so we can all catch up then. Okay?"

As they all walked down the aisle toward their assigned seats, Steph leaned close to Amari. "You sound almost as nervous as Zen. What gives?"

Amari kept her voice quiet. "She's had such a rough life and sometimes I can feel her sadness deep inside. The closer we bond, the more we can feel each other's emotions. I know today is hard for her because she still misses her parents. So I want her to have nothing but the best in life and all the love and support we can give her. She's worked so hard."

"I'll admit, I never would have guessed that rough punk had it in her. Zen was so...so different from you." Steph shook her head, still amazed at what the younger woman had accomplished in such a short amount of time.

"It was always inside her, she merely lacked the resources to bring it out. Zendara is no less a genius than me but honestly I think her background made her twice as driven as I've ever been."

"Romy says Zen has really taken to the officer training and that she's a natural leader."

Amari smiled and gazed off to where her Q'sirrahna sat with the rest of her fellow graduates. "She really is. I'm so proud of her."

"Sorry I'm late, I got off on the wrong train stop. Stupid Chicago trains!" The energetic Hispanic woman gave a little wave to the people sitting to either side of Amari. "Hey, Amari. Uh, hi to everyone else too. I'm Zen's friend, Cin."

Lingua leaned forward so she could see the newcomer better. "That's the childhood best friend from Maine?"

Cin raised a dark eyebrow at the woman who was at least ten years her senior. "That's me. What's it to you?" Her "in your face" attitude was real and bold, very much like Zendara when they all first met her.

Everyone who knew her expected Lingua's eye roll but her response had even Amari snickering. "Jesus, what are they feeding you people in backwater Maine?" She pulled out her cell phone and started typing. "Note to self, never eat the seafood on the east coast! It makes people pugnacious as fuck."

"You must be the bitchy one called Lingua. Zen told me *all* about you." She smiled sweetly with dimples evident on each cheek and everyone laughed at the interchange until they were hushed by people in the row behind them.

Amari shook her head at their banter but the smile stayed on her face throughout the entire graduation ceremony. Feeling a wash of emotion through their empathetic bond, Zen turned in her seat and gave Amari a beaming grin. She also gave a little wave when she saw Cin. Zendara Inyri Baen-Tor had finally come into her own and life had never been better.

HOURS LATER THE last of their friends left and Amari blew out a sigh as she shut the door and locked it. They had offered Cin the use of their couch before the woman had even come to Chicago but she insisted that she had a cousin in Hyde Park that she hadn't seen in forever so they were going to hang out the next day. Romy and Steph gave her a ride since it wasn't that far away.

Amari walked over and with an uncharacteristic flare of her powers, floated up into the air then dropped onto the couch with her head in Zen's lap. Zen glanced at her cell phone then back at Amari. "You can't be tired already. It's only just past eight." But even as she said the words, her fingers were in motion, running through the silky dark strands that lay across her right thigh.

Amari looked up. Her eyes fluttered with pleasure as her girlfriend massaged her scalp. "I'm not tired per se, but it is exhausting spending the entire day wanting nothing more than to crawl inside your skin." Fingers stilled. Amari watched pale eyes widen and she tried to elaborate. "It's just...I'm so proud of you, and so damned in love with you that I don't know how to hold all of this emotion in. You must feel it."

Zen nodded slowly. "I do. It's been like this warm ball sitting inside my chest all day. Every time I started to feel nervous before the ceremony, I just shut my eyes and...felt you." Her fingers moved again but instead of scraping across Amari's scalp,

Zen moved her hand lower. Fingernails made a gentle path around the edge of Amari's ear and down the side of her neck until Zen could just trace the tan flesh at the edge of Amari's shirt. Amari's breath hitched as her body warmed and hummed with an energy that only came about with Zendara's touch.

Having their crystal-carbon cells perfectly in synch with each other meant that intimacy was about more than just simple physical pleasure. They could play harmonies across each other's skin that vibrated through their bodies and minds. It was a beautiful experience that had no real words of explanation. But in that moment, lying on the couch with Zendara's hands tracing a light melody of motion across her skin, she found herself warm and wanting. Amari closed her eyes and let out another sigh as Zen's touch moved back up to trace her cheekbones, eyebrows, and jawline. "I'm glad we have the condo to ourselves tonight."

Zen smirked. "Oh? And why is that?"

"You know why." Amari sat up and stood abruptly. She moved to straddle Zen's lap on the couch.

Zen always found it fascinating when Amari took the lead. Her lover was insatiably curious and always wanted to try something new. It was never dull, never boring, and whatever Amari got into her head, it always ended with mind-blowing sex. She reached around and caressed the dip of bare skin on Amari's lower back, the space where the low-rise dress pants stopped and her sleek button down shirt had come untucked. Zen's own breath was coming faster as her body resonated in response. "What's on your mind, sirra?"

Unable to concentrate, Amari grabbed Zen's hands and pulled them from her skin. She placed them on the couch with palms flat on either side of Zen's thighs. "Be good. I want to try something." Zen had worn a crisp white shirt with a navy blue suit vest and pants for her graduation ceremony. The sleeves were rolled up shortly after the ceremony concluded and she had loosened the tie and top button of her shirt sometime in the last hour or so. Amari found the look incredibly hot.

"What do—" A finger covered Zen's lips, stifling the imminent question.

"Shh, be patient, love." Amari carefully untied the sexy lavender silk tie and pulled it from Zen's collar at a seductively slow pace. When it was free she flung it off to the side where it draped across the arm of the chair. With a naughty look, Amari slowly unbuttoned the vest then the shirt until Zen's clothes were parted down to her navel. All that was left was the practical bra that covered smallish breasts. Amari left the bra in place since it wouldn't interfere with what she wanted to try. "Okay, I want you to close your eyes and relax for me."

There was no doubt and no hesitation. Zen simply complied with a smile and a curious tilt to her head. She felt the touch of Amari's fingertips trace along her sternum and held her breath. As soon as the tingling started she let it out again in a *whoosh*. She sat forward, abdominal muscles crunching with the effort. "What are you—?" Amari effortlessly pushed her down with the same hand that had been trailing across the skin with what felt like little sparks of electricity. When she brought her other hand in and moved to cover Zen's upper pectoral muscles, the sparks radiated across her chest. The energy coursed along Zen's skin and moved in pulsing arcs across her nipples, which sent a signal much lower.

She whined at the stimulating feeling and lifted her hips unconsciously to search for some contact that would give her a measure of relief. She groaned to realize that that angle wasn't good. "Easy, just relax." Amari moved one of her hands to the center of Zen's chest and slid the other lower to caress the skin just under the top of her pants. The tingling began again much lower, like it was arcing hand to hand to radiate farther down and Zen gasped. Her body clenched as she was stimulated in an entirely different way than anything she'd ever felt before.

"Si—sirra?"

"Do you need me to stop?"

Zendara moaned. "No. Fuck."

Amari watched as her lover's eyes slipped shut and that familiar pale blue disappeared. "Is it too much?"

Zen's response was a whisper. "More."

Less than a minute later she arched her pelvis off the couch as the unexpected orgasm pulsed through her like lightning. Amari maintained contact with her skin and went along for the ride. Amari stopped pouring power through her fingertips when Zen collapsed back to the couch, twitching and limp. Amari leaned down to gently stroke Zen's bottom lip with her tongue. She was awarded entrance and they reveled in the deep and thorough kiss that had been missing at the beginning of the Amari's little display. They pulled back from each other and Zen's eyes were a pale blue beacon in the darkening room. "How the sweet hell did you discover *that*?"

"I practiced, of course."

"What?" Zen's heart hammered as her mind raced in a million and one different horrible directions.

Feeling the strange self-doubt through their connection, Amari immediately reassured her. "On myself." With their busy schedules, it was a given that they couldn't spend all their time together. Sometimes Amari's work in the lab kept her late at night, and sometimes Zen's classes kept her out the same way. At least they were on the same duty schedule as CORP agents. Rocket made sure of that, claiming that it was easier for her to train the two women if they were together. Both Amari and Zen thought that maybe their new Director had soft spot for the soul mates but they never called her on it.

Upon hearing about Amari's experimental self-exploration, she didn't get upset like a jealous or less secure lover might. Instead she was even more turned on to hear what Amari had been doing. "Show me."

Amari turned her head to look around the living room. "Well—"

It was a lucky thing Amari had not taken down Zen's pants because in that moment Zen only had one thought. Get them both to the bedroom and out of their clothes. It was a thought she put into quick action in the blink of an eye. It took seconds for her to stand with Amari in her arms and race them both into the bedroom. She deposited her lover on the bed and stood again to quickly strip. Then she slowly crawled up the comforter with a gleam in her eyes. "Show me, please?"

Amari shrugged out of her own shirt and Zen helped her remove the black dress pants that she had admired earlier. Amari lay back on the bed and Zen was on her knees between her legs. Neither had a shred of self-consciousness. Amari slid her right hand down her abdomen to rest just above her pubic bone. She suddenly tensed and sucked in a breath as she let power flow from her fingertips into her own sensitized flesh. Wanting to teach as much as show, she beckoned. "Place your hand on top of mine." Zen complied with a look of hunger on her face. "Feel how the power flows, how it resonates from my fingers to my skin."

Zen studied the resonance and felt it in her own cells then she pushed Amari's hand back. "Like this?" Amari moaned as Zen replicated the power exchange but it felt different when it wasn't her own power. It was more erotic, more energizing, and she bit her lip as her body grew tighter with imminent release. She whimpered when it was taken away. Her eyes popped open with dismay. "What—" Zen grinned at her and stifled Amari's words with the forefinger of her left hand.

"Shh, I want to try something."

Amari shuddered at the idea of whatever it was that Zen was going to try. "Fuck. I forgot how quick you were." All rational thought left her body when Zen's fingers slipped lower and slid through and into her. Then before she could think to prepare herself, the flow of power returned while Zen had two fingers inside. She brought her left hand down to rest in the same spot the right hand had been and the arcing current of power suddenly hit every erogenous spot at once. Amari cried out as the pressure built higher and higher. Sensing imminent release, Zen leaned over and stifled her lover's scream, swallowing down wave after wave of released power that traveled back and forth between them like a looping circuit. The feeling brought Zen over the edge too, which only made the loop stronger. It was only broken when she removed her fingers from inside and threw herself backward until their bodies lost contact with each other. Both were left panting and shaky. Amari had thrown an arm over her eyes and she mumbled the words "Oh shit" over and over again.

"Jesus, fuck!" Sensing that they were no longer at risk of looping again, Zen moved back up the bed and collapsed next to her Q'sirrahna. "That was..." Still panting, she was at a loss for words.

Amari sighed and turned to look at her lover with a wondrous smile. "You continue to surprise and amaze me." She pulled Zen closer and whispered into her ear. "There isn't a day that goes by that I'm not grateful I found you. I would have been so empty."

Zen laughed lightly and held up her hand to wiggle her fingers. "Not with a magic trick like that at your fingertips. Who knew we had orgasmic hands?"

"Sirra, the physical pleasure is nothing compared to how you fill my heart. That is what matters to me more than anything else."

Zen snuggled closer, warm in the quiet room. It was early still, but she knew they'd be up again in a little while. There was still too much for them to explore to sleep just yet, but she took the opportunity to simply revel in the comfort of Amari's skin. She hummed in an attempt to match the frequency she could feel between them, the one that was always there caressing their hearts and mind. Then she conceded Amari's point. "You're heart means everything to me too."

FOR A WHILE we worried for the physical safety of our heroes just as much as we did for their mental health. But a little more than two years out from the tragic Chromodec uprising found both women achieving more than they'd ever dreamed, more so in Zen's case. Some may wonder what could possibly be next for the two babes that had been born under the rose light of Q'orre and raised on Terra without the comfort of their birth parents. Some may already guess. Fear not, my friends, their story isn't quite finished yet.

Chapter Twenty-five

AT FIRST, ONLY a few people noticed when a man climbed the lighting tower near the stage at the Taste of Chicago Festival in Grant Park. As more and more people began pointing and yelling, the rest caught on and eventually the band stopped playing. Seeing he finally had an audience, the twenty-something man yelled to the crowd below. "This is for my mom who never gave a shit, and my dad who didn't love me enough to stay. This is for all those Chromodec fucks who made the world harder for me! You want to be afraid? I'll give you something to be afraid of!" His screaming devolved into basic ranting and what he was saying was alarming enough, but the fact that he also began glowing had people backing away from the stage in fear.

The police were quick on the scene at the first 911 call. Many were already in the area because of the festival. SIMoN alerted the active agents as soon as the "glowing disturbance" came across the police radios. Thanks to the newly assigned teleporter, the entire CORP team arrived within two minutes time, with the exception of Voda who was back at headquarters with a broken ankle. Rocket floated above the crowd directing the various members over their helmet com. "Vision, that kid is glowing like a star. I want power readings stat!" She spun in the air to look at the alarming number of targets below. The Taste of Chicago boasted a daily total attendance of nearly three hundred and fifty thousand people and if their Chromodec threat was powerful enough, they were all at risk. "Blink, I need portals opened that will funnel people away from the area. Voda, get him a clear visual on his HUD for the exit. And Blink, they'll have to be held open. Can you do it, kid?"

The new graduate sketched a quick salute. "Yes, sir!" The rest of the team began herding festivalgoers toward the portals that were popping up in the surrounding area.

Blox, another newer member of the team, tapped into the sound system with the help of SIMoN and tried directing the crowd. "Please remain calm and make your way toward the exits of the park. If you are near the stage, please use the portals that have been provided. They will take you to Millennium Park where you will be safe." Police were also on the scene trying to keep panic at a minimum.

An older CORP member attempted to talk the kid down from the light tower. Sift had her helmet shield filter turned up nearly one hundred percent and the light was still too bright. Her telepathy was giving her a grim picture of the young man's state of mind. "Boss, it's not looking good here. There is nothing I can do to bring him down. I'm pretty sure he's gonna go nova here in a minute."

"Someone say my name?"

The two late arrivals flew up and Rocket blew out a sigh of relief. "It's about time you slackers arrived. Can you do something about that guy?"

T'ala glanced at Rocket and scowled. It looked particularly menacing on account of the glowing black mohawk and eyes. "You're not supposed to be here!"

Rocket waved her concerns away. "I'm fine, you need to worry about *that* guy!"

"Rocky, you're eight months pregnant, your wife is going to kill you. And personally I don't want Steph's prison sentence on my hands." Nova pointed away from the stage. "If you don't fly out of here and monitor remotely I'm going to take you myself!"

"I'm the Director!"

Nova yelled back. "You're a soon-to-be mother! Go now."

"Fuck!"

Vision's voice interrupted their argument over the com. "Guys, this guy's power levels appear to be peaking, I think explosion is imminent."

T'ala and Nova met each other's eyes, then took off for the glowing man. Even though they didn't have helmets like everyone else, the light didn't bother them as much because of their continuously regenerating hybrid cells. No words were spoken, it was as if they both knew what the other was going to do. As soon as they reached the Chromodec, they grabbed him from each side, sandwiching his body between theirs. Suddenly he screamed and a great flash burst from the trio only to disappear a second later. Every bit of the man's power was absorbed by the two alien women.

The crowd went silent, staring in awe. The dichotomous light and dark glow from Nova and T'ala's hair and eyes was so enhanced that most didn't know what to think. Nova carried the unconscious man as they floated down to the ground to where the rest of the CORP team waited. Tank carefully attached the eloptic collar around his neck and Kinny telekinetically floated him through another portal that would lead them back to HQ. Rocket's voice came over the com. "Do you two need to siphon off all that power?"

T'ala answered. "Yeah, probably."

"The city finally finished the Willis Tower receiver last week. I think that's closest."

They flew off in an instant. The receivers had been the brainchild of Amari a year after Zen's graduation. She got the idea after yet another moment where the two women had absorbed a massive amount of power. Amari lamented that it seemed like a shame for all that energy to go to waste when it was technically clean and renewable and free. So they worked with engineers in the private sector to come up with power collection units. The energy industry footed the upfront cost of the receivers and their money was easily made back plus a tidy profit in the subsequent two years since it had been put in place.

Nova and T'ala had just returned to hover over the park where the CORP team was standing when a voice came across the PA system reassuring the festivalgoers that the threat had been taken care of and that they were free to remain in the park. It was then that the clapping began. The CORP agents glanced around the plaza to see what was going on and were surprised that the crowd faced them. They were applauding for the team. Amidst the roaring cheers, the same voice came over the PA again. "Many thanks for Chicago's very own CORP team. And special thanks to T'ala and Nova. Good luck in Seattle, heroes!" The crowd went crazy

THREE YEARS AFTER the dreaded Chromodec uprising, the populace was still generally suspicious of the high-powered human hybrids. Having the CORP teams help with the rebuilding process went a long way to reestablishing public goodwill. But what finally pushed them back into the citizen's good graces was a promotional ad campaign that Augur and Hatch thought up. The two years since the campaign began has proved the resilience of the people's capacity for hope, and the CORP agents had become heroes again.

They were very similar to the ad campaign of decades before that tried to drum up recruitment for the United States Marine Corp. Only these new ads were geared toward reassuring the public that CORP agents

were not a threat. All things considered, it was ridic-
ulously easy how well it worked. One ad started simple
enough. There were clips of a CORP agent's training,
including those of various people learning to use their
powers. The government had a lot of footage of different teams around the country safely apprehending criminals and some of that was included as well. But what
really hit people in the gut was the second ad.

The other video began in a training field, showing
row upon row of CORP agents in full gear standing at
attention. They had their helmets tucked under their
left arm, and they saluted with the right. As one they
recited the first word of their motto. "Peace." Voices
of hundreds rolled like a clap of thunder across the
field.

Then it switched to a teenager wearing jeans and a
hoody. His face was somber as he sat on a stool with a
black background. His dark hair was shaved on the sides
and there was small scar on his left cheekbone. "My
name is Jay Gutierrez and I used to be in a gang in
Chicago. Agent Dae-Jung Lee gave his life when he threw
himself in front of me and my sister during a drive-by
in our neighborhood. Sentinel was a hero." He closed
his right fist and placed it over his heart. "I wish to
honor him."

Back to the field and hundreds of voices echoed
with the next word of the motto. "Prosperity."

The picture switched back to that familiar black
background and a young mother with a sleeping toddler
cradled on her left arm. She looked from the child to
the camera and gave a sad smile. Her southern accent
was soft and lilting when she spoke. "My name is
Shaylee Smith. Agent Travis Washington came across a
traffic accident on Interstate Ten near Mobile, Ala-
bama. My car was on fire and I was able to get out but
I couldn't get my baby free from the car seat. He
instructed me to get away from the car, then pulled out
a knife and cut my baby free from her restraints." She
stroked the sleeping girl's soft head of hair. "I don't
know how he was able to sense that the car was going to
explode but he yelled at me to get down then he covered
little Riley with his own body. He later succumbed to
his injuries but he saved her life." Shaylee shook her
head sadly and placed the closed fist of her right hand
over her heart. "Telsen was only a telepath but he was
a hero. I honor him."

The next image of the field was expected but the

voices were even louder as they carried to the camera. "Protection."

Then it cut to an old man. He was stooped with age, and what was left of his hair had gone white and soft. His words were short and poignant. "My husband died the first day of the Chromodec uprising. I would have died too but Agent Samantha Jake gave her life to save mine. Solara was a hero." He put a shaking fist over his heart. "I honor her."

The end of the commercial showed the field again and those same men and women recited the CORP pledge of duty. "If there is war, I will do my best to find peace with honor. If the nation sees hardship, I will work to ensure prosperity. If citizens are in danger, I will lay down my life to protect them. Peace. Prosperity. Protection. US CORP!"

It was the personal stories that turned the tide in favor of the Chromodec Office of Restraint and Protection. Suddenly, Director Danes no longer had to contend with daily protests outside the CORP headquarters around the country. It was as if seeing those personal accounts took the fuel out of people's anger. Citizens realized that just like police, firefighters, and soldiers, the CORP agents put their lives on the line each day to protect and serve. The other part of the agency rebranding was to make the agents more approachable. It was actually put to a vote to see how the field agents would feel about "coming out" of the shadows to be public figures. Anyone that didn't want their images used could opt out of the field agent program, or transfer to another division entirely.

But for those that stayed, they became almost like celebrities. Companies made trading cards with the heroes of each city. And when people transferred from one team to another, it made the news. And that was how T'ala and Nova found themselves blushing despite the power glow, as thousands of people cheered. The city of Chicago would miss them, but Seattle already had billboards up with the pictures of both that said, "Welcome T'ala and Nova!" Radio stations announced the upcoming addition of Special Agent in Charge Zendara Baen-Tor and Agent Amari Del Rey months before the move was scheduled to happen. It was surreal for both women, but Amari was especially happy to be moving back to Washington and closer to her parents.

IT SEEMED STRANGELY quiet as Amari and Zen unpacked moving boxes in their new house. Granite Falls, Washington was close enough to Seattle if one had the ability to fly. It was about three minutes from their front door to the Seattle CORP head-quarters, at Mach One. And Amari's parent's lived only a fifteen-mile drive down the Mountain Loop Highway. Zen was in the bedroom pulling clothes from boxes and hanging them in the closet while Amari unpacked miscellaneous items in the living room. She pulled out stacks of black-framed pictures and set them on the couch near one empty wall. Amari got the idea for a picture wall weeks before, after touring the house one last time before they finalized the sale. It didn't take long to measure and put nails up, less time after that to actually hang the frames. When she was done she stepped back to admire her handiwork.

In the center were four frames hung in the four cardinal directions—north, east, south, and west. North and south were prints she made from the downloaded files of each pod. There was an image of her own birth parents, Queen Denii Losa Del Rey and Queen Selphan Sirre Del Rey in the bottom position. The top frame was Zendara's parents, King Calden T'al Baen-Tor and Queen Inir Allo Baen-Tor. Both couples wore clothing that would be considered strange by Earth standards but it was easy to see the uncanny resemblance between each couple and Amari and Zen. The near perfect resemblance between parents and child were made possible by the DNA merging technology both Reyna and Tora used to help conceive life.

Their adopted parents were in the left and right frames. A picture of James and Michelle Bennett that was taken at their Badge ceremony a little over four years prior was in the left hand frame. And the right was an older picture of a man and woman standing with a sweet-faced little blonde girl. Amari hadn't told Zen that she took the photo that Zen had always kept on her night-stand. She hadn't told her at all about the picture wall idea. She wanted to surprise her Q'sirrahna. While those four photos were the most important ones, the rest on the picture wall held places in both their hearts. There were pictures of Amari and Zen hiking in the mountains and at different places around Chicago. There were photos of their friends both in and out of the CORP. Each and every image was a memory they'd collected somewhere in the past thirty years of their lives. Amari straightened the photos of her birth mothers one last time then placed a closed fist over her heart. Her voice was a whisper in the big house. "I honor you."

"Babe?" Zen's voice called out from the master bedroom but got louder as she approached. "Do you know where...?" Her voice faltered and trailed off as she caught sight of the wall. "Oh." She slowly walked toward the picture display, her eyes drawn to the quad of images in the center.

"Do you like it?"

When Zendara turned to Amari, her eyes shone with glittery tears. "I—um, I'm not even sure what to say right now." She glanced back at the wall, then turned and held out her hand to her soul mate. As soon as their fingers touched, wave after wave of love and appreciation resonated through their empathic bond. Humility, respect, devotion, and sadness made themselves known and it wasn't long until Amari had her own tears falling. They moved as one to cling to each other, accepting the embrace for what it was. Home. When they pulled back, Zen wiped her eyes. "Thank you."

Amari shook her head and smiled. "These are all our people. I thought we should honor them."

"I love it and I love you." Zen looked around at the last few boxes that had yet to be unpacked. "What else is out here?" She walked over to one and pulled the cardboard flaps open. Inside was some pottery they got at an art festival near Boys Town and a bulging manila envelope. Zen pulled it out of the box as Amari walked up to hug her from behind. She peered around her girlfriend's shoulder at the strange envelope.

"I don't remember putting that in there. What is it?"

"This was all stuff from the sideboard. I'm not sure what everything is. I remember just stuffing it into boxes so we could get it shoved through the portal to the new house."

Amari laughed. "You're *so* organized."

Zen reached around and pinched her hip. "Shut it, Doc." Despite Amari's curiosity, Zen took her time unwrapping the string that held the envelope shut. Then she slowly tipped the heavy paper until two objects fell into her hand. They were the crystal pendant necklaces that they had found in Zendara's lock box more than five years before. "How the hell did *these* get lost in the shuffle?"

Amari's eyes lit up and she clasped her hand over the top of Zen's with the pendants trapped between their palms. There was a soothing feeling that traveled back and forth between each, very similar to the resonance they felt when their connection was peaking. Amari shut her eyes and knew what they had to do. She glanced at the wall and her thoughts solidified. "Look at the pictures of our birth parents. What do you see?"

Zen walked closer to the wall and leaned in to see the images better. "I don't see any—" She squinted and leaned closer. "Hey! They're all wearing crystals!"

"I think maybe the crystals were your parents' gift to us. All four of them knew we were Q'sirrahna. We read the histories but they read more like a textbook and less like personal accounts. Some of the stuff on social tradition is missing. The only thing I can gather is that bonding between two individuals was a private thing. But I did notice that all of our parents had the crystals so maybe it means something?"

Zendara cocked her head and looked from Amari back to the photographs, then down at the necklaces in her hand. "You think they're connected to the bonding ceremony?"

"Yes."

"So...do I just give you one and we put them on, or what? I mean, it's not like we have anything to guide us here."

Amari sighed and turned her gaze toward the large picture window on the west side of the house. It was about a half hour until sunset and they were emotionally, if not physically, weary from the long day. She marveled at how lucky they had gotten to have such a gorgeous view every day for the rest of their lives. Her mind jumped topics abruptly and she wished she had her cell phone to take a picture. As soon as the thought entered her head, she snapped her fingers. "That's it!"

"Babe?"

Amari turned and grabbed Zen by the shoulders. "Lake Twenty-two! We need to go right now." She grabbed Zen's free hand and tried dragging her toward the door but Zen resisted.

"Wait, where are we going?"

"We're flying to Mt. Pilchuck State Park!"

"Um, I know we're pretty remote out here but should we put on our suits just in case?"

Amari thought for a second, then reversed course and dragged them toward their bedroom. At that point, Zendara was just along for the ride. They quickly changed into their ship suits and left the house via the slider and private deck that was just off their bedroom. Barely any time had passed before Amari and Zen found themselves alighting at the highest point of a barely-worn hiking trail. "This is the place."

Zen looked around, taking in the majestic setting sun and the glory of nature all around. "Is this where−?" A bird cried out above them and Zen craned her head to look up and follow its gliding flight.

Amari took her free hand, the one not holding the necklaces. "This is where I fell off the mountain and first discovered my powers."

Zen laughed. "I think that would have been more terrifying than getting unknowingly shot." She squeezed her soul mate's hand. "So how do we do this? We don't exactly have a script or anything."

Amari smiled as she reached out and took one of the necklaces from where they were clasped tightly in Zen's palm. "We don't need one. Let's keep this simple." She pulled her other hand free of Zendara's grasp and pinched the shimmering strands between her fingers. Just like years before, the necklace separated on the side opposite the lavender crystal pendant. As the sun began its journey beyond the horizon, the sky tinged a deep pink. Unknown to the two women at the top of the trail, it was very similar to the rose light that bathed the planets of Reyna and Tora. Amari reached around Zen's neck and let the strands grasp and weave together again. "Ahna, me sirra."

When she was finished, she lowered her arms and Zen did the same for her in return. Only something in Zendara's heart made her change the words around. It was a feeling that she couldn't ignore. "Me sirra, ahna." As soon as the second necklace was sealed around Amari's neck, both crystals flashed a bright purple then faded as the sun fell into night. Each one could feel the change deep inside and were certain that their spiritual bonding was complete as the crystals thrummed with resonance. It may have taken thirty years for the two children of Q'orre to fully come together in body, mind, and spirit, but Amari Losira Del Rey and Zendara Inyri Baen-Tor knew without a doubt that their hearts had always been as one. From the beginning of time to the end of space. Q'sirrahna.

Epilogue

THE SHIP FLOATED three clicks outside Terran space and General Tal Boraan hovered over the shoulder of his ship's plotter. "Are you sure this is the last location they were tracked?"

The man nodded. "Yes General Boraan. We entered the coordinates the tracker had in their log when they returned to Reyna. But sir, that was more than a generation ago. Surely no one could have survived the self-destruct sequence of the ship?"

Tal slammed his fist onto the console very near the plotter's fingertips. "They would not have blown up the babes! I need those princesses to secure my position as supreme leader. If I come back without them I come back to nothing. Plot a course to that planet. Its people are primitive compared to ours, it should be fairly easy to cloak our presence."

"But sir, there are beacons littered throughout this galax—"

"Silence! Do as I say or I'll shove you out a waste port myself."

The communications specialist called out. "General Boraan, we are picking up an interspace signal. Should I put them on the screen?"

The general waved his hand. "Fine, do it."

The distinctive face of a Tau Ceti citizen lit up the main ship screen. Tal muttered under his breath. "Blasted Grays..."

The mouth of the Tau moved but it took a few seconds for the translator to catch up. "You are trespassing in restricted space. Terra is under Tau Ceti protection and sealed with a pact. If you do not leave immediately you will be destroyed."

The general called out to the com officer. "Screen dark." Suddenly the main screen went dark as the specialist froze the communication. "Where is the ship? Do they have the fire power to back up such an outrageous threat?"

"Sir, I don't know."

"What do you mean you don't know? The communication is coming from *somewhere*! Find it." He waited a minute as the com officer furiously clicked dials and switches then made a motion as if to say "well?" and the officer sighed.

"Still nothing sir. It's like they don't exist. Their cloaking system must be beyond anything we've ever seen."

General Tal Boraan snarled. "Screen light." The Tau Ceti image appeared back on the screen and the general tried a different tact. "We are here to search for the lost children of Q'orre. Surely you must see how important it is to bring them ho—"

The Tau interrupted, uncaring about the general's excuse. "Are you refusing a direct order from a Tau Ceti patrol ship?"

Tal's face purpled with rage and the temper that he was famous for bubbled to the surface. "Listen, d'eeshek—"

"Intention determined." The ship, along with General Tal Boraan and crew, disappeared in an explosion of light. And the mysterious explosion picked up on the surface of the planet below became more fodder for the Terran conspiracy theorists who were convinced the universe was full of aliens trying to take them over. It was ironic really.

IN EVERY WORLD across the known universe, there are multitudes of stories told to entertain the masses. This story has taken you across the whole of space and through the intricacies of time. You have watched heroes rise and fall, you have watched good triumph over evil. And in the end, we saw the brave sacrifice of two queens finally avenged with the quick destruction of one man. As for Amari and Zen, two princesses of worlds that had gone beyond the good sense of reason, they found exactly what their parents had hoped for when the journey began. Peace, prosperity, and protection. The story simply was as it had always had been for our two heroes…complete. After all, ahna means forever.

About the Author

Award winning author and Michigan native, K. Aten brings heroines to life in a variety of blended LGBTQ fiction genres. She's not afraid of pain or adversity, but loves a happy ending. "Some words end the silence, others begin it."

2019 GCLS Goldie winner
Waking the Dreamer - Science Fiction/ Fantasy

Other K. Aten titles to look for:

The Fletcher

Kyri is a fletcher, following in the footsteps of her father, and his father before him. However, fate is a fickle mistress, and six years after the death of her mother, she's faced with the fact that her father is dying as well. Forced to leave her sheltered little homestead in the woods, Kyri discovers that there is more to life than just hunting and making master quality arrows. During her journey to find a new home and happiness, she struggles with the path that seems to take her away from the quiet life of a fletcher. She learns that sometimes the hardest part of growing up is reconciling who we were, with who we will become.

ISBN: 978-1-61929-356-4
eISBN: 978-1-61929-357-1

The Archer

Kyri was raised a fletcher but after finding a new home and family with the Telequire Amazons, she discovers a desire to take on more responsibility within the tribe. She has skills they desperately need and she is called to action to protect those around her. But Kyri's path is ever-changing even as she finds herself altered by love, loyalty, and grief. Far away from home, the new Amazon is forced to decide what to sacrifice and who to become in order to get back to all that she has left behind. And she wonders what is worse, losing everyone she's ever loved or having those people lose her?

ISBN: 978-1-61929-370-0
eISBN: 978-1-61929-371-7

The Sagittarius

Kyri has known her share of loss in the two decades that she has been alive. She never expected to find herself a slave in roman lands, nor did she think she had the heart to become a gladiatrix. But with her soul shattered she must fight to see her way back home again. Will she win her freedom and return to all that she has known, or will she become another kind of slave to the killer that has taken over her mind? The only thing that is certain through it all is her love and devotion to Queen Orianna.

ISBN: 978-1-61929-386-1
eISBN: 978-1-61929-387-8

Rules of the Road

Jamie is an engineer who keeps humor close to her heart and people at arm's length. Kelsey is a dental assistant who deals with everything from the hilarious to the disgusting on a daily basis. What happens when a driving app brings them together as friends? The nerd car and the rainbow car both know a thing or two about hazard avoidance. When a flat tire brings them together in person, Jamie immediately realizes that Kelsey isn't just another woman on her radar. Both of them have struggled to break free from stereotypes while they navigate the road of life. As their friendship deepens they realize that some-times you have to break the rules to get where you need to go.

ISBN: 978-1-61929-366-3
eISBN: 978-1-61929-367-0

Waking the Dreamer

By the end of the 21st century, the world had become a harsh place. After decades of natural and man-made catastrophes, nations fell, populations shifted, and seventy percent of the continents became uninhabitable without protective suits. Technological advancement strode forward faster than ever and it was the only thing that kept human society steady through it all. No one could have predicted the discovery of the Dream Walkers. They were people born with the ability to leave their bodies at will, unseen by the waking world. Having the potential to become ultimate spies meant the remaining government regimes wanted to study and control them. The North American government, under the leadership of General Rennet, demanded that all Dream Walkers join the military program. For any that refused to comply, they were hunted down and either brainwashed or killed.

The very first Dream Walker discovered was a five year old girl named Julia. And when the soldiers came for her at the age of twenty, she was already hidden away. A decade later found Julia living a new life under the government's radar. As a secure tech courier in the capital city of Chicago, she does her job and the rest of her time avoids other people as much as she is able. The moment she agrees to help another fugitive Walker is when everything changes. Now the government wants them both and they'll stop at nothing to get what they want.

ISBN: 978-1-61929-382-3
eISBN: 978-1-61929-383-0

Running From Forever

Sarah Colby has always run from commitment. But after more than a year on the road following her musical dreams, even she yearns for a little stability. Her sister Annie is only too happy to welcome her back home. When she meets Annie's boss, Nobel Keller, she's immediately drawn to the woman's youthful good looks and dangerous charisma. The first night together leaves Sarah aching for more, but the second shows her the true price of passion.

ISBN: 978-1-61929-398-4
eISBN: 978-1-61929-399-1

Embracing Forever

Sarah Colby is a musician, teacher, lover, sister, and so much more. In the past year, she learned that sometimes life takes you places you never even knew existed. For Sarah and her sister Annie, they found out that not only were the monsters real but sometimes you loved them. Now the Colby sisters and their friends are being targeted by someone with a grudge. They must discover who is attacking the people of Columbus or risk losing all that they hold dear. Nobel Keller is with them every step of the way but will she bring salvation or merely the end of their lives in Columbus?

ISBN: 978-1-61929-424-0
eISBN: 978-1-61929-425-7

Burn It Down

Ash Hayes was failed by the system at the tender age of six-teen and suffered an addiction. As a result she lives her life weighed down by the guilt of her past. To atone for childhood misdeeds, Ash trained as a paramedic after high school and eventually became a firefighter with the Detroit fire department, along with her childhood best friend Derek. Friend, confidant, brother, he has been her light in an otherwise dark life. When tragedy strikes on the job, injury and forced leave from the department are the least of her concerns. Suffering from even more guilt and depression after the loss of her two closest friends Ash is set adrift in a sea of pain.

When Mia Thomas buys the house next door, Ash finds friendship in the most unlikely of places. It's Mia's nature to help and to heal. Many would say she has a knack for finding the broken ones and leading them into the light. But Ash's secret still lives deep inside her. Before the firefighter can even think of a future, she has to amend her past. Like the phoenix of leg-end, Ash has to burn her fears to the ground before she can be reborn.

ISBN: 978-1-61929-418-9
eISBN: 978-1-61929-419-6

MORE REGAL CREST PUBLICATIONS

Be sure to check out our other imprints,
Blue Beacon Books, Mystic Books, Quest Books,
Troubadour Books, Yellow Rose Books,
and Young Adult Books.

VISIT US ONLINE AT
www.regalcrest.biz

At the Regal Crest Website You'll Find

~ The latest news about forthcoming titles and
   new releases

~ Our complete backlist of titles

~ Information about your favorite authors

CPSIA information can be obtained
at www.ICGtesting.com
Printed in the USA
JSHW021642101219
2895JS00005B/75